PRAISE FOR *SONS OF VALOR*

"[A] solid series launch from Andrews and Wilson...Scorching action scenes and authentic technical detail...Military thriller fans will be pleased to have a new team to root for."
—*PUBLISHERS WEEKLY*

"*Sons of Valor* delivered. I highly enjoyed this novel...If you are an established Andrews and Wilson fan you will enjoy *Sons of Valor*. If you are new to this author team (or looking for that next binge-worthy read) *Sons of Valor* is the way to go."
—*MYSTERY AND SUSPENSE*

"As a veteran, thriller-writer, and fan of the genre, the *Sons of Valor* series is as good as it gets. If you liked Tom Clancy's John Clark, and if you like Brad Thor's Scot Harvath, you'll devour the Tier One series."
—ANDREW WATTS, NAVY VETERAN &
BESTSELLING AUTHOR OF THE WAR PLANNERS

★★★ **SONS OF** ★★★
VALOR

ANDREWS & WILSON

★★★ SONS OF ★★★ VALOR

BLACK STONE
PUBLISHING

Copyright © 2021 by Organic Machinery Media LLC and Jeffrey Wilson
Published in 2021 by Blackstone Publishing
Cover and book design by K. Jones

Printed in the United States of America

First edition: 2021
ISBN 978-1-0940-9356-7
Fiction / Action & Adventure

1 3 5 7 9 10 8 6 4 2

CIP data for this book is available
from the Library of Congress

Blackstone Publishing
31 Mistletoe Rd.
Ashland, OR 97520

www.BlackstonePublishing.com

Dedicated to the men and women of the Joint Special Operations Command—the Tier One operators, direct action support sailors and soldiers, leadership, and support staff who make possible the missions, rarely made public, that allow us to live safe and free.

And for their families, who wait sleeplessly at home for their warriors to return, while the rest of us sleep in peace . . .

Thank you.

NOTE TO THE READER

A glossary of the acronyms, abbreviations, and military jargon used in this novel can be found at the back of the book.

PROLOGUE

ACHIN DISTRICT OF NANGARHAR PROVINCE

AFGHANISTAN

SEPTEMBER 28, 2016

2030 LOCAL TIME

At half past eight in the evening, the musicians played *"Âhesta Bero,"* prompting bride and groom to enter the wedding hall after hours of symbolic isolation. Qasim Nadar, along with the three hundred other guests, got to his feet and turned to watch the bridal procession. Round tables and high-backed chairs with white cloth covers filled the cavernous event space, leaving a wide central passage. Gold and maroon silk drapes hung from the walls and ceiling, tastefully hiding electrical conduits and other utilitarian architectural details. The facility was not opulent, but what it lacked in luxury was overshadowed by kinship and ambience.

Qasim smiled at his sister as she walked past. Even the veil Saida wore couldn't hide her radiance. He'd never seen her so happy. Today was a joyous day, a wonderful day . . . a perfect day. The groom, Eshan Dawar, was his oldest and most cherished friend. Qasim could not imagine a more perfect union—his twin sister marrying his best friend.

Truth be told, he was a bit jealous.

The trio had been inseparable since childhood, each of them filling a distinct role. Saida, the charming one with her infectious laugh; Eshan, the prankster with his brash bravado; and Qasim, the cool-headed, cerebral one who somehow always managed to keep them out of trouble—no small feat in Afghanistan. The scarred and turbulent country—plagued by war, opium trafficking, and terrorism—was no place for happy-go-lucky children. And yet, despite this, love, laughter, and community had found a way to persevere. The sons and daughters of war were growing up, and Allah willing, they would forge a path to peace and prosperity for their children's tomorrow.

Qasim watched the ceremony with tear-rimmed eyes and a dull, happy ache in his chest. When it was over, he hung back, waiting patiently while the couple made their rounds with the elders and guests of honor. When it was finally his turn, he embraced the grinning bridegroom.

"Congratulations, brother, I am so happy for you."

"Thank you," Eshan said, slapping his back. He stepped back to regard Qasim. "I would not have thought it possible, but you've got even taller while you've been away at university. You must be at least two meters!"

"I still have a few centimeters to go, but I'm getting close," Qasim said, cheeks flushing. At six foot four, he towered over almost everyone else in the room, including his father.

Eshan, who stood a perfectly respectable five foot ten, pretended to take an imaginary jump shot. "Well, if you decide you don't like engineering, you could always try out for the NBA."

Qasim chuckled at the joke, despite hearing it constantly

from classmates. On that cue, Saida, who was perfectly matched to Eshan in more ways than height, joined them. She threw her arms around Qasim and let out a contented sigh.

"I've missed you," she said, releasing her grip and considering him. "You look thin. Are they not feeding you at university?"

"No, no, it's not that. Everything you could ever want or imagine is available—except for Afghan food, of course." He chuckled. "But you know me, when I'm lost in my work, sometimes I forget to eat."

"Well, I hope you've filled your belly tonight. Did you get some kaddo with yogurt sauce? Our aunt made it extra sweet, just the way we liked it as kids," Saida said, her skin and eyes glowing.

"Three portions, and it was delicious . . . Now, go dance and don't worry about me."

"What's that look for?"

"I'm just so happy for you," he said. Then, turning to Eshan, "For both of you. I just wish I could somehow be a part of . . ."

When he didn't finish, Saida pressed a fist to her heart. "Qasim, you are always with us in here."

"I know."

"And when you graduate and come back to Afghanistan, you can marry Diba, have children, and then we can be one giant, happy family again," Eshan added with a sly grin.

Qasim glanced at the pretty girl in the emerald-green gown and shawl who was trying not to get caught looking at him. Diba averted her eyes, but too late. They'd been playing this little game all night. Eshan was not wrong about her. She would marry him in a heartbeat if he asked her father for her hand. And Diba's father had made it known on more than one occasion that a union between the families was something he greatly desired. Qasim had fantasized about bedding Diba because she was beautiful, but the girl had very little to say. After the novelty of physical intimacy wore off, he wondered if he'd find her intellectually stimulating enough to spend a lifetime with. Thankfully, he was in no rush to make *that* decision. He still had four semesters left at school, and there was a girl in the electrical engineering program who'd caught his eye. Maybe he'd end up with her instead. The future was impossible to foresee. A star could fall from the heavens tomorrow and change all their fates.

"Time will tell," Qasim said at last, then, taking a hand from each them, "I'm just so very, very happy for both of you. The ceremony, the food, the exchanging of vows—all perfect."

"Thank you, Qasim," Saida said, squeezing his hand.

"And on that note, I think it's time to start the real party," Eshan said. "We have a surprise."

Qasim cocked an eyebrow.

"That's right, we have a DJ," Eshan said with a grin. "I can only take so much tribal music. It's time to dance!"

The next three hours were filled with dancing and laughing as the celebration continued well into the night, like all good Afghan weddings. Gradually, the older and middle-aged guests trickled out in pairs and small groups. Around one in the morning, Qasim's father bade his children good night. His embrace with Saida lasted longer than usual while he whispered in her ear. When he finally pulled away, Qasim was surprised to see Saida laughing and crying at the same time.

"What did he say?" Qasim asked once their father had departed. He'd left with two men that Qasim knew were Taliban elders. They'd not been on the guest list, but they had shown up regardless. He'd seen his father talking with them, and though he'd not heard the conversation, he understood from watching that an agreement had been made.

Bribes paid in exchange for a bride's safety, he thought. *No point pretending. That's the way things work in Taliban country.*

"He told me a story about our mother on their wedding day," Saida said, wiping her cheeks with the backs of her hands. "Something he'd never shared before."

"Can you tell me?" Qasim asked, his stomach suddenly in knots of emotion as he thought of their mother, who'd passed away nearly five years ago.

"I think I should let him tell you on your wedding day," she said, smiling and looking up at him with wet eyes. "It would be more special that way."

He nodded and went to hug her but stopped short when her eyes suddenly went wide. "What is it? What's wrong?"

"Oh my God, I forgot to thank him," she said, her hand going to her chest. "I'll be right back," she said over her shoulder as she sprinted off.

This ought to be funny, Qasim thought, striding after her.

He stopped at the threshold of the wedding hall, smiling as Saida chased after the sedan in which their father was a passenger. She ran down the dirt and gravel road in her wedding dress and fancy shoes, waving her arms like a maniac. Brake lights flashed red, and the car glided to a stop a hundred meters away, well out of earshot.

"What's going on?" Eshan said, joining him. Voice ripe with sarcasm, he added, "I figured it would take at least a *few* days before she realized she made a mistake marrying me."

"She said she forgot to—" His voice cut off as a brilliant red-orange comet streaked down from the sky. A heartbeat later, the car erupted in a ball of fire.

"Saida!" he screamed as burning debris arced in all directions. He was aware of Eshan running beside him, yelling something, but his mind couldn't process anything beyond the abrupt and irreversible shift in his reality. Not two seconds ago, his sister and father had been right there—alive and full of joy—and now they were gone.

Incinerated.

Wiped from existence.

"Turn away. Don't look," Eshan said, piercing the hysteria in Qasim's mind.

But he had looked.

"Oh God," he murmured. "It's her leg . . ."

Hands were pulling him back now, away from the heat and the carnage.

The world was spinning. He felt dizzy. Time seemed to be passing in chunks. A crowd had gathered around him. Some people were screaming. Others were crying.

"Qasim, brother," Eshan said, grabbing him under his jaw. "Look at me."

Qasim blinked and Eshan's face came into focus. He'd never seen his friend so pale. Tears ran freely down Eshan's cheeks and the look in his eyes was all wrong.

"She's gone," Eshan said. "They're both gone."

"How?" he heard himself ask. "I don't understand."

"It was a drone strike," Eshan said, his gaze tilting skyward. "The Americans did this . . . the Americans took our Saida from us."

PART I

"You have enemies? Good. That means you have stood up for something, sometime in your life."

—Winston Churchill

CHAPTER 1

Lieutenant Commander Keith "Chunk" Redman stared out at the pitch-black water as he and his teammates zipped across its surface in the series-7 Rigid Inflatable Boat. Navy SEALs were supposed to love the ocean. It was their strategic haven—a dark place from which a warrior could emerge to strike his enemies, then disappear into when the mission was complete.

Yeah, well, Chunk didn't love it. Quite the opposite, in fact—he hated it. He hated the salt and sand, he hated the way the cold mercilessly sapped his body heat, but most of all, he hated the countless toothy critters lurking in the invisible deep. Even growing up in Bishop, Texas—where chasing girls on spring break along the Gulf Coast was a way of life—he'd loathed wading out into the surf. The girls in bikinis, the bonfires with the bros, throwing back cold ones in the hot Texas sun . . . all fantastic. But hanging out in the surf, not so much. Given a choice between the beach and the woods, he'd pick the latter every time. Hunting deer, or even better, wild hogs—now *that* was his idea of heaven.

Yet despite all of that, he'd been selected for Naval Special Warfare, gone through BUD/S and SQT, and become a SEAL. Which meant here he was again, about to take the plunge into the friggin' ocean to go swimming with the friggin' sharks. Why did that asshole Steven Spielberg have to make that damn *Jaws* movie? And why had he been stupid enough to watch it? And then there was Shark Week on the Discovery Channel . . . don't even get him started. Some people might be tempted to label his condition a phobia, but that was preposterous because SEALs didn't have phobias. Nonetheless, his emotionally unhealthy preoccupation with man-eating creatures of the deep was the most closely guarded secret of his professional career—something he'd never mentioned or confessed to any of his teammates.

Thank God they don't know.

"You're looking a little green, Chunk," said Saw, the team sniper, who was sitting directly across from him on the RIB.

"Ha ha. So do you, dude." Chunk laughed, tapping his night-vision goggles.

"No, that's not it," said Riker, a breacher with double sleeve tattoos he liked to flaunt by cutting his BDU blouse off at the elbows. "I think what he means is you look nervous, bro."

On that cue, Saw started humming a vaguely familiar tune. A few measures later, Riker joined in, adding lyrics.

"'Baby shark, doo-doo doo-doo doo, baby shark, doo-doo doo-doo doo, baby shark.'"

Trip, who was seated next to Saw, started tapping his thighs and joined in. "'Mommy shark, doo-doo doo-doo doo, Mommy shark doo-doo doo-doo doo . . .'"

"Really?" Chunk said, looking back and forth between them.

"Let's eat Chunk, doo-doo doo-doo doo, let's eat Chunk, doo-doo doo-doo doo, let's eat Chunk, doo-doo doo-doo doo, let's eat Chunk!" Riker keyed his mike, transmitting over the open comms channel for all to hear.

"You guys are such assholes," Chunk said, laughing despite himself. "But I'm not afraid of sharks."

"Mm-hmm, we know," Riker said.

"Really, guys, I'm not . . ."

"Right, uh-huh, sure." Saw had straightened his right hand into a fin and was holding it at the crown of his helmet, while chomping his teeth audibly.

This earned a round of hearty laughter, at Chunk's expense of course.

All this time and they knew, he thought with a shake of his head. *Proof again that in the Teams there are no secrets.*

"Less than a kilometer, boss," Riker said, checking the GPS on his watch, his demeanor serious now that it was time to get down to business.

"Check," Chunk said.

Moments later the RIB slowed to a stop, the white, frothy wake catching up and sloshing against the sides of the boat. On this cue, Chunk's hands flew over his kit—checking magazines, counting grenades, and validating he'd packed the blowout kit he stowed in his left thigh pocket. Satisfied with his loadout, he looked across the expanse of gray-green water at the brightly lit deck of a merchant ship anchored beneath a clear sky polka-dotted with stars. He flipped his NVGs up on his helmet and could see the ship's distant lights fine without augmentation.

"Not much light discipline," he said.

Saw shrugged as he tightened the ghost-gray McMillan TAC-338 sniper rifle on his back and cinched the shorter MK18

CQBR assault rifle to his chest. "That's because nobody fucks with them out here at anchor." He slipped a pair of curved fins over his boots.

"Nobody except us," Riker said as he snugged his own MK18 and an H&K MP7 9 mm machine pistol to his chest. Next, he donned his fins and removed his helmet to lift his Aqua Sphere swim goggles off his neck and into position over his eyes before resecuring it. Riker bitched incessantly about the standard-issue SEAL dive mask, and he'd recently converted Saw and Trip to his goggles approach—but not Chunk. He hated getting saltwater up his nose more than he hated the bulky mask with its poor peripheral vision.

"Neptune Two, One—how copy?" Chunk said into the boom mike by the corner of his mouth.

"You're five by, One," Lieutenant Carlos Juarez replied. If the young Officer in Charge of Bravo Platoon was annoyed that Redman, as Task Unit Commander, had taken the helm as Neptune One, he didn't show it. Most SEAL officers continued to lead missions as they promoted, and Chunk had a reputation for getting down in the dirt with his team more than most. In fact, he hoped never to promote beyond his current O-4 rank. He hadn't become a SEAL to sit in a TOC and watch his men fight on TV. He'd become a SEAL to bring the fight to the bad guys' front doors, so that Americans at home could sleep soundly.

He keyed his mike. "Mother, Neptune One—passing Camaro."

Someone in the N3 shop had a hard-on for muscle cars, because almost every mission lately had used automobile models for checkpoint designators. The next call-in was when they reached the target ship, where he called, "Stingray," to get the green light for the assault.

"Roger, One. We got eyes in orbit. You're all clear from here to Stingray," came the reply.

The satellite had good visuals; no unexpected watercraft or counterinsurgency measures had been identified. Chunk acknowledged with a double click of his mike, then nodded to the three SEALS, who'd all repositioned into a line on the pontoon beside him. He turned to the pair of SWCC operators piloting the RIB and gave them a thumbs-up. For this op, the protocol was for the RIB to creep in behind them and be ready for emergency exfil—in other words, if they got their asses kicked and had to evacuate.

He smiled at the thought. *Not gonna happen.*

If all went well—and it would—two MH-60 helicopters would drop off a second wave of personnel—a navy boat crew and qualified merchant pilot who'd drive the Pakistani-flagged ship and its cargo to a port on the Gulf of Oman. Chunk and his boys would stay behind to play security escort on the seized freighter, and the CIA or another dark and spooky "Joint Task Force" would take over the show, inventory the spoils, and hopefully confirm whatever terrorist operation they thought was going on. They would also sort out the geopolitical aftermath of the raid. Thank God he didn't have to deal with any of that bullshit. He and his team were door-kickers, plain and simple, and that's the way he liked it.

He rolled into the water—forcing away the thought of a great white shark's giant open maw waiting for him just below the surface. Riker, Saw, and Trip rolled in behind him. Their four-man assault team was half of first squad, Bravo Platoon, SEAL Team Four. The other half of first squad was being led by Lieutenant Carlos Juarez. Dubbed "Carla" by his teammates in light of the long silky locks he grew whenever they "bearded up" for Middle East deployments, Juarez would be swimming in from a thousand yards farther northwest. The two four-man fire teams would board simultaneously on the port and starboard sides of the freighter to begin the assault.

Chunk would've preferred a deeper water infil with rebreather tanks, but finning on the surface tonight worked fine, given the moonless sky. The gray vest he wore over his kit was optimally buoyant, just enough to keep him at the surface. He swam with one arm stretched forward and the other trailing, holding his rifle tight against his side, while his legs did all the work. Now and again he'd break the waterline with his mask just enough to recalibrate his bearing on the target. The well-lit ship was growing incrementally larger with each glance. He was aware of the four SEALs behind him, staggered so that they formed a V, but they were nearly silent, too quiet to be heard over the water swirling across his earphones and sloshing around his helmet. The noise-canceling tech in his Peltor headset worked great for dampening loud, staccato sounds like gunfire or helicopter engines, but it amplified quiet noise like whispers—and unfortunately, sloshing water.

We are invincible warriors of the night, he told himself, *silent death from the sea . . . unless, that is, a twenty-foot tiger shark decides to maul our asses before we get there.*

He shoved the paranoid thought out of his head, and instantly other concerns filled the void. Rumor had it that the Joint Special Operations Command was finally ready to reconstitute the elite Tier One SEAL unit, after the previous unit had been wiped out during Operation Crusader in a horrific act of terrorism levied against US Special Forces. A high-ranking spook friend had hinted once that if that time ever came, he'd throw Chunk's name in for consideration. Getting selected for the Tier One had been Chunk's dream from the day he'd pinned on his trident. Hell, it was every SEAL's dream. But after Crusader, he'd shelved that fantasy and resigned himself to finishing out the operational years of his command with Team Four.

Now with the possibility back on the table, he wasn't sure if the Tier One was what he wanted. How could he, in good conscience, walk away from his guys? This unit worked because of the trust and bond they'd forged. As Task Unit Commander, it was his job to keep Riker from running off the rails, to make sure Trip didn't burn out from pushing himself to the breaking point, and to be that insulator between the job and Saw so he had time to be the devoted husband and father he wanted to be. Chunk was their sounding board, their mentor, and most importantly their umbrella—shielding them from a ceaseless deluge of shit raining down from above. They needed him, and the inverse was true.

They were his brothers.

They were his family.

If the CSO walked up and offered me that golden ticket, would I take it? I don't know anymore . . .

"Neptune One, Two—in position," Juarez said, the SEAL's soft whisper crystal clear in Chunk's headset.

The report snapped him back to the present. A mental picture formed of the other half of their assault force bobbing in the water on the opposite side of the freighter, and he double-clicked his mike in acknowledgment. With the ship looming, he ignored the lactic burn in his calves and thighs as he pushed through the tail end of the fifteen-minute infil. Moments later he steadied himself with a hand on the hull of the ship as his fellow operators crowded around him.

With both fire teams now in position, he made the call. "Mother, Neptune One—Stingray, ready."

"Roger, One—hold," came the calm voice of Lieutenant Commander Aveda, who was coordinating the op from their Tactical Operations Center with the rest of the command staff.

While the Head Shed assessed and deconflicted any new intel before giving them the go, Chunk pictured the layout of the ship and rapidly reviewed the assault. Phase One, board at the stern and take down any roving security elements or personnel loitering aft. Then they'd advance forward, one fire team on each side, clearing the port and starboard rails. Saw would find high ground and become overwatch, while Juarez and his shooters secured the main cargo deck. Meanwhile, Chunk would lead his team up the starboard rail to the bridge tower. At the corner of the superstructure, his fire team would split into pairs and take the bridge, using opposite stairwells and converging on the O-5 level in the middle. Once Chunk's guys had secured the bridge and Juarez's the cargo deck, the vessel would be under their control. After that, Phase Two would commence—the slow, methodical process of clearing the entire ship for bad guys potentially hiding in some nook or cranny, waiting to ambush them.

Easy day.

"Neptune, you're a go. Call Charger," came Aveda's voice over the wire.

Chunk double-clicked and nodded at Riker. The SEAL finned backward a few yards, doffed his fins, then struggled into his REBS magnetic climbing system. The foot attachments worked like crampons, fitting over the boot, but instead of spikes these had a bulky, articulating magnetic plate. The hand units were similar but smaller. After a string of quiet curses, Riker was ready and swam up to the hull, where he created his first "handhold" with a dull thud. Next, he brought his knees up and his toe-plates connected to the hull with a double *thunk thunk.*

Saw secured two dark-green ropes to Riker's kit with carabineers and gave him a two-finger salute. Like an ant defying gravity, Riker began the otherwise impossible climb up the side of the ship. When he reached the halfway point, Chunk and the other three SEALs each readied an equally badass piece of shipboarding tech—the Atlas Power Ascender. About the size of a small shoebox, the APA-3 was a battery-powered motor that would zip them up forty feet to board the freighter.

Upon reaching the top of the gunwale, Riker locked the REBS handhold devices into place. Next, he peeked cautiously over the rail, suspended like Spider-Man on the side of the ship. He looked down over his shoulder and gave Chunk a thumbs-up before unclipping the climbing ropes from his kit and tying them to the gunwale rail. After securing his harness to the rail, he silently slipped out of the REBS, leaving the toe and hand grips stuck to the hull.

Chunk locked his ascender onto the free end of a dangling rope, then squeezed the handle. The electric motor whirred into action, feeding the nylon rope through a pulley system and propelling him upward. Heels on the hull, he walked up the side of the ship as the power ascender lifted him by the harness. Soon he was dangling midair beside Riker, four stories above the water-line. Twenty seconds later Saw and Trip joined them.

Chunk let himself hang in his harness, resting his arms for the work ahead, and keyed his mike. "One is set," he whispered, knowing the Peltor would make his voice crystal clear to the team.

"Two, all set. Call it, boss," came Juarez's reply.

Chunk got nods from Riker and Trip, while Saw gave him a thumbs-up. Chunk pulled his NVGs into place, then wrapped his right arm around the rail. "Three . . . two . . . one . . ."

At the zero beat, the SEALs slipped sequentially over the top rail, landing in tactical crouches, their weapons at the ready. Chunk turned left, feeling a familiar but paradoxical calm spread over him as he cleared his corner and surged forward. Three suppressed rounds kicked off the assault, white flashes lighting up his green-hued night vision as Juarez's operators shot two men armed with AK-47s who were rising from sleeping mats on the deck. Chunk sensed motion to his left. He turned, put his green targeting dot on the forehead of the large man, eyes wide in surprise, emerging from behind a power box. The guard didn't even try to raise the rifle slung over his shoulder, but Chunk dropped him with a single shot before the man could cry out and steal their stealth. He crumpled to the deck, and Riker snatched the AK-47 and tossed it over the side. Only seconds had passed, but the eight SEALs had dispatched three armed sentries and cleared the stern.

Chunk nodded at Juarez, who nodded back, then led his team around the aft tower, as wide as it was tall at five stories above the deck. If these assholes were smart enough to have a sniper on the aft tower or armed lookouts on the forward bridge wings, then crossing and securing the cargo deck would be deadly. Aveda, call sign Mother, back at the TOC, hadn't reported any heat signatures of concern, but the thought still needled at Chunk's brain.

"Two, One—hold at the corner," Chunk said, keying his mike.

"Check," came the reply. "Problem?"

"No, but if they have a shooter in the aft tower, it could be a problem for you, and especially for Saw moving to his nest."

"Roger. How 'bout we clear around the corner and take covered positions on the cargo deck? Somewhere with sightlines up the face of the aft tower and across the deck."

"Roger, Two. Go," Chunk said and advanced his own team— but only to the corner, where he took a tactical knee and held up a closed fist. As his men bunched in behind him, he started his ten count, expecting gunfire. When it didn't come, he snuck a peek around the corner and got a glimpse of a pair of SEALs repositioning, quickstepping in low crouches.

A heartbeat later, the report came: "One, Two—we're dug in."

Chunk double-clicked and gazed out at the expansive main cargo deck. He'd seen freighters like these stacked with CONEX boxes as tall and wide as an apartment complex, but this ship was carrying a modest load—only few dozen CONEX boxes, half of them strapped down in four small distinct clusters, and the rest stacked all the way forward. He quickly scanned for threats, and finding none, his eyes settled on a loading crane in the center of the deck. He pointed to Saw, then to the crane.

The sniper nodded and crept up beside him.

"Two, One—Three is Zeus now," Chunk said, changing Saw's designator. "Hold and cover until he's in the nest."

A double click told him Juarez understood. Of all the assignments on tonight's op, Saw crossing the cargo deck and climbing up the crane tower to provide overwatch was the most dangerous: he was completely exposed and vulnerable.

Chunk turned to his sniper, and Saw flashed him an easy grin.

"Go," Chunk said and watched the SEAL streak forward along the starboard rail, a shadowy blur of lethal precision. Saw disappeared, only to reappear a minute later climbing the crane ladder with smooth, practiced efficiency. But every second his teammate was on that ladder, Chunk's guts were in knots.

Finally, the call came.

"Two, this is Zeus," said Saw's calm, confident voice. "Zeus has good eyes."

Chunk double-clicked, then said, "Two, One—clear the deck."

"Roger, One. Clearing the deck," Juarez came back.

Chunk leaned around the corner and watched two pairs of SEALs advance from their hides and fan out toward the next cluster of CONEX boxes. He turned to Riker and Trip and was about to chop a hand forward when night became day.

"Shit," he barked, flipping his NVGs onto his helmet and squinting.

Halogen floodlights illuminated the cargo deck. Chunk and his SEALs made themselves small.

"They know we're here," Chunk growled.

"Neptune, Mother—we hold two new heat signatures on the

conning tower. One shooter has stepped out onto each bridge wing, port and starboard sides," came the report from Aveda in the TOC.

The first round fired was from Saw, the distinctive sound of the .328 Lapua Magnum high-velocity round screaming across the deck. A volley of AK-47 fire echoed next, followed immediately by the staccato crack of 5.56 as the SEALs went to work with their assault rifles. A second sniper round whistled above the fray and Chunk watched a body fall from the port bridge wing.

"One, Zeus—Bridge shooters are KIA," Saw reported.

"Roger, Zeus. Mother, what else you see?" Chunk queried, while using hand signals to direct Trip to sweep the stern, thereby covering their six.

"Neptune, we've got heat sigs moving inside the bridge tower. Expect more resistance," Aveda came back.

Chunk turned to Riker. "With me," he barked and advanced across the cargo deck.

A deck hatch popped open fifteen meters away, catching Chunk's immediate attention. He hovered his green infrared target designator a foot above the opening. But instead of a head popping up like he expected, a soda can-sized object arced out of the hatch and sailed toward the middle of the deck.

"Grenade amidships!" Chunk shouted and hit the deck as the grenade flew into the gap between clusters of CONEX boxes— the exact spot where he thought one or more of Juarez's team might be sheltering.

The grenade detonated with a resounding pop, sending shrapnel ricocheting off the deck and punching holes in the sides of the shipping containers.

Chunk knelt and performed a quick self-assessment: *Nothing burning, grinding, or leaking—I'm good.* He brought his rifle up and lit up the hatch with his IR designator. "Zeus, put a round down the open hatch, starboard amidships where I'm pointing."

"Check," came Saw's reply, followed by a .338-caliber lightning bolt streaking into the hole. "That'll make him think twice before lobbing another grenade."

"Neptune, SITREP?" Chunk queried his team.

"Four is intact," Riker said, falling in tight beside Chunk.

"Neptune Two is intact," came Juarez a split second later, speaking for the entire team.

"Neptune, you've got fire teams stepping out of the bridge tower at deck level," Aveda reported.

Chunk scanned the walkway along the gunwale and saw two crouching figures duck out of the outboard hatch, moving like operators. Riker squeezed off a volley a millisecond before Chunk, and together they dropped the lead shooter. The second shooter returned fire. A tracer round sailed past Chunk's right ear as bullets sparked off the gunwale. Working together, Riker strafed the ground in front of the shooter, sending him scrambling, and Chunk dropped him with a headshot. The path now clear, he chopped a hand forward and they were advancing side by side, a heartbeat later.

"Forty Mike-Mike that hole," Chunk shouted as they passed the open hatch they'd been ambushed from minutes earlier.

"Gladly," Riker said and sent a 40-mm grenade down the hatch from the undermounted M203 launcher on his weapon.

The grenade detonated behind them with a satisfying boom and an aftershock that shook the deck beneath their feet as they ran. Gunfire echoed from the port side, where Juarez's element was engaging an enemy fire team.

"One, Two—two tangos KIA portside. Who are these assholes?" Juarez asked, his voice ripe with aggravation.

"Don't know, but they've had training," Chunk said. He put a round in the back of the head of the first enemy shooter they had dropped seconds ago. The other combatant was missing half his head and clearly out of the fight. Chunk's brain cataloged other tactical details as he sprinted past the bodies to the outboard side of the bridge tower, where he and Riker stopped and pressed their backs against the metal bulkhead.

"You expect this much resistance?" Riker asked, scanning vertically with his rifle, making sure some new asshole on the bridge wing didn't drop a grenade or worse on their asses.

"Hell no," Chunk said, thinking about the unmarked tactical uniforms the dead tangos were wearing. "No insignia on these guys."

"Yeah, noticed that. Think they're contractors?"

"No idea." Irritated, Chunk prompted Aveda for an update on enemy thermals. "Mother, Neptune—talk to us?"

"We've got lots of interference from the superstructure. Satellite can't make out anything below decks, Neptune, but I hold your team's eight heat sigs topside and six cold tangos. Also, I've got five warm bodies on the bridge."

"Copy, Mother."

"One, Five," Trip radioed, "the stern is secure. Want us to stay put?"

"No, fall in on me," Chunk said. "Two, hold the deck while my element takes the bridge as briefed."

"Check," came the reply from Juarez.

"Oh, and Two, stay frosty because that grenade-lobbing sonuvabitch below decks could still be alive and probably has friends," Chunk added.

"Copy, One."

Trip and a SEAL called Ethan from Juarez's fire team came sprinting along the gunwale and fell in beside him and Riker. The forward superstructure, or bridge tower, had two access hatches— one port and one starboard. Using hand signals, Chunk sent Riker and Ethan around to the port hatch, and he stayed behind with Trip. He stayed tight against the wall beside the starboard hatch and waited for the call from Riker.

"One, Four—set," Riker said in his ear.

Trip gave Chunk's shoulder a confirming squeeze and Chunk counted them down from three. On zero he pivoted, ducked low, and entered. Once through the hatch, he immediately slid left. While he cleared the crawlspace under the stairwell, Trip cleared his corner and took the lead, quickly advancing up the stairs to the next landing. Chunk followed, adrenaline pumping, pulse pounding in his ears, checking their six down the stairs as he ascended. They repeated the drill, reversing roles at each landing until they'd reached the O-5 level, which housed the bridge.

Within seconds Riker's amplified whisper was in Chunk's headset, "Four is set." Riker and Ethan had advanced up the por side of the pilot house with mirror-image precision.

Chunk nodded to Trip, repositioned to the opposite side of the hatch, then whispered, "Go."

They moved down the passage a short distance until they reached the bridge access door. But as they approached the door, Aveda spoke in Chunk's ear.

"Neptune, Mother—you have two insurgent fire teams advancing in pairs from the aft tower, main deck level."

The news did not surprise Chunk; he'd predicted more shooters were hanging out below decks.

"Copy, Mother," Juarez replied.

"I see them," Saw said calmly. "Make that one fire team," he added a beat later, having dealt death from his perch.

Automatic rifle fire erupted outside, but with Juarez's team covering the bridge tower access doors and Saw as overwatch, Chunk was confident they had things under control. He couldn't let himself get distracted from the task at hand, which was taking the bridge. With a nod to Trip, he yanked open the door. Trip tossed a flash-bang grenade through the gap, and Chunk held the door closed until he heard the dull *whump*. He reopened the door and followed Trip inside, sighting over his MK18 in a tactical crouch. He squeezed twice on his trigger, dropping a bearded man in shorts and flip-flops sighting over a pistol. Chunk pivoted and surged forward, aware that Riker and Ethan were clearing from the opposite side. His brain identified their kit-clad shapes as friendlies, and his rifle sights drifted past them.

Two muzzle flares flashed in his peripheral vision, and it was over.

Three men were dead at their feet, two others kneeling on the floor with hands up in surrender. Trip and Ethan held sentry positions, sighting on the port and starboard doors from the corners of the navigation table, just aft of the empty workstations flanking an elevated captain's chair.

"Bridge secure," Chunk called, hoping for a SITREP from Juarez and his team. This was the hardest part for him—when the initial shooting lulled and he didn't know if all the men he led were okay.

Without warning, the portside access door burst open and a fighter charged onto the bridge. His wide-eyed expression showed he realized his mistake a millisecond before he took a 5.56 round to the forehead. The man's assault rifle clattered to the floor, and his body hit the deck.

"Good boy," Trip said, a tendril of smoke curling from the muzzle of his weapon. He held the target on the door in case the party-crasher had a friend.

Riker moved swiftly, checking the two kneeling prisoners for suicide vests and weapons before flex-cuffing them.

"One, Two—main deck is secure," came the timely report from Juarez. "You want me to sweep below decks?"

"Roger, Two, and stay frosty. There could be more shooters." Chunk scanned their two crows. Picking the older and more grizzled of the duo, he said, "Are you the captain of this ship?"

"Yes," the man said.

"You speak English?" he said, approaching the bearded Pakistani.

"Yes."

"Why is your vessel at sea anchor?"

"We don't have authorization to enter port yet."

"Which port?" Chunk pressed.

"Gwadar," the man said, his gaze downcast.

"That's in western Pakistan, close to the Iranian border, correct?"

The captain nodded.

"How many contract fighters like this guy do you have on board?" he asked, pointing to the dead fighter in the doorway. Like the others who'd been wearing unmarked uniforms, he looked to be of East Asian descent.

Chinese . . . maybe North Korean? Chunk thought.

"Ten," the captain said.

Riker shot Chunk a wary look, but Chunk held his stone-faced expression.

"What about these guys?" Chunk swept the muzzle of his rifle across the other dead. None were in uniform, and they all looked to be Pakistani or Arab.

"Not contractors. Ship's personnel."

"Why are the contractors here?"

"Security."

"Security for what?" Chunk pressed.

The captain looked away and didn't answer.

"I said security for what?" Chunk grabbed the man under the jaw and turned his chin until he made eye contact.

"I don't know," the man answered, his voice weary and defeated. "And I don't *want* to know."

Riker tugged at Chunk's sleeve. "This ain't our job, bro. Leave it to the spooks when we get to port."

"Yeah, except I think the Head Shed screwed up," Chunk said in a hushed tone. He pointed his rifle barrel at the dead contract shooter. "That ain't no AK-47. The mag's behind the pistol grip. Look at it—that's a QBZ-95."

Riker ran his tongue between his lower lip and his bottom teeth and walked over to the doorway. With the toe of his boot, he nudged the dead man's rifle for a good look. "Yeah, yeah . . . you're right. It's actually a 97. This variant takes NATO 5.56 rounds."

"All these shooters we killed, I'm pretty sure they're Chinese."

Riker looked at him. "Yeah, so?"

"So you were at the same intel brief I was. I don't think these guys were supposed to be here," Chunk said. "If we just took out a regiment of Chinese special forces . . ."

"Shit." Riker winced. "I'll start moving the bodies below decks, and we better get the spooks here ASAFP to figure it out."

Chunk nodded, and an unfamiliar lump began to form in his throat as he keyed his mike to give the Head Shed the bad news.

CHAPTER 2

BRITISH AERO DEFENSE SYSTEMS

AERONAUTICAL DYNAMICS DIVISION

NEW MALDEN, ENGLAND

1918 LOCAL TIME

Qasim frowned at his computer as the next-generation Valkyrie combat drone on his monitor went into an uncontrolled spin and crashed into the ground. It didn't *really* crash—this was just a simulation—but if he didn't figure out the problem, his career would mirror the pixelated wreckage on the screen. He aborted the trial and reset the parameters to tweak the design change and try again.

"Qasim," a voice ripe with accusatory irritation said from behind him. "It's after seven o'clock and I'm still waiting. What's the problem, precisely?"

He turned to find his boss, Oliver Payne, arms crossed and invading his personal space. Several possible retorts popped into his head: *The problem is that the simulator software is shit and full of bugs.* Or how about: *Valkyrie is an engine masquerading as a control surface and we need to stop pretending otherwise.* Or best yet: *The problem, oh wise and powerful boss, is that you tasked me with eighty hours of work and gave me ten hours to do it.*

Qasim, of course, said none of these things. "I'm sorry, Mr. Payne. The latest design change has had rather significant aerodynamic repercussions, and I'm still trying to evaluate the impact across hundreds of flight permutations. There's an instability in certain conditions that—"

"I don't see why this should be so difficult," Payne cut him off. "Your job is to plug the change into the model and let the computer do all the work."

Qasim suppressed the reflex to laugh aloud at this moronic statement and said, "I wish it were as simple as that."

The subtle condescension was apparently not lost on Payne, because his cheeks turned red. "How much longer do you need? I don't know if you are aware, but I'm under immense pressure from senior management to finalize the design so we can commence aviation trials. This stealth aircraft is the *future* of British air defense and combat operations abroad. Getting the Valkyrie into production is the PM's number one defense priority. He personally called the CEO last week for a status update."

"Stealth UCAV," Qasim said.

"Excuse me?"

"You said stealth aircraft, but technically Valkyrie is a UCAV—unmanned combat aerial vehicle, sir."

"Are you trying to pick a bloody fight with me?"

"No sir."

"You think I don't know it's a bloody drone?"

"No, sir, it's just that semantics matter, particularly . . . with this program."

Payne took a theatrically deep breath and said, "Will you be getting the work done tonight or not?"

"No," Qasim said. "I need another day."

"Bloody hell," Payne snapped. Then, as he walked away, "You have until tomorrow, Nadar, but after that, no more excuses."

"Yes sir. Good night, sir." He turned around in his chair to face his computer, and when Payne was out of earshot, murmured, "Asshole." These simulations were helpful, to be sure, but they were still just a simulation.

If only they'd let me pilot a Valkyrie, he lamented. *For just one day. I could learn so much . . .*

But they would never let that happen. He wasn't an RAF pilot with "golden hands." He was just a lowly Afghan engineer with dual degrees in aeronautical engineering and avionics software integration. He was just the immigrant who'd designed a third of the Valkyrie's systems, debugged all the avionics software, and ran all the model simulations. They wouldn't even let Qasim see the prototype in person. He knew the closest he'd ever get to Valkyrie was on this computer screen, and that infuriated him.

"Hey, Qasim," said a cheerful male voice behind him. "Some of us are going to the pub. Want to join us, mate?"

"I've got too much work to do," he said without turning around. "But thank you anyway, Trevor."

"We'll be at Glasshouse if you change your mind," the young software engineer from Surry replied.

"If I finish, maybe I'll do that," he said, but they both knew it wasn't going to happen.

After five years he still felt like a visitor in his adopted home. No, not a visitor—a foreigner. There was a difference. His coworkers were generally nice to him and tried to include him in their social outings, but he was never going to be one of them. Not really. London had nothing for him but the job—a job that was more an addiction than profession. The irony that designing combat drones had become his life's work was not lost on him. There was a dark and twisted part inside him—a part he never talked about—that had festered and mutated ever since the deaths of his father and sister and pushed him to design the same weapons of war that had murdered them. It was disgusting what he was doing, and yet he could not help himself. Working at British Aero was his personal form of spiritual self-mortification. Like a moth to a flame . . .

He *wanted* to be burned.

He worked until eye fatigue forced him to quit, which turned out to be after 10:00 p.m. After logging out of his terminal, he took the elevator down to the ground floor and exited the building onto the wide sidewalk that ran along High Street. A red double-decker bus along the curb belched out a cloud of exhaust that made him momentarily hold his breath. As the bus rumbled away to the north, Qasim's gaze followed it. The Glasshouse was literally a stone's throw away, just a block past the overpass. He was certain a few of his coworkers would still be there . . . but their commonality ended with being young engineers. He was a brown-skinned Afghan Muslim. They were pale British Protestants. They were happy, hopeful sheep, foolishly naive about the company they worked for and the world they lived in. They lived their lives like oversized children . . . programming advanced military aviation software by day, ordering drafts at the pub by night.

None of them had seen death up close and personal.

None of them had experienced the horrors of what the machines of war could unleash.

Feeling suddenly and passionately resentful, he turned and headed south.

He walked a block to Cambridge Road, past the Domino's Pizza, which he hated. Past the Cake & Bingsoo Café, which he also hated—but not quite as much because he still had a sweet tooth—and finally past the New Malden Methodist Church, which he resented but could not articulate why. At the intersection, he turned right and walked two and half blocks to the over-priced two-bedroom flat he rented. He was so lost in thought that he didn't notice the man seated on his front stoop until he reached down to open the little gate in the fence surrounding his six-square-meter "garden" in front of the redbrick house.

He started as the man abruptly stood, but his nerves evaporated a heartbeat later. "Eshan?"

"Hello, brother," Eshan said with a grin, taking a step forward to greet him.

"What are you doing here?" Qasim embraced his oldest and dearest friend.

"It's good to see you too," Eshan said with a laugh.

"I didn't mean it that way . . . what I meant was, I didn't know you were in London," Qasim said, suddenly feeling shabby in his business casual next to the impeccable tailoring of Eshan's suit.

"I'm sorry I didn't give you advanced notice. It was a last-minute trip to try to smooth things over with an important client."

"I see. Well, no matter, it's very good to see you. How long has it been, my friend?"

"Too long," Eshan said, taking on a remorseful tone.

"So true," Qasim said, nodding. "But that's my fault, I suppose. I never visit home."

"Why would you?" Eshan threw an arm around his shoulders. "There's nothing but rocks, goats, and Taliban at home."

Qasim couldn't think of a proper reply, so he simply nodded. It was true. His nuclear family were all dead, and while he had inherited most of his father's money, he had no interest in politics, smuggling, or living under the Taliban regime. There was nothing and nobody for him in Afghanistan, nothing and nobody except for Eshan . . . And despite neither man intending it to, Saida's death had silently pushed them apart rather than bringing them together.

He retrieved his keys from his pants pocket, unlocked the front door, and invited Eshan inside. "Can I get you something to drink?"

"A glass of water, please," Eshan said, switching from English to Pashto and taking a measure of the place as he spoke.

"I know it's not much, but I'm renting and don't have the time to decorate," Qasim said. He couldn't remember the last time he'd spoken his native tongue, but it felt good—like kicking off an uncomfortable pair of shoes after a long day at work. He filled two glasses from a jug of tap water he kept in the refrigerator and walked to the living room.

"There is beauty in simplicity," Eshan said from where he stood, perusing the only decor in the flat—a row of framed photographs atop the mantel.

He watched Eshan pick up his personal favorite of the group, a candid photo of the two of them laughing while Saida, sitting between them, recounted a funny story. Angst—long suppressed but not forgotten—awoke inside him. His throat felt tight, and his knees suddenly unsteady.

"I remember this day," Eshan said, his back to Qasim. "Like it was yesterday."

After a long pause, he replaced the photo, pulled out his mobile phone, and snapped a picture of it before turning to face Qasim. To Qasim's surprise, Eshan was not choking back tears like he was. Instead, his friend's expression was clinical, almost detached. "So tell me, have you met someone yet? A beautiful Afghan expat like yourself here in London?"

Qasim felt heat in his cheeks. He shook his head.

"What about a nice English girl? I know you always secretly liked blond women with blue eyes."

"No," he said with a wan smile. "No English girls . . . There is this one girl at work, Veena, who is funny, but I don't think she's interested in me. Besides, her parents are Indian, so I don't think it would work even if she were."

"Don't tell me you've lived in London for all this time and haven't gone on a single date," Eshan said with fraternal condemnation.

Qasim shrugged. "Work is very busy. I don't have time for a relationship right now."

"I understand," Eshan said, his tone a double-edged sword. "So tell me about your work, then. What are you doing these days?"

"Systems software development and integration at British Aero," he said, handing his friend one of the two glasses of water, then walking to an armchair to take a seat. "It's classified. I can't really talk about it."

"Sure, I understand," Eshan said, nodding. "Must be challenging work—they certainly have you working long hours."

"It's my choice to work late, they don't force me," Qasim lied. "How about you? Judging by your suit, it appears you are doing very well for yourself."

"Thank you, but I'm still just a very small fish in a big ocean."

"Are you in banking? Last time we spoke, I think I remember you saying something about applying at Deutsche Bank."

"I did say that, didn't I," Eshan said with a chuckle. "But no, I'm not at Deutsche Bank. I ended up taking a position at a smaller bank that specializes in investing for high-wealth individuals, deploying capital in higher-risk markets, and debt financing for projects in Afghanistan and Pakistan."

Qasim nodded. "Sounds interesting. Where do you work out of?"

"Hotel rooms," Eshan said with a practiced laugh. "But my office is in Lahore."

"What is that like?"

"Crowded and busy like London, only not so clean and not so posh."

"I've never been to Lahore. I'll have to come visit you there someday."

"As it turns out, that's why I'm here, my friend." Eshan flashed him a wide grin. "I'm not sure how to tell you this other than to just say it—I've met a woman and we're engaged. It would mean a lot to me if you would come to the wedding."

The news took Qasim several seconds to process. His initial shock was quickly replaced with outrage. How could Eshan betray Saida's memory like that? How could he move on so quickly? Did he not still feel her loss everyday upon waking and doubly so before surrendering to sleep at night? *She deserves better!* But then another voice, steeped in reason, chimed a rebuttal. *It has been more than five years, more than sufficient time to mourn Saida's passing. A life of bitter celibacy is not the fate my sister would have wanted for Eshan.*

Qasim forced a smile. "I am so happy for you, brother. Tell me about her. Tell me about your new love."

"Her name is Aleena, and I met her in Lahore. She's Pakistani, very pretty, and a delight to be around. I try not to compare her to Saida, but that's impossible of course . . ." Eshan's voice trailed off, his gaze distant. He said nothing for a moment, then collected himself and looked Qasim in the eye. "I know it might feel like a betrayal, but it's time for me to stop grieving and move on. I think Saida would want that."

Qasim stood, walked over to his best friend, and took a seat on the sofa beside him. "Yes, that is what she'd want . . . for both of us. I am proud of you, Eshan, for you have managed to do what I have not. I ran away to bury myself in my work and brood. I might as well be a dead man walking among the living."

At first, the power and poignancy of the confession cleft the air between them, but then a strange thing happened. Like exhaling after holding one's breath a very long time, the release felt invigorating. Eshan met his eyes and nodded, the words unspoken: *I understand, brother, for I, too, know what it means to have drowned in sorrow.*

Eshan brightened. "Come to Lahore," he said, buoyant. "Meet my bride, bless the marriage, and help us celebrate this new and wonderful adventure."

"When is the wedding?"

"A month from this Saturday. It is a perfect opportunity to—what's the English expression?—kill two birds with one stone. If you fly into Kabul, I can pick you up. We'll visit home first and see the family, then drive across the border to Peshawar together."

Qasim's stomach sank, as if he'd just swallowed molten lead. "Four weeks? I don't know if that's enough time for me. I have meetings scheduled and important milestones to meet. There's so much to do. Besides, if we're driving into Pakistan, I'll need a travel visa, and then there's—"

"When is the last time you took a holiday?" Eshan said, cutting him off. "Huh?"

Qasim looked at his feet. "I don't remember."

"That's what I thought." Eshan put an arm around his shoulders. "It's okay to take time off work. It's okay to make time for family. Take a holiday, Qasim. A long one. You certainly deserve it. Trust me, the work will get done without you. The company will not close its doors and go bankrupt in your absence. Come to the wedding. Meet Aleena and spend time with us. Visit home. There are people there who miss you."

"Like who?"

"Your aunts and cousins and second cousins. They ask about you all the time. And then there's Diba, of course."

"Diba? She must be married by now. How many children does she have?"

"No children. Diba is still not married," Eshan said with a mischievous grin. "A miracle, I know."

Diba . . . now that's a name that hadn't crossed his mind for a very long time. "Is she still beautiful?"

"Even more so now that she's a woman," Eshan said with an easy smile, "but like you said, you're busy at work. If you cannot make the wedding, then I simply ask for your blessing now. You can visit us at a future date when it is more convenient."

"Why do you do that to me?" Qasim said, eyes rolling heavenward.

"Do what?"

"Put me in an impossible situation and watch me squirm until I rise to the occasion?"

Eshan smiled. "Because, brother, someone has to be the one who reminds you what you're capable of."

CHAPTER 3

Chunk watched the team of five CIA "Smiths" exit the ship down the gangway dressed in gray cargo pants and black polo shirts. They carried matching coyote-tan backpacks and wore sunglasses despite the sun not yet having broken the horizon.

"Jesus, why don't they just wear dark blue windbreakers with *spook* stenciled on the back in bright yellow letters?" Saw, leaning against the rail, spit into a plastic Coke bottle already half full of dark tobacco juice.

"I know, right?" Riker laughed and spun his stained and worn ball cap backward. Scratching at his beard, he looked at Chunk. "No, no, no, dude. Don't do it . . . don't do it."

Chunk, who was packing a fresh wad of tobacco into his lower lip, tried desperately to resist the urge . . . but couldn't. "Hey, hold up a second," he called after the spooks, who'd left without a parting word to Chunk or his team.

The lead guy, a quiet, clean-shaven forty-something case officer who'd introduced himself as J. P. Jones, stopped and looked over his shoulder. "Yes?"

"A quick word," Chunk said, waving him back aboard.

The spook debated for a beat whether to grant this request for a conversation he most certainly didn't want to have; his shoulders sagged a little. "I'll be just a minute," he said to his team, then reversed course and headed back up the brow.

Chunk moseyed over to where the brow met the ship's deck. "Given what happened on this op, I figured you'd at least provide me with some sort of after-action debrief," he said with a play-nice smile.

The CIA man made a face that Chunk interpreted to mean, *What can I tell this guy to get him off my back without picking a fight?* but all he said was, "What do you want to know?"

"Well, for starters, nobody said shit about us hitting a freighter with Chinese operators on board. I know the Chinese supply hardware to the Pakistani military, but *your* people told *my* people this cargo vessel was carrying weapons bound for terrorists. That's a pretty different scenario than the one we encountered."

"Who says they were Chinese?" the spook said.

"Well, nobody, but I think it's pretty obvious they weren't Pakistanis, you know what I'm sayin'?"

"If they were Chinese SOF, don't you think the resistance you and your team faced would have been more robust? Or are you just *that* good?"

Chunk felt heat flare in his chest, but he put out that fire quick. "Yeah, that's what's been bugging me. They were outfitted like special operations, but they didn't move or shoot like it."

The spook touched his index finger to his temple and pointed it at Chunk with an accompanying condescending wink.

"Still doesn't explain what Chinese mercenaries, or contract security, or whatever you want to call them, were doing on a Pakistani freighter." Chunk clapped his meaty paw on the man's shoulder. "Next time it'd be nice to know what we're walking into . . . if you know what I'm sayin'."

The CIA man, still wearing his sunglasses, looked at Chunk's hand on his shoulder, then met his gaze. "Yeah, I'll keep that in mind. Wouldn't want to make you *uncomfortable*."

Chunk smiled, removed his hand, and spit tobacco juice on the deck beside them. "What was in those crates by the way?"

"You know, you sure do ask a lot of questions for a SEAL." J. P. Jones clapped Chunk hard on his shoulder and turned to leave. "You guys need to wait at least fifteen minutes before disembarking, otherwise you'll draw too much attention to us. I mean really, Commander, you guys look like a casting call for a Peter Berg movie."

Chunk felt the flare of heat resurge in his chest, but he laughed anyway. "Don't forget your umbrellas," he fired back. "I hear there's a chance of rain this afternoon."

"What was that all about?" Riker asked as Chunk watched the CIA man head to an idling SUV whose front passenger door was hanging open for him.

"Just busting his spooky chops," he said dismissively. "C'mon, time to help Carla and the rest of the boys pack our stuff so we can get the hell off this tub."

"Don't gotta ask me twice," Trip said.

"Hold up, boss," Riker said, nodding at the pier. "Something's going on."

Chunk swiveled back around to see two new black SUVs pulling up, followed a few seconds later by a third.

"Looks like the spooks aren't done here after all," Saw said.

"These guys must be the cleanup crew," Riker said, as a group of different spooks unloaded big black duffels, hard cases, and a roller gurney.

I was right . . . We interrupted something major on this tub, and now somewhere out there, some serious shit is hitting a big-ass fan.

As if thinking it made it happen, Chunk's sat phone rang. Annoyed, he pulled it from his cargo pocket and took the call. "Redman," he said, holding up a finger to the boys.

"Make yourself private," said the gruff voice of Commander Bowman, the Skipper of SEAL Team Four.

"Yes sir," Chunk said, turning his back to his men and walking along the gunwale.

"Chunk, the bulk of this conversation will need to happen in a SCIF, but here's what I can tell you. Half the team will head back to the *Reagan* as planned, but I want you to pick three of your best operators—a sniper, a breacher, and TAC guy. I've arranged for you and your guys to meet me at Naval Support Activity Duqm. I'll read you in there. Clear?"

Chunk felt his head spin. He knew better than to press, but he couldn't help himself. "New tasking, sir?"

"We talk when you get here," Bowman said. "There's a fleet Seahawk waiting on the runway at Fujairah International Airport as we speak. Don't miss that flight."

The line clicked dead.

He didn't know if it had anything to do with the Chinese dudes they'd taken out, but any decent SEAL was up for a super-secret mission anytime, except for weddings and the births of their children—and even those were sometimes negotiable.

Chunk turned back to where three SEALs were now waiting for him, Trip having joined the group during his short absence. *Bring it on*, he thought with a grin.

Three hours later they approached NSA Duqm from the sea, aboard the helo Bowman had promised. Saw slept during the two-hour ride in the MH-60S Seahawk—an antisubmarine variant of the Blackhawk that, as SEALs, they'd spent hundreds of hours being shuttled around in. Even with just the four of them it was cramped, however, as this helicopter's cabin contained workstations for two sensor operators, launch tubes for sonobuoys, and a winch in the center of the aircraft for working the AQS-13F dipping sonar that was lowered from a 1,600-foot cable and used to prosecute underwater threats. Riker spent most of the ride showing Trip something on his tablet that they both laughed at, while Chunk stared out the large rectangular window on the port side, watching white caps drift by while he noodled on last night's op and his parting conversation with J. P. Jones.

John Paul Jones, he thought with a chuckle, just now connecting the dots that the lead spook had named himself after the father of the American Navy. *What a dick.*

It hadn't surprised Chunk that Jones wasn't willing to share any tidbits of value; there was an intentional demarcation between operations and intelligence. Worrying about why those Chinese dudes were onboard the ship and what type of illicit shit was in the CONEX boxes wasn't his responsibility. He was a SEAL, a door kicker . . . a weapon. Understanding the what, why, and how of the bad guys' operations wasn't part of his job description. He'd always been fine with that. But that was before he and the boys had augmented the DNI's super-secret black ops unit, Task Force Ember, a couple of times over the past two years. He'd been given a peek behind the curtain, and now he couldn't help himself.

Someone kicked his boot.

"We're here," Trip said, snapping Chunk out of his head.

On that cue, the Seahawk flared and landed on a large brown tarmac. Duqm was a walled compound on the bay side of a narrow man-made spit of land at the western edge of the Arabian Sea. Chunk looked out the open crew door and scanned the horizon. Every damn structure in sight was painted the same coyote tan as the desert. White pickup trucks dotted the compound, and other than a ghost-gray frigate flying a Union Jack on its stern a few hundred yards to the south, the facility felt like a graveyard.

The US Naval Support Compound they were visiting—three trailers in a U around a flagpole flying the Stars and Stripes—was technically located on property leased by the British Navy from Oman. As far as Chunk knew, it was a joint task force compound that functioned as a command-and-control point for American, British, Australian, and German Special Forces units operating in the area. Chunk had never actually been to Duqm, but this quick glance around confirmed he hadn't missed much.

They slung their rifles over their heads and grabbed their bags as the helo kicked up dust before its twin turbine engines shut down with a long whining sigh. Chunk jumped out the door and his guys fell into a loose group behind him as a rail-thin soldier dressed in British SAS cammies approached and extended a hand.

"Welcome to the Ritz-Carlton, mates," he said with the easy smile that confirmed he was an operator.

"Great to be here," Chunk said. "Lieutenant Commander Redman, but you can call me Chunk."

"Patch," the man replied, squeezing and releasing his hand with his worn paw. "Doesn't look like you chaps are coming in from leave."

"Ha," Chunk laughed. "Not leave, but way more fun."

"Fuck yeah," Trip added.

"I hear that," the British commando said. "Maybe you can get me an' my boys into some scraps. Going crazy doing PP up and down nowhere," he added. Operators sometimes got roped into personal protection details during slow times on deployment. "Even willing to operate next to you SEAL wankers if we can get into some scraps."

Chunk laughed. He liked this guy.

Brotherhood.

"I'll see what I can do, bro," he said as the man punched a code into the steel barrier gate. Once inside, the four SEALs followed the Brit through the middle of the compound. At the rear, a stubbier building had a hand-painted sign beside the door that read Joint Special Operations Task Force 288. Patch punched in a code, the door clicked open, and they entered a small lobby where a picture of a British Special Forces operator—full beard and fully kitted up in the desert somewhere—sat on a table beside a framed letter telling the fallen warrior's story. Beyond was a long room with workstations and computers.

Commander Bowman came from beyond the work area, no doubt from inside a Tactical Operations Center. His presence instantly filled the room.

"Lieutenant Commander Redman," the senior SEAL officer said, gripping Chunk's hand in a powerful, short shake.

"Sir," Chunk replied. "This is—"

The skipper cut him off before he could introduce his guys. "Saw . . . Riker . . . Trip." Bowman nodded at each man, knowing not only who they were, but their platoon nicknames for God's sake.

Impressive.

"Sir," they responded in unison.

"Why don't you fellas get some chow while I talk to Chunk? Patch, can you take these guys over to the canteen?"

"Delighted, sir," the SAS operator replied with a genuine smile.

While his teammates left, Chunk followed his boss to the rear of the TOC, where the CO pressed a code into a punch lock. The lock clicked open, and Bowman waved Chunk into a secure briefing room with a conference table and multiple flat-screen TVs on the walls. The SCIF was smaller than what was typical back home and modestly equipped but soundproof and stout enough to block all electronic emissions. Bowman dropped into the chair at the head of the table, then gestured for Chunk to take a seat.

Chunk followed suit and fixed his attention on Bowman, careful not to let his gaze drift to the right side of the senior officer's head, which was riddled with scar tissue. Before the IED explosion, he'd had a full head of thick black hair. Now it had gone silver-fox gray, and he wore it high and tight so the left side matched the hairless right. The VA had reconstructed an ear for him and done a pretty damn good job—but as Bowman himself was fond of joking, "The docs gave me back an ear, just not one that matches." That simple quip summed up the man in spades. Bowman wore his disfigurement like he did his trident. He was a son of valor, and his scars were overt proof that he'd answered his nation's call of duty.

"Before I begin, I can see from your expression that you've got something on your mind," Bowman said.

"Yes, sir. I'm assuming you brought me here for an after-action debrief on the op."

Bowman looked surprised. "Actually, no, but go on."

It was Chunk's turn to be surprised. "I assume you were listening in on comms or Aveda briefed you?"

"Both."

"Okay, so I'm not sure what happened, but obviously we fucked up."

"Hold on." Bowman raised a hand. "We didn't fuck anything up. We got a mission package and we executed it brilliantly. OGA is the one who dropped the ball."

"I hear you, sir, but we capped ten Chinese nationals. There's going to be consequences. And what the hell were they doing on that boat in the first place?"

"Not your problem. Your job is to execute your tasking. When reality does not match the package—which it invariably doesn't—you are expected to adapt and overcome. That's exactly what you did. Bravo Zulu, end of story."

Chunk opened his mouth to try again, but Bowman beat him to the punch.

"Not a Team Four problem," he repeated.

Chunk took a deep breath and let it go. "Yes, sir. Sorry, it's just the disconnect between ops and intel makes me . . . You know, never mind."

Bowman nodded. Then he leaned forward and put his elbows on the table. "Now, that being said, what if I gave you an opportunity to close that disconnect, to operate with a higher level of autonomy and integration with the spooks? Would you take it?"

"Sir?" Chunk said, confused . . . but intrigued.

"After the massacre of Operation Crusader in Yemen, JSOC has been without a Tier One SEAL element, leaving a heavy burden for Delta to shoulder. But that's about to change."

Chunk felt his pulse quicken.

"About damn time, sir," he said, keeping his voice as subdued as the moment would allow.

"At sixteen hundred hours yesterday, the Tier One SEAL Team was officially and confidentially reconstituted," Bowman said, with a little theater in his voice. "Commander Redman, you've been personally recommended by someone whose opinion carries a lot of weight to lead one of the two squadrons."

"Captain Jarvis?" he murmured, unable to contain himself. Kelso Jarvis was the former Director of National Intelligence, now Vice President of the United States, but before his rapid rise in the

DC power circles he'd spent his career at the Tier One, finishing his Naval Special Warfare career as the CSO.

"All those joint-mission boondoggles we lent you out for must have made an impression. 'Unflappable under pressure,' I believe were the Vice President's exact words." Were the corners of the intense old frogman's mouth bending upward? Chunk suspected Bowman knew far more about those Task Force Ember missions than he was letting on, but this was about as close to a smile as the man was capable of.

"But I want you to know, that even without the VP's input, you would have been on my short list to screen for the unit anyway. You're a natural-born operator, Chunk, but more importantly you're a helluva leader. Your guys would follow you to hell and back if you asked them to, and that sort of loyalty and respect is only earned one way—by the blood, sweat, and tears you've given for them. That's the kind of officer I want in my unit."

"*Your* unit, sir?" Chunk asked.

Bowman leaned back, his smile now exposing teeth. "I'll be commanding the new unit, so you'd be stuck with me for another few years. Hell, maybe the rest of your career—the Tier One units are hard to leave . . ." The SEAL's eyes went to the middle distance and his mind to another place and time. Then, he blinked and was back, focused hard on Chunk. "The Tier One's not for everyone, and this offer is on a strictly volunteer basis."

Chunk leaned back in his chair, needing a second to take this all in. The Tier One had always been his dream billet. Just as Naval Aviation had Top Gun, Naval Special Warfare had Green Team—a screening process to train the "best of the best" in the SEAL community for service in the covert JSOC-run Tier One SEAL Team. Less than 5 percent of all Navy SEALs ascended to the Tier One level, and now he was being tapped to lead a squadron.

Then, out of nowhere, an unexpected dread washed over him. "If I say yes, who would take over my role at Team Four?"

"What?" Bowman said, clearly confused by the question.

"It's just that my guys depend on me."

"Well, first of all, in case you haven't connected the dots, you're bringing Saw, Riker, and Trip with you. They each had by-name recommendations as well. And second, while I appreciate your loyalty and commitment to Team Four, your country is giving you an opportunity to serve at a higher level. Now if you want to stay at Team Four, that's fine; there's a long list of guys who would kill for this opportunity. But I think that commitment to the brotherhood and the well-being of your men will play an even more important part in the Tier One. The operational tempo, and the physical and mental toll this job exacts, will be significantly higher than what you and your guys are accustomed to. So yes, you may be leaving one family behind, but you're stepping in to lead another."

Bowman's words resonated with him. The idea that it was somehow a betrayal to leave Team Four for this opportunity was silly. But it was also a statement about how strong the bonds of brotherhood inside the SEAL community were. The truth was, he wasn't abandoning his family; they were just getting reshuffled—something that was going to happen with or without his blessing. That was how the military worked.

"Count me in, sir, and thank you for the opportunity."

Bowman laughed like Chunk had just figured out that jumping in a pool would make him wet.

"Now look, Chunk, this ain't gonna be like the last few decades. We lost the entire unit in Yemen. We're bringing back a few guys who served at the Tier One before Operation Crusader for staff and instructor positions, but when I say we're starting from scratch, I mean we're standing up two squadrons of guys entirely from white side teams. Green Team screening won't be like it was—we'll train the squadrons hard, but simultaneously. Only two platoons per squadron. We're going to be smaller, leaner, and meaner than before. And we're going back to being black. All the old monikers are being retired and JSOC's official policy is to deny any and all reporting that the unit has been reconstituted."

"I understand."

"And we're standing up a dedicated intel shop to support you twenty-four seven, so you won't have to be as reliant on CIA and the Activity as you've been so far in your career." Bowman raised a hand. "Don't get me wrong, we're still going to have to lean heavily on the establishment, but you're gonna have your own in-house spooks who will report to you and be an integral part of mission planning."

Chunk nodded. "I like the sound of that, but how exactly is that supposed to work?"

"We'll figure it out as we go, but one of the lessons learned from the tragedy that put us here is that intel isn't prescient. Last night's op is a perfect example. Somebody missed something and now ten Chinese nationals are dead, and that somebody has to figure out why. As a white side SEAL at Team Four, that some-body is not you. In fact, asking those questions and chasing the answers only throws sand in the gears of the machine. At the new Tier One, you'll still be a door-kicker, Chunk, but now it's okay if you question which door you're supposed to kick and why."

"I like the sound of that."

"All right then. I'm heading back to Virginia to meet with Lieutenant Commander Derek Malkin from Team Five. You know him?"

Chunk nodded. "Our paths have crossed. Academy grad. Good guy. Solid operator is his reputation."

"If he says yes, Malkin will take the other squadron—assuming everyone makes it through Green Team. You'll be operating out of the compound on MacDill. So pack your bags and prep for the move to Tampa."

"Roger that."

Bowman stood and extended his hand. Chunk followed suit and clasped his CO's strong weathered fingers. "Welcome to the new Tier One, Commander," Bowman said.

"Thank you, sir."

"So which of your guys do you want in here first for the good news?"

"Oh that's easy. Senior Chief 'I make my BDUs into board shorts' Riker. But if you don't mind, sir, let's start by telling him we've decided it's time he retires from Team Four." Chunk was unable to suppress an evil grin. "I owe him one."

"Start the screening with a stress test, huh?" Bowman replied with a grin of his own.

"Exactly." Chunk turned to fetch the SEAL.

A little payback for "Baby Shark" . . . This is going to be fun.

CHAPTER 4

"Well, how does it feel?" Eshan asked, interrupting Qasim's train of thought as he stared out the passenger window of the SUV at the lush green fields and trees of the Kameh Valley.

"It's a very comfortable ride," Qasim replied.

"That's not what I'm talking about," Eshan laughed. "I meant how does it feel to be home?"

"Oh," Qasim said, stupefied by his own thickheadedness. "Strange. On the one hand, it feels like I'm visiting an alien planet, but on the other hand, this road is so familiar to me it's like I never left."

When they pulled into the front yard of the modest house he had once called home, he saw a small crowd gathered. His aunt and uncle on his father's side waved at him, along with his four cousins, who'd grown so much he barely recognized them. Also present was a close friend from primary school who Qasim had lost touch with; his aunt Char, of sweet kaddo fame; and lastly Diba, as pretty and bashful as the last time he'd seen her.

"I assume I have you to thank for this?" Qasim said, turning to Eshan.

His friend said nothing, just turned off the engine and smiled as he climbed out of the driver's seat.

The surprise reunion morphed into a family brunch. Aunt Char had prepared an elaborate spread with all of Qasim's favorites, including spiced walnut cookies drizzled in honey. The little cousins played and squabbled, while the adults—both young and middle-aged—told nostalgic stories. When the reminiscing ran its course, the conversation pivoted to Qasim and London. They peppered him with questions about his travels, his work, and what it was like to live in the most expensive and intriguing city in the world. To his surprise, he found himself embellishing many details and outright lying about others. How could he tell them he worked on developing the very machines and weapons of war deployed against his countrymen and women? When he faltered, his tongue going to knots in his mouth, Eshan waltzed into the conversation and rescued him. Ebullient and witty, his best friend assumed the role of charming moderator, asking Qasim leading questions to get the conversation back on track while bolstering the fantasy.

The reunion ended with hugs and tear-rimmed eyes, but not before Qasim carved out a few minutes for a walk and private conversation with Diba. To his great surprise, she did not squander the opportunity with small talk as he intended to do. When he asked her why she had not married, she bluntly told him that she was promised to him, that she had always loved him, and that she wanted—more than anything else in this world—to live in

London with him. She went on to confess that on the night of Saida and Eshan's wedding, her father had spoken with Qasim's and a marriage agreement had been made.

"My father intended to revisit the conversation with you after the funeral proceedings," Diba said, her gaze fierier than he'd ever seen before. "But you left and never came back."

"And what about now? Is he still of the same mind?" Qasim asked.

"My father is dead. He died last year, caught in the middle of a skirmish between the Taliban and Americans working with the Afghan Army," she said, her jaw set. "I speak for myself now; that is, until the Taliban decides to speak for me. Please Qasim, take me with you."

"Okay, I will marry you," he heard himself say, and it felt both exciting and terrifying. He blushed. "What I mean to say is, Diba, will you marry me?"

"Oh, Qasim," she said, her eyes filling with tears. "Yes, yes, yes . . ."

He left her there at his childhood home—with a promise of marriage and no means to contact him—standing amid a gaggle of extended family waving goodbye. As he watched her disappear in the rearview mirror, a single thought replayed over and over again in his head.

My God, what have I done?

"Don't worry. The family has agreed to look after her," Eshan said, breaking the silence at last.

Qasim's jaw dropped open. "Is that what this was? Some ploy to guilt-trip me into marrying Diba?"

"Of course not," Eshan said with a wry grin. "This was a family reunion with a special guest. You did the proposing all on your own."

"You're a sneaky bastard, you know that?"

"Like you said in London, my job is to put you in an impossible situation and watch you squirm until you rise to the occasion. In this case, that occasion just happens to be reuniting you with the girl you're destined to marry."

"Do you really believe in destiny?"

"Of course, and you don't?"

"Destiny hasn't been a great friend to me," Qasim said. "I'd choose you over destiny every time."

"Thank you, my friend. That means a lot to me."

"After Saida died," Qasim said, turning to look out the window, "I ran away as fast as I could. I tried to forget this place and everyone in it. I thought if I started over, it would be easier to move on. But that's the irony. I moved away, but I never moved on. I abandoned the people who loved me in their time of need. Thank you for reminding me of who and what I walked away from."

"You're welcome," Eshan said and reached over and gave Qasim's shoulder a squeeze.

They drove in comfortable silence for several kilometers until Eshan turned off the main road.

"This is not the way," Qasim said.

"I know. We have one more quick detour. It won't take long, I promise."

Qasim checked his watch but didn't argue. Whatever Eshan wanted to show him, he would not complain. A few minutes later, the gravel road terminated at the charred and scattered remains of what was once a wood-and-stone farmhouse. Eshan parked the SUV but did not shut off the engine.

"What is this?" Qasim asked.

"This was Tef Magrab's family home. Turned to ash by an American drone strike."

"Why?"

"Because he was sheltering three Taliban lieutenants."

"What about his family? Were they present when it happened?"

"Does it matter?"

"Of course it matters."

"So if I say yes, then it is a tragedy. If I say no, then it's not? It wasn't a tragedy that your father and Saida were killed because he happened to be riding in a car with two Taliban?"

Qasim consider the question. "I don't know . . ."

Eshan shook his head. "Tef was a pragmatist. He told his wife to take the children to her family home and stay with her parents as a precaution. Thankfully, they were not present at the time of the attack." He gripped the steering wheel tightly with both hands. "But it doesn't diminish the fact that he was murdered by the Americans, making a widow of his wife and leaving his children fatherless. He was a good man, Qasim. A good man put in an impossible situation, forced to choose between capitulating to a cause he didn't support to safeguard his family and livelihood, or standing up for his principles and risking the loss of everything. He chose as your father did. What would you have done in his shoes?"

Qasim said nothing, just stared out the window at the rubble that had once been a home.

Eshan shifted the transmission into drive and executed a U-turn, spraying dust and gravel behind the SUV as they left the property for the main road. They drove in silence all the way back to Jalalabad, where Eshan piloted the Toyota onto the N-5, heading east toward Pakistan. After a long bout of silence, Qasim finally broke.

"Do you think we'll have any trouble at the border?" he asked.

"Well, it's possible, but I know how to handle these things," Eshan said, his eyes fixed on the road.

"I don't like that answer," Qasim said, shaking his head. "Explain, please."

"Pakistan discontinued the practice of issuing on-arrival travel visas for Afghans. Crossing at Torkham is not like it used to be."

"What?" Qasim fired back, his voice full of outrage. "Open travel for Afghan Pashtuns has been a standing policy for decades! Khyber Pakhtunkhwa is our people's land. We do not need permission to cross some imaginary border down the middle of our tribal home."

"Listen to you," Eshan said with a chuckle. "One day home and you already sound like a bitter old man from the village. You know it's not that simple when nations, money, and security are concerned."

"So what's your plan?"

"I pay the border guard a bribe to sign off on a thirty-day travel visa for you."

"And what if that doesn't work?"

"It will."

"But what if it doesn't? I can't afford to wind up in some Pakistani jail. I just got my British citizenship two months ago. I didn't tell them I was going to Pakistan because I was planning on using my Afghan passport for the trip over . . . What?"

"You're a British citizen?" Eshan asked, eyeing him sideways.

"Yes."

"But you've only been working in country for three years. It takes five years in residence employed and another twelve months after that to get your application approved," Eshan said. "I know this because I looked into it myself. How did you pull it off?"

"The Home Office has all kinds of deals they cut with the big companies," Qasim said through a heavy sigh. "While I was at university, British Aero recruited me for a permanent internship. Provided I went to work there upon graduation and remained employed for three years, my school visa time counted as residence time employed."

"Why would the company do that?"

"Because it is a cost-effective way for them to import cheap talent. You'd probably think that a company as important and powerful as British Aero pays premium wages."

"I would."

"Then you'd be wrong. The truth is they pay below market, and the best and brightest programmers invariably get recruited into fintech or IT consulting. I make twenty thousand pounds less than I could working at ASOS or Accenture. But I'm an Afghan immigrant with no legal prospects of making the kind of money I'm making at British Aero in Afghanistan. The company knows this. If you're from India, Pakistan, Malaysia, and so on, they dangle a path to citizenship and lock you into at least three years of employment at below-market wages."

"Very imperial of them, don't you think?"

"Yes, but shaving three years off my wait for citizenship has a monetary value. I imagine many people would pay twenty thousand pounds a year for that benefit. In fact, probably more."

"Count me as one of those people," Eshan said. "So did you bring your British passport with you?"

"Of course."

"Then we don't have a problem, and this whole conversation is academic," Eshan said.

"Why is that?"

"Because at the same time Pakistan suspended on-arrival visas for Afghans, they implemented them for Americans, Brits, and other invaders of our country."

"That's ridiculous," Qasim said, his cheeks going hot. "So Pashtuns can't travel freely in our own land, but rich Westerners can?"

"Welcome to the new Middle East, my friend. Even Pakistan is trying to open its doors to tourism."

The conversation ebbed and flowed over the next two hours, with a familiarity that Qasim had missed. Eshan was describing the dinner menu for the upcoming wedding feast when they hit the kilometer-long queue of cars waiting to cross the border.

"Is it always like this?" Qasim asked.

"No," Eshan said with a sideways grin. "Sometimes it's longer."

They crept forward, making steady progress while Eshan talked about his honeymoon plans. As they approached the checkpoint, Qasim noticed a squad of heavily armed and distinctly Western soldiers in camo fatigues, inspecting both inbound and outbound traffic.

"I didn't realize the Americans maintained a permanent contingent at Torkham crossing," Qasim said.

"To my knowledge, they don't," Eshan said.

"Then what are they doing here?"

"I think it's obvious . . . They're looking for someone."

Qasim nodded. Torkham was one of the busiest, if not *the* busiest, crossing between Pakistan and Afghanistan. And while illegal border crossings were still the preferred way for the Taliban and smugglers to move illicit goods and wanted personnel across the border, the N-5 was a well-maintained paved highway. Convenience was sometimes worth the risk.

"Don't forget to talk with that English accent of yours when they question us, and leave your Afghan passport in your bag."

A pair of American soldiers approached the SUV, machine guns slung across their chests in a way that seemed relaxed, but the weapons themselves were ominous. Qasim fished out his British passport as Eshan rolled down the driver's side window.

"Do you speak English?" the lead soldier said, glancing at Eshan, then scanning their hands and the interior of the vehicle.

"Yes, we both do," Eshan said, adopting a pronounced and convincing British accent.

"Passports, please."

In his peripheral vision, Qasim could see the other soldier circling around the back of the SUV. He handed his passport to Eshan, who passed both to the American.

"What is the purpose of your visit to Pakistan?" the soldier asked, handing their passports off to a third American who was dressed in a black polo shirt and gray slacks.

"We're attending a wedding." Eshan answered.

"Whose wedding?"

"Mine, if you must know."

"Congratulations," the soldier said, while the plainclothes American took a picture of each of their passports with a mobile phone, before handing them back to the soldier.

"And the purpose of your travel?" the soldier asked, meeting Qasim's eyes.

Qasim's stomach fluttered.

Why am I nervous? I'm not a terrorist. I didn't do anything wrong.

"I am attending the wedding as well," he managed, his accent somehow sounding less convincing than Eshan's, which was preposterous because he was the one living in Britain.

"You're a British citizen?"

"Yes."

The plainclothes American stepped up beside the soldier and said, "Look at the camera for a picture," and snapped a quick headshot of each of them before Qasim could protest.

"Why is he taking our picture?" Qasim asked Eshan, before repeating the question to the man who'd just photographed him. "Why are you taking our pictures?"

"Routine security check," the plainclothes American said with disinterest and turned to walk away.

"Congratulations on your wedding," the soldier said. "Safe travels."

"Thank you," Eshan said with a broad smile. "Have a pleasant day."

Qasim waited until Eshan had rolled the window back up. "What the bloody hell was that all about?"

"I told you," Eshan said, handing Qasim's passport back to him. "They're looking for someone."

"Who?"

"Hell if I know," Eshan said, his familiar Afghan accent returning. "But it's not us, so it doesn't matter."

Qasim's gaze ticked to Eshan's passport as his friend returned it to the breast pocket of his shirt. It seemed to be a darker shade of blue than his own Afghan passport . . . but with his tucked away in his bag, it was impossible to compare.

Is he using a fake passport?

Qasim debated asking, but decided it would come across as paranoid. Besides, Eshan hadn't seemed nervous about the border crossing or being confronted by the soldiers. Yes, he'd altered his accent, but that was just gamesmanship to smooth the way . . . wasn't it? Qasim studied the profile of his best friend of twenty years.

"What?" Eshan said with a glance, while gently pressing the accelerator.

"How do you do it?" Qasim asked.

"Do what?"

"You're like a chameleon. You completely had that soldier fooled."

Eshan shrugged.

"I wish I had your courage and confidence. You have something I'll never possess."

"Showmanship, nothing more. I'd trade my bravado for your technical genius in a heartbeat. You haven't even scratched the surface of what you're capable of. You're destined for great things, my brother. You just don't know it yet."

"Do you really think so?"

"Oh yes," Eshan said, his eyes fixed on the road ahead. "I'd bet my life on it."

CHAPTER 5

Chunk expertly worked his parachute risers, reining in the left slightly more than the right, swiveling an instant before stepping out of the air and onto the steep, rocky mountainside. Finding his footing, he quickly pulled in the lines and collapsed his chute, rolling it into a ball with practiced efficiency. He snapped open the Koch fittings on his straps and stepped out of the harness. A heartbeat later, he was sighting over his rifle from a tactical knee, scanning the green-gray desert terrain below through his NVGs. His eight SEAL teammates who'd just dropped from the heavens followed his lead and formed a semicircle behind him. He waited until movement stilled, then he keyed his mike.

"Mother, Popeye One—Popeye is Daytona."

Chunk rolled his eyes as he spoke the call sign the Head

Shed had assigned them. Popeye—as in Popeye the sailor man—
had struck a nerve and annoyed them more than most. Check
that . . . it annoyed *Riker* the most. At least the checkpoints were
beach destinations. They'd done a maritime assault recently where
the checkpoints had been wine varieties, and when he'd called
"Merlot," Riker had threatened to quit.

Ah, the little things . . .

"Roger, Popeye One—report Sandbridge," came the reply
from the TOC, instructing them to call the next checkpoint atop
the ridge.

"Check."

Chunk angled left, then started the trek up the steep rise with
Riker, Trip, George Ash, and Donnie Morales. Ash, the young-
est member of Green Team, had been dubbed "Georgie," which
chapped the kid's ass to no end. Morales, a quiet and compe-
tent 18 Delta combat medic from SEAL Team Five, was called
"Hollywood" because of his dazzling smile and perfectly mani-
cured jet-black hair. Morales was particularly valuable to the
team because prior to attending BUD/S, he'd logged two years
of medical training and been an EOD. Not only did Chunk like
and respect the hell out of the guy, but to have an operator with
two special-mission skill sets was perfect in the Tier One, where a
small footprint meant the need for lots of cross-training.

The amplified crunch of boots on rock echoed in Chunk's
Peltor headset as Lieutenant Chad Spence, the OIC of Gold
Squadron first platoon, led Saw and two other SEALs on a divergent trek to a position 150 meters down the ridgeline. Upon
reaching that checkpoint, Spence would call "Pensacola," and
Saw would set up as overwatch while the lieutenant and his other
two SEALs—Anthony "Antman" Williams and Jamey Edwards—
would prep to rope down the north face. The plan was for Chunk's
element to lead the assault, while Spence's squad capitalized on the

confusion and attacked from the rear. While the SEALs executed their two-pronged ground assault, Saw would pick off the resistance and any squirters. Calling "Destin" would signal mission success—that they'd taken the enemy compound and liberated the hostages held within. Then it was up the east slope, over the ridge, and a helicopter exfil in a pair of MH-60s from the 160th SOAR.

Classic covert SEAL Team hit.

What could possibly go wrong?

He led his team silently up the grueling mountainside, keeping radio silence and moving with stealth. Twenty minutes later they made the top of the eastern ridge and spread out in a line. Taking a knee, he pushed his NVGs up on his helmet and raised an IR spotter scope to his eye to survey the target compound, which was located to the west, inside a bowl-shaped depression at the top of the mountain. The topography reminded him of a crater or, better yet, the crown of a dormant volcano. Inside the depression, three metal buildings were arranged in a U and had a chain-link fence perimeter. The fence was pointless because the compound was wedged tightly into the narrow bowl with east and west rises so steep, they were barely traversable. And the north approach was even worse—a vertical rock wall that even a professional rock climber would balk at. Vehicle access was limited to a narrow, rocky trail on the south side, navigable only by ATV.

"Mother, Popeye One is Sandbridge—you have eyes for me?" Chunk said into his boom mike.

After a long pause, the reply came, "Negative, Popeye. Satellite coverage interrupted. We can put a Predator in orbit, but ETA is ninety minutes. Do you want to hold?"

Chunk sighed. *Of course we lost the satellite. Why would it be easy?*

"Stand by, Mother," he whispered and lifted his spotter scope.

He saw two sentries standing by the front gate, smoking and joking. He could not see a roving patrol, but he knew there was one. As far as a ranging patrol outside the fence line, the original satellite pass had not shown any thermals outside the wire, but that data was nearly an hour old. Intelligence indicated this particular group of insurgents maintained a second site—a single structure five miles to the south. Chunk had no idea if the second building housed fighters, but he did not like the idea of potential enemy QRF being located so close. Worst-case scenario, he estimated any QRF would take several minutes to mobilize and ten minutes minimum to cover the rough terrain. A Predator with air-to-ground missiles in orbit would be nice to have to provide immediate fire support just in case, but the MH-6 they had on standby could be on station in less than fifteen mikes. The little bird was equipped with an M134 Minigun and could easily hold off any QRF assaulters en route. And bonus, it also had the FRIES rope system for rapid extraction of anyone not able to make the rally point. So he had *that* in his back pocket . . .

"Popeye Three is now God," Saw announced, confirming he had found a satisfactory sniper hide on the ridge.

"Two is Pensacola," Spence said, indicating his element was in position at the crotch of the ridge to the north, setting ropes for their infil to the target.

Chunk finished scanning the compound, then directed his gaze to ridgeline on the other side of the crater. As he did, a time-proven adage popped into his head . . .

No plan survives first contact with the enemy.

What if these assholes had their own overwatch set up on the other side? What if a convoy of ATVs was already en route? He couldn't safely move on the target with enemy position data that was an hour old. And they sure as hell couldn't wait ninety minutes for a Predator to get on station. So he keyed his mike and whispered, "Four, One—send up a hornet. Survey the compound, then give me a bird's-eye look down the road."

"Check," came the reply.

Above the north face, the tech-savvy Edwards would be pulling a small black case from his pack, containing the newest model of the more widely known PD-100 Black Hornet drone. Resembling a miniature helicopter, this generation of the nano UAV was slightly larger than the original, but still fit in the palm of a hand. It was faster, zipping around at nearly twenty miles an hour, and had a control range of three miles over line of sight. Most importantly, however, it was now equipped with three cameras, HD, night vision, and a FLIR thermal imager. Chunk pulled out a small tablet from his cargo pocket and waited for it to sync automatically to the drone. The screen flickered to life, and he watched the camera feed skim across a pant leg and boot, then turn to focus on Edwards's face. The Senior Chief lifted his eyebrows three times in rapid succession and the image rocked and tumbled, then stabilized as the drone lifted silently into the sky. Chunk tracked its progress as it skimmed from the ridgeline toward the compound.

Once the drone had repositioned, Chunk's screen refreshed into a three-way split, with thermal, night vision, and HD cameras all streaming simultaneously. The HD feed on top was dark, but the middle screen showed the compound in silvery gray, and the bottom frame depicted bright yellow-orange silhouettes of humans, their body heat visible only in the IR spectrum. He saw the two sentries by the gate, still standing next each other and shooting the shit. He counted three stationary images in supine postures—sleepers—in the far building, which was designated Building One. The closest building, Building Two, showed no thermals. The rear structure, Building Three, formed the bottom of the U and held multiple occupants. The camera feed zoomed in on two thermals—one male, one female—seated close together.

"One, Four—looks like we found our hostages," Edwards said.

"Copy," Chunk said.

The video panned to two other warm bodies, one seated and the other pacing. Unfortunately, it was impossible to tell if these two guys were hanging out in a separate room from the hostages or if the structure had one big open floor plan.

"No change in intel on the compound, Mother," Chunk whispered. "Two hostages in the rear building with two guards. Two roving sentries outside. Three tangos appear to be sleeping in the far building."

"Roger, Popeye One."

"One, Four, you ready for a look down the road?" Edwards said.

"Yes," Chunk answered. The drone immediately began a vertical climb for a bird's-eye view down the southern access road. Seeing no inbound vehicles he said, "Four, One—before you pack it up, let's make a pass along the west ridgeline for snipers and take peek on the other side, just to be safe."

Edwards confirmed with a double click in his ear and the nano UAV zipped across the crater.

"Shit," Edwards's amplified whisper exclaimed in his ear. Two thermals had materialized as the drone crested the slope. "You seeing this, boss?"

"Get a closer look with IR," he whispered back.

The duo could be a sniper team providing overwatch, a wide-perimeter roving watch, or civilians not affiliated with the terrorist compound. As the drone zoomed in, Chunk saw the figures were two men armed with rifles . . . but not sniper rifles, it appeared. Since they were west and below the crest of the ridge, they didn't have a clear line of sight into the crater. At the moment they appeared to be taking a break, sitting on rocks and drinking from a shared bottle or canteen. Still, they had high ground and, called into the fight, they would be a problem.

"God, One, you got a line on these guys?"

"Negative," Saw said, "but if they pop up over the ridgeline I can take them."

Chunk tapped his index finger against the trigger guard of his rifle. He could send two guys to eliminate this threat now, but that would take time—during which any number of other threats could arise, namely additional fighters from the building to the south. The likelihood of completing the op without these two guys being alerted to their presence was extremely low. One volley of return fire from an AK-47 was all it would take to send these guys scrambling to the ridge, where they would be able to rain down lead from above. In that case, his only option would be to pray that Saw was good enough to take them out or provide covering fire until exfil.

He looked at his watch. *We've been too long on target already.* "Four, One—hover the drone over the compound."

"Check."

"Two, One," he said to Spence, "we're moving in. Be ready to rope down when we engage."

"Roger, One," came Spence's reply.

Chunk led Riker, Trip, Georgie, and Morales down the steep eastern slope, careful not to kick loose rocks that would alert the sentries to their presence. The descent was slow and painful, with his thighs burning after only a few minutes. At the bottom, Chunk took a knee with his teammates behind him, each man scanning his sector. Ten meters away, the two sentries stood inside the padlocked front gate, laughing and unaware of the shadow of death closing in from just beyond. Chunk got nods from his teammates, signaling they were ready. If they did this quietly enough, they could breach the perimeter without alerting the two shooters over the west ridge or waking the sleeping fighters, who might summon their QRF. As tempting as it was to light up the sentries from outside the fence, Chunk pointed at Riker and Morales, then at the two men by the gate, and drew a hand across his throat.

Both men nodded and moved silently toward the fence line.

Through his NVGs, Chunk watched Morales take a knee, scanning over his rifle at the base of the fence. Riker, using his teammate's bent leg like step, catapulted himself over the wire-topped fence, dropping to the ground with a thud that sounded soft, even in the amplification of the Peltors on Chunk's ears. Inside the perimeter and concealed by the darkness of a moonless sky, Riker took a knee and sighted over his rifle on the sentries. Morales cleared the fence a heartbeat later, pivoting on his chest against the concertina wire as he swung his legs over and dropped to the ground. But this time, the chain-link fence shuddered, and the sentries stopped talking and turned. Morales and Riker had instantly dropped prone on the ground, the targeting lasers of their rifles trained center mass.

One of the guards motioned for the other to stay put and began walking cautiously toward the fence. This was it, the moment that would decide how it all went down. Riker was up now, his crouch so low he could have dragged elbows on the ground. His rifle was slung on his chest, and though Chunk couldn't see it from his angle, he knew Riker's hand was holding a bowie knife. It felt like watching a leopard stalk an unsuspecting gazelle. The SEAL moved closer, ready . . .

A flashlight beam clicked on.

Morales's heavily suppressed rifle coughed out a round and the guard farther from Riker snapped back his head and crumpled to the ground, the flashlight rolling in the dirt. The guard closer to Riker froze, confused at first, before turning to run. But Riker was already on him, a hand over the man's mouth, dragging the knife across his throat. The SEAL silently lowered the body to the ground, sheathed his knife, and turned to sight his rifle on Building Two.

Chunk held position, waiting for an alarm to wail, lights to go on, or gunfire to erupt.

"Clear," came the report from Riker. "God?"

"No movement from the west ridgeline," Saw answered.

"Five and Six, move to cover Building One," Chunk commanded as he led Trip and Georgie to the fence. "Two, begin the descent. One and Seven will hit the front of the target building when you call it. Eight, join Five and Six at Building One."

In seconds, Chunk, Trip and Georgie were over the fence. Georgie went left to join Riker and Morales at the bunkhouse—the next immediate threat—while Trip shadowed Chunk as he vectored toward the building where the hostages were being held. They arrived at the door and, finding it closed but slightly ajar, knelt on either side. Chunk looked up in time to see Spence, Edwards, and Antman speeding silently down the north face of the crater.

"One, God—we've got company." Saw's voice was tight but controlled. "I have lights coming up the road behind you from the south camp. Looks like a QRF is inbound."

Shit!

"How many vehicles?" he whispered nearly inaudibly.

"Can't tell yet. Just see the lights. Two, get off the ropes."

Beyond the roofline, Chunk saw the three SEALs rappelling down the cliff wall increase the speed of descent, then disappear behind the building.

"Single vehicle, but looks like four guys . . . maybe five," Saw reported.

Time to breach. Come on, come on, come on . . .

"Two in position," Spence's report finally came.

Chunk looked at Trip, who nodded back.

"Three . . . two . . . one . . ." Chunk whispered, keeping a controlled cadence despite the stress of the approaching vehicle. On the zero beat, Trip pushed the door open and Chunk followed behind him. Trip cleared right, while Chunk cleared left. At the same time, a *whump*, followed by the sound of breaking glass, echoed from the rear of the building as Spence's team breached the wall with a small charge.

Gunfire erupted from the back room.

"One KIA, male hostage is secure," Spence announced in his ear. Then came the curveball, "Female hostage is missing."

Chunk grinned tightly. He'd expected there would be something unexpected at this point, and here was at least the first one. He surged forward with Trip covering his six, and he heard shouting and the click of the door straight ahead being locked. He increased his speed, lowered a shoulder, and plowed into the wooden slab. The door came off its hinges as he tumbled through the doorway. Ahead, a muzzle flash lit up the hallway as a pistol cracked. Coming out of his roll, Chunk snapped into a kneel, sighting over his rifle. He put his holosight targeting dot on the forehead of a bearded man pointing the pistol at him. The fighter was using the female hostage as a human shield. Tears streamed down her face, and her entire body was trembling beneath the thick forearm latched across her throat.

The man screamed in Arabic as he swept the pistol left to right and back again, shifting his aim between Chunk and Trip.

"Put down your weapon or you die," Chunk shouted in Arabic.

The man shook his head and pressed the muzzle into the sobbing woman's right temple. Chunk frowned and pulled the trigger.

"Hostage two secure," he announced, as the kidnapper collapsed.

"Shooters coming through the gate," Saw announced. "Scratch one," he said as he began taking out the arriving fighters from his hideout.

Gunfire echoed outside the building—both MK18 and

AK-47 rounds being exchanged—as Riker and his fire team engaged the fighters in Building One.

"Three KIA in Building One," Riker reported when the gunfire stilled as abruptly as it started.

"God, report on the west ridge," Chunk said, his mind on their exfil as he sighted on the female hostage, who was now on her knees and wailing. He surveyed her closely to make sure she wasn't wired up with a suicide vest or concealing a weapon.

"West ridge still clear," Saw said.

Satisfied his hostage wasn't a booby trap, Chunk raised his rifle and advanced within arm's reach, upon which the woman collapsed against him, hugging his leg. He introduced himself using a NOC and the standard hostage rescue litany.

"Courtney Tindley—I'm Tom. We are the United States military, and we're here to take you home."

"Home?" she sobbed, looking up at him.

"Contact left, contact left—QRF just breached the front gate," Riker reported in his ear. Chunk pictured the scene outside, where his men were taking fire from the vehicle at the gate.

"Moving back toward Building Two. They got a .50 cal," Morales said. "Find cover."

"Yes, home," Chunk said to the hostage, raising her to her feet with his left arm, keeping his voice soft and soothing. "Can you tell me the name of the elementary school you attended, Courtney?" he asked. He needed to confirm her identity so they could get the hell out of there.

"My school?"

"Keep him off that machine gun, God," Riker hollered in his ear.

More gunfire.

"What was the name of the school where you went to first grade, Courtney?" Chunk pressed.

"Oh . . . yes . . . um . . ." She shook her head and wiped tears from her dirty cheeks.

He waited.

"Um . . ."

"Machine gun neutralized, but we have more lights coming up," Saw reported.

"Thomas Roberts," she said.

"Fire from the ridgeline."

"I'm on it—tango down."

She smiled at him. "Thomas E. Roberts Elementary School."

Chunk smiled back. "That's right."

Spence, Edwards, and Antman entered from the back room, dragging a dazed and haggard Caucasian man. The guy could barely walk, and Edwards was holding him up, arm around his back, gloved hand under his armpit.

"We're confirmed," Spence told Chunk, moving past him and taking a position at the open door, scanning the compound.

"Five is wounded," an unfamiliar commanding baritone announced over a megaphone. "Gunshot wound to the left leg. Unable to walk due to fracture. Hemodynamically unstable."

Of course, and they had to pick Riker.

"Second shooter neutralized," Saw announced immediately after. "West ridge is clear."

Add a couple of minutes while the bad guys sort out what had happened here. Maybe we can make it, with air support . . .

"Mother, this is Popeye One," Chunk said. "Popeye is Destin. Say again, Destin. Get that little bird in tight orbit, as we may need hot extract for some personnel."

"Roger, One," came the acknowledgment from the TOC.

"God, hold overwatch. Everyone else up the hill and over the ridge to extract. Four—SITREP on Five?"

"Got a tourniquet on the leg," Morales replied.

"Conscious but in shock," the amplified baritone voice projected over the megaphone from somewhere out of sight.

"From the Almighty's lips to our ears," Edwards commented. No one laughed, but it was pretty funny.

"I can carry him out. Might need help up the hill to make it fast, though," Morales said.

"Meet you over the fence," Chunk barked. "Let's go, Popeye."

In moments, they were helping the hostages awkwardly over the fence, just as Morales arrived with Riker in a combat carry. He was moving almost effortlessly despite the hefty load. Riker looked at Chunk from under tipped-up NVGs and rolled his eyes.

Chunk shook his head in admonition. *Play along.*

As the rest of the team—save for Saw, who was still in his hide—scrambled up the hill with the hostages, Chunk slung Riker's left arm over his shoulder as Morales did the same with his right, splitting the load. Each man then took a leg, making a human palanquin of sorts for the wounded SEAL. They huffed and puffed up the hill at full speed and were still short of cresting the ridge when they heard the thrum of the approaching helicopters rising from the valley on the other side.

Then came the bad news from Saw. "Inbound enemy vehicle is in the open and approaching the gate."

Well, of course it is.

"Popeye One," came the calm voice of Mother from the TOC. "Do you want the little bird to engage?"

Chunk weighed his options as they struggled the last seventy-five yards up the steep rise. This second wave of bad guys finding missing hostages and dead teammates was still fully deniable, but if he sent an American combat helicopter to overtly engage, it could be a geopolitical problem. No, it was better to hold off, so long as they didn't get shot in the back.

"Negative, Mother. Have the little bird loiter just north of the exfil to grab God in two mikes. God, engage the tangos in the approaching vehicle to cover our exfil. Just need another minute."

"Check," Saw replied.

"How much do you fucking weigh, dude?" Morales grumbled, Riker's weight beginning to take its toll as they huffed up the hill.

"Two hundred and ten buck naked," Riker answered, grinning.

"Great mental picture," the SEAL medic grumbled in reply, but he was smiling.

"Don't drop me, dude. I don't want to get my cammies dirty," Riker added, as they crested the ridge.

Chunk exhaled with relief as they joined the rest of the team who'd surged ahead. The SEALs spread out on the steep cliff side, holding security in all directions.

"Stalker, we're ready for exfil," Chunk called and watched as the two MH-60s rose from below until they were hovering parallel to the cliff's edge, rotors lifting up shale and dust. Together, the SEALs and hostages piled aboard. "God, drop down the east side and your ride is waiting," Chunk said, following the last of his men into the helo. To the north, he watched the smaller MH-6 hover to exfil Saw. "Stalkers, stay below the ridgeline," he called, but it was unnecessary—the pilots of the Army's 160th Special Operations Air Regiment were the most elite aviators in the world. They knew the drill.

Seconds later the helos were descending into the valley at a stomach-lifting speed.

"God is clear," Saw called, the unmistakable warble from the MH-6 evident in his voice.

"Exercise is now complete," announced the same humorless baritone that had called out Riker's injury, except this time the voice came over the comms channel. "Secure the drill."

Morales leaned back from pretending to work on his "wounded" teammate and smacked Riker on his perfectly healthy leg. "Get your ass up off the floor, bro," the medic said.

"Nah." Riker crossed his legs at the ankles. "This is pretty cozy."

Chunk kicked his Senior Chief in the side.

"Okay, okay," Riker said and scrambled onto the canvas bench seat.

Across the aisle from Chunk, the woman who'd played hostage Courtney Tindley was wiping her face with a hand towel. With a weary sigh, the CIA simulation coordinator reached behind her and pulled a pair of David Clark headphones from a hook and slipped them on.

"Two hostages rescued, no lost blue members, and one wounded," she said, meeting Chunk's gaze. "Well done, Commander. Our team will do a forensic sweep of the site to see what evidence of an American presence may have been left behind, then we'll review the film with Commander Bowman. There'll be a hot wash of the op with my team of trainers at zero-four-hundred, so get cleaned up quickly. When we're done, we'll hand you back over to your command for a formal debrief."

The woman flipped her mike up, crossed her legs at the knee, and leaned her head back against the bulkhead.

"And?" said a voice on the channel. Chunk shook his head. It was Riker, unable to contain himself.

The woman opened her eyes and raised her eyebrows.

"And what?"

"And," Riker said, his gaze sweeping across his teammates, "we were pretty shit hot, right? I mean that was a tough setup, lady. Boxed-in canyon compound, HALO infil, QRF minutes away, hostages divided, spotters on the far ridge . . ."

The woman stared at him, eyebrow raised. "And what?"

"Oh, come on, lady," Riker said, laughing and summoning

his best Ron Burgundy impression. "I mean, don't pretend you're not impressed."

The CIA trainer didn't smile. "My understanding is that this evaluation is the final screening for you guys getting signed off as the new Tier One asset."

"Right," Riker agreed.

She exhaled, leaned her head back against the bulkhead, and said, "In that context, you were adequate."

"Adequate?" Riker said, then huffed incredulously before hamming it up with Morales and Trip.

Chunk looked at the woman, who made eye contact and gave him a subtle nod. Then, with an almost imperceptible smile, she folded her arms and closed her eyes—spook code for "you guys nailed it, but I refuse to add any hot air to your already inflated egos."

He'd take it because tonight's simulation capped off four weeks of Green Team evaluation. For weeks Bowman and the Green Team trainers and evaluators had put Gold Squadron through the wringer, but every member had impressed. Long days of diving, breaching, range training, grappling, ropes training, and dive, jump, sniper, and breacher requalifying were coming to a close. They'd made it through—individually, but far more importantly, as a team. As good as these SEALs had been, they were now even better. Soon they would round out the team with additional support personnel and of course their new intel shop, to be led by an intelligence expert from the civilian agencies—a woman Chunk had helped select.

He wasn't sure what the skipper had planned for them next, but whatever it was, they'd be ready.

CHAPTER 6

From a chair along the wall, Qasim watched Eshan dance with his new bride. Aleena bore little resemblance to his sister, yet Qasim's mind kept playing tricks on him, ghosting Saida's face over the other woman's. Every adoring smile, every passion-fueled glance, every seductive touch sent a stab of pain through Qasim's chest.

It was all wrong.

This was not how it was supposed to be.

But his subconscious was in control, and the gruesome flashback spooled through his mind: Saida's smile, running after their father's car, fire streaking from the sky, then her severed leg, smoldering on the ground while his father's funeral pyre burned in the distance. Panic, angst, and rage filled him, the likes of which he'd not felt since the night of the drone strike. He stood abruptly, feeling flushed and short of breath. He had to get out of the banquet hall. He needed air. He needed to breathe . . .

Trying not to draw attention to himself, he slithered through the crowd of guests and made his way outside. Despite it being a dreadfully hot day, the temperature had dropped significantly after sundown. The cool night air immediately whisked the heat from his skin and made it easier to breathe. He bent at the waist, palms pressed against the tops of his thighs.

This is a happy day . . . a good day. What are you doing, Qasim? he chastised himself.

He took one final, cleansing breath and straightened. Suddenly feeling eyes on him, he looked right and saw three men standing in a tight cluster, one of them smoking. Presumably, they'd been talking, but now they were silent, staring at him. He'd noticed them earlier, inside the wedding hall, where they'd seemed out of place beside the other guests. They wore understated tunics and trousers, a shabbiness that bordered on the inappropriate. Pakistani weddings were flashy affairs, with the women dressed in ornate and brightly colored dresses and the men frequently opting for European suits with clean lines. When men did wear tunics, they were typically made of silk and elaborately embroidered. These guys, with their heavy beards and black turbans, looked like they'd just wandered in from the Khyber Pass. But it wasn't how they looked that bothered him; it was the way they looked *at him*, the way they looked at *everyone*: with scrutiny, with judgment, with malice. It was the same malevolent stare that every Taliban lieutenant had fixed on him growing up.

A hand gripped his shoulder. Reflexively, he jerked free and whirled to face his accoster.

"Qasim?" Eshan said, frowning. "Are you all right?"

"Fine, fine," Qasim said, straightening his necktie and forcing a pleasant smile. "You just surprised me, that's all."

"I'm sorry about that; I didn't mean to surprise you. I wanted to make sure that you weren't ill."

"No, I'm not ill," he said through a sigh. "I just . . . never mind. Enough about me. Aleena looks so beautiful; she's so full of life and energy. I'm happy for you."

"She is radiant, isn't she? But I'm not letting you change the subject so easily. Talk to me. What's on your mind?"

At first, Qasim's jaw clenched, but then it all came spilling out. Like a dam break, it was impossible for him to contain the torrent he'd kept at bay all these years. He started by telling Eshan about the flashback and of his mixed emotions about Eshan moving on, how he was jealous and yet overjoyed, bitter but relieved. He talked about the guilt he carried for leaving his ancestral home to start a new life in England. And how a big part of his leaving was driven by fear—fear of the Taliban, fear of the Americans, and mostly fear about his future in a country he felt so disconnected from. The dark irony, of course, was that in his flat in New Malden, he felt more alone, afraid, and isolated than he ever had growing up. He didn't fit in, and no one loved or understood him there. He blamed the Americans for that, because if they hadn't murdered his sister and father, then leaving would have been his choice, not something that was done to him. He said this and other things. Many things, almost all of them contradictory and conflicted and childish. When he had finished, he felt better, but he was also too ashamed to look his friend in the eyes.

"Qasim, there is nothing wrong with you," Eshan said, his voice calm and steady. "I've battled with all the same feelings. I've battled with guilt and anger and hopelessness. I loved your sister—more than life itself—but she is gone, and nothing we do can change that. Nothing we do can bring her back. But that doesn't mean we must accept the atrocity. It doesn't mean we should forgive the men who murdered her and stole her future . . . our future. With our silence, we sanctify their war crimes. With our inaction, we legitimize their tyranny."

"What are you talking about?" Qasim said, sensing a new and unfamiliar tone.

"I'm talking about reclaiming what is rightfully ours from the apostates who occupy our land and murder our brothers, wives, and children. I'm talking about freedom and recompense. I'm talking about change, Qasim. Most of all, I'm talking about the future."

Qasim didn't reply. Eshan's words both energized and terrified him to the core.

"But we'll talk more about these things later," Eshan said. "Tonight is a night for celebration, not remorse. Let's go back inside. Aleena wants to meet you. If you're lucky, she might even let you dance with her."

"All right, but I'm a terrible dancer," Qasim said.

The night ebbed, the newlyweds eventually disappeared, and a few hours later, a knock on the hotel room door jolted him awake. It felt like he'd slept for no more than fifteen minutes, but the sunlit room begged to differ. A glance at the clock on the bedside table confirmed it was after noon. The knock came a second time, and with a groan he crawled out of bed. Stooping to use the security peephole, he saw Eshan's face—distorted by the fish-eye lens—staring back at him.

"What are you doing here?" Qasim said as he unlocked and opened the door. "Is everything okay?"

"Everything is magnificent," Eshan said, waltzing into the room, face freshly shaved and beaming. "I have my bride and best friend together in the same city at the same time. The wedding banquet was a huge success, and last night with Aleena was something I'll remember for the rest of my life."

Qasim grinned and shook his head. "So *that* was the howling keeping me up all night."

"Don't be surprised when I invite you back in nine months so you can meet little Eshan," his friend said with a wink.

"As long as I get to be Uncle Qasim, you have a deal." Then, after an awkward beat, he said, "Not to be rude, my friend, but why are you here? You should be in your room, enjoying the morning with your new wife."

"We already enjoyed the morning," Eshan said, grinning even wider than before. "Aleena is an early riser. We had some fun together, and now she is off for a day of shopping with her sisters. Which is great, because it gives me time to spend with you. Get dressed. I want to show you around Peshawar. It's a beautiful and vibrant city. Much to see."

Knowing that arguing was pointless, Qasim dutifully changed clothes, and five minutes later the two friends were walking away from the hotel.

"Eshan, there's something I need to ask you. Something that's been bothering me since last night," Qasim said.

"Okay, what is on your mind?"

"Those men last night, at your wedding . . . were they Taliban?"

Eshan smiled, then pulled his phone from his pocket and powered it down wordlessly in front of Qasim's face. Shaking his head in disbelief, Qasim did the same. When the deed was done, Eshan said, "Two of the men were Taliban, and one is affiliated with a different group."

"You invited fucking terrorists to your wedding!" Qasim gasped. Because of his Islamic upbringing, he rarely swore, but he couldn't help himself.

"Keep your voice down," Eshan snapped while keeping his expression pleasant. Then, in a relaxed, conversational tone he added, "They are business associates, Qasim, and they wanted to meet you."

"Meet me?" Qasim said, practically choking on his tongue. "What the bloody hell for?"

"Because of the work you're doing at British Aero, of course. And because I have spoken very highly of you. They know our story. They know what we have lost."

"Eshan . . . I . . . I don't even know what to say. You know I'm not a believer. You know I don't support jihad. And neither do you, for that matter. I don't understand," Qasim said, stopping in his tracks.

"Keep walking," Eshan said, with an uncharacteristic take-charge manner. Qasim found himself falling in step beside Eshan despite himself. "Saida was murdered. Your father was murdered. The people who murdered them have not been held accountable. The American military kills with absolute impunity. They believe themselves gods, like Zeus striking down mortals from the sky without guilt or consequence. But instead of throwing thunderbolts from Mount Olympus, they use Hellfire missiles fired from drones at thirty thousand feet."

Qasim resisted the urge to nod in agreement. There was truth in his friend's words.

"It is a shame that it takes personal loss and suffering for most men to find their courage . . . to find their principles. I count myself as one of these men. Before Saida's murder, I told myself that the Americans were not invaders, but rather arbiters of justice. Keepers of the peace. But this is the story a coward tells himself so he can sleep at night. As long as the bad things happen to somebody else's wife, somebody else's daughter, then why get involved? Why take the risk of drawing their fury down on your head? It is so much simpler, so much safer, to remain anonymous in the crowd and play the game of numbers."

"Like a bait ball," Qasim murmured.

"Excuse me?"

"A bait ball," he repeated. "Small fish, like sardines, cluster together in a tight sphere when confronted by a predator. They swim close together, at the same speed and in the same direction, each fish trying to get lost in the crowd. I saw it on a documentary."

"Exactly my point. When faced with a powerful threat, we are no smarter or braver than sardines."

"Maybe, but if you are a sardine being hunted by a shark, what other option do you have? It is not a choice, it is necessity. The sardine that breaks from the school and charges the shark is sure to be eaten."

"Ah. But what if the sardines pooled their resources and hired a shark to protect them and attack any incoming shark before it could strike?"

Qasim raised a quizzical eyebrow. "Go on."

"What if I told you that I had acquired a combat drone equipped with air-to-ground missiles, and that I could deploy it in the Afghan skies as a deterrent to the Americans."

"I'd say you were crazy."

"Crazy like a sardine, right?" Eshan said, his trademark grin returning.

"Exactly."

"Okay, then call me crazy." Eshan pulled his phone out of his pocket and powered it on. He found the image he wanted and passed his phone to Qasim.

Qasim recognized the object on the screen instantly—an MQ-9 Reaper UCAV armed with a Hellfire missile under each wing. *Wait, no. That's not a Reaper*, he thought zooming in with thumb and forefinger. The C-band radio antenna behind the sensor fairing hump was missing, as was the downward-pointing tail control surface.

"That's a Wing Loong Pterodactyl," he said, handing the phone back to Eshan. "A Chinese clone of the American Reaper but with marginally reduced range, payload, and sensor capabilities."

"Impressive. You certainly know your drones." Eshan powered his phone off and returned it to his pocket.

"Why are you showing me that?"

"It's in our possession. Would you like to see it?"

"What do you mean in *our* possession? Are you talking about those men from last night? They acquired this drone and you're working with them?"

"In a manner of speaking," Eshan said simply. "Would you like to see it in person?"

A moment passed between old friends before Qasim said, "Of course not! Are you crazy?"

"You hesitated."

"No, I didn't."

"You did, and I know you, Qasim. You're curious. You want to see it."

"I work on drones far more advanced than the Pterodactyl every day . . ."

"On your computer. But have you actually put your hands on one?"

"No," he said, not meeting Eshan's gaze.

"Have you piloted one?"

"Only a simulator."

"Would you like to?"

"You're crazy." Qasim picked up his pace and walked ahead, despite having no idea where he was going.

"It's time to stop lying to yourself," Eshan said, trotting to catch up with him. "Do you think it was an accident that you went to work for British Aero? An accident that they put you in charge of flight dynamics software integration for their next generation stealth drone? Of course not. This is Allah's hand at work. He has been laying the groundwork for this moment since the night that Hellfire missile destroyed our lives. Working through your subconscious mind to make the plans and build the foundation of our retribution."

A shiver ran down Qasim's spine, and he halted. "This is your plan, not Allah's. You're the one who encouraged me to apply at British Aero. I'd forgot that, but it was you. I bet you knew about their path-to-citizenship intern program, didn't you?"

"I didn't make any of this happen," Eshan said with a shrug. "I just gave you a nudge; the rest you did yourself."

"Bollocks. It's all your handiwork." Qasim laughed harshly. "You're not an engineer of machines, you're an engineer of outcomes. Push a little here, pull a little there, whisper this, lie about that, until you have everyone doing your bidding. Just like this visit. You show up on my doorstep out of the blue, talking about home and family. You invite me to your wedding, knowing I can't refuse, then you set a recruitment trap for me. But I'm not some poor, naive boy from the village with dreams of glory and no prospects for a better future. These are bad men, Eshan, very bad men you've tangled yourself up with. Once they get their hooks into you, you can never escape. I'm sorry, but I'm not throwing away my life, and I'm not going to live the rest of my life in fear wondering if tonight is the night men with guns break down my door and haul me away to some black site, never to be seen or heard from again. I'm not doing it."

"Okay," Eshan said with another shrug. "I understand. We don't need to speak of this again. Let's enjoy the walk, get some lunch, then you can enjoy the rest of your holiday. No hard feelings."

They walked in silence for a block, Qasim's mind a mess of contradicting thoughts and emotions.

"This place has good food," Eshan said, nodding at a sign. "Not so clean, but very tasty . . . What? What's that look?"

"I don't understand how you can be so casual about this,"

Qasim said, standing in the middle of a street crammed with vendors, scooters, and three-wheeled carts. The cloud of dust and mélange of city odors reminded him of Jalalabad.

"Look, I understand you're afraid, and it's okay," Eshan said as a bearded man on a motorbike zipped by, shooting the narrow gap between them. "There's no shame in saying no."

Qasim could detect no hint of insincerity in his friend's voice or expression, but the subtext was unmistakable: There *was* shame in saying no, and in saying no he solidified his cowardice.

"Why do you do this to me?" Qasim said, an actor repeating his lines as they played out the same old scene.

"Do what?"

"Put me in an impossible situation, watch me squirm, then act so noble and understanding when I fail to rise to the occasion?"

Eshan put a hand on his shoulder. "Because, brother, it's my job to remind you of what you are capable of."

"Then, tell me, brother, what *am* I capable of?"

"Great things . . . impossible things. One man *can* make a difference. All we need you to do is look over the drone's programming and make sure it's operational. We need this drone for protection. It levels the playing field and will make the Americans think twice before they launch missiles from the sky at someone else's wedding."

"You're not going to use it for terrorism?"

"Of course not. It's for protection . . . Spend one day with the drone, that's all I ask. Then you can go back to England and your life."

"And Diba?"

"And Diba, of course," Eshan said, nodding. "Don't worry, she knows nothing of this."

"That's all? I look at the drone, check the programming, make sure it can fly without crashing?"

"That's all."

Qasim felt a lump form in his throat. He swallowed, but it persisted. "Okay," he finally said. "I'll do it."

"Good." Eshan turned toward the restaurant. "Let's go get some kebabs, and you can ask anything you want about our Wing Loong Pterodactyl."

CHAPTER 7

UNITED STATES SPECIAL OPERATIONS COMMAND (SOCOM)

MACDILL AIR FORCE BASE

TAMPA, FLORIDA

1307 LOCAL TIME

Whitney Watts combed her fingers through her espresso-brown hair, pushing the tousled sweep of bangs out of her eyes. The very last thing she'd done before leaving DC was to chop twelve inches off. It had been a spur-of-the-moment decision, but a symbolic one—a fresh look for a fresh start. The old Northern Virginia Whitney was over. Say hello to Florida Whitney.

When Reed Lewis, her boss at the National Counterterrorism Center in McLean, Virginia, had informed her that he'd recommended her for a big promotion, she'd thought he was messing with her. Despite him being two decades older, they got each other's humor, but it hadn't been a joke. Apparently, some nameless, secret direct-action activity was being stood up in Florida, and the NCTC Director had been asked to recommend candidates for an analyst to run their intel shop. Out of everyone in the department, Lewis had recommended her—a twenty-seven-year-old tattooed millennial with unicorn professional dreams and a sorry-not-sorry attitude.

Go figure.

And now she was here, with absolutely no friggin' idea what she'd gotten herself into.

"You said Lieutenant Commander Redman?" The man beside the check-in desk looked up at her from his computer.

"Yes, Lieutenant Commander Keith Redman," she said, resisting the urge to check her notes. She was positive that was the name she'd been given. "This is SOCOM HQ, correct?"

"Yes ma'am, this is SOCOM, but there's nobody by that name working here. Are you sure he's not over at CENTCOM? You could try there," the young Marine Corporal said.

"Okay, thanks for checking."

She stepped away from the reception desk and walked out of the building. She'd dressed to make a good first impression, selecting her nicest professional business attire: a slim-fitting black pantsuit, crisp lavender V-neck blouse with an open collar, and a trendy pair of black pumps she'd never worn. She raised her hand like a visor to cut the glare from the high noon sun as she scanned for an approaching Naval officer in uniform who might be her new boss. Finding no one fitting the bill, she sighed and wiped a bead of sweat from her brow with the back of her hand.

Nothing like getting left high and dry on your first day on the job . . .

The sound of off-road tires growling over asphalt got her attention, and she looked right to see a stingray-gray Jeep Rubicon four door approaching at high speed. She watched the driver brake to a hard stop along the curb fifteen feet in front of her. The Jeep was outfitted with a lift kit, an integrated front-bumper winch and skid plate, and splattered with dried mud from the midline down. It also had no doors. Without killing the engine, the driver hopped out, squinted at her, and waved.

"You Whitney Watts?" he called, flipping the of bill his backward-facing ball cap around to the front.

"Yeah," she said. "Are you . . . Lieutenant Commander Redman?"

"Nope, I'm Riker. Redman sent me to pick you up. Sorry I'm late," he said, but his body language said otherwise.

She looked him up and down. He wore flip-flops, a pair of cut-off BDU board shorts, a frog skeleton tattoo on his left calf, a threadbare "Bars of Virginia Beach" T-shirt that showed off sleeves of tattoos on both arms, and a ragged red ball cap with a giant *N* on the front.

There is no way in hell this guy is a Navy SEAL, she thought while trying her damnedest not to screw up her face in irritation. She was just about to question him when his mobile phone rang.

"Yeah . . . yeah . . . she's here," he said, taking the call. "Yeah, I know, dude . . . Well, she's looking at me like I'm nuts, and I don't think she wants to go anywhere near my Jeep . . . Yeah, all right, I'll tell her. Uh-huh, see ya in a few." He shoved his mobile back in his pocket. "That was Redman. He wanted me to tell you that next time he'll make me wear my whites to pick you up, but if you could please make an exception and ride in my filthy-ass jeep back to the compound, because y'all got several hours of indoc paperwork bullshit to take care of and happy hour ends at eighteen hundred, so we gotta rock and roll."

Then, he flashed her a toothy tobacco-stained grin and made a low sweep of his arm toward the Jeep.

"I can't even . . ." she mumbled under her breath and walked to the passenger side of the Rubicon. The suspension lift on the Jeep demanded that she use the mud-crusted tubular step that ran along the undercarriage of the vehicle. *At least I didn't wear white*, she thought as she brushed off the seat cushion, which thankfully—unlike the outside of the vehicle—was not covered in dirt.

"Somebody probably shoulda given you a heads-up," Riker said as he packed his bottom lip with Copenhagen snuff. "We're a business casual shop."

"Yeah, I gathered that," she said absently, reaching to close the door that wasn't there. Riker chuckled. "You got something against doors?" she quipped with a sideways glance.

"Doors are superfluous," he said, shifting the transmission into drive. "We're in Florida and this is a Jeep."

He at least did her the courtesy of letting her click her seatbelt before he sped away from the curb. Clutching the handle on the A pillar with her right hand and her shoulder satchel to her chest with her left, she tried to ignore the sensation that she would be flung out onto the pavement at any moment. After one particularly erratic swerve, she glanced over to see Riker steering with his knees while unscrewing the lid from a mostly empty soda bottle. The plastic crinkled loudly in his grip as he raised it to his lips and dribbled tobacco juice inside. Deposit made, he stuck it in the cup holder behind the gearshift.

"Dip?" he said, presenting her with the tin of wintergreen smokeless tobacco.

"No thanks," she said, but the grin on his face told her the offer was tongue-in-cheek.

"Where you from, Whitney?"

"Northern Virginia."

"*Northern* Virginia, huh?" he echoed, flipping his ball cap backward. "Trying to make sure you don't get confused with them real Virginians, huh?" He grinned.

"Yeah, actually," she said with an unapologetic nod. "I suppose. What about you? Nebraska, I assume?"

"Hot damn, you are intel."

"The giant red *N* on your cap tipped me off," she said, laughing.

"That's the kind of actionable intelligence gathering that could have prevented 9/11," he said with a wry grin.

"So you're with the Tier One?" she said.

"I don't know what you're talking about, Whitney. To my knowledge there is no unit with that designation," he said, his expression turning dubious. "I do, however, work for a group within Naval Special Warfare on classified special projects that require overseas travel."

Her cheeks flashed crimson at her rookie gaffe. "Understood," she said. Lewis had told her that this unit took operational security *very* seriously—more so after the catastrophic loss of the original team in Yemen, she imagined.

Riker drove to an access road that skirted the airfield, driving past rows of KC-135 aerial refuelers belonging to the 927th Air Refueling Wing. About halfway down the west side of the two-mile-long runway, they turned onto an unnamed road with a sign that read "Authorized Personnel Only. Use of Deadly Force in Effect." After fifty meters or so, the road doglegged right and disappeared into a thick grove of brush and mangrove trees. On the other side of the thicket, a series of concrete barriers forced Riker to slow and weave the Jeep through a serpentine gauntlet—a passive security measure designed to force a vehicle to a crawl. Once they were through, the road opened into a large blacktop parking lot beside a small brick building. A desert-camo Humvee armed with a .50-caliber machine gun was parked nose out, with clear lines to strafe an approach.

As they drifted past the sentry vehicle, Riker gave a little nod to the Humvee. Whitney didn't see anyone inside the vehicle, but clearly this was by design. Riker drove another hundred meters, then braked in front of an intimidating security checkpoint. Like

MacDill's main entrance, this access point was equipped with twin hydraulic metal barriers, but here the massive steel plates were flipped up at forty-five-degree angles, completely blocking access to the road beyond.

Riker stopped short of the barrier, shifted his Jeep's transmission into park, and turned to face her. "I need your ID."

She'd expected as much and was already wearing it in a plastic case on a lanyard around her neck. She slipped it over her head and passed it to Riker as a guard clad in black Nomex, finger poised on the trigger guard of a short barrel SOPMOD M4, approached the driver's-side door.

"Good afternoon, Senior Chief. What do you think of the commissary?" the guard asked, his steely gaze locked on Riker.

"The prices are good, but the parking sucks," Riker answered—no doubt one of a handful of acceptable responses that conveyed he was not under duress. Had Riker answered differently, she wouldn't be surprised if a half dozen shooters converged on the vehicle from invisible hides in the nearby woods.

"Hers is probably going to flash," Riker said, handing over their IDs. "It's her first day, so I wouldn't be surprised if you have to make a call or two."

The kitted-up sentry frowned at the news, then checked their IDs with his handheld scanner. Riker's ID earned a green light, and to their collective surprise, Whitney's got a green flash as well.

"Well, that's a first," the guard said. He nodded to a second guard standing in the tiny security shack just ahead. The steel panels lowered into the ground, clearing the path for them to enter.

With wide-eyed anticipation, Whitney stared through the windshield as they drove onto the compound. Her anticipation, however, quickly deflated as they rounded the corner. The "compound," as it were, turned out not to be the modern, high-tech complex she'd imagined would house the most elite special operations team in the world, but instead three office trailers—the same elevated double-wide variety contractors used on construction sites—arranged in a U-shape. In the middle, a simple wooden deck spanned the gap between the trailers, forming a "redneck courtyard," replete with picnic tables, benches, and an oversize gas grill. She counted seven vehicles parked in a gravel lot that began where the paved road ended. Riker parked at the end of the line, killed the engine, then turned to look at her, his bottom lip bulging.

"Welcome to the Tier One," he said.

"You were pretty explicit earlier that no such unit existed," she said.

"Outside the gate it doesn't, but we're inside the gate now."

"Ooookay," she said, not sure how to take this comment.

"Might wanna ditch those heels. You're likely to turn an ankle on that gravel," he said before flinging himself out of the driver's side like an acrobat.

She looked down at her feet, then at the coarse gravel, and sighed with irritation. He was probably right, but walking barefoot across the gravel was a nonstarter. With her luck, she'd step on a shard of glass or piece of metal and slice her foot open so bad, she'd need stitches and a tetanus shot.

So far, her first day had all the makings of a practical joke worthy of some hidden-camera television show.

"Screw it," she murmured and climbed out of the Jeep. She walked—shoes on—methodically across the coarse gravel, keeping her weight on the balls of her feet. Halfway across, Riker offered her his arm, but she shook her head. Still, she was relieved when she reached the deck and sure footing.

The door to the trailer on her right flew open, and a bearded thirty-something operator stepped into the sunshine and squinted at her. He was thick, built like a rugby player, with at least thirty pounds on Riker. He wore gray tactical cargo pants, a black polo emblazoned with a logo she didn't recognize, and a gray snake-skin camo ball cap with a Punisher patch on the front. He walked straight up to her with an easygoing smile and extended his hand. She shook it, noting how fragile and insignificant her hand felt inside his grip. She looked at his massive forearms, rippling with muscle. This man could crush the bones of her fingers to shards with the same effort it would take her to squish the hand of a toddler.

"You must be Whitney," he said, pumping her hand once and releasing it, fully intact and decidedly uncrushed.

"Whitney from Northern Virginia," Riker chimed in before she could answer.

"Well, Whitney from Northern Virginia, I'm Lieutenant Commander Redman, but you can call me Chunk. Everyone here does."

"We call you other things too," Riker said, deadpan. "Behind your back."

"I know," the SEAL officer said, hamming it up with a wink at Whitney. "Handsome, charming, brilliant—all the things they're too embarrassed to say to my face and in public. It's like I'm Bradley Cooper to Riker's Lady Gaga. It's awkward sometimes, but we all have our crosses to bear. Mine is this face and body."

She wasn't sure whether to laugh or roll her eyes. He *did* have a Bradley Cooperish look about him . . . if you crossed the actor with a bear. "You want me to call you Chunk? Is that, like, your SEAL call sign or something?"

"SEALs aren't like pilots. We don't really have call signs, just terms of endearment."

This comment earned a snort from Riker.

"Take Riker here, for example . . ."

"Is it a *Star Trek* reference or something?" she asked.

Chunk screwed up his face with incomprehension. "*Star Trek*? No. We call him Riker because he looks like someone who just got out of Rikers Island prison."

She nodded and said, "Why do they call you Chunk?"

Riker laughed but held his tongue.

"That's a story for when we, uh, have gotten to know each other a little better," Chunk said.

"That crude, huh?" she said.

"Crude or childish, that's pretty much the only two choices with this crew."

"So can I expect a crude or childish nickname in the near future?" Whitney said, now becoming acutely aware of the heat from the bright Florida sun beating down on her face.

"Nah, I think it'll be a while before one of us comes up with something that'll stick," he said with a crooked frat-boy grin. "Don't ya think, Riker?"

"Yeah, I'm sure it'll be a while, if it even happens at all."

"All right," Chunk said, turning and waving for her to follow him into the trailer. "C'mon, Heels, we've got a ton of indoc paperwork to do inside . . ."

She frowned. *I'm gonna be Heels? Really?*

She followed the SEAL officer across the wooden deck, painfully aware of the loud sound of her heels clicking on the wood, as if each step confirmed her new and obnoxious nickname. As they approached the door, she realized immediately that the trailer was far more than it appeared, from even a few yards away. The aluminum skin was clearly something much more, and the door itself was twice as thick and heavy as the faux exterior suggested. She glanced at the air conditioner hanging out the window to her left and realized now that it was not an air conditioner at all, but a shell facade around some sort of electronics suite—cameras and listening devices, she could only imagine. What also appeared to be the twin barrels of some sort of weapons system were visible on the fake air conditioner.

Chunk saw her eyeing the unit and gave a double lift of his eyebrows as he placed the palm of his hand on the glass plate of a biometric security scanner. The scanner chirped, something clicked, then the door broke loose from magnetic seals. She felt cool air whisk across her sweat-dappled skin and exhaled with relief.

She followed Chunk into the surprisingly roomy lobby of the building—a far more accurate label than the trailer she'd seen from outside.

"Is this better?" Chunk asked with a smile.

"More to her *Northern* Virginia tastes, I expect," Riker added as he pulled his spit bottle from the cargo pocket of his improvised surf shorts.

"Clever," she said, taking it all in. "From the air or a satellite pass, this would look like a pretty unremarkable collection of trailers, maybe a maintenance facility for the base or something."

"Exactly. Also, the Tier One unit is rumored to be in Virginia, but that's just a training facility. Only a very small number of military personnel are aware of the existence of a new Tier One SEAL team, and nobody is looking for us here in Tampa," Chunk said.

The "lobby" was actually more of an antechamber, a narrow hallway-like space with myriad pictures on the walls to either side of a heavy frosted-glass door: SEALs exiting the rear of a C17 at night, SEALs taking a beach from the water, fast boats with fully kitted-up operators, SEALs in a jungle somewhere, SEALs in the desert . . . and so on.

The space to the right of the door reminded her of the

memorial wall at Langley, except instead of black stars in white marble, this display had several rows of gold tridents on a black backdrop. An American flag hung to the left of the memorial and a United States Navy flag to the right. Above the rows of tridents was an inscription in gold lettering that read:

REMEMBERING THE MEN OF OPERATION CRUSADER.
BRAVE MEN HAVE FOUGHT AND DIED BUILDING THE
PROUD TRADITION AND FEARED REPUTATION THAT I
AM BOUND TO UPHOLD.

Below the rows of tridents were two lines from the SEAL creed:

THE LEGACY OF MY TEAMMATES STEADIES MY
RESOLVE AND SILENTLY GUIDES MY EVERY DEED.
I WILL NOT FAIL.

A heaviness enveloped her, almost as if God had turned up the earth's gravity. Chunk and Riker stood beside her, hands clasped in front of them, staring at the wall. She glanced at them each in turn. The silly frat-boy grins were gone, replaced by a warrior's solemn stare.

Chunk turned to her and gave a sad smile.

"I know that sometimes it might not seem like it, but I assure you, Ms. Watts, we take what we do here very seriously. I don't know how much you know about Operation Crusader, but the loss affected everyone in Naval Special Warfare in a deeply personal way. It's taken two years to bring the Tier One back from this tragedy—a tragedy born of an intelligence failure that was entirely preventable. This time around, we're going to do things differently. That's why you're here. Word on the street is that you're Rhodes Scholar smart, able to make connections and notice details that other analysts miss."

She met his gaze and fought the urge to interrupt and state, for the record, that she was not a Rhodes Scholar, nor had anyone ever compared her to one before. Instead, she let him keep talking.

"What we do now, we do for our country, our Constitution, and for the men whose tridents are hammered into that wall."

Whitney looked at the tridents of the fallen and, in that moment, felt a connection with them. She had her own ghosts that haunted her—ghosts born from an intelligence failure of her own that she never talked about but could not escape either. Like a pack of wolves on her tail, the mistake drove her relentlessly to do better. To be better. To never make a mistake like that again . . .

"C'mon, let's go," Chunk said, waving her to follow.

As she stepped away from the memorial, the moment was gone and she was back beside the two men-children taking turns ripping each other. They led her on a tour of the support facility where she'd be working—including a conference room, a computer center packed with workstations, a break room with a kitchenette, and a hall with individual office spaces.

"This is you," Chunk said, opening the door to a modest office with a modern task chair behind a vacant desk. "I'm not sure how much has been explained to you . . ."

"Nothing has been explained to me," she said, feeling very much the fish out of water.

"I figured as much as, uh, technically your job and this organization itself do not exist. But the short answer is that you're our chief intelligence analyst, and it's your job to figure everything out so me and my team don't get killed in the field because somebody in some cube somewhere had to leave early for a chess match, or a cappella practice, or whatever it is that spooks do in their spare time. You're gonna have a team working for you headed by a Naval Intelligence officer and his four enlisted subordinates. Technically, you're not their boss, as you're not in the chain of command, but I've made it clear to them that they work for you. You'll have twenty-four-hour support from them as well as unrestricted access to two cyber experts. We have real-time access to everything percolating at Langley or NCTC, but we try not to rely solely on those data streams. Also of note, Naval Special Warfare now has its own intelligence asset management team, but the network is not as robust as CIA and DIA. You're not going to be running any assets right out of the gate, but I could see us getting there in the not-so-distant future."

"Really?" she said, her head spinning at the idea. "I hadn't heard that."

"Yeah, we'll get into that more during your full brief." He looked at his watch. "That's coming up in just two hours, so we better get cracking." He pulled her office door closed and led her back to the conference room with its long mahogany table flanked by tall-back leather chairs. Two men in civilian clothes and a woman dressed in khakis with the insignia of a Lieutenant Commander sat in chairs across from them.

"Is this the SCIF?" she asked.

Chunk laughed. "Nah, you ain't read in yet, so the SCIF is still of limits. We'll take you downstairs later, and you'll see the rest of the compound."

She raised an eyebrow at him. "Downstairs?"

That explained a lot. Of course there was more than just these three trailers.

"Later," Chunk said.

"Hello, Ms. Watts," the woman said and rose and shook her hand. The men nodded but stayed seated. "I'm the command JAG attorney and these gentlemen head up the unit's counter intelligence branch. We're going to brief you on the details of security for the unit, and I'll discuss your rights—or more accurately the rights you forfeit—by being fully read into the Tier One unit."

"Enjoy your trip down the bunny hole," Riker said with a laugh. He and Chunk departed, closing the door behind them.

"Have seat, Ms. Watts," the JAG attorney said, taking her own seat and opening a thick blue file folder. "We have lots of paperwork for you, but first we have a video you're required to watch."

One of the two CI guys typed something on the laptop between them, and the screen on the far wall lit and music started to play.

A video, she thought with a silent chuckle, remembering the mandatory video she'd been forced to watch at NCTC that in no way captured what she'd signed on for. *Of course there's a video.*

CHAPTER 8

Qasim had never been to Mingora, but a strange familiarity washed over him as he looked at the lush green countryside and the towering mountains beyond. The city was situated in a fertile valley on the eastern edge of the mighty Hindu Kush mountain range, which stretched five hundred miles west across Afghanistan. The last third of the three-hour drive from Peshawar had them on the N-95, snaking along the eastern side of the Swat River. The Swat, like all the life-sustaining rivers originating in the Hindu Kush, was glacier fed and provided irrigation for the six hundred thousand Pakistanis who called the valley home.

"Did you know that a great and ancient civilization once flourished here?" Eshan said from the driver's seat.

"Which civilization is that?" Qasim asked.

"The Gandhara. They occupied the entire Peshawar Basin from the Kabul River to the Swat. This place was the crossroads of Asia," Eshan explained, "an epicenter of trade, connecting China in the east to Macedonia in the west."

"Makes sense," Qasim said, doing his best to feign interest.

"They were Buddhists, which is why there are so many ancient stupas in this area," Eshan continued. "Stupas are dome-shaped temples they built in the mountains. Some people say that a Gandharan teacher named Guatama was Buddha incarnate and that he lived and walked the enlightened path until he was eighty years old."

"Oh," Qasim said. He'd never cared about history, and even less so about Buddhism.

"What's wrong? You seem nervous," Eshan said, eying him.

"That's because I *am* nervous," Qasim said. "This was a mistake. I shouldn't have agreed to come." When Eshan didn't respond, he added. "Aren't you going to say something?"

"What do you want me to say? I can turn the car around if you like, but we've come this far. We both know you want to see the drone, and like I told you before, there's no commitment. Help us with the interface, then you can walk away."

I should tell him to turn the car around, Qasim thought. *I should do it right now.*

But he didn't.

They soon arrived in Mingora, where Eshan piloted the sedan through the city, over a bridge crossing the Swat, and into the Kanju district. With the aid of GPS, he navigated to a dingy-looking warehouse on the Saidu Sharif Airport grounds. He parked behind the building and turned off the engine. Qasim's stomach became an acid bath of nerves. Even in the aftermath of the American drone strike that took his sister and father, he'd not been this frightened. Then, he'd been numb with shock. Now, he was petrified, and primal urges for self-preservation made him want to fling open the door and run away.

"Before we go in," Eshan said, his expression turning serious, "some advice . . . Do not say anything to antagonize or potentially offend these men. They are true believers. If they challenge you about your faith or allegiance to the cause, you need to speak with conviction. Speak from the heart. Talk about what you've lost. Communicate your pain and suffering and desire for retribution, but be humble. Do not place yourself on a pedestal because of your education, British citizenship, or job. And don't ask too many questions."

Qasim tried to swallow, but his mouth had gone dry. Eshan's little speech had just confirmed that this entire thing was a mistake. "I want to leave. I-I . . . I can't do this," he stammered.

"That time has passed, Qasim," Eshan said. "We've arrived, and that means they've seen us. We have to go in now."

Qasim said nothing, just stared straight ahead like a statue.

"It will be okay," Eshan said, giving his arm a squeeze. "Now let's go see that drone."

He climbed out of the hired sedan and waited until Qasim did the same before closing his door and walking toward the run-down building, which was in desperate need of a fresh coat of paint. Qasim followed him to a metal door. Eshan rapped three times, and to Qasim's surprise, the door immediately opened. No challenge-response question, no secret code—just a bearded man wearing a black turban and tunic.

"Eshan," the man said, a smile stretching the sun-leathered skin of his face.

"Bacha!" Eshan embraced the man with a hug, then addressing him in Pashto said, "How are you, my brother?"

"Good, good," Bacha answered. "Is this your friend?"

"Yes, this is Qasim."

"An honor to meet you," the older man said, extending a hand.

"It's no trouble," Qasim said awkwardly in Pashto while clasping the stranger's hand. "I mean, it's an honor to meet you too."

"Come in, come in." Bacha waved them inside.

Qasim followed Eshan, ducking his head to stoop under the low doorframe and into the warehouse. Bacha locked the door, then stepped around them until he was back in the lead. The warehouse was not dark, but it wasn't well lit either, and Qasim's eyes took time to adjust. As the world came into focus, he counted four—no, five—men armed with assault rifles watching them from different strategic positions inside the cavernous space. Two of the guards flanked the door they'd just come through. Despite holding their weapons in a relaxed carry, such close proximity to firepower made Qasim nervous, and he crossed his arms.

"This way," Bacha said and set off toward a tarp-covered object in the middle of the warehouse floor that could only be one thing.

Without hesitation, Eshan followed. Qasim froze for a second, his legs leaden, but a reproachful backward glance from Eshan got him moving.

"Welcome, gentlemen," a confident voice said in a British accent colored with Pakistani undertones.

Qasim turned in the direction of the voice and saw a man, no older than thirty, approaching. He was dressed in casual modern clothes, something a Pakistani college student might wear out with his mates. His face was bearded but undeniably youthful, and he walked with confidence.

"Eshan, it's good to see you again," the man said, extending a hand.

"You too," Eshan said, shaking hands.

The man turned. "And you must be Qasim."

"Yes," Qasim said.

"Welcome. My name is Hamza. I understand that you're an aerospace engineer."

"Yes. Well, actually I'm an aerospace engineer *and* avionics software specialist," Qasim said, uncrossing and recrossing his arms over his chest.

"You're with British Aero in New Malden?"

Qasim hesitated. "Yes . . . Do you know the area well?"

"Certainly not." Hamza laughed. "But I have traveled to London."

"I see. Your English is excellent. From your accent, I might have thought you'd lived in Britain," Qasim said.

"I was educated in the private school system in Saudi Arabia, then later here in Pakistan," Hamza said with a smile. "I've been fortunate to have very good teachers . . . Well, you didn't come all this way for idle small talk. Let's take a look, shall we?"

Hamza ordered that the tarps be removed from the drone, and a minute later Qasim was staring at a sleek gray fuselage. It was astonishing how similar the Pterodactyl looked to the iconic American Predator B. Like the Predator, it had a fairing blister on top of the nose to house its synthetic aperture radar and SATCOM hardware, and beneath hung a gimbal-mounted infrared optics and targeting system. The craft was supported by a retractable tricycle landing gear, sported a V-shaped tail, and had a three-bladed propeller at the rear. At nine feet tall by thirty feet long, with a wingspan of forty-five feet, the Pterodactyl was no child's toy. Despite being incrementally smaller than the Predator, the Chinese-made UCAV still took up most of the open floor space of the building.

Hamza looked at Qasim expectantly, asking the question with his eyes.

"This is a Wing Loong Pterodactyl drone, if I'm not mistaken. Designed and manufactured by Aviation Industry Corporation of

China, which is the same aerospace conglomerate behind the J-20 fifth-generation stealth fighter," Qasim said, his first move in what he assumed would be a dance to prove his expertise.

"That is correct," Hamza said with an approving nod. "What do you know about this aircraft?"

"Well, it's the second generation, with improvements in instrumentation and the satellite array comms package. This one you have here looks like the GJ-1 variant, because you've got the reconnaissance and targeting pod under the chin and a hard point on each wing for carrying payload." Qasim walked in a slow circle around the drone, lightly dragging his fingertips across the carbon-fiber reinforced polymer skin. "Twenty-two-hour endurance, twenty-thousand-foot operational ceiling with a hundred-and-fifty-knot top speed and an operational range in the neighborhood of twenty-five hundred nautical miles."

"I'm impressed. You certainly know your drones, Qasim."

Qasim nodded. "How did you manage to acquire—" But then he caught himself. Eshan had told him not to ask questions, and he suddenly understood why. Regardless of how these men got the drone, it was not information that Hamza would be keen on sharing. In fact, knowing such information arguably made Qasim a bigger liability than his knowledge of the existence and location of the drone. He tried to unwind the error. "I'm sorry, what I meant to say was this is a very impressive piece of hardware. Have you had an opportunity to take it up?"

Hamza glanced at Eshan—who Qasim realized had been uncharacteristically quiet—before responding. "I agree it is very impressive, but unfortunately we have not been able to deploy it. As you might imagine, doing so poses significant risk to our operation. There is a very high probability that the maiden flight will be its only flight. The Pterodactyl is not a stealth drone, as it does not evade radar. Also, it requires a runway for takeoff and landing, and communication and control pose a counter-detection risk. Which leads me to the reason that you are here, Qasim."

Qasim stopped circling the drone and looked at their host. For the first time since their arrival, his fear seemed to fade into the background, ceding control to the analytical part of his mind. Epiphany struck, and he suddenly understood the quandary Hamza and his masters undoubtedly found themselves in. They had acquired a truly powerful military asset, undoubtedly at great financial cost, only to realize the crippling constraints on their ability to use it. An American Predator drone was not a formidable weapons platform because of its inherent capabilities; it was formidable because of the infrastructure that the American military had created to support it: Kandahar Air Field provided a dedicated runway for operations and maintenance. Creech Air Force Base in Nevada housed an untouchable command-and-control center on the other side of the world. The US global satellite communications network allowed control of the drones from space and provided a virtually unlimited operational footprint. And the American global supply chain allowed for the transport and armament of UCAVs as required to adapt to changing tactical and strategic conditions in the field.

Hamza and his bosses had none of these things. What they had was an aircraft with a forty-five-foot wingspan that was difficult and risky to transport, store, maintain, and most importantly, to operate without being seen.

"I understand the predicament you're in," Qasim said, then proceeded to communicate all the liabilities and problems he'd just mentally outlined to Hamza.

A flicker of a smile crossed the man's face. "My expectation was that you would quickly recognize our constraints. You have not disappointed."

"Did the Chinese sell you the mobile ground control station?"

Qasim asked, feeling suddenly and brazenly confident enough to violate Eshan's advice about not asking questions.

"We have access to a unit," Hamza said vaguely, "but it is presently being kept in a different location for security purposes."

"The Pterodactyl variant you have here is SATCOM capable, but I can't imagine the Chinese are going to give you uplink and transmission authorization on their network."

"That is correct."

"So you're limited to using a line of sight data link?"

Hamza nodded.

"At maximum ceiling, what sort of operational radius are we talking about?"

"You tell me. You're the drone expert."

"Hmm," Qasim said, rubbing his chin. "At max altitude of five kilometers, I would estimate a two-hundred-kilometer operational radius, but that gives you only a one- or two-degree angle of elevation. If we were in a flat desert, maybe you could maintain control without interference, but here in the Hindu Kush, there are mountains in the way. Worse, the Afghan border is probably a hundred fifty kilometers from here. Even without the mountains to contend with, you couldn't engage targets in Afghanistan so long as you are operating from Mingora."

"Exactly," Hamza said, frowning. "And the mobile command center is containerized. It is ten meters long. There is a difference between mobile and portable. We need another way. Can you help us?"

Qasim looked from Hamza to Eshan and back again. "I . . . I think so. The Chinese copied the Predator command center design. Like you said, these units are mobile, but they were designed to be parked on a military base or airport tarmac. Functionality and reliability were the governing design criteria, not portability and simplicity. But in theory, every function performed by the command center could be performed on a laptop computer connected to a Thrustmaster aviation simulator joystick and a portable antenna array with enough power to transmit line of sight over long distances."

"Could you do this?" Hamza asked, his voice hopeful. "If I provided you with the materials, could you make a highly portable control unit for the drone?"

"In an ideal world, yes," Qasim said, "but I would need a programmer who was fluent in English and Chinese. Also, it would take time, potentially a lot of time. This is not something that can be accomplished in an afternoon."

"How much time?" Hamza pressed.

"I don't know. Two weeks minimum, but it could be two months. It all depends on how the system is configured and how much code the Chinese pirated from the Predator program."

Hamza met his gaze. "What if I told you that the command-and-control module we have obtained is the Chinese export model and that the interface is in English?"

Qasim slowly nodded. "I would say that greatly improves the likelihood of success and should reduce the time required to make the conversion. But if the back end is all programmed with Chinese notations, then it will still be a challenge."

"But not an insurmountable challenge?'

"No."

Hamza smiled broadly. "So it is agreed? You will help us?"

Qasim's stomach went to knots. He looked at Eshan, who gave him an encouraging nod. "Okay . . . I'll help you."

"Excellent," Hamza said, then turned to Eshan. "Why don't you take Qasim out for something to eat, and when you're ready, come back and we can get started."

Bacha escorted them to the door and saw them out.

Once back inside the sedan, Qasim said, "I've never seen you so quiet as you were around Hamza." He looked sideways at his friend. "Who is he?"

"Are you kidding me?" Eshan said, meeting his gaze. "You don't know?"

"No . . . should I?"

"That was Hamza al-Saud."

"Dear God," Qasim said, his hands suddenly trembling in his lap as the car pulled away. "You're working with al-Qaeda?"

"Not exactly. Hamza has split from al-Qaeda and formed a new, more enlightened faction. We call ourselves *al Qadar*— Power and Destiny."

"We?" Qasim said, astounded.

"Yes, I am a member."

"Oh my God," Qasim said, revulsion creeping over his entire body like ants crawling across his skin.

"Listen to me, Qasim. Hamza is not like the others. While ISIS and al-Qaeda are busy perfecting the art of savagery, we are building a different kind of organization. As you can see, Hamza has charisma and vision. He is not like the old guard. He's like us—young, smart, educated. He understands geopolitics and technology. More importantly, he understands that tomorrow's jihad is not strapping suicide vests onto desperate souls and sending them into some market to blow themselves up. Jihad is not about savage brutality and murdering our fellow Muslims. Jihad is about inspiration. It is about tapping into the minds and skills of the younger generation. It is about sustainable Islamic values and building a movement that Muslims the world over can rally around."

"Are those your words or his?"

"I'm not a spiritual leader, but I recognize wisdom when I hear it," Eshan said simply.

Qasim's mind was a whirlwind of contradictory thoughts

and emotions. On the one hand, he'd just agreed to help Hamza al-Saud. Technically, that made him a terrorist. *A terrorist*, he thought, shaking his head, *I'm a bloody terrorist thanks to Eshan.* And yet on the other hand, he felt a catharsis, the likes of which he'd never experienced. The invisible yoke of cowardice and shame he'd been carrying on his back since that wedding five years ago suddenly felt lighter. The Americans had assassinated his family, and he'd done nothing. Nothing! Worse than nothing—he'd gone to work for America's greatest ally, helping them further cement their iron grip on his homeland.

All this time he'd thought of his tenure at British Aero as a twisted penance, born of weakness and psychopathy. But what if he had it all wrong?

What if there was such a thing as destiny?

CHAPTER 9

Surveying the smiling faces around him, Chunk tipped back his bottle of Corona and took a long gratifying pull. Tonight's cookout was as much a celebration as it was a team-building event. The selection process was over. They'd passed the final exercise, completed Green Team evaluations, and were now, officially, Tier One SEALs. The enthusiasm was palpable. They'd reached the pinnacle of Naval Special Warfare, and Chunk felt like a kid in a candy store with a hundred-dollar bill.

Across the counter, Ellie Sawyer, wife of Navy Senior Chief Nicholas "Saw" Sawyer, held a two-year-old on her hip while she added hot dogs and bratwursts to a platter of seasoned burger patties ready for the grill. "You're gonna keep them from burning down our new house, right, Chunk?" she said with a wary glance toward the back patio, where grilling preparations were underway. The handsome Craftsman-style home—located in a historic neighborhood in South Tampa—had been a financial stretch for the couple. But to Chunk, its purchase was a statement of commitment: *We made our decision, and we're here to stay.*

Chunk smiled and was just about to give her his rock-solid assurance that the Tampa Fire Department's services would definitely not be necessary, when a flash of light and a *whoosh* from the pool deck made him wince.

"Fire in the hole!" Trip hollered, followed by a howling laugh from Georgie.

"Chuuunk, please," Ellie said, her tone insistent now.

"I'm on it," he said, double-timing out the back and onto the patio.

"Dude, you're going to burn down Ellie's dream house," Saw growled, swiping the bottle of lighter fluid from Trip's hand.

"Don't worry, bro, I got this," Riker said. Imitating the sound of a fire truck siren, he capped his longneck Budweiser with his thumb, shook it, then sprayed down the three-foot inferno engulfing the charcoal grill.

"Dude, you're making it worse!" Saw snapped, swatting at Riker to stop. "Just let it burn out. You're getting beer everywhere."

"Now, look fellas," Chunk said with a paternal grin. "I've been sent by CINC-Home to contain this escalating situation . . ."

"Don't look at me, boss. My ass has been planted over here the entire time," Georgie said from where he sat on the deck railing, watching the chaos.

Riker responded by hooking his arm around Trip's neck and fashioning a friendly headlock. "Papa One, Two—I put out the fire and apprehended the insurgent. What do you want me to do with him?"

"Throw him in the pool so he can cool off." But when Riker

started dragging Trip toward the water for real, Chunk stopped him. "Kidding . . . I'm just kidding."

Saw leaned in to whisper in Chunk's ear, "Is Ellie pissed off?"

"Nah. When I left, she was still smiling."

"Thank God," he said and took a swig of his beer. "She loves this house. I don't think I've ever seen her so happy."

With the lighter fluid burned off and the fire back under control, Saw visibly relaxed. Riker gave the top of Trip's head a playful noogie, then released his headlock. Trip apologized by means of a two-finger salute to Saw, then sauntered toward the back of the patio, where his date was sitting in a deck chair. The girl was pretty, young, and clearly enamored with Trip. On his arrival, he kissed her on the cheek. Then they swapped places. He took her seat, and she got comfortable on his lap.

"I see Trip has found time in the training schedule to make a new lady friend," Chunk said to Riker with a grin.

"He always does," Riker said and chuckled.

While they talked, Chunk surveyed the scene. Half the SEALs were chatting around the pool deck in twos and threes, and the rest were in the backyard, tossing Nerf balls around while toddlers tugged at their legs. The wives and significant others loitered in the kitchen, chatting over appetizers. Only Trip's new girlfriend, Val, was outside, too uncomfortable in this unfamiliar setting to venture inside with the spouses.

Chunk turned to Riker and caught a glimpse of something in the frogman's eyes.

"So what's the deal with Michelle, bro?" he asked. Riker's girlfriend of two years had moved in with him before the last deployment, and Chunk had heard rumblings of a proposal . . . but apparently it hadn't happened. "Is she coming to Tampa or what?"

Riker shrugged. "Not sure. She's got a great job in Virginia

Beach. She offered to come, but with the Green Team pace and then not knowing how our deployments would unfold, it seemed unfair to have her leave her job, come here, and be alone for six months. We're gonna see how things shake out and decide later. Too many unknowns for now."

Chunk nodded, watching Riker's face carefully. The man seemed content with the decision, but he could see there was more.

"Best for the team," Riker said without prompting. "So long as she's cool up in Virginia, I can focus on Gold Squadron. She's strong and tough, which is why we're together. We talked about her making a trip down to Tampa for a visit, you know, when the time is right."

"Cool," Chunk said. "Tell her hi for me. I'm excited to see her."

"Will do, bro."

He gave Riker's shoulder a squeeze and headed back into the house, pretty sure he would never see Michelle again.

"Situation contained, ma'am," Chunk said, reporting to Ellie in the kitchen. She was laughing about something with Spence's wife, Olivia, whose burgeoning belly was undeniable proof she was just weeks away from giving birth to their first.

"Thank you, Chunk," she replied with a genuine smile. "I'm—"

"Mommy, where's Daddy?" Saw's young son asked, pulling at her arm.

"He's out back, buddy," she said, "but he's with his team, okay?"

Chunk set his beer down on the counter and took a knee beside the boy. "Hey, Connor, your dad said you're part of the team and he needs your help. Do you wanna help him get some food on the grill?"

"Yay!" Connor said.

"Thank you," Ellie mouthed silently.

Chunk winked and was about to grab the platter of burgers

and dogs from Ellie when the doorbell rang. Conner, redirected by this new development, sprinted toward the front door.

Ellie rolled her eyes and moved to set down the platter to answer it.

"I got this," Chunk said, stopping her. "Grab your minute of peace."

He found Connor fumbling with the doorknob. "Need my help, buddy?"

"I can do it," the little guy said and then somehow managed to get it unlatched. With a kiddie grunt, he swung the door open wide.

"Well, hello there," said a surprised, but smiling Whitney Watts as she glanced down at the little doorman.

Conner crossed his arms and looked up at her. "I'm Connor Sawyer, and this is my house. Who are you?"

"Nice to meet you, Mr. Sawyer," she said, crouching down. "I'm Whitney, and I'm here for the party."

Connor looked up at Chunk, who nodded his approval, and then back at Whitney. "Okay," he said, stepping aside to let her in. "But I'm just Connor, not mister anything." Then he turned on a heel and marched away. "I gotta go . . . The team needs my help outside."

"Hi," Chunk said, turning back to Watts. "C'mon on in."

"Now *that* was pretty adorable," she said, stepping inside as he closed the door behind her.

"Saw's wife, Ellie, is in the kitchen." He glanced at the bottle of wine in her hand, then at the fleeing toddler, "I think you misjudged your team by bringing wine—we're more of a beer crowd here. Let me chase down the little guy. Back in a sec . . ."

He hustled after Connor, scooping the youngster up just before he ran into the screen door leading to the patio. Behind him, he heard Ellie say, "Oh, you must be Whitney . . . and you brought wine! Thank God. These guys only bring beer."

"Hey, bro," Chunk said, walking up to Saw, holding Conner's hand. "You got a swim buddy here who wants to help out."

Saw took a knee and wrapped the little man in a bear hug. "I was just coming to get you, buddy. These clowns don't know how to help me on the grill like you do."

As Chunk watched father and son bond, a silent prayer took shape in his mind: *Lord, help me keep these guys safe and bring them back to their families every time.* He scanned the patio and backyard for any new figurative fires to put out. Seeing nothing urgent, he remembered his abandoned beer and headed back into the house.

"'Sup, Heels?" he said, grinning his best school-boy smile as he joined Watts at the island, where his half-drunk bottle of Corona remained untouched, the glass beaded with condensation.

Watts wore a strained smile on her face, reinforcing the vibe he'd gotten from her on her first day. *Not particularly adept at new social situations*, he decided. Now, at the mention of her nickname, she sighed heavily and shook her head.

"Heels?" Ellie asked with a chuckle, sipping at her wine. "That's gotta be a fun story."

"For the guys," Watts said with a good-natured laugh. "Not for me."

"Sounds like this crew," Ellie said. "Don't worry, I've got plenty of ammunition I can give you to even the score."

After a few minutes of small talk with everyone, Chunk gestured with his head, and Watts followed him out of the kitchen and into the living room, where two groups of young kids were playing and giggling on the floor. He took a seat in a large, worn easy chair, gesturing for her to have a seat on the sofa facing him.

"So how are you doing?" he asked, leaning back in the

comfortable chair. "Getting settled in yet—pictures hung and boxes unpacked?"

"Yeah, well, I'm not much of a decorator," she said with an easy smile and seemed to relax a touch. "I found an apartment not far from here, actually. It's in Hyde Park Village, so I have access to restaurants and stuff. Takeout is kinda my thing since, you know, long hours and all."

"So," he said, shifting gears, "Whitney Watts from *Northern Virginia*. What made you want to be a spook?"

"Analyst, not spook," she said, arching an eyebrow and sipping her wine.

"Same thing, isn't it?" he teased, then watched as she seemed to consider the comment.

"Not really. But you know that."

"Yeah, I'm just messing with ya," he said. "But seriously. I know a little about your background—political science major at GW. But intelligence analyst is quite a detour from policy work. How did you make the pivot?"

"Hmm. Well, becoming an analyst certainly wasn't my dream job. What most people don't understand, much less appreciate, is that it's policy decisions made by elected officials that govern their daily lives. Health care, public safety, education, personal liberties, employment standards, and on and on—all policy matters. Which means that the heart of every debate, every movement, every conflict, every war . . . it all boils down to one thing: policy. I wanted to understand it. I wanted to untangle it. All the violence in the world, all the inequity—solving those puzzles starts with—" She stopped abruptly and stared at her glass. "Anyway, that's the direction I was headed until, one day, this guy approaches me on campus and says he's a recruiter for the CIA and would I like to put my special skills to work for the country." She looked at him as if she'd just shared a joke.

"What did you say?" Chunk asked, fully drawn into her story now.

She laughed. "I told him to piss off. I thought he was full of shit," she continued. "He was young and good looking, and I thought, 'There's no way this guy is with the frigging CIA. He just wants to get in my pants.' But he gave me a card with his contact information and a link to a recruiting website. Later, I checked it out, and it was for real, so I gave him a call."

"What happened next?"

"I told him no thanks, I was interested in helping to create policy, not finding ways to circumvent it."

"Nice."

"Well, you want to know what he said?"

Chunk nodded and took a pull from his beer.

"He said, 'The CIA is not in the business of circumventing policy, it's in the business of safeguarding it.' And then he proceeded to make the most compelling damn argument and recruitment pitch imaginable. He concluded by telling me that if unraveling puzzles was truly my gig, the intelligence world was the place I needed to be."

"And?"

She shrugged. "I bought it hook, line, and sinker, and now . . . here I am."

"Here you are," he agreed. Then a thought occurred to him. "So who was right? You or the recruiter?"

"What do you mean?"

"Is the CIA in the business of safeguarding policy or circumventing it?"

She gave him a tight, noncommittal smile, and he couldn't help but feel something beneath haunting her.

"Both," she said finally. "With a bias toward the former."

"Well, if safeguarding American policy is what gets you up

in the morning, then you definitely ended up at the right place. Because this unit is the government's policy-enforcing tool of choice—stopping evil twenty-four seven, three hundred sixty-five days a year."

"To stopping evil," she said, raising her glass.

"To stopping evil," he echoed and clinked bottle to glass.

"What about you, Lieutenant Commander Keith Redman?" she said, turning the tables. "What makes a college-educated, Texas redneck want to be a Navy SEAL?"

Chunk laughed. Her description of him was one he used frequently, and he wondered if he'd already said it to her, if she was psychic, or if she was just that good at reading people.

"You read my personnel jacket, so you already know all about me," he answered, shrugging off her attempt.

"No, no," she said, wagging a finger at him. "You read mine too, and you still asked. And anyway, our files only answer the what, not the why."

"Okay, that's fair," he conceded. "Mine's not a particularly inspiring journey, I suppose," he said as he tried to articulate the answer to a question he'd never fully answered for himself. "I come from a very patriotic family. We love America and Texas—which we love more is the topic of many Christmas gathering debates," he said with a chuckle. "But seriously, everyone in my family has served, most for just a single tour. Give back to the home and community we love. I know that sounds trite, but it's who we are. I suppose I never imagined being career military. My dad served in the Navy JAG Corps after law school, before going into private practice. My grandfather was a Marine in Vietnam, then started his own business. So from the time I was a kid, there was really no question about whether I would serve."

"Yeah, but you didn't just serve—you chose to be a SEAL, which is pretty much, like, the hardest pipeline in the military."

He nodded. "Only about ten percent of the guys who pursue it actually pin on a trident, with most washing out from BUD/S. But I knew I wasn't joining a peacetime military. We were a nation at war. I guess I figured if I was going to fight the war on terror, I wanted to do it with the best warriors in the world. If I was gonna do my part, it had to be in a way that really moved the needle, and to me, that meant being at the pointy tip of the spear." He stopped, having answered her question, but to his surprise the next words came out anyway. "And then there's that *other* part of me."

"What other part?" she asked.

He hesitated, not sure why Watts was the one he'd finally chosen to open up to. Maybe it was the pull of reciprocity, her having shared her inner self with him. Or maybe this was a necessary step for her joining a brotherhood in which she would otherwise always float at the fringe. He leaned in, resting his elbows against his thighs, and met her eyes. "I love this community. It's how I define myself . . . it's become my entire identity. And I want it that way. I love these men. I love operating. I can't think of anything in the world that would give me more personal satisfaction, sense of purpose, and pride of accomplishment than being a SEAL. In this job, I get to make a difference in the world every day. It's not just words on a T-shirt. And the people you see here tonight—not just the SEALs, but also the spouses, the kids, and the significant others—they are my family. And now . . . so are you."

Watts stared at him for a long moment, then said, almost in a whisper, "Wow."

"Wow what?" he asked, suddenly feeling like he'd shared too much, that he'd come off as corny.

"I didn't know you felt that way. Thanks."

"For what?"

"For sharing," she said, and with a wry smile added, "and for admitting you're an actual deeply feeling and introspective human being."

"Don't tell anyone," he said with a grin and got to his feet. "And now, I should probably help Saw get the burgers and dogs on the grill. I hope you're not a vegetarian."

She laughed and stood. "Don't worry. I can carnivore with the best of them."

"In that case, I think you're gonna fit in around here just fine," he said. Happy, as he headed off to join the others, to find her walking beside him.

PART II

"With our silence, we sanctify their war crimes.
With our inaction, we legitimize their tyranny."

—Eshan Dawar

CHAPTER 10

WING LOONG PTERODACTYL UCAV GROUND CONTROL UNIT (GCU)

KANJU, PAKISTAN

TWELVE DAYS LATER

0312 LOCAL TIME

Qasim sat in the pilot's seat, while Hamza and several other al Qadar members crowded behind him, watching his every move. A bird's-eye view of a valley flanked by towering jagged peaks filled the primary monitor as live imagery from the Pterodactyl's chin-mounted optical array streamed over the data link. Despite the pressure of the situation, Qasim was having the time of his life. He was piloting a combat drone, something British Aero would never let him do, no matter how high he rose in the Valkyrie program. And in that moment, he realized that Hamza al-Saud had given him two things that Oliver Payne never would: opportunity and respect.

"Commencing test maneuver," Qasim said, speaking into the boom mike of his headset.

"We are ready," a gruff voice replied in his ear.

Qasim shifted his gaze to the drone's avionics display, which was located directly below the primary monitor. Digital instrument gauges—depicting airspeed, pitch angle, altitude, turn rate, vertical speed, roll angle, and heading—provided real-time flight dynamics for the unmanned aircraft. Gripping the throttle in his left hand and the control stick in his right, he eased the Pterodactyl into a sweeping turn. A surreal feeling washed over him as he made adjustments to maintain airspeed and altitude as he executed the maneuver.

"We're tracking your turn," the remote pilot said from his mountaintop position in Afghanistan. He rattled off avionics data from his laptop, which Qasim compared to what he was seeing on his screen.

He had no idea who the pilots were, but they sounded far more educated and professional than the brutish fighters he'd been exposed to. He assumed they'd been handpicked and trained by Hamza, just as he had been. Training them on controlling the aircraft would be no more difficult than teaching someone to fly a plane in a video game, though clearly the stakes were insanely higher.

From what Qasim understood, a deal had been made for the Taliban to "host" the two-man remote pilot team in a secure cave complex in the Hindu Kush across the border. Supposedly, this cave was just below the tree line, had sleeping accommodations, and had generator power. The benefits of the arrangement were obvious—the remote team could prestage for the operation while under Taliban protection, recharge equipment batteries as needed, and quickly access a position with the unobstructed line of sight required for the mission.

"Steady on new course, heading two-one-five," Qasim said as he brought the UCAV out of the turn. "Ready for handoff."

"Copy," the other pilot said. "We have a good signal, good LOS connection. Commencing handoff maneuver."

"Roger," Qasim said, removing his hands from the controls. "Standing by."

"Coming to new heading two-seven-zero . . ."

On-screen, the scenery below began to change, and the digital gauges indicated the other pilot was turning the drone north. The turn wasn't as smooth as Qasim's had been, with the pilot struggling to maintain altitude and overshooting the new heading, but eventually he got it sorted out. This was, after all, the other pilot's first flight, and he was using an Xbox flight simulator controller. A comical image popped into Qasim's mind: a terrorist dressed as a goatherd sitting cross-legged on a mountaintop, flying a combat drone with a joystick in his lap. He resisted the urge to chuckle at the ridiculousness of it all and, instead, gave himself an imaginary pat on the back for what he had accomplished over the past two weeks. Migrating the drone's operating system and interface from the Chinese Ground Control Unit to a notebook computer was nothing short of a miracle, and it had already earned him accolades and respect from Hamza.

"Steady on heading two-seven-zero," the other pilot said, leveling the wings out of the turn.

Qasim turned and looked over his shoulder at Hamza. "Ready for drone handoff . . ."

"Are you confident that he has reliable control?" Hamza asked.

"We can do a few more test maneuvers if you like," Qasim said, then tilting his boom mike away from his mouth added, "but either way, I'm planning on staying in this chair until we lose our data link."

"All right. In that case," Hamza said, "make the handoff."

"Understood." Qasim repositioned his boom mike to the corner of his mouth and said, "Saladin, this is Mecca. Thunderbolt is your asset."

"Copy, Mecca," the other pilot said. "I have control of Thunderbolt."

"Handoff complete," Qasim said over his shoulder.

"Very well," Hamza said. "Now, we wait and we watch . . ."

The next hour was extraordinarily stressful, with the portable Ground Control Unit losing connection with the drone multiple times, each time fraying Qasim's nerves and requiring the drone to circle until the remote data link could be reestablished. Steadfast, Qasim remained in the pilot's chair, even after the drone had flown well beyond his control range. With nothing left to see, the other al Qadar lieutenants retired for the night. Hamza dismissed his bodyguard—a sinewy, hollow-cheeked man who gave Qasim the creeps—leaving the two of them alone.

"What's wrong, Qasim?" Hamza asked, placing a hand on his shoulder. "You seem very agitated."

"I think we should bring the drone back," he said. "The laptop GCU is too unreliable. What if the pilot loses connectivity during the strike? What if he can't execute the mission? What if we can't recover the asset? There are too many variables. We should bring it back. I can try to boost the signal strength on the portable antenna and write better code to manage loss-of-connectivity scenarios."

"Oh, Qasim," Hamza said with a patronizing smile, "that's the engineer in you talking. I appreciate that you want everything to be perfect and the operation to function with all the precision and reliability of an American military strike, but we are not the American military. We are a small operation, and we must exploit every opportunity afforded us to the maximum extent possible. Strategically, we risk as much, if not more, trying to recover the drone for you to upgrade the controls as we do trying to complete the mission. It could crash; it could be identified by the enemy and shot down, or traced back to us here. Also, who knows when another convoy movement will be scheduled. This was difficult intelligence for us to obtain. We can't squander the opportunity. So don't fret, my friend. The drone is airborne and en route to the target. I consider this a tremendous success already."

Hamza is right, Qasim thought. *I'm thinking like a test engineer.*

"That being said," Hamza continued, his voice contemplative, "as I stand here now, having watched you fly the drone from the pilot's seat, the superiority of this control suite is obvious. For the next mission, I want to be able to stand in the GCU, watch the live imagery of the strike on the monitors, and make tactical decisions in real time. I don't want to have to rely on mobile phones to talk to the pilot. Also, without a data link, we can't watch the strike on our monitors. I want to see it happen."

Qasim nodded. "What you're talking about is satellite relay control. We would need a dedicated data link with a satellite in a geostationary orbit."

"Yes, I know," Hamza said. "Can you do this?"

"Doubtful," Qasim said and felt all the blood drain from his face. "Highly doubtful."

"But is it possible?"

"Yes, well, anything is possible given enough time, money, and resources, but I wouldn't even know where to . . ." His voice trailed off as something occurred to him. He rubbed the two weeks' beard growth on his chin. "I do have one idea, but I'm reluctant to mention it because it would . . . No, it's preposterous. Never mind."

"Preposterous is the fuel that powers all great accomplishments. Just tell me, Qasim."

"All right," he said through an exhale. "The Americans and the British operate their regional drone fleets out of Kandahar Air Base. They are flying sorties twenty-four seven, three hundred sixty-five days a year. They have multiple drones in the air at any given time with comms being relayed via dedicated satellites over the region. If we could somehow hack into one of those satellites and properly configure the data link to mimic that of an operating Predator, our drone could theoretically—"

"Disappear in the traffic," Hamza said, finishing his sentence. "Precisely."

"Oh, that's very clever, Qasim," the terrorist said, the wheels now clearly spinning in his head. "But how long before somebody noticed? Certainly, they would see this drone in their airspace and figure out it was not one of their own."

"Maybe, maybe not. Remember, most of the drones are being controlled by pilots in Nevada. Each has its own tasking, and there are multiple groups involved, all operating different missions. The British RAF doesn't care what US Army is doing with a Predator along the Iranian border, so long as it doesn't impact whatever operation they're supporting in the Hindu Kush. And I suspect that while someone is responsible for deconflicting satellite traffic, this is not the same person monitoring Kandahar airspace. My point is that the system is complex, and most of the players are myopically focused. They are only concerned about the reliability of *their* comms, clearance to operate in *their* sandbox, and whatever is necessary to complete *their* mission objective. If we configure our Pterodactyl to look, squawk, and operate like one of their drones, I think it could conceivably go unnoticed for hours—possibly even an entire day."

"It's brilliant. What are the next steps? How do we make this happen?" Hamza said, his expression brimming with excitement.

"Therein lies the problem," Qasim said. "I'm an engineer, not a hacker. I don't know the first thing about how to hack into the US DoD satellite network."

"That's okay," Hamza said, unfazed. "I have people who might be able to do this, but they will need your expertise with protocols and transmission configurations."

"Okay, I can help with that," he said, then, stifling a yawn, checked his watch. The digital display read 04:42. He'd been up for nearly thirty-six hours, and with his adrenaline now fully depleted, exhaustion was weighing on him like a two-hundred-pound blanket.

"When is the last time you slept?" Hamza asked.

"I don't know. The day before yesterday . . ."

"Go get some sleep, Qasim. You deserve it."

"I'm going to stay up. I don't want to miss the strike."

"There's nothing to see, remember? We don't have a data link," Hamza said through a laugh. "When I get the call, I'll have someone wake you with the news."

"Are you sure?"

"Yes. Take advantage of this lull, because if anything goes wrong you'll be the first person I summon."

"Okay," Qasim said. Ducking his head, he stepped out of the GCU and made his way to the folding cot he'd been using as a bed. Without even bothering to empty his bladder first, he collapsed on his stomach and fell asleep.

In his dream, he was piloting the Pterodactyl drone from the GCU, but instead of being hidden in the outskirts of Mingora, the CONEX-box-sized control unit was in the living room of his apartment in England. Hamza was there, standing behind him, and Eshan sat in the sensor operator's chair next to him. They looked at him with wide, preternatural smiles. Police sirens wailed in the distance, but they didn't seem bothered. His palms were sweating, and the throttle and control stick felt slick in his hands.

"There 'tis," Hamza said, his accent distinctly more British in his dream. "Our target . . ."

Qasim looked at the primary monitor and saw a three-vehicle convoy—one truck flanked front and back by armored Humvees—kicking up dust as it traveled on Highway A1. The live-streaming video of the vehicles was overlaid with targeting data as the drone's fire-control system automatically tracked the convoy.

"Which vehicle should I target?" Eshan asked.

"The middle one," Qasim answered.

In his dream, he used a trackball controller to select the middle truck as the primary target for one of the Pterodactyl's two HJ-10 missiles. The AR-1B variant loaded onto the UCAV was specifically designed to be carried by drones and attack ground-based targets using lock-on-before-launch and semi-active laser guidance technology.

"Target acquired," Eshan reported.

"Fire," Hamza said.

Qasim squeezed the trigger on his control stick, and a brilliant streak of flames momentarily washed out the drone's video display. The missile streaked away at Mach 1, closing the distance between the drone and the convoy in seconds. He watched it silently impact the American transport vehicle, which exploded in a fireball. A black cloud of smoke and dust engulfed the convoy. Once it cleared, he scanned the carnage. Some of the bodies were moving, some were not.

Some of the bodies were whole.

Some were not.

The camera feed began to zoom.

"What are you doing?" Qasim said to Eshan, his gaze glued to the monitor.

Eshan didn't answer immediately and instead just kept zooming in and in and in until a dismembered limb—a hunk of leg from knee to boot—filled the screen. "Eye for an eye, leg for a leg," he said and began to laugh.

Qasim sat bolt upright, gasping for breath. For several seconds, he was disoriented and wasn't sure where he was. Then, it all came back to him. He'd been so sleep deprived for the past ten days that everything blurred together. Had he ever been truly awake, or had this all been one vivid sleepwalking event? Is this what it felt like to be brainwashed? Had he *really* joined al Qadar and helped plan and prepare a drone strike against the Americans?

He felt nauseated.

"I have to stop it," he murmured, checking his watch. "There might still be time . . ."

CHAPTER 11

When it came to convoys, anywhere was better than the middle.

Staff Sergeant Mirin Taylor had learned that the hard way on her two tours in Iraq, when she'd seen more carnage than she cared to contemplate. Her unit had supported both conventional and SOF units with convoy operations—moving fighters and materials all over Anbar Province. The Wild West, they had called it back then, and the euphemism had been accurate. Lawless, dangerous, and dusty . . . yeah, the Wild fucking West indeed.

Over the years, she'd developed a fatalistic view of life. If it was your time, then it was your time. Plain and simple. As one of two combat medics on this convoy, traveling from ISAF headquarters in Kabul to Forward Operating Base Fenty beside Jalalabad Airport, it was Mirin's job to provide first responder medical support in the event the convoy encountered an IED or was attacked by insurgents. She'd lived through both scenarios multiple times, and she was good at her job. She'd do whatever it took to keep an injured soldier alive, but in her heart, she felt it was fate or God or the universe that made the final call. And yet, despite feeling entirely secure outsourcing her destiny to a higher power, as her Humvee rumbled along the dusty A1, one thought played a loop in her mind . . .

Anywhere is better than the middle.

When a convoy was targeted by insurgents, the middle always took the brunt of the attack. Today she'd avoided the proverbial short straw and was riding in the rear vehicle of their three-vehicle convoy: Humvee, truck, Humvee.

"Whatcha thinkin' about, Mimi?" a soldier beside her said, using the nickname she hated.

She looked over and shook her head. "Just scan the road, Cortez." She searched for movement among the boulders littering the rocky hills on both sides of Highway A1. "We're in Tali country; these guys can climb and blend in like effing mountains goats."

"Five, it's One—you there, Mimi?"

"'Sup, LT?" The Mimi handle didn't bother her from the Lieutenant. Maybe it was because he was an officer. Maybe it was just that he wasn't trying to get in her pants like these new boys.

"Just got a drone-pass feed—we're all clear between here and J-bad. Got no one tucked in the hills waiting for us that we can see and no thermals."

"Good to go, sir," she replied. Of course, you were never really safe in the 'Stan. Green on blue was the favored method of killing infidels after IEDs, and FOB Felty had been the site of an insider attack a few years earlier. Just because a passing soldier was dressed in an Afghan military uniform, didn't mean he was friendly.

As the Humvee rattled and shook over the pockmarked dirt road, she thought about the decisions she'd made to wind up in this seat and what her future held . . .

It is what it is, she decided after beating herself up for a good long while. *What am I gonna do? Work at Target and drink beer at the VFW? Like they even want women soldiers hanging around in towns like mine.*

No. She was career Army now. It was just math. She was already over the hump at twelve years in, and it would be stupid to stop now. She had once thought about going to medical school on the GI Bill, but that window of opportunity was behind her. Best option was to tough it out and retire at twenty.

I'll still be under forty years old. Just two years of school and I can become a PA.

She knew plenty of medics who had done that.

Seven and a half years . . . plenty of time to get ready for my next—

Something streaked across the sky ahead of them—like a big brightly lit shooting star. At first she thought it was a magnesium flare falling from above, but it was too big.

And it was too fast.

She realized it was a missile just before the world in front of her became a fireball and both of her eardrums burst in pain. Then it was like being under water—hot water—but for some reason she could breathe it in. It hurt, but she could breathe.

She couldn't see though.

The world had gone bright white. The glare soon began to fade, and she thought she saw shadows moving around her. Her left side hurt and so did her left collarbone. The right side of her face felt tight and numb.

She blinked. Twice more.

She heard a sound like someone shouting from inside a

bucket. It sounded a little like "Mimi," but she wasn't sure. Hands tugged at her.

Time warped.

She saw light, then black.

Then light again after minutes, maybe hours, or even days.

She blinked, and the world came into slow focus.

She was dangling from the shoulder harness of her seatbelt, and she was sure that her collarbone and several ribs were broken. The Humvee was on its side, and someone was pulling her out of the door, which was above her.

It hurt like hell.

She let herself be lifted, grunting when her knee hit something hard. As other senses returned, she gagged on the overpowering stench of burning fuel. Burning fuel and burning flesh.

It was the same smell as in Fallujah in 2005.

Her face and neck on the right began to burn in pain, and she realized the charred odor was coming from her.

"This one is urgent surgical," someone said.

She thought of those burned, disfigured bodies she'd treated in Fallujah. She couldn't tell the men from the women because their hair was gone and only black flesh tinged with red blood remained.

Her stomach heaved, and she tasted blood and bile.

"Who next?" another voice said.

"No one else. Top gunner was cut almost in half when the damn thing flipped. Driver is dead. All the others are crispy critters."

She let her head loll as she gazed at the charred and bloody bodies, just like those in Fallujah.

Am I one of them? One of the bodies? Just throw me on the pile . . .

The pain was terrible, and she was ready, but there was something she needed to do first. Something she needed to tell them, so they understood what had happened here. She had to tell someone about the missile she'd seen. It took all her strength, all her will, but she forced her head up. Forced her mouth to form words.

"What's she saying?" a male voice said.

"I don't know. Take it easy, Staff Sergeant, we got you," another said.

"Dro . . ." she said, the word little more than a gurgle. With great effort, she pointed at the sky and tried to say the word again.

"I can't understand her. What's she—oh shit, I think we're losing her."

Suddenly, she couldn't feel the arms supporting her anymore. She was falling, falling, falling to somewhere. Which was good because the pain was unbearable now. She said a silent prayer to God or the universe or fate that the dark pit she was plunging toward was death.

CHAPTER 12

Before he could get to Hamza, Qasim knew it was too late.

Everyone was awake and crowded around the charismatic al Qadar lieutenant, cheering, shouting, and backslapping.

Hamza was all smiles, and when he saw Qasim, he waved him over. "Qasim, your timing is perfect. The strike was a success!"

Qasim squinted as Hamza showed him a grainy image of a large explosion in the middle of a military convoy.

"The pilot took this picture of the laptop screen at the moment of impact." Hamza threw his arm around Qasim's shoulders. "We did it, Qasim. We executed the world's first drone missile strike against an American military target. Allah is smiling upon us today, my brother."

Looking at the image, a quizzical emotion washed over Qasim, one he did not expect: pride. The disgust and anxiety he'd been feeling in his dream was unexpectedly displaced. He was glad the Americans were dead. He was glad the operation had been a success. And in that moment, he wondered if he was losing his mind. How was it that he could flip-flop between revulsion and excitement so readily? How was it that two personas could occupy his thoughts at the same time? Which reality was true—Qasim, the law-abiding naturalized British aerospace engineer, or Qasim, the Afghan drone pilot and terrorist? Is this what it meant to be trapped in a duality?

He looked up from the image and met Hamza's eyes. "We really got a hit?"

"Yes!"

"Have the Americans shot the drone down yet?"

"No, the pilot is flying it back into the Hindu Kush. The plan is to keep it airborne and as far north as line of sight will permit. If we can make it to nightfall, we will attempt to fly it across the border and land it at the Mingora airport. Do you want to pilot the landing?"

Qasim nodded, eager to get back in the pilot's chair.

He joined the group, talking little but accepting words of praise and congratulations from the other al Qadar men, most of whom he recognized but still did not know. He'd made a point of not fraternizing with anyone other than Hamza these past twelve days. He didn't feel comfortable with these men and suspected he never would.

A breakfast of chai and paratha was served, prepared, and delivered by women he also did not know. It was that way with all the food since Qasim had arrived; it just showed up, and he'd never once been asked to pay for his share. Hamza maintained a strict policy of limiting traffic in and out of the building. Only Eshan seemed to be permitted to come and go freely, and Qasim wondered when his best friend would return. It had been three days since they'd spoken.

After the meal, Hamza pulled Qasim aside, leading him to the boxy GCU, where he closed and locked the door from the inside.

"So that we are not disturbed," he said, turning to look at Qasim.

"I figured as much."

"How are you feeling about all of this? The first operation can be . . . emotional for thoughtful men like yourself."

"When you sent me off to get some sleep, I had a nightmare," Qasim said, looking down at his hands. "I dreamed about the strike. There were bodies, and pieces of bodies, everywhere. Charred and smoldering. I woke up in a panic. When you waved me over, I was coming to ask you to call it off."

"Mmm-hmm," was all Hamza said.

Qasim looked up. Instead of judgment, he found empathy in Hamza's eyes. "Are you angry with me?"

"With these other men," Hamza said, gesturing outside the walls of the GCU, "I would not tolerate such behavior. But from you, I would be concerned if you were *not* conflicted. You have suffered great tragedy in your life. You have lived through a drone strike. You know the cost. You know the carnage. You're not an evil man, Qasim, and neither am I. Only a sadist enjoys the torture and mutilation of others. That is not what we're about. That is not what jihad is about. Under my leadership, al Qadar will not follow the path of al-Qaeda or the Islamic State. This was a tactical strike on a military target. We are professionals, Qasim. We do not blow up women and children. We do not murder our fellow Muslims. I know such things have weighed heavy on your mind, but now you can sleep easy. You have my word on this."

"I'm not sure I can go back," Qasim said, shaking his head. "Not after this."

"You mean back to work? Back to England?"

Qasim nodded, the duality of his personas strained to the breaking point.

"Why?"

Qasim shrugged. He worried that if he said more, he would undermine all the goodwill he'd built with Hamza.

"Because you're a terrorist now? Is that it?"

He nodded.

"Does that make you ashamed?"

He looked away, unable to hold the other man's gaze any longer.

"Do you think that an American soldier, a Navy SEAL, for example, is ashamed of the work he does? Do you think he calls himself *terrorist* in his own mind? No, of course not. He calls himself *patriot*. He calls himself *warrior*. He is a soldier fighting his enemy with a mandate from his country. We are soldiers too, fighting our enemy with a mandate from God. Which mandate do you think holds more weight? Which mandate do you think is more just? The one from Allah, or the one from President Warner?"

"God's mandate," he whispered.

"That's right," Hamza said, his voice hardening. "I want you to strike this word *terrorist* from your personal lexicon, Qasim. You are not a terrorist. Do you understand? Look at me." Qasim found it difficult to lift his gaze, and for a moment felt like a child, his eyes now rimmed with tears. "You . . . are . . . not a terrorist. You're a drone pilot and engineer. You're a patriot and warrior in Allah's army. These are things to be proud of. It's time to purge your shame. It's time to purge your guilt. When you go home to England—and you will go home, my friend—be proud."

Qasim nodded, empowered by the other man's words. "Okay, I'll try."

"Good," Hamza said, giving Qasim's shoulder a squeeze. "It won't happen overnight, but think about my words. A man's personal truth is the only truth that matters." Hamza released his shoulder, then pulled a folded envelope from his pocket and handed it to Qasim.

"What's this?" Qasim asked, accepting it.

"For your work, of course," Hamza said with a laugh. "You don't think I expect my people to work for free, do you? You're a professional with an extraordinarily valuable skill set. You deserve compensation."

Qasim's heart rate picked up as he opened the flap and peeked at the stack of notes inside.

"Twenty thousand euros," Hamza said. "I counted it myself."

Qasim refolded the envelope and stuffed it in his pants pocket. To his surprise, his mind went to Diba. He could buy a very nice wedding ring for her with this and still have money left over to pay for an extravagant, romantic holiday when this was all over.

"Thank you," he said, not sure what else to say.

"You're welcome," Hamza said. "But that's only the start. Assuming we recover the drone, if you and my cyber team can succeed in hacking the US satellite network and configure the drone for another mission, I'll give you access to an account in Dubai with a starting balance of one hundred thousand."

"One hundred thousand?" Qasim said, his jaw agape.

Hamza nodded. "As I rise, so do those who help me fulfill my vision. As your role and commitment increase, so will your bank—" Hamza's mobile phone vibrated in his pocket, stopping him midsentence. He checked the message and his expression darkened.

"Is everything okay?" Qasim asked.

"It doesn't concern you," Hamza said. Then, tone softening, he added, "Why don't you take the rest of the day off? Eshan should be arriving within the hour. Just make certain you're back after sundown to pilot the drone . . . assuming it lasts until then."

"You can count on me," Qasim said and meant it.

CHAPTER 13

TEAM INTELLIGENCE SUPPORT

TIER ONE COMPOUND

MACDILL AIR FORCE BASE

TAMPA, FLORIDA

0635 LOCAL TIME

Whitney massaged her temples, then looked at the Casio G-SHOCK watch the command had issued her. It was a huge and hideous thing and looked ridiculous on her slender wrist. As she unfastened it and put it on her desk, she wondered if wearing it was obligatory.

Well, if it is, too bad . . . I'm not wearing that friggin' thing.

She shifted her attention back to her monitor and the photographs documenting the aftermath of yesterday's convoy attack outside Jalalabad. The preliminary reports were that a three-vehicle Army convoy had encountered two roadside IEDs, but something about the battle damage didn't sit right with her. There was one picture that she couldn't get out of her head, and it had ushered her down a bunny hole of sleep deprivation and speculation. She'd promised herself when she'd accepted this job that she'd stop doing this sort of thing and stay in her lane, but she simply couldn't help herself. The more challenging the knot, the more driven she was to figure out how to untie it.

It was in her nature to snoop.

And it was why she'd pursued a career in intelligence in the first place.

Her propensity to stick her nose into other analysts' business—some might even label it a compulsion—had annoyed her contemporaries at NCTC. And it might have possibly, probably, earned her the nickname Woke Whitney, an honorific certainly born from envy at her uncanny ability to see connections that others were blind to. But for all the teasing and complaining it might have earned her from her peers, she was convinced it was the primary reason her boss had recommended *her* for the promotion. She worked longer hours, excavated more intel from background noise, and simply outperformed the other analysts. Know-it-alls with a respectable batting average were annoying. But a know-it-all who bats close to a thousand was downright despised.

That person was Northern Virginia Whitney.

Florida Whitney needed to chill . . . but could she?

A rap at her door gave her a start. She swiveled in her chair to find Petty Officer Michelle Yi, dressed in green digital cammies unique to Special Warfare and EOD, standing in the door frame holding two cups of coffee.

"You're here early, Michelle," she said, looking at the petite Asian American who Whitney suspected wasn't a hair over four feet eleven. "When did you get in?"

"I'm here when you're here, ma'am," the enlisted intelligence specialist said, addressing her as she would any officer.

"Well, I've been here since two forty-five."

"Yes, ma'am," she said, her voice and expression professional.

"How do you even know . . . never mind," Whitney said, shaking off the thought. "Come in."

Yi stepped into Whitney's little office. "I brought you a coffee, ma'am. I figured you could probably use it. Take your pick. Either a mocha or a latte with two shots of espresso."

"The double latte, definitely." Whitney graciously accepted the double-cupped creation that looked like it came from the "robo-barista" machine in the break room. When Yi remained standing, Whitney motioned for her to take a seat. "Michelle, how long have you been at this command?"

"Just a couple of weeks, ma'am. I got here two days before you arrived."

"Look, this is my first military command, but from what I've observed around here, I think you can ixnay on the 'am-may.'"

Yi screwed up her face with incomprehension.

"Sorry, pig Latin, just something stupid that me and my old boss used to do. What I meant to say was that you don't have to call me *ma'am*. I don't hear anyone using honorifics around this place. The SEALs all call each other *bro*, and my boss has insisted that I call him Chunk." She shook her head. "I think we both might fit in a little better if we, you know, just chill."

"Okay," Yi said cautiously. "I'll try. Are those pictures from the convoy attack outside of Jalalabad?" She sipped her mocha, leaning in to look at Whitney's monitor.

"Yeah," she said, angling her monitor for a better shared view. Pictures filled the screen of burned-out military vehicles on route A1 in Afghanistan. The rear Humvee was the most intact, lying on its side, with a body splayed beside it. The transport vehicle was completely incinerated, however, little more than scattered parts inside a wide crater. It was the worse IED scene she had ever seen, but something else about it bugged her. She tapped the side of her coffee cup with a finger as she stared at the pictures. At the bottom left, two medics from the recovery team were leaning over someone on the ground, one of them holding a bag of saline for an IV in the air.

"Did we get tasked to look into it?" Yi asked, her tone cautious.

"No, but I saw the report in flash traffic and I got curious . . ." She hesitated, debating whether she should let Yi into her head. *What the hell. We're a team, right?* "Michelle, do you see anything odd in this picture?"

Yi leaned in for a closer look. "Um . . . nothing that immediately catches my eye. Just looks like a typical IED attack. Middle vehicle gets the worst of it. Why, do you?"

"Maybe," Whitney said, then zoomed in on the image of the injured soldier being tended to beside the wreckage. "From this angle, it looks to me like that soldier is pointing at something."

"Yeah, you're right, it does. What do you think she's pointing at?"

"I don't know, but from the look on her face, I'd say it's important."

"Maybe we can find out. Do you want me to do some digging and try to figure out who she is and get a message to the command?" Yi asked.

"I already know who she is—Staff Sergeant Mirin Taylor."

"Okay, great, that makes things easier."

"Not really. She didn't make it."

"Oh . . . that's too bad," Yi said, looking down into her cup.

"Yeah, it is," Whitney said, zooming the image out to full frame, then reclining against the backrest of her chair while she stared at it. She took a sip of the latte, which had finally cooled enough to drink, then said, "What if it wasn't a roadside IED that took out this convoy? What if it was missile strike?"

Yi laughed nervously at first, then said, "Oh, sorry, you're serious, aren't you?"

"Dead serious," Whitney said. "I mean, I'm no explosive ordnance expert, but this crater looks different than an IED blast. The vehicle damage looks different too. Whatever did this got really hot. Reminds me of pics I've seen of vehicles after getting hit by a Hellfire."

"Interesting theory," Yi said. "You don't think this was friendly fire, do you?"

Whitney winced. "I think it's a possibility we shouldn't ignore."

"I have some connections with aviation types up at Oceana. They do Battle Damage Assessments following airstrikes. If you want, I can get a BDA opinion on these pictures. And at the same time, I can also float the question to see if they've heard any rumors about a blue-on-blue event."

"You were at Oceana in Virginia?"

"Yes, ma'am—I mean, Whitney," Yi said, smiling. "I was at VFA-31 as a new-intel specialist right out of school at Dam Neck, before I ended up at SEAL Team Ten."

Whitney nodded and saved several images into a file and labeled it *Oceana*. "I'm sending you these pictures. Let me know what you hear back, then we can decide where we want to go next with this."

"Roger that," Yi said and got up from her chair.

"Thanks for the coffee, Michelle."

"You're welcome, Whitney," Yi said with a smile and left.

During her indoc, Whitney had been briefed by Commander Bowman—*Captain Select* Bowman, she'd been informed—that hers would be a job of short fuses. Her primary function was to pull together important bits of relevant intelligence to prepare the team when orders hit, then unravel streams of actionable intelligence when they were down range, to keep them safe on the hunt. When she was not supporting tasking, her job was to maintain a thirty-thousand-foot perspective of ever-evolving intelligence on the terrorism hot spots around the globe, to be ready at moment's notice to support action against any number of targets when an opportunity presented itself. So given the latter mandate, she'd decided to do what she always did—snoop around. When she found something that piqued her interest, she would peel back the fragmented layers of information until a story began to take shape. At NCTC, she'd had access to counterintelligence data streams, but nothing like she had here. At the Tier One, she felt like the proverbial kid in the candy shop. With a click of her mouse she could peruse the daily intelligence briefs from all the Unified Combatant Commands in DoD with high levels of terror threats—which in today's world was practically all of them.

In her peripheral vision, someone big stepped into her open doorway.

"Morning," said familiar voice.

She looked up from her monitor to see Chunk dressed in running shorts and a "Don't Tread on Me" Gadsden flag T-shirt. He smiled at her from under his battered backward ball cap.

"Good morning," she said, flashed him a don't-you-dare-ask-me-to-go-running-with-you smile, then took a long sip from her coffee.

"Glad to see you're here early. I'm headed out to do a PT run with Riker, Trip, and Spence. Got your PT gear?"

Are you friggin' serious?

"I do, but I have a few things I'm working on," she said, not moving a muscle.

She'd stuffed workout clothes and a pair of Nikes in the bottom drawer of her desk after the fourth time Chunk had mentioned that PT was a part of the workday for everyone.

"Delegate," he said and smiled at her.

She sighed. "Chunk, I don't know how to say this, but uh . . . I don't run," she said, using her best it's-settled tone. "Sorry."

"Say again?" he said, cupping a hand to his ear theatrically. "I thought I just heard you say you don't run, but that couldn't possibly be, because you're at the Tier One SEAL Team and physical readiness is one of our core principles here."

"Yeah, about that. I'm an analyst. You're the Navy SEAL. You work out there"—she gestured to the beyond—"jumping out of helicopters, swimming in the ocean, and chasing down the bad guys. And I work in here, at this desk." She tapped the desktop and took another long, slow sip of coffee, just to drive the point home.

His response to this was not what she expected. He laughed—a legitimate, pitying laugh, at her expense. "Did nobody tell you?"

"Tell me what?" she asked, feeling her cheeks blush with heat.

"Your billet is not a desk job. Yes, you're our lead analyst, but where we go, you go."

As quickly as the blood had gone to her cheeks, she felt it drain away. "Whaaat?" was all she could manage.

"Yeah, you're part of the team. When we deploy, you deploy."

"I thought you guys were just screwing with me."

"No," he said through a chuckle. "Why do you think we gave you all that gear?"

She did a quick mental inventory of all the shit they'd outfitted her with. Tactical clothes, backpacks, boots, socks, hats, rain gear, two sleeping bags, pocket knives, and that ridiculous G-SHOCK watch. She'd even made a joke at the time that she was grateful for the free swag, but as a taxpayer she was starting to get enraged.

"And we still need to get your kit set up and weapons issued. Saw is gonna help you dope up your rifle with sights and lights, and help you select a pistol or two. Any preferences?"

It wasn't a charade. He was serious.

She wasn't sure what to say. She hadn't shot a firearm since her indoc course at the Farm, and that had been more than a couple of years ago.

"You gonna say something, or just stare at me with your mouth open?"

"Yeeeaaah, I haven't really kept current with my firearms training like I probably should have. And the last time I did PT was at the Farm."

Chunk nodded. "All right, at least you're being honest. Here's the thing, Heels—working out together is a big part of team building here. This is more than a desk job for you. You'll need to stay fit and be proficient with a firearm if you want to be part of this unit."

"But I'm not a SEAL, and I have no aspirations of trying to become one," she said, making no effort to hide the incredulity in her voice.

"Oh, don't worry, we know that. But there's no room for baggage at the Tier One. You don't need to be an operator, but like I said, where we go, you go, and we don't stay at the Ritz much. Shit happens in this line of work. You need to be able to run and to shoot, if only for personal protection. We won't always be there to carry you. Do you understand?"

She nodded and felt her heart flutter. "No baggage . . ."

"That's right."

"Okay," she said and exhaled. "How far is the run today?"

"Probably six, no big deal."

"Six? Like, six *miles*?" she gasped.

"Yeah," he said with a sadist's grin. "Is that gonna be a problem for you?"

"Yes, Chunk, it's going to be a problem for me. And for you, when people see me puking along the side of the road."

"Nah, it's good to clear out the pipes once in a while. Meet you on the barbecue deck in five," he said and was gone.

She leaned back in her chair and looked up at the ceiling.

He's not joking. They're going to run me until I puke or die from heatstroke. Whichever comes first.

Probably death.

With a resigned groan, Whitney "Heels" Watts pulled her workout clothes from her desk drawer and began to change.

CHAPTER 14

Chunk jogged in place along the curb as he waited for Whitney to finish puking in the grass. He'd sent the rest of the guys and Yi on without them, because, well, contrary to popular belief, SEALs *were* capable of empathy.

"Is that really necessary?" she asked, on all fours, not looking at him, her voice both weary and agitated.

"Is what necessary?"

"Running in place while you wait for me. It kinda feels like you're rubbing it in."

He gave a genuine laugh. "This is just good physiological science. I'm keeping my muscles warm and my heart rate up so I don't fall into a resting lull."

"Mm-hmm," she said, wiping her mouth with the back of her hand. "'Cause it feels like you're rubbing it in."

"The first run is always the hardest," he said. "You're going to be sore as hell tomorrow, but three weeks from now, you'll be shocked at how far you've progressed. The human body is an amazingly adaptive machine."

She spit one last time, got to her feet, and turned, red faced, to glare at him.

"Your color looks better," he said with a smug smile. Then seeing the reaction he was hoping for added, "It's okay, go ahead and say it. That's how we roll around here."

"You sure?"

"Yeah, hit me with both barrels."

"Fuck you and your fucking six-mile run."

He nodded approvingly. "Feel better?"

"Much better," she said and finally flashed him the defiant smile he'd been waiting for.

"We're past the halfway point. It would be longer to turn around and go back than to finish the loop. So . . . you ready?"

She let out an exasperated sigh. "Fine, but I get to set the pace."

"Sure. It will give us a chance to talk."

Despite the compulsion to push her, he kept his promise and let her set the pace, which was so slow he could almost walk.

All in good time . . .

They jogged in silence for a quarter mile or so before he said, "So, Whitney, I haven't heard much from you over the past two weeks . . ."

"I've been working," she said with a defensive edge.

"I know, I've seen you burning the midnight oil in your office . . . Let me rephrase. What have you been working on?"

"I started by familiarizing myself with the old Tier One

after-action reports—beginning a year before and up through the Operation Crusader incident. Next, I reviewed every team member's personnel files, including yours, and after that, I studied the last twelve months of operations that you conducted at Team Four."

"Oh," he said, her initiative and brazen candidness catching him off guard. "Makes sense, I suppose. You got any questions?"

"Dozens . . ."

"Great, fire away."

"Your last op with Team Four, that Pakistani freighter in the Arabian Sea, particularly got my attention."

"Oh yeah?"

"The assessment CIA prepared has some holes. Maybe you could help fill them in for me?"

"I can try," he said, his mind taking him back to that very unusual night.

"Reading between the lines, I take it you encountered resistance commandeering the vessel, but the assessment was light on specifics."

"Threat assessments usually try to keep it at a higher level, but yes, we did face resistance. Ten contract security personnel in unmarked uniforms were on board to protect the cargo. I wasn't able to confirm their identity or employer, but to my eye they looked to be of East Asian descent."

"Chinese?"

"That's where I'd put my money, but I never followed up."

"Do you know what hardware was recovered from the cargo hold?"

"Nope. We turned the ship over to the spooks and didn't stick around for the unboxing."

"You curious to know what it was carrying?" she said, glancing at him as she jogged.

"Yeah, actually, I am."

"Chinese military hardware. HJ-10 air-to-ground missiles, portable SAM units, and boxes of what CIA believes to be drone components."

"We all know the Chinese have defense contracts to supply the Pakistani military with hardware and systems, so on its face that's not surprising," Chunk said. "But what's odd to me is that the Chinese guys we capped were armed, but definitely not SOF. They performed like mercenaries, not operators."

"That's the sort of detail that was missing in the threat assessment," she said, squeezing out the words between heavy pants. "That ship was bound for Gwadar, a small seaport in western Pakistan. If this was legit defense contract fulfillment, then I would expect delivery to happen in Karachi by a Chinese-flagged cargo ship. The ship you hit was a Pakistani freighter."

"Agreed. So you think it was illegal arms trafficking?"

"Yeah, and given the port, probably bound for a jihadi client," she said. "And there's something else . . ."

"Go on."

"I don't have shred of proof for what I'm about to say. It's pure conjecture."

"Okay. I'm listening."

"There was an Army convoy that got hit en route to J-bad yesterday."

"I heard."

"Preliminary assessment is that they hit an IED, but I think it was a missile strike."

"On what basis?" He had already learned enough about her to know not to dismiss anything she said as out of hand. Still, this seemed far-fetched.

"I've seen lots of pictures of IED hits and missile strikes, and the aftermath here looks like the latter to me."

He pursed his lips as he jogged beside her at a snail's pace. It seemed pretty thin. On the other hand, she did have a reputation for having near-perfect instincts regarding intelligence assessment, which was why they had hired her. And the implication that terrorists in theater might have access to Chinese air-to-ground missiles was too chilling to ignore.

"You think it's connected to my last op at Team Four?"

"Not directly, obviously," she said. "We confiscated those weapons. But I'm not a believer in coincidences. The Chinese-made missiles on the freighter you intercepted were headed to Pakistan for some illicit purpose. Have there been other shipments we missed, and if so where did those weapons end up?"

"You have been busy," he said, turning to look at her while they jogged. If she was right about this, the implications for their forces in the Middle East were gut-wrenching.

"Told ya."

"Tell you what," he said. "Keep working on trying to connect the dots, and if you come up with something concrete, we can bring it to Bowman."

"Roger that," she said—the first time he'd heard her use military speak.

A good sign, he chuckled to himself as he jogged ahead. *She's already beginning to talk like us.*

CHAPTER 15

Chunk pushed through the tinted glass doors, jogged past the row of SEAL pictures, and ducked into his office just long enough to dump his cell phone and keys into the top drawer. Bowman had told him to "hurry his ass over" because they had an important guest in the SCIF and he'd moved Watts's intel brief up to accommodate. He headed down the hall to the rear corner of the building, where an elevator door seemed curiously out of place. He swiped the ID hanging from his neck across a scanner plate, the LED indicator light changed from red to green, and the door opened. Inside, he punched the bottom of the two unmarked buttons and the elevator dropped rapidly, like he'd just stepped out of a C-17 for a HALO jump. The real and hidden heart of the Tier One unit was fifty feet underground—a watertight steel-and-cement bunker located below sea level on the tip of the peninsula sticking out into Tampa's Hillsborough Bay.

Crazy . . .

The doors opened, revealing a steel door five paces away, painted green and labeled Sensitive Compartmented Information Facility. Flanking the stout green door were two armed guards, dressed in full battle rattle, rifles slung combat style across their chests.

"Identification, sir," the guard on the right said in a practiced monotone.

The perfunctory "sir" was all Chunk would ever get out of this guy.

The guard scanned his badge, then presented the scanner to Chunk for his left thumb and right index finger. The scanner flashed green—his fingerprints a match—and the stone-faced guard entered a rotating code into the keypad beside the door.

The door hissed open, and the guard on the left waved him through.

A star-shaped conference table dominated the center of the dimly lit SCIF—the six spokes formed by three long tables joined in the middle. Computer workstations were set up at each of the seats around what Chunk had come to think of as a star-shaped version of King Arthur's famous table. Only one station was occupied, however, with Watts seated and typing, while Yi leaned over her shoulder and pointed to something on the screen. Chunk had given Whitney the green light to brief Bowman on her theory about the convoy attack. He wasn't fully convinced she was right, but he'd decided to let her run with it—if for no other reason than that if she was right, the cost of missing this was too terrifying. In doing so, he'd stuck his neck out for her, but what better way to embrace the ethos of the new Tier One where spooks and operators were teammates under a single banner, as opposed to the divisive separate-but-equal paradigm that had grated on his nerves at Four?

In his peripheral vision, a man dressed in a dark-blue suit stood talking to Captain Bowman. Despite seeing him only from the back, Chunk recognized the visitor instantly. He'd first met Kelso Jarvis while the former SEAL was serving as the Director of National Intelligence. In the time since, Jarvis had been tapped by President Warner to serve as Vice President after Warner's former VP was killed in a terror attack in Kiev.

Jarvis had an unmistakable presence about him. Wherever he went, he pushed an invisible bow wave in front of him, parting a room full of people just like an aircraft carrier parted the seas. To see him here for this brief, defied all logic and expectation.

Bowman spotted Chunk and waved him over. En route, he couldn't help but glance in Whitney's direction. She caught his eye, and her face was a portrait of nerves.

Oh shit, he thought, suddenly regretting his decision not to be more hands-on with her. *What have I done?*

Jarvis turned to greet him and extended a hand.

"Mr. Vice President," Chunk said, returning the firm grip. "It's an honor to serve here, in the house you built."

"Good to see you again, Commander Redman," Jarvis said, his voice coarse gravel. "I was in the neighborhood and I couldn't resist the opportunity to drop by and visit the new Tier One. It's been a long time coming."

"Yes, sir," was all he said, deciding to keep it simple rather than risk waking old ghosts.

"Chunk, we'd like to hear your opinion of Gold Squadron's readiness," Bowman said. "The trainers have already given us their assessment, but you know the men better than anyone. Are they ready for field work?"

Chunk weighed his answer carefully. The line between

confident and overconfident was a fine one in this business, and the White House certainly was not interested in a cowboy leading a squadron of the most lethal operators on earth.

"Got a few boxes left to check, sir," Chunk said, walking that line, "but to a man the operators are five by. The skills and readiness are already there, and group cohesion is coming together remarkably fast. I'd say we're damn close to operational."

Bowman looked to Jarvis, who folded thick arms across his chest and nodded.

"Which platoon do you think could pull the trigger on a deployment right now?" Bowman asked.

"First Platoon, without a doubt. We've been mixing up the squads in training to flesh out the best combinations. I have First Platoon whittled down to two fire teams: Riker, Saw, Trip, and Morales in Alpha; Edwards, Georgie, Antman, and Lieutenant Spence in Bravo. Second Platoon is gonna be badass, sir, but First Platoon has already meshed."

"Good," Bowman said, then glancing over Chunk's shoulder added, "Looks like the rest of the leadership team is here, Mr. Vice President. We can start whenever you're ready."

Chunk turned to see the N3 Ops Officer arriving, along with the N2 department head, Lieutenant Commander Day. N2 was Navy shorthand for the Intelligence Department, while N3 was Operations. Both officers, who wore matching gold oak leaf insignia on their collars, looked as surprised as Chunk had been to see the Vice President in attendance.

Jarvis glanced at his watch, then made his way to the table and took a seat, cuing everyone else to do the same.

Bowman shifted his gaze to Whitney. "Watts, you're up."

"Yes, sir," she said and tapped something on her computer. One of the screens on the wall flickered to life with the opening slide of a presentation Chunk had, unfortunately, not seen yet.

Watts moved to the front of the room as Yi took a seat behind the computer. Chunk shot her a little smile and a thumbs-up, and he saw her shoulders visibly relax.

"Mr. Vice President, Captain Bowman, gentlemen," she said with a nod to the assembled brass, "this photo was taken by CIA during inventory of a freighter seized last month off the coast of Pakistan." Chunk immediately recognized the ship as the one he'd hit in his last action at Team Four. The image showed not the CONEX boxes on the cargo deck, but a series of crates in the hold. Another photo filled the screen, this time looking inside an opened box. "Half the crates contained electronics and drone components." The screen split in half, the first image moving left while a new image popped up on the right. "And the rest contained weapons and ordnance, like these Chinese-made HJ-10 air-to-ground missiles."

"I've been briefed on this," the VP said from beside Chunk. "You can skip the appetizers, Ms. Watts, and serve up the main course."

Whitney nodded, but Yi advanced to the next slide anyway.

"The electronic components were manufactured by the Aviation Industry Corporation of China, the Chinese equivalent of, say, Boeing or Lockheed Martin," she continued, her voice cracking with nerves. "Because of their uncanny similarity to their US-manufactured analogs, these components were identified as navigation, communications, and control modules for UCAVs. Aviation electronics is not my area of expertise, but my understanding is—"

"We'll stipulate that those parts are what you say, Ms. Watts," Bowman grumbled. "Like the Vice President said, please, let's just get to the meat and potatoes."

Yi quickly advanced several slides, stopping on an image of burned-out military vehicles along a road. Chunk's stomach tightened. They'd all lost too many brothers to gutless IED sneak attacks over the years. An IED didn't care whether you wore a trident or not.

"This image was taken in the aftermath of the recent convoy attack in Afghanistan," Watts said.

"That's one hell of an IED," Lieutenant Commander Day said. Chunk didn't know him well, but knew his impeccable reputation. "Jesus, look at the blast radius."

"The same thing caught my eye," Watts said, and the screen zoomed in on the crater surrounding the second and third vehicles. "The blast radius is big, but what really got my attention was the blast *pattern*. We ran these images past several experts in the tactical aviation community, and the feedback we received contradicted our initial battle damage assessment. The convoy did *not* hit an IED. What we're looking at here is the aftermath of a missile strike, with a blast pattern similar to what you'd expect from a Hellfire. Now I know what you're thinking, because it was my first concern as well—but we have confirmed that this was not a friendly-fire incident. We are not looking at a blue-on-blue scenario, gentlemen."

This conclusion was news to Chunk. He'd known Whitney was working on a theory, but he hadn't had a chance to dialogue with her before this brief, the VP's surprise visit having thrown the proverbial monkey wrench into both of their days. He looked at Bowman, who held his gaze as Watts began to narrate a series of slides on the technical aspects of buried charges versus aerial missile blast patterns. But everyone already knew where she was headed, and Chunk felt his pulse quicken.

"Miss Watts," Jarvis said, stopping her.

"Sir?"

"My time here is at a premium. I know you're used to making a case to your bosses—of giving evidential details to support your conclusions—but I'm willing to accept that proper due diligence occurred. We've got people looking into this in parallel. So if you could please jump ahead to your conclusions and recommendations . . ."

"Yes, sir," she said, and Chunk saw she was flustered at having her rhythm broken yet again. She rocked from one foot to another.

First she looked over at Yi, as if to tell her what slide to fast-forward to, but then made a "never mind" motion with her hand and put the laser pointer she'd been using down. Yi advanced the slides anyway, stopping on a photograph of an injured US Army solider lying next to a burned-up Humvee and pointing at the sky. The poignant image raised gooseflesh on Chunk's forearms.

"I believe that terrorists—either the Taliban or perhaps an al-Qaeda offshoot—have obtained an operational Chinese drone from the black market. I'm talking about a Rainbow Five or Pterodactyl-class UCAV capable of firing HJ-10 class AGMs, probably similar to those confiscated by Team Four on the Pakistani freighter. I believe that such a drone was used against our convoy, and I believe we should expect additional, and potentially deadlier, strikes against US military personnel in the very near future."

"And where do you think they are operating this drone from?" Bowman demanded.

"The Hindu Kush, sir," Watts said. "On the border between the Kunar and Nuristan provinces in Afghanistan." She looked at Yi and held up one finger, then flashed five more—slide fifteen, Chunk surmised.

A satellite view of eastern Afghanistan and western Pakistan filled the screen, with the midline centered on the border between the countries. A series of overlapping colored circles spread out over both areas. Most of the circles were blue or green and fell on the Afghan side. A smattering of yellow and red circles, however, extended into northwestern Pakistan. The region was almost entirely Pashtun and a place where tribal law reigned and national government influence was severely lacking.

"These colored circles mark areas where our signals and cyber experts identified radio and telecommunication transmissions temporally relevant to the convoy attack. The blue dots are confirmed to be friendly transmissions by American coalition operations." She nodded to Yi and the blue circles disappeared. "The green are our Afghan partners." These also disappeared, leaving only three yellow circles and three red circles. Two of the yellows were located in southern Afghanistan and the third over a town labeled *Mingora*, in the Swat Valley of Pakistan. "Yellow dots are mobile communications from suspected terror groups at the time of the attack, and the red circles are transmissions that fall inside the command-and-control frequency bands for a drone." She nodded at Yi and the yellow circles disappeared, followed a split second later by two of the three reds. "If we drop the mobile comms and the two command-and-control frequencies completely outside the target radius, we're left with this."

A single red circle hovered alone in the mountains of the Hindu Kush, on the southern edge of the range overlooking Jalalabad. Chunk knew the area intimately. He had conducted countless operations in that region; Taliban forces had lived and fought in those mountains for generations.

"That's Taliban territory," Chunk said. "There's a large village in the foothills just southeast of that point. Mano something-or-other."

"Mano Gai," Yi said.

"Right—Mano Gai. We used to run ISR on that shithole once or twice a month looking for HVTs. A lot of bad guys transit through there."

"It's a hornet's nest," Bowman agreed.

Jarvis folded his hands and waited for Watts to continue, but Day couldn't contain himself.

"Hold on, Watts, don't tell me you're suggesting that a bunch of goat-herding Taliban fighters somehow conducted an aerial attack against an American convoy—undetected, no less—just a couple miles outside of one of our major military compounds? The Taliban is, like, a thousand years from having an air force."

Watts pursed her lips, and Chunk was curious to see how she handled the challenge. From what he'd seen so far, she wasn't afraid to speak her mind or stand her ground . . . but she hadn't been staring down three O-4s, an O-6, and the Vice President of the United States.

"For the record, Commander, I'm not suggesting the Taliban has an air force. What I'm suggesting is that they have gained custody of a combat drone. The Chinese are offering their version of the MQ-1 to regimes throughout the region, and the bargain-basement prices mean they're selling like hotcakes at Denny's on Sunday morning. Saudi Arabia, Egypt, the UAE, Kazakhstan, and Pakistan all have Chinese drone programs. Is it really that big a stretch to imagine these same platforms making their way into the hands of terrorists? A million dollars, Commander; that's all it takes to buy a Chinese Predator clone."

"Your theory is both sobering and compelling, Watts," Bowman chimed in, "but I've been up in those mountains. It's rugged territory—just rocks, goats, and a few caves. There are no runways where you could launch or land a Predator drone, Chinese copy or otherwise. Besides, I can say with one hundred percent certainty that the Taliban do not have a satellite network of their own, or access to one necessary for piloting these drones—nor do they have people with the education and training to operate this kind of equipment."

Watts nodded and looked down. Chunk read in her face that

she had anticipated these arguments and was weighing whether she was willing to die on this hill or not. He hadn't known her long, but he knew a gifted intellect when he saw it. She'd done the mental math on this already, or she would have balked when Bowman asked her to present her findings.

Before she could answer, Jarvis stepped in. "I want to play this out," he said to Bowman. "Whitney, tell us how you think it could be done."

She nodded at him, then looked to Bowman. "You're correct when you say that the Taliban deploying a UCAV using satellite relay control is highly unlikely. But remember, these drones can also be controlled using a line of sight transmitter. Our default paradigm is to think of pilots flying Predators from bases on the other side of the world. But with the right antenna, a laptop, and a two-day training course, it's feasible that even the Taliban could pilot one of these drones."

She was pacing now, and Chunk could see her confidence building.

"Our overflight reviews show nothing up there right now, that's true, and we have no imagery from the time of the attack. But there are several caves very close to the signal we pinpointed. And . . ." She turned to face the satellite image on the screen. Using her laser pointer, she drew an imaginary line between the ridge in the Hindu Kush and the site marked Convoy Attack. "Keep in mind, every foot of elevation extends the operating range of the drone. The radio horizon for an operator standing at ground level is five kilometers. Standing on the side of a mountain at five thousand feet, however, that radius grows to a hundred and sixty kilometers—well within reach of the convoy."

She retraced the invisible line twice more, staring at it as if reinforcing the conclusion.

"What do you propose we do next, Ms. Watts?" Jarvis asked,

but Chunk sensed the Vice President had already made up his mind on how he intended to proceed.

She turned to face him.

"I propose an ISR operation into this area to inspect the transmission site, including searching the caves, along with a HUMINT push to see if assets in the area know anything about the existence of a Taliban-controlled drone." Two green stars appeared on the screen, both within less than two kilometers of the red circle. "How many Taliban have died as a result of our UCAV program? Hundreds? Thousands? What if what we're seeing now is just the beginning of a move to level the playing field? I think the days of sending fifteen-year-old boys into markets to blow themselves up are coming to an end. We've been lulled into a false sense of security by the technological gap between our military and the terrorists, but the Chinese have closed that gap, and we need to start acting accordingly."

Jarvis cleared his throat. "I, for one, find Ms. Watts's theory pretty damn compelling. We have plenty of Special Operations Forces in Jalalabad, including a detachment from the Army's Fifth Special Forces and a platoon from SEAL Team Three. But our activity in and about J-bad is constantly surveilled and scrutinized by the enemy. If they see an operation moving toward them from the JSOTF compound there, they'll scatter and we'll hit a dry hole. I'd like to see the Tier One enter covertly and cut their teeth on this operation."

"Easy day, sir," Bowman said, his gaze going to the middle distance as his mind worked the problem. "We'll deploy Gold Squadron's First Platoon to Kandahar, do a HALO insert from the north, move in undetected, and sweep the caves. At the same time, we'll have OGA query their assets in the region, and we'll start a satellite search for potential landing sites."

Jarvis nodded and looked at his watch. "The plane's waiting on me. Get a copy of your plan to my Chief of Staff, Petra Felsk, when you have something concrete put together, and I'll take a look when I'm back in DC and discuss it with the President. Assuming he gives the green light, consider this a historic day, ladies and gentlemen—you just pitched and sold the first operation for the reborn Tier One."

"Yes, sir. We'll have something to you by tonight."

The Vice President fixed his steely eyed gaze on Whitney. "Nice work, Watts, and don't let these knuckle-draggers convince you otherwise."

"Thank you, sir," she said, folding, then unfolding her arms across her chest.

He nodded at Chunk, then excused himself and headed for the elevator door, where he waited—presumably to give Bowman a moment to wrap up.

The Tier One CO looked at Chunk. "No bullshit, Chunk. Are you good with the timetable?"

"Absolutely, sir. Let me gather my team, and we'll start planning with Watts and Yi right away."

"Assuming we get the green light—which I guarantee we will—I don't have to tell you how flawless the first operation needs to be," Bowman said. "If the convoy attack was only a warm-up, God only knows how many American lives are at risk when they choose their next target. We're playing catch-up, Commander, and that's my least favorite game."

"Understood, sir," Chunk replied. "That's why I'd like to lead the mission myself."

Bowman nodded. "The SCIF is yours. You have three hours to put a plan on my desk. I want you ready for wheels up by tonight. If there's a trail to follow, it's gonna get cold fast."

When Bowman had left to join the Vice President at the elevator, and the rest of the room began to clear, Chunk crossed to Whitney's side of the star shaped table. "Nice work."

"Thanks," she said and blew out an unsteady exhale. "But you could have warned me Bowman was calling the friggin' Vice President of the United States for the brief."

"I didn't know," he said, holding up his hands. "I swear, Heels. I had no idea."

She narrowed her eyes at him. "If you say so." Then, shaking her head, she added, "What a crazy AF day."

"Better get used to it, because that's gonna be your new normal at the Tier One."

"Wonderful."

He nodded toward the satellite slide with the red dot. "You made a good start. I'll meet you back here in an hour to finalize all the details. In the meantime, I need to give my guys a heads-up. If you have a roommate or a significant other, you should probably do the same."

He wasn't surprised when her mouth fell open.

"What are you talking about?"

Chunk grinned. "Remember? You go where we go, sister. Pack for a ten-day deployment. Oh, and why don't you bring Yi from your shop? I can see that you two work well together."

He turned and headed for the steel door of the SCIF, feeling her wide eyes on his back.

"Might want to have Saw or Morales help you pack your tactical gear," he said over his shoulder. "My plan is to park you guys in the Tactical Operations Center in J-bad, but I still need you kinetic in case we need to move." He stopped, hand on the door handle, and shot her his best Texas smile. "Shit changes fast in this world. Time to buckle up, because here we go."

CHAPTER 16

The "cyber shack," as Qasim had dubbed it, was about as out of place inside the dilapidated warehouse as a strip club in Taliban country. It was the only room inside the building with air conditioning, actual chairs, and proper lighting. It was also the only place where he felt comfortable enough to relax and let his guard down. Despite the camaraderie Hamza's men had expressed after the successful drone strike, he still didn't feel he meshed with the rest of al Qadar. He didn't have the foggiest idea what any of them actually did, other than carry around assault rifles. The lone exception was the hacker sitting in the chair next to him, typing away at a computer with two monitors.

With Hamza pressing him to make quick progress, Qasim had spent every waking hour with al Qadar's hacker in residence—a

kid everyone called Fun Time. When first introduced, the black
hat had described himself as the "badass Uyghur from East Turkestan." East Turkestan, Qasim had since learned, was what ethnic
Uyghur dissidents called China's Xinjiang Province. Through
vague and dubious means, Fun Time had fled China and ended
up in Pakistan. He was fluent in Mandarin and the Uyghur
dialect, but also could speak passable English and middling
Arabic. Despite only having just met the guy three days ago,
Qasim knew the kid's entire life story. Five years ago his father
and uncle had been rounded up in one of the government's mass
incarceration sweeps and were now living in detention camps run
by the Chinese government.

"My father no terrorist," Fun Time had exclaimed emphat-
ically when telling the story. "*I's* the motherfuckin' terrorist,
bitches."

Despite his over-the-top personality, Fun Time was unques-
tionably the best hacker Qasim had ever crossed paths with. His
tool kit of exploits and cheats was unlike anything Qasim had
seen. At first, he wondered if Fun Time had worked for China's
government cyber programs, but on reflection the kid seemed too
raw and rough around the edges for that.

"Gazaaaa," Fun Time said with a fist pump to the air.

He did that a lot.

Qasim turned to look at him. "Something good?"

Without taking his eyes off the monitor, the hacker answered,
"Ya, something really good, man. We in RTS Diego Garcia."

"Are you serious? You got in?" Qasim said, his eyes going
wide. "How?"

Fun Time didn't answer him, just started bobbing his head
to the beat of whatever he was listening to on his chunky headphones.

Qasim was about to slide his chair closer to watch what he was doing, when shouting outside usurped his attention. He popped out of his chair and walked to the door that led to the main floor of the warehouse. The door had a rectangular inset window, but Fun Time had taped brown paper over it. Qasim hesitated a moment. It technically wasn't any of his business what was going on out there, but this was the first conflict he'd witnessed since he'd agreed to work for Hamza.

He opened the door.

What he saw next made his heart skip a beat. A man knelt beside the tarp-covered Pterodactyl, begging for his life while Hamza pointed a pistol at his forehead.

"Search him," Hamza ordered.

Hamza's bodyguard and another al Qadar fighter forcibly stripped the man naked, searching for hidden transceivers and destroying his clothes and shoes in the process. When they finished, the man's belongings were tossed into a steel barrel and set on fire.

"Two men from Pakistani Intelligence came to your store. What did you tell them?" Hamza asked, his voice cold and clipped.

"Nothing, I swear," the man said, naked and trembling. "I've never seen them before in my life."

"The ISI cannot be trusted. They work very closely with the Americans. You never know if an agent is a true believer or a traitor."

"I told them nothing. I swear! I followed all the protocols you taught me."

"How can I believe you, Mohamed, when you tried to hide the meeting from me? Even worse, once you suspected you'd been caught in your lie, you decided to come directly here, potentially compromising this location."

"I'm sorry, I was afraid, but I am loyal. I swear. Have mercy, please," he begged.

"There is no place for lies and incompetence in my

organization," Hamza said, his voice hard, but at the same time he holstered his pistol.

"Thank you, oh, thank you. Allah truly rewards the merciful," the man said. But Hamza's sunken-cheeked bodyguard had stepped into position behind him. "Wait? What is this?"

Hamza folded his arms across his chest and nodded.

With practiced efficiency, the bodyguard grabbed the condemned man by the hair and sliced open his throat. The cut was so deep that, at first, Qasim thought he'd decapitated the man. Bright-red blood sprayed from the wound, pouring down the man's chest and abdomen and pooling on the concrete floor. He made no sound, just clutched at his ruined neck as he fell into the puddle. Only then did Hamza look away, his gaze settling on Qasim.

Qasim locked eyes with the terrorist, and in that instant, his perception of Hamza fractured. "Is this the price of failure?" a voice asked, and only once it was too late, did he realize it was his.

"No. This is the price of deceit, the price of cowardice . . . the price of willful incompetence," Hamza said without a trace of malice or ire. "Do you think I should have let him go?"

Qasim didn't answer.

"What would you have done in my stead?"

"I don't know, but I would not have murdered him, that's for certain."

Hamza nodded, his expression cynical. "How magnanimous of you. Thankfully, you're not in charge, or we'd all be dead or strapped to a board with water being poured down our throats. This is not a game, Qasim. It's a war. Of all people, you should understand this by now. The Americans murdered your sister. They murdered your father . . . just as they murdered mine." The terrorist then shifted from English to Pashto and asked the assembled fighters how many of them had lost a parent or family member to war. Every fighter present raised a hand. "You see, Qasim, we are all sons of war, come together for a single, unified purpose. And through that purpose we become a family. Mohamed was tested and he failed. His weakness jeopardized all of our safety, and I refuse to let *anyone* hurt my family."

Qasim heard Fun Time curse inside the cyber shack. He looked over his shoulder as the hacker jumped out of his chair and darted toward him.

"We have big problem!" he cried, beckoning Hamza with a wave.

"Tell me," Hamza said, striding over.

"Soldiers in the mountains. The Americans are approaching the cave. I see them on the camera," the hacker said.

Qasim's knees started to quake. *Will Hamza be furious and blame me for the Americans tracing the signal? Is it my turn to have my throat slit? No, he can't kill me. Fun Time can't configure the drone-satellite data link without me . . .*

"What you want me do?" Fun Time asked.

"We knew this was a possibility," Hamza said. "Quite frankly, it took the Americans longer than I thought it would. Did you sever the data link to the camera?"

Fun Time shook his head. "Signal is encrypted and running through a hundred blinds. Impossible to trace."

"Nothing is impossible. Sever the connection," Hamza said. "And I will warn our Taliban partners that the Americans are launching an assault. If we're lucky, our brothers in arms will usurp the Americans' full attention and hopefully kill some Navy SEALs and Army Rangers in the process."

The hacker nodded and ran back into the cyber shack, while Hamza shifted his gaze to Qasim.

"How is the work coming along?" he asked. "Have you made progress penetrating the American satellite communications network?"

"We just breached RTS Diego Garcia," Qasim said. "That is the first step."

"We need to accelerate the timetable," Hamza said through a heavy exhale. "They're hunting us now, and the Americans are very good at hunting. It won't be long before they shift their spotlight from the Hindu Kush to Mingora. Tell Fun Time to work quickly and keep me posted."

"Okay."

Hamza walked several paces before he stopped and turned back. "And Qasim?"

"Yes?"

"I don't blame you for the Americans detecting the line-of-sight transmissions from the remote pilot team. It was an inherent risk of the operation."

"Okay," Qasim said, heart still pounding.

Hamza smiled. "I'm not a monster, Qasim. Reason, not emotion, guides my decisions. I would hope you that you recognize that by now."

"I do," Qasim said unconvincingly.

"Okay," the terrorist said, his gaze flicking to Qasim's quivering knees. "Now go finish the work so that we may, *inshallah*, get the drone airborne again before the Americans find us."

CHAPTER 17

OPERATION JACKAL

HINDU KUSH MOUNTAIN RANGE

TWENTY-FIVE MILES NORTHWEST OF JALALABAD, AFGHANISTAN

0335 LOCAL TIME

Chunk scanned the mountainside terrain through his NVGs. The rugged beauty was hard to appreciate in the monochrome night vision, but he'd watched more than his fair share of sunrises in the Kush over the years. When the sun crested the ridgeline and lit up the white rocky peaks above and the lush green valley below, it was a sight to behold . . . but the only way he and his team would be here at dawn was if they were dead.

And that wasn't going to happen.

The op was straightforward—hike in, hit the target cave, and exfil by helicopter without alerting the sizable Taliban contingent hanging out at the compound in the valley below. The hope was Chunk and his team would find a small contingent of Taliban fighters in the cave, dispatch them with minimal resistance, confiscate all mobile phones and laptop computers, and exfil with a crow or two for questioning. With the help of their spooky friends at Ft. Meade, Watts and Yi had narrowed down the transmission site to a specific location on the southeast face of this mountain. Unfortunately, the spooks on the ground had not been successful at harvesting any confirming intelligence from their local Taliban-connected assets.

For those keeping score: SIGINT one point, HUMINT zero.

There was a lot riding on this op for everyone involved. Fair or not, it would set the tone for the new Tier One. Succeed tonight, and it would instill faith and confidence among the JSOC brass, the power brokers on the National Security Council, VP Jarvis, and President Warner that the Tier One was back and more capable than ever. Fail, and a stigma could follow Bowman, Chunk, and Watts for the rest of their respective careers. They'd put their collective necks on the line pursuing Watts's Chinese black-market drone theory, and they needed providence to have their back.

He shook the distracting thoughts from his head and checked his watch.

Still on time, on target . . .

For this op, Riker had lobbied for whisky codenames for all the checkpoints, which was a big step up from wines and cartoon characters. The target cave, Dewar's, was located on the eastern face of the mountain. The primary exfil—a ledge outcropping a half mile north of Dewar's at elevation—was Maker's Mark. And predictably, the emergency secondary exfil down mountain was Johnny Walker. Assuming all went well, they would be home at Redneck Riviera for breakfast—Saw's pick because his favorite country-music star had created the line of whiskey—aka the base in Jalalabad, where Captain Bowman, Watts, and Yi were manning the TOC.

First Platoon was split into two fire teams, Chunk leading four men and Spence leading three. The hike in had been uneventful so far, but Chunk knew that could change any minute. The Taliban had an extensive scout network, which included goatherds and teenage boys who could move as silently and swiftly up and down the slopes as mountain goats. All it took was crossing paths with, or getting spotted by, the wrong kind of mountain man, and the peak would suddenly be teeming with Taliban fighters.

"Jackal, this is Mother," came Yi's voice over the secure channel. "We might have a problem."

And there it is, Chunk thought with a sigh.

"Jackal One," Chunk replied, scanning over his rifle with renewed concentration as they crossed a narrow pass bisecting two large rock formations. The geometry created a perfect kill zone if the enemy set up a crossfire, and he hoped this call wasn't her reporting any new thermals nearby.

"Jackal, we have movement in the valley. Two trucks have left the Taliban compound. One that left about three minutes ago, moving north out of Mano Gai. And now we have a second truck—this one a transport with over a dozen thermals in back—looping just south of Aranas. Thermal imagery indicates they are heavily armed. Hard to say for sure, but looks like they might have RPGs and crew-served weapons, in addition to assault rifles."

"You think they've been alerted to our presence?" he asked.

"That's our concern," she said. "We didn't report the first truck, but that second really got our attention. They're heavily armed and—hold on . . . it looks like they're turning to head up the mountain."

Chunk cleared the gap between the two rock towers, then moved left, back into cover. Spence came up beside him and took a knee, scanning over his SOPMOD M4. In a moment he would lead his half of the team right, to offset Chunk's squad so they could cover one another during the approach. As a former enlisted SEAL sniper, Spence had the mental geometry that made him perfect in his leadership role in the squadron.

"How long do you estimate it will take on those switchbacks for the trucks to get to our position, Mother?" Spence asked.

"From satellite imagery, the roads look pretty shitty and they don't appear to go all the way up. They're gonna have to hike the last thousand feet over rough terrain," Yi said.

In the background, Chunk heard Whitney say, "I'd estimate two hours, maybe a little less."

"These guys are friggin' mountain goats," Spence said. "Let's call it an hour and a half."

"Jackal is ten minutes from target. It shouldn't be a problem," Bowman said in the background, his voice transmitting over Yi's mike, which apparently she had on vox. "They will be long gone by the time these assholes arrive on target."

Chunk gritted his teeth. Maybe, maybe not—this new wrinkle definitely impacted the tactical picture. Taliban reinforcements coming up the mountain meant two things. One, his team had just lost the ability to descend to their emergency exfil checkpoint. Second, and perhaps more significant, he'd just lost his most important tactical advantage—the element of surprise. Now, almost certainly, any Taliban sheltering in the cave knew the Americans were coming. What if they turned the tables and ambushed Chunk's team? Also, the primary exfil checkpoint was a ledge on the west side of the range. If the reinforcements were carrying RPGs, the helos would be vulnerable during the pickup.

If, if, if . . .

"Whaddya think, Spence?" Chunk asked.

Spence flipped up his NVGs. "I say we still go for it, boss. If these assholes have a command-and-control compound in these caves for drone ops, God knows what they could hit next. They could launch those Chinese Hellfires into the compound at A-bad or J-bad. Hell, even Kabul is potentially within their operating range. We gotta shut this site down."

Chunk nodded and gave Spence a thumbs-up, then watched him disappear to his right on the other side of the path. Chunk made the call. "Mother—Jackal One. Jackal is inbound to Dewar's."

"Roger that, Jackal One," came Yi's tense voice.

They fanned out and moved silently, Spence driving his team forward with urgency. Chunk scanned his sector in the modified V formation he led with Riker, Georgie, Morales, and Trip. The minutes ticked by, the only sound: his heavy breathing amplified through the mike into his Peltor headset.

"Jackal, this is Mother. The second truck is making better time than we thought. They've closed a third of the distance up the mountain."

Chunk didn't reply immediately. The second truck was the one with more fighters and the heavy weapons.

Shit . . .

"Jackal, we recommend you abort and proceed directly to Maker's Mark. We can have exfil there in eight mikes." It was Watts's voice now. He wondered where Bowman fell on the question. In general, the skipper would defer to the team for a final decision, unless he had a strong opinion.

"Mother—Jackal One. Negative. We are one minute from Dewar's. We will proceed as briefed and exfil at Maker's Mark in fifteen to twenty mikes. Have Stalker flight move to a standby position north of Dewar's and close in."

Stalker flight was three MH-60s for exfil, supported by two "little birds" or MH-6 light attack helicopters. Just like during the training op, these little birds had FRIES rope systems and could be used for rapid extraction if Chunk and his guys were really in the shit. Though small, the MH-6s were the Special Operations' variant of the MD 500E with FLIR capability, two .50-caliber guns, two 7.62 Miniguns, two 70-mm rocket pods, and two Hellfire missiles. With all that firepower, they could rain down hell on earth if need be, and he felt a helluva lot more comfortable knowing he'd have them just minutes off station if needed.

"Roger, Jackal," came the belated reply from Watts.

She sounded nervous, but that was to be expected. Yi was a proficient radio talker and had supported ops from a TOC during her time at the white side Teams. Watts, however, had no previous significant experience in the field or running things from a TOC. She'd studied the after actions from some of the old Tier One missions, but that was a far cry from being in the hot seat and coordinating in real time. Nonetheless, she'd taken the initiative and told him she wanted to learn. So he'd instructed Yi to take her underwing and share the comms tonight. Watts's brief with the Vice President showed she was good under pressure, but this would be a different kind of pressure test.

Chunk personally found sitting inside the TOC, watching brothers that he knew and cared about, a thousand times more stressful than fast roping into a hot LZ. For a SEAL, being powerless to pick up a rifle and join the fight created a special kind of angst . . . and that angst was amplified in the TOC.

"Jackal Two—position?" he said.

Spence had his team offset forty-five degrees from where Chunk's team would be in moments. Chunk could feel his men pulling in tight again as they approached the edge of the woods just above the mouth to the cave. The opening was larger than he expected. Anecdotal intelligence held that this cave was mammoth, extending deep into the mountain, with multiple antechambers linked by interconnecting passages. Watts had not specified the source of the information, but Chunk assumed it was from OGA assets who lived in the village below.

"Jackal Two—in position," Spence reported.

"Five is moving to overwatch," Saw added immediately after.

Hearing that Saw was getting into position as their sniper eased Chunk's nerves as he scanned through the trees, assessing his approach to the cave entrance. From his current angle, he decided that Spence's element would have a slightly better approach, being below him and another twenty yards east.

"Two, One—we'll execute Bravo," he said, announcing to everyone which assault plan he wanted to use.

They'd briefed two plans to hit the cave. Plan Alpha involved moving into position on either side of the cave mouth and breaching as they would a building, with two fire teams rushing in and sweeping the cave. Alpha used the element of surprise to increase the likelihood of taking crows off the target alive for interrogation and to reduce the time the Taliban had to wipe valuable information off phones and computers. But he now had to assume that the element of surprise had already been lost. No way would he risk rushing his guys into a death trap to be mowed down by a half dozen waiting machine guns. So he went with the backup plan—Bravo—which was to fire rocket-propelled grenades, then CS gas, into the cave. The riot gas would flush the surviving Taliban outside and into the rifle sights of the waiting SEALs. It would be a turkey shoot. After that they could enter the cave with NVGs and gas masks to sweep for salvageable electronics.

"Jackal Two, roger," Spence said, acknowledging for his squad. A moment later Saw checked in. "Jackal Five is now God."

They had briefed a position on a slight rise east of the target, where Saw could have cover in a garden of boulders and only light vegetation interfered with his line to the entrance of the cave. He wouldn't have the height advantage he liked, but he would have a nice line on fighters exiting the cave. And a short move south put him in position to have the high ground on any fighters climbing from below, should that become an issue.

"Mother, SITREP on Stalker?" Chunk asked.

"Stalker is on station. Available in less than two minutes. Tangos ascending from the valley are still pressing, but forty-five minutes away. We have no thermals except Jackal outside the cave, but no eyes inside the cave," Yi said.

This, of course, made sense as their overflight Predator drone's thermal imager would be unable to penetrate hundreds of feet of rock to see thermals inside the cave. The Taliban knew this, which was one of the reasons they continued to use the caves.

That's what a thousand years of adapting to enemy after enemy does, I suppose.

Chunk pulled out a compact mask to protect his face from the CS gas, hung it from his neck, then said a simple prayer—the same words he'd prayed before every mission since he'd become a SEAL.

Lord, protect my guys. And by your grace, let us win.

"Jackal Two—go."

Chunk heard a *whump whump*, then saw the smoke trail of the grenades disappearing into the cave entrance. He closed his eyes as twin explosions belched light, heat, and sulfur gas from the cave's maw, and the air reverberated with a horrific echo. A moment later he heard two more *whumps* as Spence's guys fired riot gas into the hole. Through his NVGs, he saw three green targeting dots crisscross over the entrance, hunting for targets as smoke billowed out and rolled upward into the night.

He tightened his grip on his MK18 assault rifle, blinked hard, and steadied his green dot, ready to put it onto the forehead of the first asshole fleeing the cave. Any second, Taliban fighters would come pouring out, driven by the intolerable CS gas.

Any second . . .

The silent counter in his head kept clicking.

Fifteen seconds passed.

Then thirty.

"One, Two—might be a dry hole. Should we move in on masks?" Spence called.

But Chunk's spidey sense told him it wasn't a dry hole. *Something isn't right.*

"Give it thirty more seconds. If nothing, we breach," he said.

A double click in his ear was Spence's acknowledgment.

Chunk felt Riker's questioning gaze on him, but he didn't look over, concentrating instead on keeping his green dot at the floating ready.

CHAPTER 18

TACTICAL OPERATIONS CENTER

JOINT SPECIAL OPERATIONS TASK FORCE COMPOUND

JOINT BASE JALALABAD

AFGHANISTAN

0420 LOCAL TIME

Whitney paced back and forth behind Yi, who was sitting at the primary workstation.

Like Yi, she was dressed in coyote-colored tactical cargo pants, a slim-fitting button-front shirt, and Oakley boots. Unlike the operators that rocked this look, she felt like a military wife who'd reluctantly been dragged by her husband to the 5.11 store and walked out looking like Three-Gun Katie and sporting a frown of regret. On the plus side, at least nobody would call her "Heels" dressed like this.

Yi sat rigid at her terminal, swiping between views from the drone and the satellite feeds, seemingly unsatisfied with both. Whitney looked at the monitor mounted on the plywood wall, streaming the same imagery in split-view simulcast. Three feet away Bowman stood like a sentinel, his muscular forearms crossing his chest, his right foot tapping a battle march cadence on the cement floor of the converted hangar.

She'd watched videos of Special Forces hits just like this dozens of times—glowing, ghostlike silhouettes creeping over otherworldly terrain, white muzzle flares creating a strobe-effect while gunfire was exchanged, and bright green spray as falling bodies gave up their warm contents to the earth. It was chilling to watch.

But not like this.

Because tonight it was personal. Her convoy-drone-strike theory was the reason they were here. She had brazenly recommended this op to Vice President Jarvis, and he'd taken her assessment to President Warner and lobbied personally to make this hit in the Hindu Kush happen. Just thinking about that made her head spin. In just one month, she'd gone from being a rank-and-file NCTC analyst whose insights and recommendations were simply fed into the machine and digested without noticeable effect, to someone whose opinion single-handedly impacted policy. She felt the weight of that squarely on her shoulders.

She'd studied Operation Crusader ad nauseam. She'd watched the classified satellite video of the explosion that wiped out two platoons of SEALs as they hit a compound they believed to be hosting what amounted to a jihadi VIP summit. The analysts had gotten the summit part right; they'd missed the part about the suicide pact and the trap. Gooseflesh rose on the back of her neck. This op had the same sort of vibe. Something wasn't right . . . Had she led the new Tier One into trap of the same design that had wiped out its predecessor? Was Operation Jackal going to be her Operation Crusader?

Did I miss something, and if so, what?

Every one of those ghosts creeping over the rocks was a

colleague. And despite not knowing these men well, she was shocked to realize that she could already recognize most of them by their roles and silhouettes. The thick, stout one just west and above the cave entrance, that was Chunk. The figure beside him was Riker, because Riker was *always* right beside his friend and boss. Saw was the one to the east by sixty or seventy yards, because he was the sniper. The lean silhouette at the north edge of the cluster of three SEALs, that was Spence. And the SEAL on his left, who was constantly tweaking his position, was Georgie. Jamey Edwards was on Spence's right shoulder, probably cracking jokes despite the danger of the situation.

"What the hell is going on?" Yi asked, irritated. "Why is no one coming out of the cave?"

"Dry hole," Bowman grumbled.

"Hold on," Whitney said, new movement catching her eye on the zoomed-out satellite feed. "We've got activity to the north."

One hundred yards northwest of the cave mouth, yellow-orange silhouettes began materializing out of thin air, like enemy avatars generated from the mist to join the melee on a video game. She counted twelve—make that fifteen—men streaming out of the mountainside, moving in a line to the south. It was definitely not a dry hole. A Taliban presence like this could only mean one thing—she'd been right.

"And movement south," Yi gasped as the same thing began to happen seventy yards southwest of where Chunk's team was dug in.

"Oh, shit," Watts cried and ripped Yi's headset right off the other woman's head.

"It's a trap. It's an ambush. You have enemy fighters!" Whitney said in a panic, her voice cracking. "Fifteen shooters north of you and twelve more seventy yards southwest. They're converging on your position. Get the hell out of there, Chunk."

"Shit! That cave has multiple entrances," Bowman hollered. "Yi, get me the team leader for the Ranger QRF right fucking now. And get those little birds moving in to provide fire support."

"Yes, sir," Yi said, flipping open her satellite phone.

"Jackal One, Mother—do you copy?" Whitney said, this time remembering her call sign.

"Mother, Jack—" came Chunk's reply, but the rest was drowned out by an explosion and the sound of gunfire.

She looked up at the big screen where streaks of white fire zigzagged in all directions across the green-gray background. Silhouettes of SEALs and Taliban moved in complex vectors as each repositioned to engage the other. A cold bead of sweat trickled down from her armpit and ran over her ribs as she handed the headset back to Yi.

"Oh my God, they're going to die," someone said, then she realized it had been her.

CHAPTER 19

CHECKPOINT DEWAR'S

HINDU KUSH MOUNTAIN RANGE

AFGHANISTAN

And just like that, with one cosmic flip of the coin, everything went to shit.

Chunk had been here before. Times like this were what separated a leader from a shooter. In the chaos, the team would cue off his response. If he kept a cool head, so would they. If he didn't let the chaos of battle distract him, neither would they. If he ate the shit biscuit the universe had just served them and kept on going, so would they. The only way to turn the tables and regain control was through sheer force of will and Tier One–level determination.

"Contact, right! Contact, right!" Riker shouted in Chunk's ear.

This was followed by two three-round bursts of rifle fire. Chunk spun left and pedaled backward, following his Senior

Chief as they descended off the rocky rise, toward the "courtyard" by the cave entrance.

"Twelve fighters south and spreading out west," came Yi's voice. "Less than sixty yards. You have fifteen more moving quickly from the north. They shifted east and will come down the hill right on top of you."

Enemy rounds exploded the boulder beside Chunk's head. Rock shards peppered his right cheek as he sighted and returned fire on the muzzle flash across the way. After squeezing off a three-round burst, he ducked low and found barely functional cover behind a rocky rise, his back now to the cave mouth.

If fighters come out of that cave mouth, we're fucked, he realized.

"God, One—how are your lines?" Chunk asked, working the problem.

"One, God—I got no line yet on the southern assaulters pressing you."

"How about the cave mouth?"

"Good lines."

"Put a few rounds to keep heads down and make them think twice," Chunk answered. "Just in case."

Because the Tali were pouring out the other exits to escape the CS gas, odds were the cave was empty, but a little insurance would be nice so his guys could focus on the enemy in front of them. He heard three throaty pops from Saw's sniper rifle, firing deadly 7.62 rounds into the cave.

"Three rounds down the throat," Saw came back. "No movement."

"Check," Chunk said and turned to Riker, who was firing his assault rifle, the Mk 48 machine gun still strapped to his back. "Let's put the heavy gun to work. I'll cover you."

"Roger," Riker called to him, firing from a crouch. "Cover."

Chunk popped up and fired several blind bursts into the

woods, then targeted the area where he'd last seen enemy muzzle flashes, aware that Georgie was firing from beside him and Trip was still in the fight at the overhang above the cave. He felt, rather than saw, Riker sprint across the courtyard, unstrapping the Mk 48 as he ran.

"Shit," Yi said. "Looks like three more fighters emerging from the south. That's fifteen south, and the fifteen north will be on you in seconds."

"Hang in there, Jackal," came the cool baritone voice of Captain Bowman. "Stalker is inbound to clear the woods in less than two mikes."

"Roger, Mother. Jackal, pop IR now. Pop lights for Stalker," Chunk ordered his team.

Chunk fired again, reached up and snapped on the IR strobe on top of his helmet, then clicked the MBITR radio on his chest two clicks left and switched to vox, letting his voice now activate the boom mike.

"Stalker flight—Jackal One."

"Jackal, Stalker Three—we're on target in forty seconds. Stalker Four in trail," the helo pilot answered, rotors thrumming the air in the background.

"Roger, Stalker. We're being overrun. Popping lights. Anything without a strobe is a shithead. We have fifteen tangos between us and Maker's Mark, and another fifteen engaging us from the south."

"Hurrying," came Stalker's deadly serious voice in his ear.

"Contact left!" someone called.

A fresh burst of enemy fire ricocheted all around him as Taliban fighters from the north came into range and joined the fight. The controlled staccato cracks of the SEALs' 5.56 rounds were drowned out by a wave of throatier, chaotic AK-47 fire from the new arrivals.

"Two, this is God," came Saw's calm voice. "Shift left two meters."

Chunk scanned the woods and rocks to the south. A head snuck around a boulder and he dropped his green IR dot onto the face and squeezed. Three rounds tore apart the bearded face and the insurgent pitched forward onto the pine needles. Chunk switched to a single round with his right thumb as someone reached around the boulder and pulled at the downed fighter, only to collapse on top of him after Chunk's bullet hit him in the chest.

In the background, Chunk heard Saw finally going to work with his sniper rifle as the Taliban encroached into his sight lines.

"Two—you got two tangos bearing down on your left," Saw warned Spence. "And you got three more trying to flank you, Jackal Two."

Several more cracks followed.

To Chunk's left the tree line suddenly exploded with muzzle flashes. The ground in front of his face exploded and dirt sprayed his face. He tried to raise his head to engage a target but was forced back down by another barrage from the woods.

"Shit, shit, shit," he heard Trip grumble.

Fire and move. Fire and move . . .

He dropped low and shuffled to the left, smashing his elbow painfully into a rock. Then the air began to vibrate around him as he heard Riker, behind him, light up the night with the heavy machine gun. He peered above the rock, aware that warm blood trickled down his right cheek and was collecting in his beard. The stream of 7.62 from Riker's Mk 48 tore through the pine trees, dropping branches and chunks of wood to the forest floor and forcing the fighters back. Chunk pulled his rifle up, sighted, and with three rapid squeezes of his trigger, dropped two retreating fighters, shooting them in the back.

Then the world exploded to his right.

"Oh, fuck," came Spence's voice. "Heavy contact. Five, shift fire right. We're in deep shit."

"I got no line," Riker said. "Moving back."

"Stalker Three and Four are on station," came the pilot's voice. "We see you in heavy contact, caught in a crossfire from north and south, Jackal."

Chunk imagined the battle from the attack helicopter pilot's perspective. His half of the SEALs were on the west side of the courtyard, bunched up with limited cover. Spence and his team were even less protected on the other side. They were completely boxed in and, yes, caught in a wicked crossfire.

Chunk was confident he could hold the south, especially with Riker on the Mk 48. Unfortunately, reaching their exfil required them to go through the heart of the Taliban force bearing down on Spence's squad. The minute Chunk turned his team north, the Taliban shooters behind them would pursue, flanking them the entire way.

First things first . . .

"Stalker Three, we need you to clear a path north to Maker's Mark," Chunk said to the helo pilots.

"You're danger close, Jackal. Closest fighter is less than ten yards."

"Roger, danger close. Stalker, standby—we'll reposition and clear you in hot." He squeezed off several rounds south. Then, he pressed a button on the MBITR and clicked twice to the left, merging the channels. "Jackal, fall in on the cave mouth. Close ranks right fucking now. Stalker is coming in hot, danger close. Move now."

A steady thump of sniper fire echoed from Saw's position, but it was quickly drowned out by a prolonged strafe from Riker's heavy gun.

"One more down to your north," Saw called.

"God, cover our six to the courtyard. Once we're repositioned, we'll cover your move to rejoin," Spence called.

"Jackal, I count ten tangos surging from the south tree line," Yi said.

Despite the bad news, Chunk felt a paradoxical calm come over him, warm and familiar from dozens of other firefights he'd survived. He'd repositioned his team and had Stalker engage. Now, they just needed to exfil.

Muzzle flashes lit up in the trees south of him like fireworks.

In response, he, Georgie, and Trip, popped up and poured fire into the tree line. A moment later a serpentine tongue of orange fire licked over his shoulder as Riker sprayed the advancing fighters with 7.62 rounds. Chunk watched several tangos bite the dust, unable to withstand the maelstrom of bullets.

When the barrage ended, he made an adjustment. "Three, shift fire to the north to cover Two."

"Check," Riker replied and brought the heavy machine gun around to work the flanking Taliban fighters.

Thighs burning, Chunk duck-walked back to the right, then popped up and fired into the trees. In that moment, he noticed the muzzle flashes opposite them had all but stopped as the surviving enemy retreated from Riker's prolonged assault. A heartbeat later, the Taliban redoubled their efforts and unleashed a coordinated barrage.

"Ah, shit," he heard Georgie holler to his left.

Then he felt something hot tear through his left arm.

Awesome. Now I'm fucking shot.

"Four, Six, and Eight—stagger movements now," he ordered.

Chunk ducked and counted to three, ready to pop up again, and pictured Morales, Edwards, and Antman covering each other as they moved one by one. He popped up and fired, ignoring the burn just above his elbow. His arm appeared to be working, so whatever wound he'd taken, it wasn't mission critical.

"Four's in the courtyard."

Another strafe from Riker sent rounds and tracers into the tree line.

"Eight is moving," Antman replied.

"God's gotcha," came Saw's calm voice, then the *whump whump* of his sniper rifle.

"RPG!" someone shouted.

Chunk's throat tightened at the call and he dove down behind the rise of rocks, feeling Georgie do the same beside him, uncertain which fire team was being targeted. An explosion rocked the earth behind him. An acrid smell filled his mouth and nose, and AK-47 gunfire cracked all around them.

"Man down, man down!"

It was Edwards's voice.

Chunk realized it was all going to hell . . . he had to get Spence's guys to the courtyard so Stalker could strafe the north slope and clear a path to the exfil. Dug in like they were, it would be impossible to accomplish from the ground.

"Covering fire!" Spence shouted, more a plea than an order.

The desire to spin around and engage to the north to cover his men was almost unbearable. But if he shifted north now, they would be overrun from the south. *Hold the line*, said the voice in his head as he popped up again and fired two three-round bursts into the woods where he'd last seen enemy muzzle flares. Georgie and Trip followed his lead, and the return fire flashes in the woods fell off.

"One, we have an urgent CASEVAC. Eight is down," Edwards reported.

"Down but not out," came Antman's tense reply.

"Two, call the air strike," Chunk barked.

Spence's fire team had still not made it to the courtyard, and Chunk couldn't cover the rocky rise to have Stalker engage without risking friendly fire. The AK-47 fire from the north was relentless now as Spence and Edwards tried to drag Antman back to the courtyard without getting shot in the back.

"Two, you gotta call it, dude," Saw said, now the lone covering fire. "Or you're fucked."

"Stalker Three, Jackal Two—you're cleared hot on the tangos north. Danger close. Danger close."

"Roger, Jackal. Targets north. Danger close," the helo pilot said, then unleashed hell.

Chunk ducked and covered as the MH6 engaged. The unmistakable *brrrrrrrrrttt* of the Miniguns strafing the hillside sent a shiver down his spine. He couldn't see it, but his mind's eye imagined the scene—Taliban fighters scrambling for cover as twin tongues of fire turned the mountain into a pile of rubble, bone, and blood. The Miniguns went quiet and a half dozen squeals shredded the silence as the pilot fired his Hydra 70 rockets. In that moment, night became day, even behind Chunk's tightly closed lids, and a wave of heat rolled over his back as the rockets exploded in near-simultaneous precision, engulfing the northern approach in a wall of flame.

"Two," Chunk said, keeping the strain out of his voice as best he could, "move north toward Maker's Mark. We'll cover your six until you're clear, then pull up. Three and Five, covering fire when we move, then fall in on us."

Several double clicks followed, along with Saw's calm voice in his ear, "Rog."

Chunk fired a burst, then glanced over at Georgie, who leaned in on his rifle, jaw clenched and shredding the tree line. A wet oval the size of a football soaked the kid's left pant leg at thigh level.

"How's that leg, Georgie?" he called.

"I'm in the fight," the SEAL yelled back over the roar of his weapon.

"Can you run?"

"Yeah, boss."

"All right, get ready. We're exfilling to Maker's Mark," he said, then into his mike, "Stalker Three, Jackal One—you cool repeating that performance and sweep south?"

"Make the call and we'll light them up," the pilot came back.

"They've got at least one RPG in the mix. Be careful, Stalker," Chunk warned.

"Roger that, we'll light 'em up with rockets first in that case."

"God," he informed Saw, "covering fire, then fall in. Let's move, people." Chunk led the retreat. Georgie followed in a hobbled backpedal, rifle up and firing behind them. As they crossed in front of the cave entrance, Chunk scanned over his rifle into the blackness. Thank God, the hole was still empty, or they would have been cut to pieces. And yet, with the Taliban maintaining this kind of presence, and mounting such a tenacious defense, it all but confirmed these caves had played a role in the drone attack. With that thought, he snapped the IR beacon off the left shoulder of his kit, turned it on, and tossed it to the ground at the entrance to the black hole.

They pushed through a gauntlet of boulders and bullets.

Overhead, the helo's engines whined and Chunk glanced up in time to see the Stalker pilot execute a truly badass maneuver. Like a drift racer, he swung an arc over top of the cave while gaining altitude and repositioning to fire down mountain on the Taliban to the south. The pilot opened with a rocket barrage, emptying the eight remaining Hydras. The explosion that followed completely washed out Chunk's night vision. Light blind, his toe caught a rock and he stumbled, banging his knee painfully. A heartbeat later his vision returned. He scanned ahead and saw Spence and Edwards helping Antman, who was buckled over at the waist, across the rocky terrain on the final push to the X. Glancing behind him, he saw that Georgie was limping now, taking a skip instead of a stride every few steps, so Chunk ducked beside him and hooked an arm around his torso.

"Stalker Lead," Chunk said, calling the Blackhawk pilot. "Jackal will make Maker's Mark in less than four mikes. One urgent surgical."

"Roger, Jackal," came the reply.

"Jackal One, Stalker Three," came the little bird pilot. "Clearing the woods for you."

"Copy. Thanks for your help. Just one more package for you. You should see a strobe on station at Dewar's," he said, referring to the IR beacon he'd tossed into the mouth of the cave.

"Stand by, Jackal . . . Roger we've got it."

"Turn it to dust when we're clear."

"Roger that, Jackal."

He liked the pleasure he heard in the pilot's voice.

With the woods behind them, Chunk and the others reached a wide cliff ledge, less than forty feet across, with a hundred-foot drop-off to the east and a sheer thirty-foot wall of rock to the west. The outcropping had barely enough clearance for the fifty-four-foot rotor diameter of the Special Operations variant 160th SOAR Blackhawks.

He eased Georgie to a knee. The others followed his lead, all taking tactical knees and scanning all directions in a defensive circle at the edge of the thin woods.

"Mother, Jackal is Maker's Mark," Chunk announced, a hint of triumph creeping into his voice.

"We see you, Jackal. It's clear around you. Stalker, Mother— clear for pickup of the package."

In seconds, a Blackhawk materialized at the very edge of the cliff ledge, the tips of the rotors sparking green with static electricity in the NVGs. Spence and Edwards sprinted forward, Antman in between them, then Morales, all scanning over rifles as they stepped backward into the helicopter, which hovered expertly just inches from the ledge. The Blackhawk nosed forward and headed south, dropping below the ledge as a second bird moved into position.

Chunk scanned behind them as Riker and Saw helped Georgie into the helicopter. Then they stepped backward into the bird, never stopping the scan over their rifles. Chunk's stomach lurched as the helo dove steep and fast. Then it rose rapidly and banked east, climbing higher into the sky, then sharply south toward J-Bad.

"Stalker Three, Jackal One. Send it."

He flipped his NVGs up just as the entire east side of the mountain exploded. A mushroom of flame lit up the twilight sky as the Hellfire missiles fired by the MH6 turned the mouth of the cave into Dante's Inferno.

Chunk grinned.

Anyone left in the cave was a crispy critter now. The Talis wouldn't be launching drone attacks on US convoys from that mountainside stronghold ever again.

CHAPTER 20

Chunk watched two Air Force PJ medics from "white"—the AFSOC's 24th Special Tactics Squadron—tend to Antman and Georgie. Antman's wounds looked pretty superficial, despite his blood-soaked cammies. More blood than bone, as Riker liked to say.

"It's just cuts and scrapes," Antman protested as the medics tried to lay him back after helping remove his kit.

"Don't give me that 'it's only a flesh wound' Tier One operator bullshit," the medic barked, pushing Chunk's teammate backward as his partner set up an IV. "This was done by an RPG, right?"

Antman nodded.

"So you could have a frag in your belly or your liver, or shit leaking out of your colon into your abdomen, for all you know. You could have a vascular injury, or a—"

"Yeah, fine, fine. I get it," Antman relented. He reclined on the plywood table and stuck out his arm.

"We'll get X-rays, and if everything looks good, the JSOC surgeons will stitch you up and clear you, bro. Just chill out with that macho shit and let me do my job, okay?" the PJ said.

Chunk couldn't help but grin as he knelt beside Georgie, who was leaning back on his elbows while Morales cut away the blood-soaked pant leg around his right thigh.

"How's it look?" Chunk asked the medic.

Morales pressed on Georgie's thigh and dark blood dribbled out of a round hole.

"Ow, shit. Stop it, asshole," Georgie complained.

"Suck it up, dude," Morales said. "You got fucking shot. Let me look at it, you big baby."

Morales probed behind Georgie's knee, looking for an exit wound—talking as he worked. "Normal popliteal pulse below the entry wound. I don't feel an expanding hematoma or an unusual mass, so I don't think the bullet clipped an artery. Doesn't seem like the bone's broke, but you know, adrenaline is the great concealer—anything's possible. You need an X-ray and maybe an angiogram for a vascular injury. Does your foot feel normal, bro? Pins and needles or anything?"

Georgie wiggled his foot around in his Oakley book and shook his head. "Leg feels normal. Just hurts in my thigh."

"Good, good, probably no nerve damage." Morales turned to Chunk. "Overall, he got lucky. Seems like minimal damage for a 7.62. Probably a ricochet or a piece of frag rather than direct impact. Congratulations, kid," he said, turning back to Georgie. "You're a gunshot wound *underachiever*."

"Mama always said as much about me," Georgie said with a shit-eating grin.

Chunk liked what he was seeing. Morales was gonna be great on the team.

To his left, the PJs were loading Antman into a Humvee parked at the head of a line of white pickup trucks. Georgie would be next, which meant this was the opportunity to talk to the whole team before they got split up.

"Listen up, Jackal," he said, raising his voice. "The op did not go as anticipated, but we adapted and overcame. You guys stayed tight, focused, and took care of business. Stalker saved our asses tonight, but that's okay because it means the Head Shed did their job and planned a good op. Watts and Yi were clearly onto something, because that turned out to be a convention of assholes inside that mountain. Good work tonight, fellas. Drop your shit here and secure it inside the compound. Then, I want everyone in the trucks and over to medical."

"The surgical team is meeting us at the base on the other side," one of the PJs called from the back of the Humvee-turned-ambulance.

"You heard him. Everyone goes to the Forward Surgical Team, but you get checked out by our JSOC docs—no one else. No one comes back to the compound without their nod. Hooyah?"

"Hooyah, boss," Spence said. "You heard the man. Let's go, boys."

Riker appeared at Chunk's side, and Saw came moseying over for a sidebar.

"I'm good, boss," Saw said. "Never left my hide. Don't have a scratch."

"Fine," Chunk said. "Big boy rules for you, but go over anyway and stay with our guys, okay?"

Saw nodded but sighed audibly as he started stripping off his kit.

"I'll stay behind and secure the gear, boss," Riker said, then eyeing Chunk's blood-soaked left sleeve: "You probably need to get that checked out, right?"

Chunk opened and closed a fist. His upper arm ached, but not too bad. And his hand felt fine.

Still—*Lead by example.*

He nodded. "Yeah, just gotta check in with the Head Shed first, then you and I can go over together."

The Humvee was already rumbling off with Georgie and Antman, as the other SEALs began stowing their kits inside the open gate and behind the tall Hesco barriers. The compound—with its double row of chain-link fence topped with razor wire—looked more like a fenced-in junkyard than a high-tech base for America's most elite warriors. Presently, it was occupied by the Army's JSOC team, and Chunk's guys were the guests. He watched as his SEALs swapped out spent magazines for fresh ones and slipped spares into cargo pockets—a habit from years and years in the suck. Then, with rifles slung, they lumbered over to the pickup trucks. Chunk recognized Yi behind the wheel of one, and one of the IT guys from the N2 Intel shop driving the other.

Chunk gathered two kits over his right forearm, then one over the left, wincing as the plate carrier bumped into his upper arm. Come to think of it, his arm was burning like shit now. Riker was right to call him out on getting it checked. When the bullets stopped flying it took a long time for the adrenaline to boil off enough for an honest self-assessment. He often collapsed pain free and tired after an op, only to wake up the next day barely able to crawl out of bed. On one such occasion, he'd had a shoulder separation and two cracked ribs and not even thought to go to the docs the night before.

After dropping the last of the kits, Riker secured the compound gate. It had been a couple of years since Chunk had been to J-bad, and he remembered this little compound within a compound, but back then he hadn't been a Tier One operator and had not been permitted inside. Weird to finally be on the other side of this wire. With a nod to Riker, he headed off to talk to the CSO and Watts.

"How are our guys, Chunk?" Captain Bowman asked, greeting him at the door to the TOC.

"Antman is the wild card. Shrapnel from an RPG in his gut, but he's stable. Provided there's no organ damage, he'll be okay."

"Is he operational?"

Chunk shrugged. "We'll see what the JSOC surgeons say. And Georgie got shot in the leg, but Morales thinks he's gonna be fine. Still, I made everyone else go over to get checked out, and Riker and I'll head over in a bit. Got time for a data dump first?"

"This way," Bowman said, nodding, then led him down the hall. At the end, he tapped in his personal code on the keypad, watched the reader turn yellow, then pressed his palm against the pad. The magnetic lock clicked and they entered the SCIF. It was much like the SCIF back in Tampa, but smaller. Still, it was a decadent technical luxury compared to what the compound's outside appearance suggested. Watts was hunched over a laptop, but looked up immediately when he entered. He saw a symphony of emotions play over her face, but the concert ended with an angry, irritated stare. Whether it was more anger than irritation or vice versa, he couldn't tell, but either way it was not the greeting he'd expected.

"What's up, Heels?" he said.

"Why did you do that?" she snapped. No *Hey, Chunk, are you okay?* or *Nice work out there surviving that maelstrom of bullets and death.*

"Why did I do what?" he replied, his smile fading.

"Reduce our intelligence-rich target to its molecular components."

Chunk glanced at Bowman; it was still not clicking.

"She's talking about the Hellfire strike on Dewar's you ordered at the end," Bowman clarified, then took a seat across from him at the long wooden table.

"An unscripted, emotion-driven decision that wiped out any hope of us obtaining actionable intelligence—hell, any intelligence at all—from inside those caves. What am I supposed to do now?" she said, red-faced and advancing on him.

He resisted the unfamiliar urge to take a step back and stood his ground until she was standing toe-to-toe with him, hand on hips, left eyebrow cocked. He glanced at Bowman, who had his hands clasped on the table, just watching the show.

All he needs is popcorn.

Chunk inhaled through his nose and, with as much composure as he could muster, said, "You are aware that my team was boxed in by a numerically superior force and took heavy fire from two directions? That's called a crossfire, Watts, and for the uninitiated like yourself, it is a tactical fucking nightmare. We were fighting for our lives just to get back to the exfil point for extraction. I have two wounded SEALs en route to see the surgeons as we speak, both of whom are lucky to be alive." But while he made his rebuttal, his mind was multitasking, reviewing the sequence of events that had happened almost too fast to catalogue at the time.

Why did I order Stalker to nuke that cave? he wondered momentarily. *Oh, I remember, because it was a friggin' hive of assholes swarming out of the cracks and trying to kill my men.*

She let out a deep sigh and her expression softened, but only a little. "I know, I was watching and terrified for you guys, but then Stalker cleared a path for you to the exfil and hosed down the fighters to your south. There was nobody left, Chunk. We could have . . . I don't know, done another op to sweep the cave or taken somebody off the X for questioning. But now, there's nothing left up there but char. The signal intercept on this mountain was the only data point I had, remember? We have nothing to take us to the next step, and I'm no closer to finding the drone than I was before we ran the op."

One of the things Chunk had always prided himself on was his ability to resist letting his emotions get the better of him. The metaphor he liked to imagine was a lighthouse on a rocky island getting pounded by the surf—like the one they used in all the motivational posters. Yeah, that was him. Steadfast. Incorruptible. Unbreakable . . .

But if that was true, then why was Watts get under his skin?

"In the Teams, we trust our senior operator on the X to make the hard calls. We don't armchair quarterback from the TOC. Not even my boss second-guessed my decision. But maybe more importantly," he said, resisting the urge to step closer and speak down on her, "you work for me, not the other way around. You're not at the NCTC anymore. Your job here is to generate and analyze intelligence to support our operations, not for us to generate intelligence to support your hunches. You copy that?"

Watts's face flushed, but she didn't break eye contact. "I know that, Commander. I just . . . I just don't want any more Americans getting blown up because we didn't execute when we had the window of opportunity to do so. That drone is still out there, and we have no idea where it is, who's operating it, or what their next target is." With a little unexpected fire in her eyes, she added, "Do *you* copy *that*?"

"That's enough, Watts," Bowman said in a calm, even tone. "We're all very impressed with the sleuthing you did to get us here. The fact that we're even having this conversation should speak volumes to you about how we value your input. But it goes both ways. I suggest you try taking off your spook hat for five minutes and swapping it for an operator helmet. These guys are the best operators in the world. They know the stakes. They know the mission. In the field, in the suck, they make the kinetic calls. Not you."

"I get it, but—"

"Watts, can you give us the room for five minutes?" Bowman said. It wasn't a question. "When you come back, we'll talk about where we go next with this investigation. Clear?"

"Yes, sir," Watts said, and only as she turned to leave did she finally notice Chunk's blood-soaked left arm. "Oh my God, Chunk, you're bleeding all over the place! Did you get shot . . . holy crap, why aren't you in the hospital?"

He forced a smile. "I'm good, Heels. It's only a flesh wound," he said in his best Texas version of a Monty Python British accent. But when she screwed up her face in confusion, he simply said, "It's all good."

"The room, Watts," Bowman said, and his gaze flicked from her to the door.

"Yes, sir," she said with a cordial nod and made for the door. At the threshold, she paused. Looking over her shoulder at Chunk, she said, "I *will* find them," in a voice that made him believe her.

He nodded at her, then took a seat across from Bowman, leaning all the way back in the chair while letting out a too-long groan.

"Yeah, you got that right," Bowman said with a knowing smile.

Chunk rubbed his face, closed his eyes, and took a single deep cleansing breath.

"You're gonna need to fix that shit with Watts," the CSO said.

"I know," he said through a sigh.

"You're right to remind her that she works for you, and we can't have her second-guessing operational decisions, but . . . that one is smart. She thinks differently than the other intel pogues.

Her brain makes connections other people don't see. I spoke with the head of NCTC when we were screening for this billet, and he says she's a genius. They poached her from CIA to the Joint Terror Task Force because she was generating that kind of buzz as a newbie. 'Elon Musk smart,' I believe were his exact words."

"I know, she's sharp."

"Well, keep in mind, she wasn't even tasked to investigate the convoy hit. She did that all on her own—one hundred percent initiative—and then she had the balls to present her theory to the Vice President. We can't shut that down. We need her smarts and critical eye, but it's useless if she can't tell you what she thinks. She needs to fall in line, but still be able to speak her mind—the same rules you apply to the rest of your guys. Make her part of the team. Got it?"

"Got it, sir," Chunk said. "You're right. I'll fix it."

Bowman knitted his fingers together, rested his hands on the table, and leaned in. "I, for one, think she's right about this hunch, as you called it. We have OGA assets working this problem too, and while they were quick to dismiss her drone theory as crazy, no one is offering another explanation. After what we just witnessed on that mountain, I believe she has us on the right trail. If the Taliban have the capability to launch a drone, we have a serious, balance-shifting problem with global fucking implications. I can only imagine that the terrorist underground is watching very closely to see how we respond to this new development. If we fail to neutralize this threat quickly and completely, then every jihadi with cash in the bank is going to be lining up to buy Chinese drones."

"Understood."

"Now give me your thoughts and highlights for the after action, so we can get Watts in here and back to work."

CHAPTER 21

The rhythmic scratch of a mechanical pencil on paper was an elixir for Whitney's nerves. She often did her best thinking while sketching, when both hemispheres of her brain were fully engaged. Strands of rope looped and crossed, playing hide and seek on the page as they became impossibly interwoven. The design was of her own creation, meticulously imagined, then brought to three-dimensional life as only someone who'd spent far too many hours contemplating and sketching knots could do. She pulled her hand away to look at the knot, then blew graphite dust off the page before continuing.

I have to find a new thread to chase . . . but how? Where?

The door opened and Petty Officer Yi walked in. Whitney looked up and acknowledged her with a close-lipped smile. Yi joined her at the table, parking her uber-petite body in the vacant chair beside her.

"What are you sketching?" she asked, leaning on her elbows for a look.

"A knot," Whitney said, shading. Then, preempting the unspoken question, "Because I like knots."

Yi smiled at this. "It's quite an intricate and complex knot."

"Intricate, yes. Complex, not so much."

"Well, it looks complex."

"To the untrained eye, but that's an illusion. This knot is simple pattern repetition—seven interlocking trefoil knots."

"What's a trefoil knot?"

Whitney stopped sketching and rotated her forearm to show the other woman the triangular, beautifully inked three-lobed knot tattoo on the inside of her wrist.

"It kind of looks like a clover leaf."

"That's the origin of its name. Trefoil is the common name for Trifolium, which is the genus of three-leafed plants including clover . . . A trefoil knot is the simplest non-trivial knot."

"What's a non-trivial knot?"

"A knot that can't be untied without cutting it."

"Oh, I see, it's one continuous strand," Yi said, tracing her fingertip through the air while looking at the tattoo.

"Exactly. Trefoil knots are chiral." Yi nodded, but Whitney could see from her woman's expression that she wasn't familiar with the word. "A figure has chirality when it's not identical to its mirror image. For example, our hands are chiral," Whitney explained holding up both hands—palms out, fingers up, and thumbs extended at right angles.

After a moment, it clicked for Yi. "Oh, I see, it's like how you can't wear a glove from your right hand comfortably on your left hand just by flipping it around. The thumb gets all wonky."

"Precisely," Whitney said, then moved her hands to align the back of her right hand to the palm of her left so the fingers closed in the same direction but the thumbs were on opposite sides. She then rotated her left hand so that the backs of both hands were touching. Now the thumbs were aligned, but the fingers and thumbs bent in opposite directions. "No combination of rotations or translations will achieve symmetry with chiral pairs," she explained.

"I guess I basically understood that, but no one ever formally explained it, theoretically, I mean."

"Whether a configuration is chiral or achiral is fundamental to knot theory."

"Knot theory?" Yi repeated and screwed up her face. "Don't tell me you're some sort of math genius."

"No, I'm definitely not," Whitney said with a laugh. "One day I decided I wanted to get a Celtic knot tattoo, so I started trying to sketch one. No matter what I did, I couldn't get it to look right, so I looked up Celtic knots online. One twist led to another—no pun intended—and I discovered there's this entire field called knot theory. Mathematicians and puzzle makers have studied knots for thousands of years."

"So basically, you're a knot geek?"

"Yeah, pretty much."

"Cool," Yi said, returning her attention to the sketch. "Now that I see the pattern, I think it's kind of beautiful."

"For me, these knots are like a metaphor for working in the intelligence community. In order to properly draw a knot, you first have to understand how it's woven, and if you understand that, then you can untangle it."

"Is that how you feel right now?"

"Yeah." Whitney sighed. "This case is just one giant knotted mess. I thought I was untangling it, but I don't know . . . maybe

I've been pulling on the wrong strand. What if we hit the wrong target? What if the Taliban doesn't have a drone? What if they had nothing to do with the attack?"

"The 'what if' game is one I try to never play. You can beat yourself up all day asking those sorts of questions, and it won't change anything," Yi chided. Her expression suggested she knew what she was talking about, no doubt from years of experience working intel for Special Warfare.

"I know, but Chunk and the guys risked their lives because of our hunch. I can't help thinking maybe I screwed up—trying to force a correlation between the convoy attack and the drone parts and Chinese missiles confiscated from that Pakistani freighter."

"If we continue that line of reasoning, that would mean the battle damage assessment done by the guys at Oceana was wrong. Also, we've looked at the other scenarios and ruled out a mortar attack, RPG, and a surface-to-surface missile strike. Instead of second-guessing your initial conclusion, why don't we focus on trying to find the drone? The question I keep asking myself is where did it go after the strike?" Yi said.

"Well, obviously poststrike they would want to fly it somewhere they could evade radar and try to land. The mountain valleys are a logical place to do that. Also, if the pilot flew it any direction but north, back toward the cave they were controlling it from, then he would eventually fly out of range and lose connectivity. The drone would cruise until it ran out of fuel, then crash, but we had people looking for drone wreckage, scouring the Afghan countryside, and we haven't found anything."

"What about in the mountains?"

"Bowman had eyes tasked to look for anything even remotely resembling a landing strip inside a hundred kilometer radius of the transmission site. The search turned up nothing."

"What about outside a hundred kilometers?"

"Well, it's kind of pointless to look outside a hundred kilometers," Whitney said.

"Why?"

"Because a hundred kilometers is a reliable line of sight radius for a drone cruising at altitude. But try to land the drone and that range goes out the window. The moment the drone dipped below the mountain, they'd encounter interference. There's no way they could have pulled off a landing in the Hindu Kush that was even a hundred kilometers out from the cave. And there's no runway or wreckage in that valley below the Taliban stronghold we hit."

"All right, then there's your answer."

"Huh? Explain, please."

"They didn't land it in the Hindu Kush," the petty officer said with a victorious smile. "They landed it somewhere else."

Whitney wasn't sure whether to laugh or get angry with Yi, so she took a deep breath and said, "What do you mean *somewhere else?*"

"I don't know. That's what we've got to figure out."

Whitney was about to fire back a snarky reply when her gaze fell on her knot sketch and an epiphany struck. "I know how they did it!"

"You do?"

She tapped her finger on her sketchbook at the junction between a pair of interlocking trefoil knots she'd drawn. "They used multiple line of sight transmitters to extend the operational range. Pretend each of these trefoil knots is the geographical area the drone can fly for a single LOS controller. Where two adjacent knots meet is a hand-off zone, if you will."

"I'm with you. They didn't have to land near the control station that executed the attack, they only had to fly the drone to the edge of another transmitter's hundred-kilometer range and transfer control. After the handoff, the drone could be flown somewhere else to land."

"Precisely," Whitney said and shoved her notebook to the side to make room for a paper map of eastern Afghanistan and the Hindu Kush. Yi helped her smooth the map flat, then Whitney went to work, drawing with her mechanical pencil. "Okay, so this dot is the cave, which was also the location of the last recorded LOS signal in a drone-compatible frequency band. Now, if we draw a hundred-kilometer radius around the dot . . . we have this area of operation when the signal went dark."

"Almost half of the circle is in Pakistan," Yi said.

Whitney nodded and sketched three other circles that bisected the original circle: one northeast, one due east, and the third southeast. "Everything to the north and west inside Afghanistan is all Nuristan National Forest—rugged terrain, high altitude, and virtually uninhabitable. But east, across the border, the Khyber is packed with people and infrastructure. Look at all these cities: Peshawar, Mardan, Timergara, Batkhela, Mingora . . . not to mention the dozens and dozens of other Taliban-friendly villages scattered about. Those sneaky bastards," she said, slamming her pencil down on the table triumphantly. "They flew it into Pakistan."

"Okay, so what do we do now?" Yi said.

"We look for another source transmitting on the same frequency inside one of these three circles, close to the time the original signal went dark," Whitney said, getting up from the table. "And we're going to need some help to do it."

"Are you going to Chunk with this?"

"Not without data," Whitney said, retrieving the satellite phone from her pack and thinking about who in her existing network she could call who was senior enough to have inter-agency relationships she could leverage without running this theory up the Tier One command first.

"Then who are you calling?"

"My old boss at NCTC, Reed Lewis," she said with an ironic grin. "Technically, he's the reason I'm in this mess, so he can help me get out of it."

"And if that logic doesn't work?"

She shrugged. "Then I'll beg . . . One must never underestimate the power of begging."

CHAPTER 22

TWO HOURS LATER

"So this DIA contact of yours—Theobald," Whitney said, shifting the sat phone from her right ear to her left. "What exactly is his role in Pakistan?"

"As far as the world at large is concerned, he's the in-country coordinator for IBC," Lewis said, his voice as clear as if they were on the phone at NCTC instead of eight thousand miles apart. "IBC is a federally subsidized NGO designed to encourage entrepreneurship and small business development in Pakistan and Afghanistan. Really, it's an evergreen NOC the Defense Intelligence Agency uses to maintain a supported presence in the region. Theobald oversees a small team tasked with running assets and collecting intelligence on arms dealing, intelligence sharing, and back-channel cooperation between the Taliban and sympathetic elements inside the

Pakistani government. If what you're theorizing is true, and the Taliban is somehow operating a UCAV out of the Kush, then Theobald might have confirming intelligence."

"And what did he say?"

"Not much, until I told him your theory. Then he suddenly got real interested."

"Why?"

A heavy pause hung on the line as Lewis seemed to choose his next words carefully. They were talking on a secure connection, so she wondered if he was apprehensive to share for other reasons.

"Well, he said he has an asset running scared. Apparently, the asset's brother has recently gone missing in Mingora. They think he was murdered. The brother was in deep with local Tali and some al-Qaeda splinter group trafficking Chinese arms on the black market. Theobald was pretty tight-lipped about it. What he did say, Whit, is that he's been monitoring the proliferation of Chinese weapons to terror groups in western Pakistan, and he sees a strong possible connection to the drone theory you're pursuing."

"What connection?"

"I can't answer that," Lewis said. "That's a question you'll need to ask him when he calls. I gave him your number."

She looked down at the table, her eyes going back and forth between her trefoil knot sketch and the map with overlapping hundred-kilometer circles. Her gaze drifted east, from the cave in the Hindu Kush to an adjacent circle in Pakistan. Inside that circle was the city of Mingora, home to DIA agent Theobald's operation and the asset fretting about his missing brother. She looked closely at the map, and at the single long runway at Saidu Sharif Airport across the Swat River and north of the city at the base of the mountains. A runway long enough to land a UCAV, with big enough hangars to hide a drone with a forty-five-foot wingspan.

"All right, I appreciate you making the connection," she said. "Oh, and Reed?"

"Yeah?"

"Ixnay on the haring-say, okay? I'm playing this one close to the vest."

"Of course, you know me," he said, chuckling. "My mouth is a SCIF."

"Thanks."

"How's it going down there, or over there, or wherever the hell they have you working?"

"It's . . . different," she said with a tight smile, leaving it at that. "Different, but good."

"All right. Well, be careful, kid."

"Always. And I owe you one."

She ended the call and dropped the sat phone on the desk. She absently began tracing the infinite knot tattooed on the inside of her left wrist with her finger.

"I found the thread to untangle you, bitch," she murmured.

"Who you talking to?" a voice said.

She started and looked up, dropping her left hand under the desk for some reason.

"Sorry," Chunk said, grinning at her from the doorway. "Didn't mean to scare you."

She considered what to tell him. He'd made it clear he was interested in actionable intelligence, but wild-goose chases were clearly off the table. Which criteria did this meet? Maybe she should wait until she'd had the call with Theobald to say anything about Mingora.

"Listen," Chunk said, dropping into a chair beside her desk. "About before. We can't operate the way we need to if we don't trust each other, and while what I said is true, the way I said it was totally off base. I want you to know you can talk to me about anything, run shit by me, brainstorm together—whatever you need. You need to be able to speak your mind about stuff, and what I said before, or at least how I said it . . ."

Geez, he's like my high school boyfriend trying to apologize after I caught him staring at Kimmy Knowles's ass junior year.

"It's all good, Chunk," she said, meeting his gaze. "Sometimes I get too carried away with my part of the equation, and I lose sight of the forest through the trees. What you said was true. During an op, you're the person best qualified to make decisions on the ground. Especially with respect to getting everyone home safely. I'm sorry for second-guessing you. The lives of your team come first."

"*Our* team," he corrected. "You're just as much a part of this unit as Riker, Trip, or Saw. Maybe I haven't done a good enough job making that clear, or at least, making you feel that way . . . and if not, then that's on me. The Tier One is not a democracy, but it is a family. Everyone has a voice. Everyone gets to speak their mind, and that includes you. But . . ."

"You're the boss?"

"Yeah, and I'm in charge for a reason. I didn't get this billet by accident. Just like you didn't get yours by accident either. I trust you to do your job; you have to trust me to do mine."

"I don't *not* trust you," she said. "I just . . . oh, never mind."

"Uh-uh," he said, wagging a finger at her. "You don't get to 'never mind' me. Spit it out."

"On my first day, do you remember the thing you did to make an impression on me?"

Chunk grinned. "Sent a tattooed redneck to pick you up a half hour late in a Jeep with no doors to try to rattle your nerves?"

"No, after that."

"Gave you a misogynistic nickname to see if you had the self-confidence and sense of humor to survive in this unit?"

"No, after that too . . ."

His expression shifted from playful to serious. "Made you stop at the Operation Crusader memorial so you would understand the stakes of what it is we do and the cold reality of the enemy we face?"

"Yeah, and in case you couldn't tell at the time, that resonated with me, probably more than you realize. And do you know why?"

"Because you have your own demons?"

She nodded. "I know I'm young and I haven't been in the counter-terror community as long as the rest of you have, but I've been an analyst at NCTC for five years. I've worked a lot of cases, and two years ago I royally fucked up. I failed to properly assess the data, and as a result, innocent people died. If I had done my job properly, then a unit like this would have been tasked and the attack could have been stopped. But I failed to follow the thread. I failed to connect the puzzle pieces, and that's something I have to live with for the rest of my life." She sighed and looked down at the trefoil knot tattoo. "It's the reason I accepted this job in the first place—because feeding my theories and conclusions into the giant bureaucratic machine wasn't good enough anymore. I figured the more links of the chain I could remove between me and the decision makers authorizing direct action, the better chance I had of saving lives. And then last night happened . . . I'm watching you on the screen, swarmed by an enemy force we did not contemplate, and I'm thinking, '*Oh my god, I just killed them. I walked them into another Operation Crusader. What the hell have I done?*'"

Mortified at the naked admission, she shuddered and looked away from him.

He placed his bear paw of a hand on her shoulder. "This might surprise you, but when I was on that mountain getting ambushed by Taliban fighters, do you want to know the one thought that never crossed my mind?"

She nodded.

"The one thought that never crossed my mind was, 'This is Whitney Watts's fault.' In fact, I don't know if that would have entered my conscious if you hadn't said it."

"Really?"

"Really," he said. "Yes, we're chasing your thread, as you call it, but we planned the op together. This is the exact point I was trying to make before. We all have a stake. We all have a voice. I wasn't assaulting that cave because you had a hunch. I was assaulting it because you put together a compelling case and leadership agreed. If in hindsight it turned out to be a bad call, then we made the bad call collectively. That's the beauty of the Tier One. Neither of us was satisfied working in silos—you at CIA and then NCTC, me at Team Four. Now we have the integration of intelligence and operations, and we're just figuring out how to manage the friction that comes from that. It's gonna take some time, but I think we're on the right track."

"Me too," she said, finally meeting his gaze again.

"All right," he said giving her shoulder a squeeze, then releasing it. "Now that we have that out of the way, let's talk drones and Taliban. When I wandered in here, I interrupted something . . . where are you with all this? What are all these sketches and circles on the map?"

She tapped her finger on the circle in Pakistan, east of the Hindu Kush.

"I think we need to go to Mingora." She bit her lip. Could they even do that? Could they send a SEAL Team into Pakistan without permission? They'd likely have to run it through not just JSOC, but the Pentagon and maybe even the White House. It would take days—maybe even weeks. They didn't have the time. Regardless, she explained to Chunk the theory that she and Yi had come up with, then what she had learned from Lewis about Theobald and his asset.

"All right," Chunk said, not questioning her, not telling her she was crazy. In fact, he was rubbing his hands together as if he were already relishing the upcoming op. "Pick this guy's brain when he calls, then put together a short brief for Bowman and the team. Think you can have something together by fourteen hundred?"

"Okay, but wouldn't we have to notify the Pakistani government that we were coming? I mean, sending a SEAL Team into Pakistan is a big friggin' deal, international relations wise."

The inscrutable look on his face prompted a new and dreadful thought. She swallowed hard. "Unless you're planning on sending me alone to meet this guy?"

Just the mere prospect of traveling into Pakistan on her own made her stomach turn to acid. *I'm an analyst, for God's sake, not a field agent.*

Chunk flashed her that grin again, and in that moment she found it less irritating and possibly, maybe, slightly endearing.

"You're with the Tier One now, Watts. Captain Bowman has the Vice President on speed dial, remember? If you need to go to Pakistan, then by God, you're going to Pakistan." He headed for the door, but at the threshold he turned and said, "Oh, but don't think you can get rid of us that easy. No way in hell I'm letting you have a boondoggle in Pakistan without me and the boys." He grinned again and shot her a two-finger salute that became a thumbs-up. "Hooyah, Intel."

And with that he was gone.

Did he just call me Intel?

Shaking her head, she dialed Yi's number and put the phone to her ear.

"Hey, Whitney? What's up?"

"Where are you?"

"Working out. Have you seen the gym here? It's almost as nice the one back at MacDill."

"No, I haven't. Remember, I don't do exercise . . . Anyway, I need you back over here, Michelle. I've got something, and we need to put a brief together for the team."

"On my way." And the phone clicked off.

She looked at the map with the overlapping circles.

Then she stared at the satellite phone beside her laptop, almost willing it to ring. When it did, her eyebrows shot up in surprise.

"Watts," she answered, annoyed to hear the nerves in her voice.

"Ms. Watts, this is Bobby Theobald. Sounds like we might both be chasing the same boogeyman. We definitely need to talk. If we can meet in person we can share what we've both got and pool our resources, though it was a little unclear to me just what your resources are. How soon can you be in Mingora?"

CHAPTER 23

RELAX HILTON PALACE HOTEL

FIZA GHAT BYPASS, ALONG THE SWAT RIVER

MINGORA, PAKISTAN

1020 LOCAL TIME

Chunk was no expert on luxury hotels, and he was sure as hell no expert on urban Pakistan, but he was absolutely positive that the Relax Hilton Palace was not in any way affiliated with the actual Hilton brand. The small hotel did have a certain charm, he supposed, with its oversized bright-green tinted windows—designed, perhaps, to cast the muddy brown Swat River in a more palatable shade when viewed from inside.

He stepped from the van and looked north, across the river toward Saidu Sharif Airport, where they'd landed a half hour ago. He slung his pack, a black civilian North Face number, and resisted the urge to go to the rear of the van and start pulling out gear.

Civilians don't hump their own luggage at hotels, he reminded himself as Pakistani hotel staff descended on the vans en masse.

The porters were dressed in bright and festive *shalwar kameez*—baggy trousers tight at the ankles and long, tunic-style shirts—complete with Sindhi caps and colorful round-toed silk *khussa* shoes. He caught Riker's raised eyebrows and just smiled and shook his head. Chunk had been deployed in a nonofficial cover only once before, and that was as part of an ISR advance team in Iraq in 2014. He and his three men had posed as journalists and provided physical security for some OGA types. Today, he'd had the flight over from Jalalabad to get into character, or whatever spooks called it. During their predeparture brief, they'd conducted a video chat with a DIA man on Theobald's team, Peter Brusk, whose advice had boiled down to: Don't be afraid to be uncomfortable.

"You're Americans working on an urban development plan for the region because your companies want to invest over here. You're sniffing out places for manufacturing plants and call centers, evaluating infrastructure, that kind of thing, an effort that will create the best jobs in the region," Brusk explained, "This makes the NOC basically one of royalty, since everyone here wants those western dollars. No one will expect you to divulge individual company details—which is a gift because you don't have to remember shit, except your fake name. It also means your shitty language skills and obvious discomfort won't raise any eyebrows. We'll start with a tour of the area. If you stay long enough, we'll need to arrange meetings with local business leaders so you seem legit."

"Discomfort" wasn't the problem. Chunk and his team were used to sleeping in tree hollows, riding in cramped helos and SDVs, and getting chafed raw in every place a body can chafe. "Not raising eyebrows," now that was another animal altogether.

"You must be Harry Anderson," a man in blue jeans and a black sports shirt said, walking up to greet him. Chunk took the man's proffered hand and shook it tightly.

"I am," he said, remembering his fake name and programmed response. "You must be Peter—good to meet you in person."

"You too," Brusk said with a thick Texas accent that to Chunk sounded like home. "I work for Robert Theobald, but everybody calls him Bobby. I'm the IBC coordinator for Pakistan's western provinces. Y'all arrived in country yesterday?"

"Two days ago," Chunk replied, staying on script. "We spent yesterday in Faisalabad. We were supposed to have a few tours, but honestly, we just mostly slept off the jet lag. Faisalabad is probably a little more expensive than my bosses are looking for. I was told to look deeper here, in the Swat Valley area. Problem is, most people hear Swat Valley and think Osama bin Laden."

Brusk laughed a big genuine laugh and put a hand on Chunk's back, talking while directing him toward the hotel entrance. "Yeah, that's about right. But it also means the real opportunities are here. The area around Mingora is just good people looking for a better life. Bad guys are everywhere in the Middle East, I guess, but that's true in London these days too. We've got lots to show you, but first we have a little presentation for y'all. Let's get you checked in, then we can meet in the conference room for a quick overview of our goals and opportunities before stepping out. That sound good?"

"Sounds great," Chunk answered.

"The whole third floor is rented out by IBC, so we'll get the bags sent right up to the conference room, then y'all can grab your individual stuff and pick out your rooms. The bags will be with my guys until you get there, so don't worry about that."

Brusk held his eyes with the last comment, perhaps sensing Chunk's discomfort at being separated from their bags—bags which were full of weapons, ammunition, body armor, and communications gear.

Chunk nodded, figuring he didn't have much choice in the matter.

The surprisingly modern lobby, with its immaculate white-marble tile floor and brightly colored walls, took him by surprise. An attractive young woman behind the check-in desk smiled at him and greeted him in English, while an attendant served them cups of ice water with cucumber from a silver tray.

"Is this what you expected?" Watts said, stepping beside him, voice tense. He looked at her and was met by an expression he had decided to nickname her "stress face." It was the same expression she'd had during the briefing with Jarvis.

Instead of answering her immediately, he parried her expression by relaxing his own and smiling at her. Then, raising the paper cup to his lips, he said, "Ahhh, pickle water. Now that's a treat you just don't get every day."

This broke her immediately, and he heard her real laugh for the first time since they'd met.

"If you see a potted plant I can pour this in, let me know," he said in a conspiratorial whisper, before adding, "Don't worry. We're in good hands here. I promise. Now let's get our 'merica on."

When she shot him a quizzical look, he gestured at a woman in traditional clothes, a bright-pink pashmina around her shoulders, tending to a buffet laid out in a dining room beyond the lobby. "Biggest risk for you on this trip, Rebecca, is that you might put on a little extra weight. I know how you like to eat when we're on the road."

He saw comprehension flash in her eyes, and her expression immediately soured as she shifted into character. "What's sad, Harry," she fired back, remembering to use his fake name, "is how naturally being misogynistic comes to you."

"Nice one, boss," Saw chuckled as she walked off with Brusk. "You sure have a way with the ladies."

"What?" Chunk said, throwing his hands up in a *don't-look-at-me-she's-the-crazy-one* shrug. "Seriously, what did I say?"

Five minutes later they were checked in and gathered on the third floor, inside a large but simple conference room, their bags and boxes stacked along one wall. Chunk slid into a chair beside Watts, and Riker dropped in on the other side of him, with Saw taking the seat next to Yi. With Antman in the ISAF hospital in Kabul and Georgie on his way home to Virginia, that left just Spence, Morales, Trip, and Edwards to join them at the table.

Once they were all seated, Chunk took the temperature of the room. Other than Watts, nobody seemed nervous. *Damn*, he thought, looking around. It was so surreal. Seven SEALs at a DIA black ops site inside Pakistan, surrounded by a citizenry known to be Taliban sympathizers. Add to that their disavowed State Department, no air support, and no QRF.

Chunk grinned. *Now this is some real Tier One shit.*

Brusk returned with a new, rather benign-looking guy in tow. The DIA man closed and locked the door behind him while his partner passed out thick green folders.

"Hey guys, and thanks for coming. I'm Peter Brusk and this is Earl McAllister. We're the onsite team for IBC, and we'll be taking you on the tour of Mingora shortly. First, though, we have a briefing for you on the region, the economic opportunities we see here, and some ground rules and courtesies you should observe while in Pakistan."

McAllister keyed up a PowerPoint on a laptop, and a TV monitor on the wall refreshed with the first slide. Brusk walked to the head of the table, and with all eyes on him tapped his ear and looked up, spinning a finger around in the air. The message was clear: Don't know who could be listening.

"As I go over this material," he said, "feel free to look through the folders we prepared for you that highlight much of what I'll be saying over the next twenty minutes . . ."

While Brusk droned on, Chunk opened his folder and found a

cover page stamped with TS/SCI Eyes Only. As Brusk and McAllister put on their show for anyone listening in, Chunk and his team read through the *real* brief—a classified overview of Theobald's brilliant DIA operation in Mingora. Their NOC, as a well-funded international NGO sponsoring economic development in the former FATA region, was perfect. It gave them unfettered access in the community, and also allowed them to run local assets who served as their eyes and ears throughout not just Mingora, but the Khyber. Everyone wanted to make the westerners feel welcome—and safe—and open the deep purses of foreign investors and corporations that could pour lifeblood into the struggling region.

Very friggin' clever.

Their "tour" would allow them to perform real-time ISR on a variety of highlighted areas in Mingora and across the bridge in the communities around the airport and north into the foothills of the Hindu Kush. And it would give them access to a variety of trusted assets more read in to IBC's counter-terror mission—those individuals and their rough histories with the operation were also outlined in the file.

Chunk looked up and saw Spence flipping through his folder, a broad grin on his face suggesting this was some pretty cool shit. Riker looked bored, but then again, he never did care much about the minutiae. Watts was taking notes, of course. Next, he caught Saw's eye. The SEAL raised his eyebrows and nodded. This was the kind of shit that made a difference. Kicking in doors was awesome, but it was ten times more gratifying when you were kicking in the right doors at the right time.

Brusk spoke for another ten minutes before wrapping up. "And so, in conclusion, I think we have several sites that will be of interest to you. Go ahead and get yourselves settled, have some lunch, then we can regroup and finalize our afternoon itinerary. Any questions?"

Riker raised a hand, a stupid grin on his face, but Chunk caught his eye and shook his head. The Senior Chief lowered his hand, still grinning like a schoolboy, and said, "Nope. No questions."

"Great. Feel free to take your personal belongings to your individual rooms, but any *team*-related items will be perfectly safe here in our conference room," Brusk said. Then, turning to Watts, he added, "Ms. Taylor, I understand you're having lunch in town with Mr. Theobald?"

"Uh, yeah, so it would seem," she said, tucking a sweep of bangs behind her ear.

"Great. I'll get you the address for the restaurant."

"Thank you, Peter," she said and looked over at Chunk, eyes wide, her face one big question: *Are you coming with me?*

He'd contemplated escorting her, but she'd told him that Theobald had been explicit she come alone so as not to spook his asset. He knew it was the right call and understood the man's conundrum. Having a big, burly operator show up unannounced was all it would take to ruin the interaction, or worse, cause the asset to bolt. Whitney, on the other hand, would appear to pose no threat. She'd agreed at the time, but now—facing the actual moment of truth—she looked scared.

This, unfortunately for Whitney, was one of those kick-the-baby-bird-out-of-the-nest moments.

Time to test those wings, Heels.

He leaned back in his chair, smiled, and gave her a thumbs-up that seemed to say, "Go get 'em, tiger."

CHAPTER 24

Whitney sat on the edge of the bed in her hotel room, trying not to hyperventilate. She understood why she had to go alone to meet Theobald, but it didn't change the fact that the prospect terrified her.

What if Theobald doesn't show up? What if the terrorists know we're here and kidnap me? What if it's a trap and we get shot or blown up?

She blew air through pursed lips and tried to put the thoughts out of her mind.

Remember what Yi said and stop saying what if!

The trip to Afghanistan had been her first to the Middle East and her first time in a third world country. But from the moment she'd stepped off the plane in Kabul, she'd had a platoon of heavily armed Tier One SEALs around her. As much as she hated to admit it, she'd taken great comfort in that fact. Now she was in Pakistan, no longer safe and secure on a US base, and she had to go meet a spy at restaurant alone.

I feel like one of those idiot girls in a horror movie, bumbling her way toward an obvious and bloody demise that only she didn't recognize.

Her mobile phone rang. It was Chunk.

She answered it. "Yes."

"You should probably get going, or you're going to be late."

"I know."

"You can do this, Heels."

"Okay," she said, her voice hollow as she debated asking Yi to come with her.

"Would it make you feel better if you knew that me and the boys are going to be driving loops in the van in case you need to call in the cavalry?"

"Um, hello, yes!"

"I thought so. We're just a phone call away. Now, get your intel ass moving."

"Roger that," she said and ended the call. Feeling like nine million pounds had suddenly been lifted off her back, she got to her feet and headed downstairs.

In the lobby she asked one of the hotel's young porters to get her a taxi. He repeated the word "taxi," and when she nodded, he smiled and stepped outside to the parking courtyard. While she waited, Chunk and three of the boys showed up, but they walked past her like she didn't exist and headed out, ostensibly to the van. This knocked the edge off her nerves, until she noticed a bearded man wearing a black knit cap standing next to the reception desk, staring daggers at her. She glanced at him but didn't hold eye contact, resisted the urge to wait outside for the taxi, and tried her best to look relaxed. The next two minutes were the longest of her life, with the stranger's eyes boring into her the entire time. When the porter returned, grinning, she practically jogged to meet him.

"Taxi, taxi for you," he said and led her to a little white sedan idling in the courtyard.

"Thank you," she said and tipped him five hundred rupees when he opened the door for her, a sum that earned her gushing, incomprehensible gratitude.

"Hello," the driver said, greeting her in heavily accented English. "Where you go?"

"Hujra restaurant, please," she said, nervously folding her arms across her chest.

"Hujra close," he said, cocking a quizzical eyebrow at her.

"Are you sure it's closed? I'm supposed to meet someone for lunch."

"No, uh, it close . . . close. You understand? It not far."

"Okay," she said, nodding. "Please take me there."

He shrugged, put the transmission in drive and pulled away.

As the taxi accelerated onto the N-95, the paved two-lane thoroughfare that skirted the southern bank of the Swat River, she debated whether she should buckle her seat belt. *If bullets start flying, I need to get low and possibly make a run for it. Trying to get out of a seatbelt will cost me precious seconds. On the other hand, if we have to evade at high speed and we get into an accident—*

The taxi unexpectedly braked, interrupting her thoughts and sending adrenaline surging into her bloodstream. She looked up as the driver activated his turn signal, turned left across the oncoming lane of traffic, and pulled into a restaurant parking lot. Screwing up her face, she looked out the window and verified the name on the sign: Hujra.

"See, close," the driver said, turning to her with a comical smile. The ride had lasted no more than ninety seconds door to door.

Feeling ridiculous, she pulled two five-hundred-rupee notes from her pocket and handed them to him. "Is this enough?"

"Yes, yes, thank you," he said, happily taking the money. "You want me pick you up?"

"Um, no . . . thank you," she said. "I think I'll walk back."

"Okay, bye-bye," he said as she climbed out.

A Caucasian man standing on the other side of the N-95 caught her attention. He was dressed in a short-sleeved button-down shirt and khaki pants. The smiling, clean-shaven man was trying to get her attention with a large exaggerated wave.

"They always drop off on the wrong side," he called to her. "The owners expanded across the street for waterfront dining."

"Mr. Theobald?" she called back.

"Yeah," he said, beckoning her. "C'mon over."

She hesitated a heartbeat, then walked to the roadside to wait for a break in traffic. Fifteen seconds later she was jogging to meet her DIA contact.

"Robert Theobald," the American said, extending his hand. "But you can call me Bobby."

"Whitney," she said and shook his hand, noticing how similar his grip was to Chunk's, a hand that felt more like ironwood than flesh.

"I'm sorry we couldn't have this meeting at the hotel, but I couldn't risk spooking my asset. His antennae are up, so I wanted to keep things small and intimate," Theobald said. "How much experience do you have running assets?"

"None," Whitney said, scanning over her shoulder. In her peripheral vision, she saw a van approaching from the north and recognized it as Chunk and the guys making good on their promise to stay in the area.

"You look nervous," he said, his gaze following hers, then returning to her face. "Something got *your* antennae up?" He seemed to take a measure of her before saying, "First time in Pakistan?"

"Yeah," she said, glancing over her other shoulder.

"This place is solid. I personally know the owner, and I had his family vetted and surveilled."

"Mm-hmm." His assurances did little for her nerves.

"I know what you're thinking—what the hell is this yahoo talking about? This is the Swat River Valley in friggin' Pakistan, where every other face you pass on the street could be a terrorist in hiding. It ain't that way, I promise. Mingora is a good city—a community of mostly small and family-owned businesses. The people here aren't bent on jihad and taking down America; they're just scraping out a living and trying to make a better life for their family."

"Understood," she said.

Except those aren't the people I'm worried about, she thought. *I'm worried about the ones with a drone armed with missiles that just blew up an Army convoy.*

"Please follow me," he said and turned.

She followed him to an expansive deck filled with outdoor dining tables. A small crowd was scattered at the tables, enjoying the nice afternoon weather. Theobald had chosen a corner table along the deck railing, with a view of the muddy Swat and its rocky bank. The table was conspicuously outside the eavesdropping radius of other patrons. He gestured for her to take the seat with the best view of the river, while he took the chair opposite, with unobstructed sightlines and nothing behind him. A waiter promptly brought them a basket of naan and tea service.

"I've been thinking a lot about my last conversation with your former boss at NCTC. How about we start with you laying out your drone theory for me, then I'll try to fill in any blanks with the intelligence my team has collected," the DIA man said, kicking things off.

Whitney kept her voice low but dove in, explaining her theory that the convoy attack outside J-bad had been executed by a UCAV. Next, she read him into the raid Chunk's team had conducted on the Taliban stronghold in the Hindu Kush, and finally, walked him through her LOS hand-off theory. All the while, he listened without interrupting, nodding periodically.

"The Pakistani military recently signed a contract for forty-eight Wing Loong combat drones with the Chinese aerospace conglomerate CAIG," he said, leaning in to close the gap between them.

"Interesting," she said, wanting to hear more.

"Prior to signing that contract, Pakistan had a Wing Loong Pterodactyl model in the country for extensive testing. This was not widely publicized, but what did make the headlines was that the drone was reported to have crashed six months ago, a report which, interestingly, the Pakistani military *confirmed* in the aftermath. But what if that report was manufactured? What if the drone didn't crash, but certain corrupted elements within the Pakistani military wanted the world and the Chinese government to believe that it did? Assuming bribes were paid, is it really much of stretch to imagine that drone secretly finding its way into terrorist hands?"

"About a month ago," Whitney said, "US Navy SEALs raided a vessel in the Arabian Sea suspected of carrying WMD precursor components, but what they found instead were Chinese-made HJ-10 air-to-ground missiles and crates of electronic parts which have since been identified as drone components manufactured by CAIG. The cargo was bound for the port of Gwadar in western Pakistan. What if these parts were purchased by the Taliban after they got their hands on the drone? I mean, they would need the parts and the missiles, right, if they had acquired the drone?"

"I don't think it's Taliban, or I would have heard something supporting by now. But there is another nascent organization here in Pakistan that's more likely to be involved—an al-Qaeda splinter faction I've been trying to penetrate, operating right here in the Swat River Valley."

Whitney scooted her chair closer. "What splinter faction?"

"They call themselves al Qadar."

"I don't speak Arabic. What does it mean?"

"It means, roughly, a goal or event which is predetermined to happen."

"You mean destiny?"

"Yeah. In their case, the predestined goal is a global Islamic caliphate," Theobald said, his gaze ticking left, over her shoulder. "My contact has arrived. Why don't you pull your chair around to the end of the table?"

She did as instructed, guessing that good tradecraft meant using geometry to make it difficult for everyone to be photographed, in case they were being surveilled.

"Hello, my friend," Theobald said, standing momentarily to greet a young Pakistani man who looked nervous as hell.

"Hello, Bobby." The man took a seat but didn't move to shake hands with either of them.

"Bezerat this is Rebecca," Theobald said. "She works with my group."

Bezerat nodded at her. "Hello."

"Hi," she said and forced a smile.

"Have you heard anything from your brother, Mohamed?" Theobald asked, his voice ripe with concern.

"No, nothing. I'm very worried, Mr. Bobby," Bezerat said, his expression pained. "I think they killed him."

The compulsion to jump into the conversation and ask, "Who killed him?" was almost overpowering, but Whitney forced herself to just listen.

Theobald nodded. "I'm nervous too. I have my people and other trusted friends looking for him, but we need to take precautions now. Especially with you. This should be our last meeting for a while, and so I need you to tell me everything you know, including rumors and details you might have withheld before."

"Okay, okay," the nervous Pakistani said, scratching at his thin juvenile beard. "I think Mohamed had a run-in with ISI." When Theobald said nothing, Bezerat said, "Did you know about the meeting?"

"No," Theobald answered.

"You swear you did not tip them off?"

"I swear," Theobald replied. "You know how I feel about ISI."

Although she'd never had any dealings personally with Pakistani intelligence, Whitney understood the subtext. Inter-Services Intelligence, Pakistan's version of the CIA, was an uncomfortable bedfellow for any foreign intelligence service to work with, because for every honorable officer or agent, an equal number of snitches, thugs, and terrorist sympathizers worked there.

"Well, ISI came to see my brother. Unannounced. Two agents showed up at the store."

"Were you there at the time?"

"No. I was out making deliveries. My brother told me. He called me and sounded quite agitated."

Theobald nodded. "Go on."

"When I got back, Mohamed was gone."

"Where did he go?"

"I think he went to see Hamza."

"Why?"

"My cousin said that my brother was convinced Hamza was watching him. He wanted to head off any problem."

Whitney looked at Theobald, the question poised on her lips.

Theobald met her gaze and said, "Hamza al-Saud, the suspected leader of al Qadar."

She nodded and committed the name to memory.

"Did you ever tell your brother you were working with me?" he asked Bezerat.

"No."

"What about your cousin?"

"No."

"Are you certain? Not even in a moment of weakness?"

"No, I swear. Never," Bezerat said with conviction.

"Okay," Theobald said and blew air through his teeth. He didn't say anything for a long moment, then turned to Whitney. "Rebecca, I know you have some questions for Bezerat."

"Um, yes I do," she said, swallowing. "Do you know of, or are you aware of, the brokering of, HJ-10 air-to-ground missiles to al Qadar?"

Bezerat screwed up his face at her. "I don't even know what that is, HJ-10?"

She cleared her throat, silently chastising herself for the way she'd asked the question.

Theobald probably thinks I'm an idiot.

"It's a drone-fired missile. We have a working theory that Hamza has either acquired or is trying to acquire a drone capable of firing missiles at US military targets."

"Okay, this is interesting," Bezerat said, nervously knitting his fingers together and cracking his knuckles. "I overheard my brother and cousin just a few days ago. They were talking about a drone."

"That's good, Bezerat. What exactly did they say?" Theobald pressed.

"I . . . I don't know. It was hard to hear, and I didn't want them to know I was listening. I was behind the shelves in the back of the store, and they didn't know I was there. Mohamed was talking about a drone shooting a convoy. I assumed it was the Americans blowing something up—the Taliban, maybe, like they always do. I'm sorry, but I was very nervous and that's all I could hear."

Theobald glanced at Whitney, his gaze speaking volumes.

"Did your brother sound excited or upset, talking about the drone?" Whitney asked.

"Now that you make me think about it, when I came into the store, my cousin and my brother were in very happy moods," Bezerat said.

"What did your brother do for al Qadar exactly?" she asked.

"My family has an electronics store in Mingora. My brother is—well, he is not a terrorist, but he's a true believer. He wants to see Muslims rise. He wants a world where the West is not the boss. My cousin is in the middle. When he is around me, he is not caring about politics, but around Mohamed he is supporting a strong Muslim rise. I think my cousin has always looked up to Mohamed and tries to impress him."

"I understand," she said, nodding, "but do you know if your brother was an active member of al Qadar? Was he supporting operations or involved in the planning of operations?"

"No, I don't think so. But he was trying to make a profit from Hamza. He wanted to be a supplier of components and information."

"Why do you think ISI came to see your brother? I mean, how would they know to suspect Mohamed was working with al Qadar?" She felt herself getting drawn into the spider-web now.

"I don't know," Bezerat said, then nervously began looking over his shoulder. "I have been here too long. I . . . I need to go."

"One more question," Theobald said, calm and languid as a lullaby. "Did you ever make electronic component deliveries on behalf of your brother to Hamza or his people?"

"Maybe, I don't know. They don't tell me about all the customers, and I don't ask."

"Okay, I understand, but if Hamza al-Saud does have a drone, and we're talking about a big drone, a machine the size of a small airplane, do you have any idea where he might hide it? It would need to be in a warehouse or a big garage . . . somewhere near the airport, maybe?" he coaxed the young Pakistani.

Bezerat's eyes flashed with epiphany. "Yes, yes, possibly. During the last few weeks, Mohamed was making deliveries to a building in Kanju, the area just west of the airport. He was taking them himself instead of having me make the trip."

"Do you have an address?" Whitney asked.

"I maybe could find it for you. I need to look through the papers. See if my brother kept a record or not."

"Will you do that for us?" Theobald asked.

"It is a big risk, if my cousin sees me. What will you do for me if I do this for you?" Bezerat said.

"What do you want?" the DIA man said.

"You know this. I've told you many times, Bobby. I want to go to university. I don't have the money or the connections. You need to get me in."

"Yes, but we've talked about this. A big reward requires a big win. So here's what I can promise. If you get us the address and it is valid intelligence that leads to a successful counter-terror operation against al Qadar, then I will make good on my end of the bargain." Theobald's gaze was earnest and unwavering.

"You swear?" Bezerat said, his jaw tight.

"I swear, and you know I always keep my promises."

"If I succeed, I text you the address." Bezerat shoved his chair back from the table and stood up. "Okay?"

Theobald nodded but stayed firmly planted in his seat.

"Okay, goodbye," the young man said, and with a curt nod to Whitney, he departed.

"So what do you think?" Theobald said, turning to look at her.

"A couple of things. First, if Bezerat gets us an address, we can compare it to the transmissions we collected during the time leading up to the drone strike. If the coordinates match, then we have compelling reason to conduct ISR on the facility and potentially make a move against it." The gears in her head were really churning now.

"Okay, and second?"

"Maybe you query your network of assets about the crashed Wing Loong drone and see if anyone might have heard whispers about that. And maybe question airport employees about late night or unauthorized aircraft flying out of the local airport."

A broad smile arched across Theobald's face.

"What's that look for?" she said, suddenly feeling self-conscious.

"Oh, just that if I didn't know better, I'd say you caught the bug."

"What bug?"

"The field ops bug," he said with a smile. "It's exciting, isn't it?"

"Yeah, maybe a little," she said, her lips curling up at the corners.

"You were having so much fun there at the end, you forgot all about being nervous. Didn't ya?" he teased.

He was right, she had, but the recognition of this lapse in attention mortified her and instantly sent her stomach fluttering with renewed anxiety. "Yeah. Rookie mistake. Won't happen again."

"Ah, don't be so hard on yourself. For your first field engagement, you did pretty damn good," he said, ripping off a hunk of naan and stuffing it in his mouth. "Now let's scarf down some lunch, then I'll get to work shaking some trees and we'll see what falls out."

CHAPTER 25

AL QADAR WAREHOUSE AND DRONE HANGAR

MINGORA, PAKISTAN

2050 LOCAL TIME

Qasim looked at Eshan, then back at the Pterodactyl drone and its new paint job. The Chinese eagle emblem on the nose of the drone had been covered and a US Air Force roundel insignia had been expertly added onto the fuselage and the wings. A retired Predator tail number and squadron insignia shield had been stenciled onto the tail fins to complete the deception. He hadn't seen Eshan in nearly two weeks, and the initial excitement of his best friend's arrival had soured to acrimony born of abandonment.

"It looks exactly like an American drone," Eshan said walking to stand at Qasim's side. "It's remarkable."

"A trained eye would recognize it as a counterfeit, but it's good enough to fool most people," he replied, trying to keep his voice neutral.

"Hamza told me you were able to penetrate the satellite network and now we can fly the drone using satellite signal relay instead of line of sight," Eshan said.

"That's not entirely true. We weren't successful piggybacking off the Americans' satellite network like I'd hoped. Hamza's hacker got into the Relay Tracking Station at Diego Garcia, but he couldn't figure out how to hack into the uplink. So I suggested he try hacking into the PakSat-1R. It's a DFH-4-type satellite in a geostationary orbit, giving it signal coverage for all of Pakistan and Afghanistan. Moreover, it was built by a Chinese contractor, which I thought might make both the encryption and firewall easier for Fun Time to crack. Turns out I was right."

"So it's a Pakistani military satellite?"

"Technically, the satellite was procured by the Space and Upper Atmosphere Research Corp. And SUPARCO has made a point of publicly downplaying the military applications of the 1R in the press, but it's no coincidence it has eighteen Ku-band transponders."

"I don't understand."

"It's the same frequency band that Predator and Reaper drones use, and it's the same band this Pterodactyl drone uses as well. The Pakistanis have been planning on integrating Chinese UCAVs for years now. Getting that satellite in orbit was the first step."

"Well, regardless of the specifics, Hamza seems pleased." When Qasim didn't answer, Eshan said, "What's wrong, Qasim? I can tell something is bothering you."

"Hmm, I wonder what it could possibly be?" Qasim said, his voice ripe with sarcasm as his gaze drifted to the maroon stain on the floor, not two meters from where they stood. In a harsh whisper he added, "Maybe it's that I watched a man have his head cut off right over there."

"Let's go for a drive," Eshan said with an easy smile, while eyeing a group of bearded fighters who were talking in a cluster, just out of earshot. "This is not the time or place to have this discussion."

"Maybe you're free to come and go as you please, but I certainly am not," Qasim said, looking at his feet.

"Not true. Follow me and I'll prove it," he said and started walking toward the exit.

After a moment's hesitation, Qasim followed, positive he would be detained. But when they reached the door, Bacha greeted them both and let them pass, asking only if they would be coming back and the approximate time. Eshan explained they'd be back before sunrise. They departed without incident.

"Where are we going?" Qasim said after climbing into the passenger seat of Eshan's car.

"To my hotel. I'm giving you my room for the night. You can take a hot shower, sleep in a real bed, and have some time alone. Allah knows you deserve it."

"What are you going to do?"

"I'll sleep at the safe house in Kanju. It's fine, Qasim. I insist."

"No, don't be ridiculous," Qasim said, stubbornly shaking his head.

"I won't take no for an answer."

Qasim sighed and looked out the window. Despite his protestations, he reveled at the prospect of privacy and sleeping in an actual bed. He didn't feel safe at the warehouse, and the stress of being trapped with so many hypermasculine, gun-toting fighters was doing terrible things to his nerves.

Several minutes passed before Eshan broke the silence. "What's wrong, Qasim?"

"Where have you been? It's been forever since I've seen you."

"I'm sorry, Qasim," he said, with a parental, almost patronizing tone to his voice. "I've been very busy with work and trying to spend some time with my bride."

Qasim nodded but didn't offer any grace.

"Do you remember that day when we were kids and you challenged me to a breath-holding competition?" Eshan asked after a moment.

Despite his best effort to remain stoic, Qasim began to smile. He did remember it, as clear as yesterday. How ridiculous they'd been. "I remember that you tried to cheat."

"True, but only after my lungs were on fire and my eyeballs felt like they were going to pop out of my head," Eshan said with a laugh. "I remember looking at you—cheeks puffed and pinching your nose—wondering if you were really holding your breath or just pretending to. That's when I realized that if I eased the pressure off one nostril just a little, I could breathe a tiny bit without you noticing."

"But I did notice."

"Eventually, but not until you were on the verge of passing out."

"Why did you cheat?" Qasim asked, suddenly feeling a little sad at the memory.

"Because I knew it was the only way I could beat you," Eshan said. "Why did you challenge me to a breath-holding competition in the first place?"

"I think it's obvious. You were better than me in everything we did. Running, wrestling, backgammon . . . so I started practicing holding my breath to build up my endurance so I could finally beat you at something." Qasim turned at last to look at his friend. "But, of course, you couldn't even give me that."

"What do you expect? We were eleven!"

"Well, thankfully, I found a procedural solution you couldn't cheat your way around. Remember?"

"Oh, I remember the bucket of water all right. And you got Saida to be the judge and timekeeper. Losing is bad enough, but losing in front of a girl . . ." Eshan shook his head. "That's the ultimate humiliation."

"Actually, losing in front of a girl *and* puking your guts out is the ultimate humiliation," Qasim said, finally allowing himself to laugh. "Even now, I still can't believe you vomited."

"I know! At least after that I had the good sense to stop, or who knows, I'd probably have given myself an aneurysm trying to beat your record."

"But in the end, it didn't matter, did it? You lost the challenge but got the girl anyway."

"Yeah, I suppose I did," Eshan said, his voice trailing off before adding, "I'm sorry I manipulated you, Qasim. It was not my intention."

"Yes, it was," he said, the levity draining from his voice.

"You're right, it was, but I didn't know what else to do . . . I couldn't stomach watching you hold your breath anymore."

Qasim cocked an eyebrow at Eshan. "What the hell are you talking about?"

Eshan let out a long, slow exhale. "I woke up one morning and I realized we were still playing that damn game. Ever since Saida died, we've been holding our breath—both of us. Chests on fire, brains silently screaming for oxygen . . . torturing ourselves for years. Then I met Aleena, and it was like I could finally breathe again. It felt so good, Qasim, so good to purge all the toxic ether I'd been holding inside and to inhale life again. That's why I came to see you in England. You're my best friend. You're my brother. I love you, Qasim, and I couldn't let you suffocate in silence any longer. So yes, I might have manipulated you by taking you to your family home. And by arranging for Diba to be there. And by introducing you to Hamza. But before you condemn me, answer me this—do you not feel alive? For the first time in years, do you not feel energized with purpose? Do you not feel wanted and valued and respected?"

Gooseflesh stood up on his arms as Eshan spoke. The

profundity of his friend's words touched the very core of his being. And yet . . .

"I thought Hamza was like us. I thought he and I were building a friendship," Qasim said. "But then I watched him have a man brutally murdered in front of me. And for what, not doing his job well enough? In England if I cock something up at work, I get sacked. If I screw up here, I get my throat slit! I don't want to work for terrorists, Eshan. More importantly, I don't want to be one."

"You need to stop," Eshan said, his words as hard and jolting as a gunshot.

"Stop what?"

"Stop using the rhetoric of the enemy. They call us terrorists, but I ask you, which organization is the one firing missiles at wedding receptions? Which one uses their drones to target civilians, and which one is targeting soldiers? They invaded our ancestral home. They built bases, imported their machines of war, and maintain an occupation force of thousands. We are not the terrorists, Qasim, they are!" Eshan took a deep breath and collected himself before continuing. "But it's not your fault. Your mind has been conditioned with their lies. Since our childhood, we have been bombarded with propaganda. I thought Hamza had explained all of this to you. We are not ISIS. We are not the Taliban. No. We are al Qadar. We are honorable Muslim soldiers, and we are at war."

"If the cause is so righteous, then why did Hamza have that man executed?"

"Because he was a traitor. For so long as there have been armies on this Earth, military commanders have executed traitors and spies in their ranks. They do this not for the joy of killing, but because they must. Spies and traitors must be dealt with swiftly and decisively, or their future actions will lead to loss of life on a grand and catastrophic scale. The Pakistani man you saw executed, Mohamed, had the potential to bring down the entire organization. If he had been followed, or if he had been wearing a wire or a tracker, the Americans would have been tipped off and you'd be dead right now."

"It's only a matter of time, isn't it?" Qasim murmured, his gaze going back out the window. "My fate was decided the minute I stepped into that warehouse and saw the drone. This is one decision I can never walk away from."

"That's where you're wrong," Eshan said. "Your fate was decided the minute an American drone pilot decided to squeeze the trigger on your sister's wedding night. Hamza is not your enemy. I am not your enemy. We are your brothers, Qasim . . . Someday, I hope you'll understand that."

CHAPTER 26

NORTH OF THE SWAT RIVER

KANJU, PAKISTAN

0140 LOCAL TIME

Chunk adjusted his helmet, headphones, and boom mike. Something seemed crooked and he couldn't get it to sit right. As he fidgeted with it, he felt Riker's eyes on him.

"How do I look?" he said, winking at the SEAL.

"A little chunky, but pretty," Riker said. Then with a reference to Morales, he added, "You're no Hollywood, but I'm sure there's plenty of dudes who would do you."

Morales shook his head and grinned, and Chunk laughed and shifted in his seat to look out the van's windshield at the darkened cityscape. Less than a day in-country, and Watts had already come through. Her lunch meeting with Theobald and his asset had yielded actionable intelligence. By that evening, Theobald had supplied them with the address of a possible al Qadar safe house near the river. Both he and Watts theorized this was the possible center of operations in Mingora because satellite imagery showed the house had a parabolic dish on the roof, but it could also simply be for television service. Was it a slam dunk? No. Did they have a location where the drone was being stored? No. But it was enough for Chunk, so he'd made the call and notified Bowman, who'd remained in Jalalabad, that they were going to hit the house. He was playing by big boy rules now. If the op was successful he'd get an, "Attaboy." But if things went bad, well . . . then he held the bag of shit. The downside risk was almost always bigger than the upside payoff in Special Operations. And that was doubly true in the Tier One.

As a white side SEAL, he'd had seven major deployments under his belt, and that didn't include multiple short-fuse, small-scale operations. He'd participated in hundreds and hundreds of Special Warfare operations—hell, maybe over a thousand by now—but he'd never once been so isolated from any support. Always, there was a QRF of Rangers or other operators, or conventional forces *somewhere* nearby. There was at least an MH-6 helicopter—if not a squadron of F/A-18s—a radio call away, ready to mete vengeance from above. They had eyes in the sky, AC-130 spooky gunships, as well as Predator and Reaper drones to watch their backs. Level two medical and surgical support and level one trauma assets were just a short hop away. And they had a high-speed TOC coordinating all of those assets. In the past, he'd always had someone, somewhere with the means and authority to bail him and his team out.

Not tonight.

Tonight, if the shit hit the fan, it was just them—and the DIA guy, Jackson, in the driver's seat of their shitty white-panel van. Their CASEVAC was a Beechcraft 1900 to Jalalabad. The Beech was sitting chocked on the tarmac at the airport. That bitch was no Blackhawk, and there was no one swooping in to extract their asses if things went bad. They had to get themselves and their gear to the airport. And if somebody got shot, their surgical support was Donnie Morales and his med kit.

He leaned forward, angling to talk to the DIA man in the driver's seat of the twelve-seat van—six of which held his teammates and their gear. Not a great vehicle for a high-speed getaway, but plenty of extra room for any crows they pulled off the X.

"How long you been in Mingora?" Chunk asked.

"Three months," Jackson answered.

"You know the roads? Can you get us to the airport without NAV support?"

"Yeah, man. I gotcha."

"Cool," Chunk said and settled back into his seat.

"Show you approaching Cadillac," Watts said softly in his ear.

"Check. Jackal is Cadillac," he said, resisting the urge to point out that usually the operator called the checkpoint, in this case the right-hand turn north onto Deolai Road. Maybe Watts was worried they would miss the turn. More likely she was just nervous. She was whip-smart and confident, but slow and rigid at adapting to the unfamiliar.

Once the residential development thinned out, the driver had killed the van's headlights. They crept north until they reached the target house. The front drive was flanked by two metal posts with a chain hanging between them, a minor impediment to accessing the dirt road beyond.

The driver slowed the van.

"Drive past and circle back," Chunk said.

"Jackal, we show no one on the access road. It's two hundred yards to the target, though, and plenty of hides, but we show no thermals on the approach. Two roving sentries are circling the building and two more are in a truck beside the front door on the east side."

He wanted to tell Watts to limit her comms to new and changing information, instead of reiterating status quo tactical data they knew from the last update. Instead of lecturing her, he double-clicked his mike. Their TOC for tonight's op was the hotel conference room. And since Yi was more proficient working the computers, that left radio communication and coordinating duties to Watts.

You go to war with the army you have . . .

He looked over his shoulder at his men, whose lives were in his hands. He reconsidered their opponent—a terrorist cell that had the smarts and wherewithal to procure, operate, and hide a Predator-class drone. This was not his father's terrorists they were up against, which meant he should expect modern, if not advanced, security countermeasures at this site. Night vision-capable security cameras, proximity motion sensors on the driveway and potentially scattered around the compound, maybe even a QRF standing by at a nearby location? Any of that was possible.

Decision made, he turned to the driver.

"We'll execute plan B. Take us to the dead end of the next road, slow and quiet. We'll drop and begin our infil. I want you to loiter until we call Jaguar. At that point, start a six-minute count, then crash the gate and drive to the front of the house. We'll load our crows and whatever gear we can pull of the X. From breach to exfil, I want ten minutes or less on-site."

Jackson nodded without a hint of nerves. Chunk felt pretty sure this guy was a former operator, and this was not his first rodeo.

Good.

"Mother, Jackal will execute Bravo on the infil. We'll call Jaguar. Call any changes or relevant information, but otherwise let's keep comms nice and quiet," he said, dropping the hint without ripping Whitney a new one for her propensity to chatter.

"Roger," came her reply.

Message received.

Minutes later Chunk led Riker and Edwards up a short rise in a V formation, while Spence, Morales, and Trip maneuvered north to approach the rear of the house. The terrorist safe house was a western, ranch-style design—made of cement blocks and painted bright yellow—in an otherwise drab landscape of smaller stucco homes clustered to the north. Saw peeled off from both groups to set up as overwatch, positioning himself between the two groups on a rocky elevation that looked directly on the house, enabling him to cover all but the south side of the property, where he would be obstructed by the house itself.

Chunk kept low in a combat crouch, scanning left and right over the rolling green-gray night-vision landscape. His boots crunched loudly through his Peltor headset, though he knew he was all but silent in the real world. He kept them weaving around rocks ranging from softball sized to boulders as big as a Volkswagen. Plenty of low cover up here in the hills.

They crested the rise and he dropped prone, hearing the amplified *thunk* of Riker and Edwards dropping in on either side of him.

"Jackal One is set," he whispered into his boom mike.

He scanned the flat, open area where the dirt road widened into a courtyard in front of the house. It looked just like Watts described—a blue pickup truck beside the main door, the occasional white glow of cigarettes belonging to the two fighters in the cab. He could see one of the two roving sentries at the rear corner of the house, forty-five degrees to his right, the other perhaps obstructed at the south rear corner. He watched as the man outside the truck paced toward them, scanned right up at them, then spun on a heel and shuffled toward the rear of the house.

"Five is now God," Saw said, reporting he was in position and set.

Chunk double-clicked his mike.

The activity at the target house was low, which was a good indicator the leadership inside was blissfully unaware of what was coming. At some point, there would be a changing of the watch and the men inside would be up to relieve the sentries outside. They had no historical data to predict when that would be, so their best bet was to hit soon, while half the security detail was asleep.

"Five, One—do you have a line on the truck out front?"

"Affirmative, One. I can get both tangos from here."

Chunk scanned again and nodded to himself. He'd noticed during load out that Saw had selected the semiautomatic M110 sniper rifle tonight over the bolt action M40. *Good foresight,* Chunk thought, *because I need him to drop both the assholes in the truck before either can sound an alarm.* Saw's range was good too, less than half of the eight-hundred-yard limit where accuracy dropped off.

"And the sentries?"

"I've got the north guy pacing back and forth, but I'm only getting short glimpses of the guy on the south side."

Chunk double-clicked.

"Jackal Two—in position," came the report from Spence to the north.

Chunk scratched his beard with his gloved hand, the moving lines in his head taking shape as the plan turned into an action.

"Two, One—close range as possible. God will take the guys in the truck, but I want you to take both walkers, and do it quiet. We'll breach through the front and you hold the rear and be ready for squirters."

Double click.

Chunk estimated he, Riker, and Edwards could make it to the front door in under fifteen seconds, maybe a few more seconds more to account for the rough terrain. He didn't want to lose the element of surprise before they breached the door. With the advanced suppressor on the M110, Saw's shot would be quiet, but the glass breaking in the truck's window would make some noise. Spence taking out the roving sentries would not be silent either.

"Two is set," Spence reported, indicating they'd repositioned.

"God, stand by. One is calling the shot." Chunk scanned the house one last time before giving the order. "Three . . . two . . . one . . . go."

He heard the dull thump of Saw's first shot and he was up, clearing as he rose, scanning left and right as his legs churned beneath him. He swept the green dot of his PEQ-4 IR target designator over the terrain, searching for enemies on the approach. A second thump reverberated less than two seconds after the first, and this time he heard the soft sound of Saw's round penetrating the tempered glass windshield.

"Jackal, God—two tangos in the truck are down."

Chunk descended the hill in the lead, with Edwards fanning right and Riker tight on his left. He heard two more rounds, this time fired from suppressed MK18s—Spence's squad killing the sentries—but the house stayed dark.

"One, Two—both tangos down," came the kill report from Spence as Chunk and his guys reached the front door. Chunk slid close behind Riker on the left side while Edwards pressed against the wall on the right. Riker pressed a small charge beside the door handle—only a few ounces of explosive. Chunk took a deep breath, pictured Saw on the long gun and Spence, Trip, and Morales fanned out and taking knees, focused on the rear exit for squirters. They were set.

He tapped Riker's left shoulder.

Riker fired the small charge, then kicked the door open, tossing a flash-bang grenade into the room and turning toward Chunk, eyes shut tight. A dull *whump* pulsed the night air, and the windows flashed with white light. Riker breached the door and moved left, with Chunk following tight behind and turning right. He cleared the empty corner behind him, then spun back to face front, aware of Edwards surging into the gap between him and Riker.

His brain instantly assessed the room and catalogued the contents:

Two long sofas facing each other with a coffee table between. A desk along the back wall, covered with multiple laptops charging. Simple round dining table in the corner. And three tangos . . .

As he silently advanced, the room's occupants—who had presumably been sleeping just before having their world rocked by a flash-bang—looked left and right in confusion, one man sitting up on each sofa, and one on hands and knees on the floor. Then, they all moved in unison. The man on the floor reached for an AK-47 leaning against the coffee table. The man closest to Chunk on the sofa dove for a rifle propped against the end table beside him, and the third man popped to his feet with a pistol in his hand.

Chunk fired twice in rapid succession, aware of matching, almost simultaneous fire from his teammates. Both would-be shooters crumpled. The man standing beside the sofa—who was dressed in business attire as opposed to a fighter—froze. He'd raised his pistol, but instead of sighting over it, he was looking at the red flower of blood growing on his chest, as if searching for something he'd lost. He looked up just as Edwards fired again, the second round tearing through the center of his closely trimmed bearded face. The man pitched forward, landing face down on the floor at Chunk's feet.

Chunk scanned the bodies for signs of life and finding none announced, "Clear."

"Clear," Edwards echoed.

Riker, who'd arced around the sofas, scanned over his rifle and advanced on a door that led into what appeared to be a bathroom.

"Clear," he confirmed a heartbeat later.

Chunk felt his shoulders drop, and only then did the burn in his neck and shoulder muscles register.

"Mother, Jackal is Jaguar," he reported. "Off the target in five."

"One, Uber," Jackson radioed in from the van. "Through the gate and to you in one mike or less."

"Check."

Chunk slung his rifle, pulled a tablet computer from his cargo pocket, and rolled the dead terrorist in dress slacks onto his back. He sighed with aggravation as he snapped a picture of the man's ruined face.

"Why do they always have to go for their guns? Stupid, stupid bastards," he murmured, positive that had they been able to take this dude alive, they would have been able to extract information of value.

Watts is not going to be happy with me, he thought as he photographed the other two tangos. *Looks like we did it to her again.*

"Facial recognition is unlikely from this mess," Edwards said, standing over the body of another man. "Sorry about that, bro. Want me to get a DNA sample?"

"Yeah," Chunk said, and Edwards quickly took a smear of blood onto a cloth, put it into a zip-lock bag, then grabbed samples from the other guys. Meanwhile, Riker swept phones and laptops into a cinch sack.

"Grab everything of potential value—notes, scraps of paper, anything Mother can use," Chunk said as he scanned the room for useful bounty. "Out of here in four minutes." Then he switched off vox, but keyed his mike. "Mother, One—I hate to be the bearer of bad news, but we got no crows for you. Just electronics. The target is definitely not a nerve center for operations like we'd hoped. Just a standard safe house. Looks like we're gonna need to keep digging."

CHAPTER 27

SERENA HOTEL
OFFICERS COLONY ROAD
MINGORA, PAKISTAN
0205 LOCAL TIME

Loud pounding on the door woke him.

Qasim sat up in bed, disoriented and unsure where he was.

"Qasim," a familiar voice shouted. "Qasim, wake up."

He glanced at the digital alarm clock on the nightstand, as his brain tried to claw its way out of the REM abyss he'd been swimming in. He remembered reclining on the bed, fully clothed, intending to relax before showering, but apparently he'd fallen asleep. The blurry green numbers on the clock came into focus: 02:05.

"Just a moment," he called.

"Hurry, Qasim, we have to go right now!"

The urgency in Hamza's voice sent a jolt of adrenaline through his veins. He swung his legs off the side of the bed and stumbled in the dark to the door. After fumbling with the latch, he got the door unlocked and opened. A pale-faced Hamza grabbed him by the upper arm.

"Did you bring anything with you? A bag, a computer, anything?" Hamza asked.

"No, nothing but my phone," Qasim said, "which is in my pocket."

"Okay, we're going," he said and jerked Qasim into the hallway.

"What's going on?" Qasim asked, jogging to keep up.

Hamza ignored the question and just kept striding toward the stairwell. He rapidly descended to the first floor and pushed his way out a side exit door, where a car sat idling at the curb with the rear driver's side door open. Hamza jumped into the back seat and Qasim followed, and the driver peeled away before he'd even gotten the door shut.

Qasim tried again. "What's happening?"

"We've been compromised. The Americans are here. They're coming for us."

"Is it because of Mohamed?"

"I don't know. But what I do know is that Mohamed knew the location of the hangar. Whatever he told ISI, we have to assume the Americans know, which means we have to get the drone in the air immediately." Hamza turned to look at him. "Are you ready?"

"Yes, of course. I completed all the preflights yesterday. The satellite link was good. Assuming our network incursion hasn't been detected we should be fine . . ."

Hamza nodded and glanced nervously over his shoulder out the rear window.

"Where's Eshan?" Qasim asked. "Shouldn't he be with you?"

"He's indisposed," Hamza said, then turned his attention to the driver. "Go faster."

The driver nodded and pressed the accelerator. He piloted them through the darkened streets of Mingora, then over Airport

Road Bridge across the Swat River, weaving at a lunatic pace east of the airport, around the airfield to the warehouse where the drone was housed. When they arrived, Qasim was surprised to see a flurry of activity. A large flatbed truck was backed up to the open hangar, while three other trucks were already loaded and idling. At the loading bay, men were winching the GCU onto the back of the truck. Qasim then noticed that the other three trucks appeared to have GCUs strapped to their beds already.

"You have multiple GCUs?" he asked, surprised.

"Yes, the other unit has been in storage. Contingency options and redundant resources are the two hallmarks of successful strategic planning."

"But I count four."

"Two are decoys. I had them made from shipping containers and modified to look like the actual thing," Hamza explained.

"So they're empty?"

"Not exactly." Hamza gave a grim smile and got out of the car. "Time to go. We're riding on the second truck in the primary GCU, the one you've been using."

"Hold on a second," Qasim said, but Hamza had already slammed the door. Qasim climbed out the other side and chased after him. "Wait," he said as he caught up. "How am I supposed to pilot the drone while the GCU is in transport? It needs power."

Then, as if the universe were answering his question, a diesel generator fired up on the idling truck. "Portable power," Hamza said. "Once loaded, you're looking at the world's first fully functional and truly *mobile* drone control unit."

"That's bloody brilliant," Qasim gasped in awe.

He trotted after Hamza and climbed onto the bed of the truck, where the workers had just finished securing the GCU and were now connecting the power cable. Hamza opened the door to the unit and gestured for Qasim to go inside.

"I have to direct traffic out here for a few more minutes, but then I'll be joining you. Take the pilot's seat. I ordered the drone pushed out on the runway while I was en route to pick you up. If it's not in position already, it will be any minute. As soon as it's ready, start the engine and get it into the air. Don't wait for me. You have full unrestricted authority over the drone."

Qasim stepped inside, nodded once, and said, "I understand."

Hamza slammed the door, and all the shouting and frantic commotion outside instantly disappeared, leaving him alone inside the sound-insulated command station. The air inside had grown warm and humid during the time the GCU had been offline, transitioning from grid to generator power, but cool air from the AC unit was just beginning to circulate. In their haste to relocate, whoever had disconnected it before loading had not performed a proper shutdown sequence, instead opting for simply tripping the master breaker. The GCU's battery backup—an Uninterrupted Power Supply rated for twenty minutes—had managed to weather the transition, and Qasim was elated to see that all systems were still online.

He slid into the pilot's chair and donned his headset. The Pterodactyl's chin-mounted FLIR camera system was streaming in night vision on the primary monitor, showing a long, unimpeded stretch of gray runway ahead. He flipped a switch to transfer camera control from the sensor operator chair to his station and rotated the gimbal-mounted camera in a slow, three-hundred-and-sixty-degree arc to make sure the drone was clear before starting the engine. As he swept through the port forward quadrant, he saw two figures standing side by side, looking at the camera. One of the men extended a thumbs-up at him. Qasim paused the pan momentarily in acknowledgment, then resumed the sweep until he was looking down the runway again.

He successfully started the drone's engine, quickly completed his preflight checklist, then did something he hadn't done in a very, very long time . . . He prayed.

Allah, I know you see all—past, present, and future—but I am just a man. I know you have a plan for me, and that taking my sister was somehow part of that plan, but it has been very difficult for me to accept this. You know I carry great pain, and you know that I have been lost in that pain for many years. Over these last few weeks, I have started to walk a new path and I don't know if it is the right one or not. All I ask of you now is that you give me the wisdom and courage to make the right choices, so that I might fulfill my destiny and make you proud. Please guide my hand and heart and know I am forever and always your faithful servant . . .

He exhaled, opened his eyes, and placed his hands on the pilot's controls.

The door to the GCU swung open and Hamza stepped in just as he engaged the throttle. Qasim did not turn to look, just kept his focus attuned to the task at hand. The video feed streaming from the drone started to shake as the UCAV accelerated. The runway soon blurred as the drone gained speed. At the same time, the pilot's seat jerked and wobbled as the truck carrying the GCU began its journey. The combination of the drone's *projected* movement and the truck's *actual* movement messed with his sensory proprioception, and for a moment he had the distinct impression that he was sitting in an actual aircraft taking off. He pulled back on the control stick and the Pterodactyl nosed up into the night sky.

"Good job, Qasim. Very, very good," Hamza said and clasped a hand on his right shoulder.

He nodded, checking the drone's flight dynamics instrumentation. "Five hundred meters and climbing . . ." Hamza settled into the sensor operator's chair beside him. Over the past few days, Qasim had been training him on all the GCU's systems and how to pilot and operate the drone. "Would you like to take her up the rest of the way?"

"Yes," Hamza said and placed his hands on the control stick and throttle in front of him.

Qasim flipped a switch that swapped flight control to the other chair and sensor operations to his. He watched as Hamza maintained the aggressive climb rate he'd been using until the drone gained the necessary altitude to safely clear the mountains for the transit over the Hindu Kush and into Afghanistan.

"Your next heading is two-eight-one," Qasim said, after checking the NAV screen.

"Change of plans," Hamza replied. "I want to keep the drone in Pakistani airspace. Find me a new valley in the Khyber."

"Why? We have satellite control now. We don't have to worry about line of sight anymore."

"I know," Hamza said. "But the Americans will think twice before entering Pakistani airspace to shoot down the drone. They do not own the skies like they do in Afghanistan. Loitering on this side of the border increases the drone's survival probability."

"Okay, give me a minute," Qasim said, scanning the topography. Eventually, he found a promising valley south of Ghochhar Sar mountain. He gave Hamza the new heading and watched him expertly steer the drone onto the new course.

"You seem to be a natural at this," he said as he watched Hamza fly.

"A good leader is capable of competently executing the tasks he delegates to others. How can I accurately assess your performance if I don't have the knowledge to do so?"

Sage words, Qasim thought.

"I don't want to crash into a mountain. What altitude do you recommend?

"The highest mountain in the Khyber is Tirich Mir, and it is seven thousand seven hundred and eight meters tall. We aren't going that far north, but I recommend taking the drone up to eight thousand meters, just to be safe until we reach the target valley," Qasim said as he entered a new waypoint on the nav screen.

Hamza nodded and maintained the ascent until the drone reached eight thousand meters, at which point he leveled off and said, "Okay, Qasim, you can take the controls back."

Qasim flipped the switch to swap the controlling station back to his chair, then engaged the autopilot, which would fly the drone to the waypoint. Once on station, Qasim would spiral the drone down to a radar-evading altitude in the valley and turn donuts in the sky until Hamza chose the target. Only then would they reposition the drone.

"Have you decided on a target?" he asked.

"Yes," Hamza said, getting to his feet. "We're going to hit Kandahar Air Base."

"Kandahar? But that's seven hundred kilometers away. Depending on how long we loiter, fuel could be an issue. Also, that is a lot of distance to cover without being detected."

"I know."

"Maybe our chances will be better if we target Jalalabad," Qasim said, confused by Hamza's selection. "It's very close to the border."

"No. Kandahar will be our next target, because Kandahar is the heart of the American and British drone operations for the entire region. A successful strike on Kandahar will cripple the Americans' capabilities. Also, this might very well be our last chance. After this sortie, the Americans will figure out how we're controlling the drone. They will put pressure on the Pakistani government, and they will start patrolling the skies for enemy drones. We've already lost the element of surprise. They're hunting us as we speak."

Dread washed over Qasim at this last statement. Now that the drone was airborne and the adrenaline of the escape had worn off, his brain began to contemplate the danger he was in. Like an annoying pop-up window in his mind, he suddenly understood just how tenuous his situation was. He was—or at least this GCU was—the Americans' primary target. Mobile or not, an American drone carrying Hellfire missiles might be locking on to them at this very moment.

"And Eshan?" Qasim asked. "Are we going to pick him up, or has he already disappeared into the night?"

Hamza sniffed once and fixed his gaze on Qasim. He said nothing for several long seconds, before pulling his mobile phone from a pocket and cuing up a video clip. He handed the phone to Qasim, a grave expression chiseled on his face.

"What is this?" Qasim said, taking the phone.

"Just watch."

Qasim pressed the triangle icon on the media player and a grainy grayscale video began to play. Qasim quickly deduced he was watching security camera footage recorded from a mount in the upper corner of a living room. The space was furnished with two long sofas, a desk, and a dining table with chairs. Three men were asleep in the room, one man on each sofa and a third on the floor. Nothing was happening . . . then the door on the opposite wall was blown off its hinges. Something arced into the room and a brilliant flash of light washed out the picture. After a second, the feed refreshed and Qasim watched in horror as three operators, dressed in tactical gear and wielding assault rifles, entered. The three men who had been sleeping were up now. Two of them scrambled for AK-47s, while the third man—who Qasim now recognized as Eshan—reached for a pistol. The infiltrators opened fire, with each shooter using an identical pattern: two rounds center mass, followed by a single round to the head. Qasim watched Eshan get shot in the chest and look down, almost in surprise. Then the back of his head exploded. He collapsed face first onto the floor and did not move again. In less than four seconds, it was over and the operators advanced out of frame.

A lump formed in his throat, and he felt like he'd just been punched in the stomach.

"I'm sorry, Qasim," Hamza said.

"Was that . . . was that Eshan?" he asked despite knowing the answer.

"Yes. The Americans hit the safe house less than one hour ago. I would have been there, except I had decided to . . . it does not matter. Allah intervened to change my path tonight, just as he did for you," Hamza said.

A crushing weight descended on Qasim, and he was suddenly finding it extremely difficult to breathe. "I . . . I . . . can't breathe."

"You're hyperventilating," Hamza said. "Put your head between your knees and try to slow your breathing."

Qasim swiveled the pilot chair ninety degrees and did as Hamza instructed. Panic morphed into fury as he slowly recovered from the shock of what he'd just watched. Then, he felt Eshan's ghost and heard his best friend's parting words in his head:

"Your fate was decided the minute an American drone pilot decided to squeeze the trigger on your sister's wedding night. Hamza is not your enemy. I am not your enemy. We are your brothers, Qasim . . . Someday, I hope you'll understand that."

A dark switch flipped inside him.

Why had it taken him losing everything before he finally accepted his fate?

Because I am a fool.

"I'm going to kill them," he seethed. "I'm going to burn the flesh from their bones for this."

He felt a hand come to rest on his back as he stared at the floor, consumed with rage.

"Allah will see it done, my brother," Hamza said, his voice as flat, cold, and self-assured as Qasim had ever heard it. "And we're going to do it together."

CHAPTER 28

IMPROVISED TOC

RELAX HILTON PALACE HOTEL

MINGORA, PAKISTAN

0220 LOCAL TIME

Whitney sat on the edge of the bed, pulled her headset off, then collapsed on the mattress. "I don't know about this," she murmured, looking up at the ceiling.

"You don't know about what?" Yi said.

"This," Whitney said, waving her arms in an all-encompassing gesture.

"You mean this hotel?"

"No," she said with a laugh. "I mean deploying with the unit, being Mother on this op. Maybe I made a mistake joining the Tier One. I'm an analyst. I'm good at analyzing stuff, not calling the play-by-play in some makeshift Tactical Operations Center. This job has me dead."

"What are you talking about?" Yi said, collapsing on the bed beside her in solidarity. "You did amazing."

"No, I didn't. The second I open my mouth, Chunk gets irritated. I don't even have to see his face—I can tell from the sound of his voice. I think you should be the radio talker from now on. I'll be your support."

"You have to understand, when these guys are on the X, if they could execute the mission with only hand signals and telepathy, they would. They don't want to hear opinions or concerns or questions from us. They only want what they need," Yi said.

"What does that mean—they only want what they need?"

"Imagine you're a race car driver, and you're driving two hundred miles an hour around some twisty track. If you lose concentration or get distracted and take your eyes off the road for even a millisecond, you're guaranteed to crash and die. That's what it's like for them. They're like race car drivers. They don't want some Chatty Cathy in the passenger seat talking about stuff they can plainly see with their own two eyes, and they don't want a backseat driver telling them how to drive the car. All they want is pertinent information—information which they *don't* have access to—conveyed in a timely and succinct manner."

Whitney nodded. "Like when the pit boss radios his driver to warn him about a crash that's unfolding around the next bend."

"Exactly," Yi said with a smile.

"Yeah, makes sense, and deep down I knew that. There's just so much dead time on the line. It's nerve-wracking, and I feel compelled to fill the void."

"I know, I hate it too."

"And I suppose I wanted Chunk and the guys to know that they're not alone out there, that I have their back, and that we're watching out for them. You know what I'm saying?"

"Of course I do," Yi said. "And I promise there's a part of Chunk—specifically the part that will never verbalize it—that knows that and appreciates that."

"I don't know."

"Think about it. Why else would he drag us to Pakistan, insist on setting up this barely functional TOC, and have you play Mother if he didn't trust and value you? Look Whitney, with these guys, actions speak louder than words. They're all the same. This is exactly what it was like for me at Team Two. Trust me, Chunk wants you on his team. If he didn't, you wouldn't be here. The day he stops giving you shit—that's the day you should start to worry."

"Thanks. I needed that."

"Of course. That's what teammates are for," Yi said, then added a wry, "ma'am."

Whitney grimaced and was readying her retort when the sat phone buzzed. She popped to her feet and scrambled to get it from the desk. "Watts," she answered while bending at the waist to fend off a bout of light-headedness from standing too quickly.

"Hey, it's Lieutenant Commander Day," said a baritone voice. "Sorry to hit you up so late, but I thought you guys would want this ASAP."

"Yes, sir. I'm all ears," she said, looking wide-eyed at Yi.

"NSA deconflicted a gazillion transmissions, and believe it or not, they got a hit in Mingora that matches the criteria you gave us."

"Are you serious?" she said, a kaleidoscope of butterflies taking wing in her stomach. She wasn't sure whether she hoped this would confirm they'd indeed hit the right target, or if it could give them a new target.

"Dead serious," he came back. "You ready for the coordinates?"

"Yes . . . go," she said, grabbing a pencil and flipping to an open page in a notebook. She scribbled the latitude and longitude down, while repeating the digits aloud in confirmation. Yi entered the coordinates into the mapping application on her tablet.

"I did a search for satellite footage recorded during the transmission period, but unfortunately American eyes were fully tasked and committed to other locations at the time," he said, preempting her next question.

"Damn," she grumbled. "What about now? The team is in the field as we speak. Can you get me real-time coverage?"

"Sorry, Watts. I checked on that too. Everything is committed."

Yi held up the tablet to show her the new coordinates on a satellite map of Mingora.

"That's right on the airport property," Whitney said, looking at the green dot just north of the single runway nestled at the foothills of the mountain. "That's, like, three miles from where Chunk is." She looked over the tablet at Yi. "Call up Kandahar and see if the drone we just released has enough fuel to come back and support another op tonight."

"Roger," Yi said, slipping her headset back on.

"Thank you, Commander," Whitney said, gearing up emotionally for what she knew needed to happen next. "I owe you one."

"No worries," Day said. "I'll just put it on your tab." She could practically hear the grin on his face. "Good hunting. Everybody back here in N2 is pulling for you guys."

She ended the call and traded her sat phone for her radio and headset. With a deep breath, she called Chunk. "Jackal, this is Mother. Do you copy?"

"Go for Jackal," the SEAL Commander's voice came back a few seconds later.

"If you're not too tired, looks like we might have one more errand for you," she said, making eye contact with Yi, who nodded.

"We've got less than three hours until sunrise," he said, with a measure of strain in his voice. "What exactly did you have in mind, Mother?"

"A second location of interest," she said, trying to keep the pride out of her voice. "It's on the airport and only a couple of miles from your present location. High degree of confidence we found the control station for the drone."

"Based on what?'

"SIGINT collection. Commander Day has had NSA crunching signals for us and they got a qualifying hit in the target frequency band."

"Well, hot damn, Heels," Chunk said, fire returning to his voice. "Are they transmitting now or is this based on historical data?"

"The latter. I don't have real-time collection going, but NSA found a transmitter broadcasting during the window of opportunity." Then, balling her right hand into a fist, she said, "This is it, Chunk. We've got them dead to rights this time. I can feel it."

"Good work, Mother," he came back, with what definitely sounded like respect in his voice. "Coordinates received. We're on our way."

CHAPTER 29

"We need to strike them now," Qasim said, glaring at Hamza. "Let me use the drone to kill the Americans who hit the safe house."

"They're already gone, Qasim," Hamza said, shaking his head. "This raid was an unsanctioned operation on Pakistani soil. They did not ask for permission, nor did they bother to inform the Pakistani government. The American operators won't take any chances of being discovered. Quick. In and out. That's how it goes."

"And how do you know all of this?" Qasim asked.

"I have connections within the Pakistani and tribal governments, as well as informants inside the Pakistani National Police," he said to Qasim's surprise. Revealing this information now said much about the relationship they had built over the past weeks. "I would have been notified if it had been sanctioned."

"Then let's reposition and hit the primary target. The Americans are looking for us as we speak. We need to act before they find us or shoot down the drone."

"Sunrise is in two hours. Kandahar is over seven hundred kilometers away, which means we can't make it in time. Our greatest probability for success is to reposition the drone and loiter until after sundown so we strike during the cover of darkness."

"That gives them twelve hours to find us," Qasim argued.

"They don't even know what they're looking for. From the sky the GCU looks like a CONEX box. And thanks to the autopilot subroutine you wrote, we're not transmitting. So long as we stay dark for the next twelve hours, they'll have no signals intelligence to exploit. The other trucks are diverging, each going in a different direction. Even if the Americans were watching when we evacuated the warehouse, they only have a twenty-five percent chance of picking the right truck. You might have noticed I didn't split the convoy until after you put the drone on autopilot and we stopped transmitting."

Qasim *had* noticed, and somewhere in his mind he understood that Hamza's plan made sense, but he was just so damn angry. He wanted vengeance and he wanted it now. Then, as if his fury had somehow beamed itself into Hamza's mind, he watched the terrorist's expression harden.

"But there is something we *can* do," Hamza said, his voice a low growl. "I was so focused on fleeing and salvaging the operation that I did not think of it until this moment."

He pulled a mobile phone from his pocket, a different mobile phone from the one Qasim had seen him use before. He dialed, greeted the caller in Arabic, then conducted the remainder of the conversation in Pashto. "*As-salāmu ʿalaykum*, Abdul . . . No, things are not well. The Americans just hit my safe house in Mingora . . . I was not there when it happened . . . No, I vacated the other facility with the hardware intact . . . That is correct . . . I believe it is the same group who hit the mountain compound . . . One of my informants reported that a group of Americans checked in at the Relax Hilton Palace Hotel . . . Operator types, which tells me it is a very high probability it was them . . . Yes . . . Go with God, my brother. May he grant you courage and victory." Hamza ended the call and looked at Qasim. "It is done. You may get your vengeance yet, Qasim."

"What is done?"

"Our Taliban brothers in Mingora are going to strike the Americans at their hotel. Thirty Taliban fighters died when the Americans hit the cave stronghold our remote pilot team operated from. Taliban leadership was very angry about this devastating loss and blamed me. Abdul argued on my behalf and prevented a schism between our organizations. He understands the big picture."

"Does Abdul know our next target?"

Hamza nodded. "Yes. In fact, I will tell you a secret—a strategy you would do well to remember as you rise. To appease Taliban leadership and preserve the relationship, I let them select the next drone target."

"The Taliban chose Kandahar?"

"Kandahar has always been my ultimate target, but they didn't know this. I put the notion in Abdul's head many months ago, but during the negotiations I let him take absolute credit for the idea. He championed the selection and fought to convince the others. All I had to do was say yes."

"I do not have a strategic mind like yours," Qasim said, turning away to look at the primary monitor on the drone pilot's station. "Aerodynamics, avionics, computer programming—these are things my mind understands. Relationships have never been my strength . . . that was Eshan's specialty." A wave of fresh angst roiled his guts. The security camera footage of Eshan being shot in the face played unbidden in his mind—a waking nightmare that he couldn't turn off. "I can't believe Eshan is gone. Gone! First my father and sister, and now my best friend . . . all murdered by the Americans."

"I am very sorry about Eshan," Hamza said, laying a hand on his shoulder. "I know my words are no conciliation now, but his death has hit me very hard as well . . . in more ways than you realize."

"How long have you known him?"

"We met two years ago, in Lahore. Quite by accident, I thought, but now I understand it was destiny. I was lost at the time, and it was Eshan who encouraged me to pursue my true calling."

Qasim's heart skipped a beat, and he slowly turned to look at the other man.

"You thought it was the other way around, did you? That I had recruited Eshan," Hamza said with a chuckle. "No, Qasim. Eshan was managing money and fundraising for the Taliban when we formed al Qadar."

"We?" The word escaped his lips like a dying breath.

"I know it is upsetting that he kept this from you, but al Qadar was his vision. We built it together, as partners."

"Partners? No, no, no . . . that can't be."

"It's true, Qasim."

"I don't understand. He told me you were the leader. He took direction from you."

"Quite a convincing illusion we maintained, don't you think?" When Qasim couldn't find the words to answer, he continued. "It was all by design, and only because Eshan put the cause before his own ego. For him, it was never about power or titles or ruling other men. It was always and only about the mission, about changing the status quo . . . about changing the world. This is the agreement we had, and it took incredible trust on his part."

"You mean nobody in al Qadar knows he was the founder?"

"Cofounder," Hamza said with a smile. "And no, the rank and file had no idea that the true visionary behind our movement was hiding in plain sight. It was my job to inspire and lead operations—that is my strength. It was his job to build the global infrastructure, recruit talent, and fund our mission. You didn't really think he was an investment banker, did you?"

"I always took what he said at face value," Qasim said, his gaze going to the middle distance. "I trusted him completely, that's what best friends do . . ."

Hamza looked at him, his gaze earnest. "Eshan told me that you would someday be the third partner in our movement. He said that I needed to be patient with you, that you were a man of great intellect and inner strength, but you did not recognize those things in yourself. He also said you were living a life of denial. 'Trapped in a hall of mirrors,' I believe were his exact words. But that the day was coming when you would break those mirrors and escape the torture chamber you'd built for yourself, and I needed to be ready to embrace you with open arms. Well, Qasim, that is today."

Qasim wasn't sure how long he sat in silence, contemplating the other man's words. He felt decoupled from time as he processed the revelations that had just turned his entire life upside down. All of their interactions since Eshan had appeared on his doorstep in London played back like scenes of a movie. With the context of hindsight, the clues were there—he'd just missed them. Eshan's knowledge of his work at British Aero, the fake passport he carried, the way he managed the border crossing, the Taliban lieutenants at his wedding, the way he came and went freely from the warehouse like he had special privilege, and on and on . . . Hamza was telling the truth. Eshan had been a visionary and a chameleon, and he'd known Qasim better than Qasim had known himself. And now he was gone . . . another son lost in a war of ideologies that would never end.

He refocused his gaze to a backpack resting on the floor between the seats and nudged it with the toe of his boot. "Maybe it's time we do something more productive than talk about my feelings."

"What did you have in mind?" Hamza said with a hopeful smile.

"How about coming up with a backup method for controlling the drone should the Americans force us to abandon this GCU before the drone is on target?"

CHAPTER 30

Chunk tapped his boot on the bare metal floor of the van, waiting.

They needed eyes in the sky for this op. No way he was going in blind on a target facility occupied by an enemy that, in all probability, knew they were coming. The drone they'd had on station for the safe-house hit had been released and was flying back to Kandahar when Watts had called the new hit on the airport warehouse. He wasn't hitting anything until they got it back. He might be crazy, but he wasn't stupid.

Outside, under a moonless sky, Riker, Saw, Edwards, and Spence set up a four-corner perimeter on the van. Again, he wasn't taking any chances.

Morales paced back in forth in the aisle between the double

seats, his rifle in a combat carry on his chest. They locked eyes, both deadly serious.

"You good, bro?"

Morales shot him his signature white-toothed smile. "Easy day, boss."

Chunk nodded, tapping the trigger guard of his assault rifle. He was itching for real-time intel. They might be the best damn operators in the world, but seven of the best SEALs still didn't stand a chance against a terrorist army who knew they were coming. Just when he couldn't stand it anymore and was about to press Watts for an update, his headset crackled to life.

"I've got eyes back, Jackal," Watts said.

Thank God.

"Roger that, Mother," he said.

"Stand by, One . . ." After a long pause, Yi gave the SITREP, "We show two pickup trucks in the north lot of the hangar, flanking the single entry door about twenty feet apart. Four tangos—two in each cab. One more beside that single door on the north side. Hangar doors are halfway open to the south, facing the runway. No tangos outside the south of the hangar. Thermals show at least seven in the structure, appear to be working, packing stuff up, we think. Large truck with its motor running, based on the heat signature. Roof is clear. No obvious organized QRF anywhere on the perimeter of the airport, but there are dozens of houses in the vicinity—especially north—with multiple heat signatures in each. They're probably all civilians, but any could be tangos in a secondary safe house."

Chunk closed his eyes and pored over the mental picture she'd just built for him. At least twelve bad guys on-site, multiple vehicles, and a possible quick reaction force nearby. They had no air support, but their Beech 1900 was at least fueled, preflighted, and ready to get them the hell out of Pakistan, if need be. To operate in such close proximity to the airport, though, probably meant these guys had inside support. The airport was technically closed until zero-six-hundred, but that didn't guarantee anything. If these assholes had eyes in the tower or other buildings, the SEALs would be blown before they were on target. Still, the assault was doable, and a plan formulated in his head.

"Two, One," he said, calling Spence. "Pull it in. I got a plan."

He briefed the hit inside the van. After taking questions and input from the team, Chunk modified the plan accordingly and they were ready to roll. The van dropped off Chunk's element first, then took Saw and the DIA guy, Jackson, who would serve as a spotter, to a high spot Mother had selected across from the airfield. The second DIA man, McAllister, would stay in the van, keeping the engine running, ready to exfil them on a moment's notice.

Chunk and his team vectored north, around the approach end of the east-to-west runway. Upon reaching the fence line, he took a knee while Edwards cut quickly through the woven wire. The runway lights were off at present, and he didn't expect them on until a half hour before the airport opened for business. Even so, the ambient light level was higher than he would have liked, compliments of that amorphous background luminosity that went hand in hand with development. Big cities, he knew, slept with one eye open.

"We've got you in real time, Jackal," Watts said, taking the lead back. Since she'd put this together on the fly, they'd not briefed checkpoints to call. "No change—five tangos outside the hangar to the north, four shooters still in two trucks, and one guy beside the door smoking. Seven tangos working inside. No driver in the truck, so they're not leaving yet."

He double-clicked.

Edwards completed cutting the hole, pushed through the

fence, then held up the section he'd cut to allow his teammates through. Chunk followed Riker, who was right behind Morales. He felt Trip's hand on his shoulder, and Spence brought up the rear.

Saw would be in position any minute.

They fanned out into a V, with Riker in the lead, advancing in combat crouches. They moved low and quick, scanning through NVGs as they glided over flat terrain. Chunk felt the familiar burn in his thighs as he quick-stepped, leaning forward into his rifle, the buttstock tight on his right shoulder. Over the years he'd come to crave the burn as a prequel to the action, and it excited anticipation rather than pain.

"Jackal—Five is God," Saw called in his ear.

They passed the runway and headed directly toward the east side of the hangar, moving quickly now in a modified, crouched sprint. The crunch of booted feet was amplified in his ears, as was his own heavy breathing. Fifty yards from the hangar, he chopped his left hand toward a point in the wide corrugated-metal wall that was devoid of windows and doors. He took the lead with Riker, Edwards, and Spence, as Morales and Trip peeled off right. Seconds later, his back was pressed against the outside wall of the hangar, three SEALs beside him and two others seventy feet away, on the northern corner.

"Jackal—hold," Watts called just as he peered around the corner.

He pulled his head back before he could get a good look and waited for her to explain.

"Jackal, a tango just stepped outside the hangar on the north side to have a smoke, I think." Her voice was soft and calm—soothing even. "He's looking at the airfield."

For this op, she was bringing her A game. Apparently, Yi's coaching was starting to rub off.

Hooyah, girl.

"No movement on the south side," she continued. "Wait . . . a second guy just stepped out on the north side. He's talking to the smoking guy . . . Stand by. . . . Okay, tango two just went back inside."

He looked down the line at his SEALs, all on one knee, scanning in different directions along the wall.

"God has a line on all five tangos south side," Saw said in his ear. "What a bunch of dumbasses these guys are."

Chunk double-clicked.

"Shit," Watts said in his ear, tension up a notch, but still in control. "Jackal One, the tango outside of the hangar door is on the move. Still smoking, but definitely heading your direction . . . He's one meter offset from the wall, four meters from the corner."

Riker started to rise beside him, but Chunk held up a fist and the SEAL dropped back on a knee.

"Two meters."

Chunk tipped up his NVGs and eased the rifle onto his chest until it hung by its sling, then silently pulled a SOG bowie knife from its well-oiled sheath. He raised his left hand beside the knife hand, spreading his fingers wide.

"One meter," Watts reported. "He's armed. Looks like an AK-47."

Chunk tensed, his body becoming a coiled spring.

"He's at the corner. He just stopped . . ."

Chunk pressed up onto the balls of his feet, ready to launch himself into an attack. An orange pinprick tumbled in space as a flicked cigarette butt whizzed by in the darkness.

"He's going for his zipper. Oh shit, I think he's gonna take a piss."

Chunk entered a state of hyperawareness he always did the instant before a kill. He heard a raspy exhale, the shuffle of fabric, and the uncinching of zipper tines. The miasma of body odor, cigarette smoke, and stale curry wafted around the corner. Then a booted foot appeared.

Before the man registered what was happening, all the energy stored in Chunk's muscles exploded into a kinetic firestorm of precision aggression. His left hand clamped onto the man's windpipe. A barely audible "ehhh" was the only sound as he pulled the sentry around the corner by the throat, then drove his blade up through the man's neck, just below his chin. He pulled the stunned fighter onto his stomach and, with brutal force, slammed his right knee onto the man's neck, pinning him. With the speed and precision of a lightning strike, he drove the point of his knife through the man's temple. Bone fractured with a sickening crunch. He twisted the blade a quarter turn, finishing the kill strike, then withdrew the knife. He felt the terrorist shudder beneath him in an involuntary spasm as he cleaned and sheathed the bowie. The stench of urine filled the air as Chunk dragged the corpse around the corner and out of sight.

"You're clear, Jackal," came Watts's relieved voice in his headset.

"One, God—I have a line on tango two and a good angle on the dudes in the truck to the west," Saw reported.

"God, One—take them," Chunk said, dropping his NVGs back into place and giving Saw the green light to kick this thing off.

A double click came back, and it started a heartbeat later.

He didn't hear the first shot, but he heard commotion from behind the building and assumed Saw had just dropped tango two by the door.

"Sentry down," came Saw's whisper.

Chunk heard two cracks, like glass breaking on cement.

"Two more down in the truck."

Chunk raised a hand, then chopped it forward, and the three SEALs in his fire team fanned out behind him as he moved. Despite no audible call, he knew that Morales and Trip were rounding their corner, primed to engage the sentries in the second enemy truck on the other side of the building.

"Six, I got no line on your tangos," Saw reported.

Trip would be setting a breacher charge on the door now, leaving Morales to engage the sentries in the pickup on his own. Chunk felt Riker move behind him, shifting southwest, getting his own line on the inside of the hangar through the open door. Spence stepped up beside him, taking a knee.

"God, Six—last tango down." Morales's voice was a firm whisper.

"Nine is set."

Nine was Trip, who had the breacher charge set on the door. Chunk couldn't see the door from his angle, but he saw two enemy shooters run past the hangar door, rifles at the ready.

"Now, Nine. Blow it . . ." he called out and rose from his knee, surging forward as the explosion from the breacher charge rocked the night. White light exploded from the hangar doors, followed a microsecond later by two soft *whumps* from flash-bang grenades tossed by Riker and Edwards.

"Hold outside, Six and Nine," Spence called.

Spence was right, Chunk realized, holding Morales and Trip to cover anyone trying to exit south, without risking walking into heavy fire in the process. Chunk and his fire team would take care of that, turning the hangar into a kill box when they entered from the north.

Two enemy shooters fled out the wide open hangar door, where Chunk was still holding. Both tangos broke left, and once they crossed the threshold, he fired at the lead runner. The man crumpled to the ground in a heap, and the other terrorist stumbled over him. Riker's 5.56 round took the second insurgent in the chest before the man hit the ground.

"Two more down," Chunk called.

At least five more inside.

He was at the edge of the open hangar door now, and the air exploded with the sound of rifle fire. He dropped low—knowing AK-47 rounds would easily penetrate the hangar door. The terrorists were confused, shooting in all directions.

"They're firing through the walls," Morales reported.

Chunk surged forward as Yi fed him a tactical picture in his ear.

"Three thermal images in a line at the north side, firing through the wall. One to your right by the truck and one in the northwest corner, maybe in an office."

He flicked up his NVGs as he entered the hangar, breaking left and clearing the corner. A man was climbing into the truck and Riker grabbed him, pulling him hard to the concrete floor. Chunk's corner was clear, so he took two giant strides to Riker, kicked the side of the terrorist's head, and heard a crack. *Shit, too hard.* He took a knee beside the dying man and put the red dot of his holosight on the side of the bearded fighter's head. He exhaled and squeezed, killing the man dead beside the truck. Three bursts of fire from his right, and the other two men fell. Chunk was up and moving a heartbeat later, Riker matching him step for step. He was aware of another shot from behind him and to the right—the ever cautious Spence seeing movement from the three terrorists on the ground, no doubt.

A large CONEX box sat in the northwest corner of the hangar, where Mother had called a lone thermal image. He shifted left as Riker moved opposite, flanking either side of the unlit shipping container facing them with its double access doors wide open. Muzzle flashes inside the container lit up the dark void as somebody inside fired at them. Chunk dodged left, slipping outside the line of fire, as Riker moved in mirror image to his right.

"*Wadareja!*" Chunk commanded, keeping clear of the opening of the box. "*Wadareja ka ne daz kawam!*"

The gunfire stopped, and Chunk leveled his weapon at the opening, then nodded to Riker.

Chunk stepped out as Riker rounded the edge of the box, sighting over his rifle into the void. Then, he froze. "Bomb! Bomb! Everyone down!" he shouted and dove at Chunk, arms out like a linebacker making a flying tackle.

The instant Riker slammed into Chunk, he wrapped his arms around Chunk's waist and drove him to the ground. Chunk landed flat on his back, clutching his rifle, his helmet hitting the cement hard enough to make stars in his vision. The entire world became light. Then heat. The concussion hit them, and a pressure wave sucked the air from his lungs as he felt himself skidding across the cement floor, Riker riding him like a wakeboard. He couldn't hear anything, but somehow sensed the debris impacting around him, shrapnel from the metal box likely mixed with bone and body parts from the suicide bomber inside.

Then everything went dark.

And quiet.

He shook his head to clear it and felt Riker struggling to get off him.

Riker's alive. Thank God, he's alive.

He squeezed his eyes shut and opened them again. He could see the shadow of his teammate over him gel into a blurry image. He blinked again, and the face was clear. Blood trickled down Riker's cheek in a little stream, bending past his nose and disappearing into his beard.

"You okay?" Riker asked. "Chunk, are you okay?"

The question was muffled, but he heard it. "I think so," he said, his own voice much, much clearer. He ran his hands over his face and neck, then his body, patting and feeling all his pieces and parts. Finding himself intact, he smiled and struggled to his knees. "I'm good, dude. You?"

Riker blinked twice, eyes wide after each. Then he laughed manically. "Holy shit, the streak lives on. I thought this time I was fucking dead for sure," he said, then tilted his head back and howled.

"Dude, your mama must have dipped your naked redneck ass in the River Styx as a baby," Chunk said, wrapping his best friend and teammate in a bear hug. "I don't know how you do it."

"I'm indestructible, yo. Accept it."

"Jackal, it's me . . . I mean this is Mother! SITREP? What the hell just happened?" Watts said, her voice tight with fear.

Saw broke in over top of her, "Jackal One, God—is everyone okay?"

"Jackal—sound off," Chunk said as he clasped Riker's outstretched hand and let the SEAL pull him to his feet. "One."

"Two."

"Three," Riker said, wiping blood from a laceration on his cheek.

"Four."

"Five is God."

"Six."

"Nine. Oh shit, dude. How are we all alive?"

With his wits back, Chunk brought his rifle up and started a sweep. An enormous hole gaped in the side of the CONEX box where there had once been solid corrugated steel. Deformed metal shards curled out like flower petals from the black iris where the blast energy had been most concentrated. Had he been standing a few paces back, he would be part of the black streak on the cement. The box had vomited out fire, smoke, and other things, leaving a charcoal afterimage on the ground. Chunk's gaze followed the blast line to the far side of the hangar, where half of a desk was embedded in the hangar wall, suspended fifteen feet off the ground. Had they been in front of the box . . .

God loves operators and the very stupid, often at the exact same time.

He chuckled, then stopped himself before the laugh became hysterical.

"Mother, Jackal is all good," he said, finally answering Whitney's question as he swept his gaze across the dead bodies strewn about. "But you're gonna be mad, 'cause we got nothing again but a bunch of dead crows and some blown-up electronics."

"Thank God," Watts breathed in his ear.

"Six and Nine—hold security to the north," he said. The tinny, muffled echo in his voice was already ebbing a bit. "Three and Four, security to the south. One and Two will inventory and collect what we can quickly, then we move out. Uber, this is Jackal One . . ."

"Go for Uber," came McAllister in his ear, relief evident even over the radio.

"Uber, we made a hole in the fence where you dropped us. Breach the fence and drive right up to the south side of the hangar for pickup. Off the X in four mikes. We'll exfil the same way, then pick up Five and Uber Two."

"Roger, One. Uber is on the move."

"Mother, One—watch our perimeter. You see any thermals moving our direction, any at all, you call out."

"Roger, One," Yi came back.

No MH-6 with a Minigun to beat back an enemy QRF. No white side 75th Rangers to ride in and clear our six. No calvary to the rescue if things suddenly go to hell . . .

They desperately needed to vacate the premises, but heading back to the hotel was something he needed to think through carefully. They'd made a shit show of this hangar, and Chunk was wary of risking a trace back to Theobald. If they blew the NOC, it would force DIA to fold their operation.

Probably best to have Yi and Watts grab the rest of the gear and meet us at the Beech 1900, he thought. *I'm getting ahead of myself. After we're off the X . . .*

He followed Spence into the black hole in the side of the wrecked CONEX box, clicking on the rarely used white light on the side of his rifle, scanning the chaos. His boot stepped on something soft, and he shined the light down, seeing a hand still wrapped around a detonator button under his toes. The hand ended in a stump just above the wrist.

"Oh, that's fucking nasty," Spence said.

Chunk was about to make a joke, thinking his junior officer was talking about the bloody hand, but then followed Spence's cone of light to the corner. Three-quarters of a head and bearded face stared back at them with empty eye sockets.

"Shit," he breathed and suddenly felt claustrophobic, wondering what other gore they were gonna stumble upon. This was almost as bad as slipping into shark-infested waters.

He moved his light around the floor, looking for anything of value. The back wall of the CONEX box looked like it had been a workstation of some sort, and he could see fragments of computers and monitors on the floor. Spence took a knee and dug a charred hard drive out of what was left of a computer tower. Chunk passed his light over something black with a flash of red.

"Bingo, dude," he said, bending to pick up the item.

"Whatcha got, boss?" Spence said, pocketing the hard drive.

"Look at this shit," Chunk said, holding up an aviation joystick. "Looks like it came out of an F/A-18."

"Must be how they were flying the drone," Spence said, then backed up and pointed to the top of the CONEX, where a small parabolic dish was bolted to the bulging hump of roof. "That looks like a radio dish up there. Watts was right, bro. This CONEX was their command-and-control unit."

"See what other electronics you can grab," Chunk said, scanning the rest of the hangar, not seeing any salvageable gear, but plenty of body parts. He stepped over what looked like a thigh, complete with an intact knee.

"You wanna grab some DNA, Chunk?" Spence asked, reading his mind.

"Yeah, I guess," he said. "There's no shortage of DNA around to grab."

"Jackal, Mother—Uber is coming through the fence. Two minutes. Be ready to bug out."

"Check," he said. "Three, One—get pics for facial rec of all the dead shitheads in the hangar. And take a picture of that parabolic on top of the CONEX."

"Check boss."

"Six, One—get pics of the five dead crows outside," he said.

"Already done," came the reply.

Chunk checked his watch, then headed toward the hangar doors. "Jackal—rally on the runway side by the hangar doors. Exfil in thirty seconds."

Double clicks echoed in his Peltors as he held the joystick up for another look. "Mother, Jackal—good call on the hangar. Looks like you were right. They had a CONEX box set up with a computer, a radio, antenna dish, and flight control joystick. This hangar appears to be the drone operations center."

Spence fell in behind him as he exited the hangar. In the corner of his eye, Morales and Trip appeared around the corner, both scanning over their rifles in a combat crouch. And ahead on the hangar skirt, Edwards and Riker held a loose perimeter, looking for targets in the dark.

"Say again, Jackal," Watts excited voice said. "Repeat your last."

"I said you were right . . . al Qadar was definitely operating the drone out of this warehouse." Chunk said as he watched the ridiculous white van bounding toward them. He stuffed the joystick into his kit and raised a left hand to McAllister. "But there's no time to celebrate. Start packing for exfil, Mother. When the sun comes up, everyone is going to know we were here, and they're going to come looking for us."

CHAPTER 31

Watts looked at the live video streaming on the laptop's upper left screen and leaned in close, her heart beating with excitement.

"Here," Yi said and moved the cursor, converting it to full screen.

The gloved hand—Chunk's hand, she assumed—held the control stick up to the light, rotating it slowly. It looked like it could have come out of a military fighter jet, appearing heavy and sturdy rather than plastic like a video-game controller. It projected out of a blocky black base perhaps six by six inches, one corner bent and a chunk of charred wood dangling from the screw still in place in that corner.

She felt Theobald lean over her shoulder for a closer look. "Looks like an aviation control stick to me," he said, his voice full of contagious excitement. "Or a remote controller for a drone?"

"They had it secured to a tabletop," Chunk said over her comms. "The inside of their little operations center looked like it had multiple monitors and chairs—pretty sophisticated, I guess—but it was hard to tell because of the explosion. We got as many pictures for you as we could, but I can tell you this, Heels—you were right about this one. That was some sort of drone-flying center, or else the jihadists are entering one helluva video game competition. Nice work, Watts."

She couldn't help the grin that spread over her face. She felt Yi looking up at her from her seat at the desk and squeezed the woman's shoulder warmly.

"It was a team effort," she said and winked at Yi, who smiled back. Then Watts jerked, like someone had just thrown a bucket of cold water in her face. "Jackal—what about the drone?"

"What do you mean?" Chunk came back.

"I mean where is it?"

"No idea."

"It's got a forty-five-foot wingspan. You can't miss it."

"Uh, the drone's definitely not here," Chunk said, the tenor of his voice changing from celebratory to something else. "I thought you said these dipshits crashed it in the Hindu Kush."

"That was before we figured out the LOS hand-off protocol," Watts said, her heart starting to race. "There's a very good chance they recovered it after the first attack."

"Well, it's not here, sister," he said. "Shit . . . do you think they got it airborne in the time between when we hit the safe house and this hangar?"

"Maybe," she said, running her fingers through her hair.

"Well, the pilot just blew himself up, so if it's up there, ain't nobody at the controls. It's either already crashed, or it'll turn donuts on autopilot until it runs out of fuel."

"All right, I'll inform Bowman. We're gonna need to sweep

the skies for this thing—a dedicated ground-based radar and satellite search," she said.

"Agreed, but our work here is done. That explosion just drew a lot of attention to this site, and we need to exfil before the Pakistani police show up. RTB in twenty so be prepared to pack up and head back before sunrise if possible. Jackal out."

"Copy all."

She turned to Yi and was about to ask her to patch a call through to Bowman when Theobald's mobile phone vibrated on the conference table. He picked it up, looked at the caller ID, and took the call.

"What? When?" he said, popping to his feet. He shuffled around the table to the row of windows and opened a gap in the heavy gold drapes for a look outside. "How many? Oh, shit . . . Okay, calm down, Ahmed. No, you did real good, man. Real good. *Deri, deri manana.* Thank you, my friend. There is a case in the trunk of your car—yes, that one. One-three-one-three opens the lock. Cash and a passport for you inside. No, no, Pakistani papers, but a different name. Get your wife and kids, get in the car, and head south to Mardan. There's a phone in the case and a number to call. My friends will help you."

Theobald snapped the phone closed and turned to face her, his skin ashen.

"What's going on?" she asked.

"Enemy fighters headed this way," he said. "We're blown. My most trusted local asset says they're Taliban—a lot of them. We need to pack up and go."

"Too late," Brusk said, coming in from the hallway. "They just arrived."

Watts felt her heart almost explode with terror, and she squeezed Yi's shoulder tighter than she meant to.

Theobald whirled and peeked between the gap in the curtain

panels again. "Oh fuck," he said. "Kill the lights. Move out of the conference room—hurry."

Yi snapped the laptop closed, but slipped her headset back on as she led Watts from the room.

"Where are we going?" Watts asked, her voice cracking.

"We'll set up in the corner room," Theobald said. "Peter, grab Stan and Andy and get the boxes. I want Andy and Stan on the roof. Have them set up comms and a sniper nest. And alert KPP. They need to send SCU immediately. Tell them there's a terror attack on Americans here. And call Virginia. We're gonna be in deep shit in a minute and we're gonna need some help."

"How many incoming?" Brusk called over his shoulder as he sprinted down the hall, then banged on a door halfway down.

"At least thirty," Theobald called.

Watts stood beside Theobald, who took two pelican cases from Brusk at the door, then hurried down the hallway.

"What's KPP?" she asked.

"Khyber Pakhtunkhwa Police," Theobald answered. "Grab anything sensitive out of the rooms you guys are in and haul ass to the last room on the left."

She couldn't get her key into the lock with her hand shaking. Yi put her steadier hand on top. Together, they somehow slipped the key in and opened the door.

"Leave your personal shit," Theobald called from down the hall. "Sensitive material and weapons only."

Watts stood in the doorway of their room and watched Yi grab two backpacks and a pelican case. Her brain refused to cooperate and tell her what she should grab. Behind her she heard feet pounding and looked over her shoulder to see two men in cargo pants and T-shirts sprinting down the hall, each with an assault rifle on their chests and longer rifles over their shoulders. They wrestled a big black box between them. Peter Brusk was headed toward them, pulling a combat vest over his head, rifles over both shoulders, and a pelican case in each hand, waddling down the hall under the weight.

"Shut down the elevators and bar that fire escape," Theobald hollered.

"On it, boss," a man she assumed to be Stan or Andy shouted. Then they were through the door at the far end of the hall.

"Here," Yi said with a trembling voice. "Take these."

Whitney slung a backpack over her left shoulder, then took the heavy, short-barreled Sig Sauer Rattler in her right. She had rolled her eyes when Chunk had picked it out for her, but now her life might depend on it.

"Vests and extra magazines are in the backpack," Yi said. "I've got the comms gear from the conference room and the pelican case with our other weapons and satellite gear." She squeezed past Whitney. "Let's go."

She followed Yi down the hall, shaking off the dreamlike feeling. If she could just wake up, right? Only this wasn't a nightmare, was it?

It's just like Benghazi. We're going to die and get dragged through the streets. Or we'll get captured and suffer far more. I'll be raped. I'll have my head sawed off for an internet video.

She clenched her jaw and jogged behind Yi. There was no way in hell that was happening. She pulled back the charging plunger and checked to see there was a 5.56 round in the chamber, then she slipped the rifle sling over her head, onto her right shoulder and across her chest, just like Saw had shown her on her one day of firearms training at MacDill during indoc. The terrorists might kill her, but not without a fight.

And they will not ever take me.

She felt a strange paradoxical calm come over her as she followed Yi into the corner room.

"We need the lights out," Theobald said into the boom mike that now stretched from the earpiece in his right ear. "I need it black, guys."

She stood still, her right hand already sweaty on the grip of the assault rifle. Yi elbowed her and she looked over.

"Night vision," Yi said, handing her the helmet with ear holes cut out to accommodate headphones, and NVGs locked into the stowage position above the brim. Watts slipped the helmet on just as her entire world went dark. Her finger fumbled to secure the chin strap, then find the release to the goggles, and she dropped the night vision into place.

And saw the same black through the goggles.

A green glow appeared beside her and she saw Yi's pretty eyes lit and magnified in two soft circles of green light, hovering in the black, looking at her.

"Here, let me help you," the petty officer said.

She felt Yi's hand on her helmet and a moment later she could see, the world now bright and clear in gray-green monochrome. She turned her head and saw Theobald kneeling by the two windows that formed the corner of the room across from twin beds.

"There's thirty fighters massing out front. They have the road closed and—of course—they have a technical."

"A technical?" she asked, her voice calm but far away. It felt more like a dream than ever.

"A truck with a really big fucking gun on it. Better tell your guys. It's dead center by the entrance."

My guys? Oh shit, Chunk doesn't know!

"I've got it, Whitney," Yi said. "Jackal, this is Mother. Urgent message."

"Jackal One," Chunk came back. His voice sounded calm—because it always sounded calm.

We could be in a helicopter without engine power, plummeting toward the earth, and he'd pack a dip, shrug, and say, "Well, this sucks."

"Jackal, Home Plate is under attack. I say again. We're under attack. Copy?"

"Copy, Mother. Say force and give me a SITREP."

Theobald's voice came on next. Whitney didn't even know they could share frequencies.

"Jackal, Home Plate. We have thirty heavily armed fighters outside the front of the building, assembling for an attack. They have at least one technical across from us dead center—looks like a DShK in the back—blocking the road. They'll counter any approach by vehicle on the N-95. I have a team of two up top—let's call them Eagle One and Two."

She knew what a DShK was—a Soviet heavy machine gun that could fire more than five hundred 12.7-mm rounds a minute. She'd watched videos of the thing cutting a car in half.

"Jackal, Eagle One—Confirming that report to the north. Looks like our tangos are arguing with two uniformed KPP who just pulled up in a police cruiser, but don't expect them to lay it down for us. Tali owns this town. SCU is supposedly en route, but we're not holding our breath."

"What's SCU?" Watts asked before she could stop herself.

"Special Combat Unit—it's like the SWAT team of the Pakistani KPP, but counter-terror experts," Theobald said from the window. "They'll come, but not until it's too late to matter. Eagle Two, you checking south?"

"Yeah, boss," came a thick southern drawl Whitney didn't recognize. For some reason, she found herself wondering which voice was Stan and which was Andy. It didn't matter, she supposed, but she almost desperately wanted to know. "We got two pickups at the corners, bunch of Talis in both, just watching the rear.

Probably covering a rear exit on our part, but looks like the fight's coming inside."

"Home Plate, Jackal One—We're fifteen mikes out, ten to get in the area, then we'll have to move in on foot from the west. I'll have Uber loiter west and a block south. If we can clear the rear for an exfil, he can move in."

"Eagle One, you got Virginia?"

"They're working it. Trying to link me to the OGA guys to the south."

"Any air nearby for dust-off?" Chunk was still in complete control—calm AF.

"Just the Beech 1900, but she ain't landing on the roof," came the southern drawl from the roof. Watts randomly decided that was Andy. "OGA has nothing in town."

"OGA is working on an asset from KPP to get us off the roof, but them fuckers ain't coming to us if it's hot. We need some real-ass American shit."

"Mother, Jackal—get the Head Shed at A-bad and spin up air from there."

"Got it boss," Yi answered. "That's an hour probably."

"Forty-five if they have something on short fuse on the pad. We can turn 'em if we don't need 'em, but brief Bowman and get 'em up."

"Roger."

Watts took two long, slow breaths, just like Saw had shown her at the range. It was gonna be okay. Chunk and his team would save them. He'd beat the Taliban on the mountain; he would do it again here.

But they had attack helos for fire support on that mountain, a voice rebutted in her head.

Shut up. He's going to get here and everything's going to be okay.

A gunshot echoed, followed by a scream.

She realized the scream might have been her, but she really wasn't sure.

There was a second gunshot and she began to shake.

"Oh, shit. Home Plate, Eagle One—the Tali leader just executed both of the KPP cops right in front of the crowd. They're coming, boss."

Theobald turned to look at her in the gray-green nightmare she was trapped in.

"Stay away from the windows if I start shooting, okay?"

She nodded. Bile burned her throat.

"And push that dresser near the door. Crouch behind it and cover the hall. Anything moving down that hall, you shoot it unless I tell you to stand down. Clear?"

"Clear," she said, her voice a hoarse whisper.

"Clear," Yi added beside her.

"Thin the herd, Eagle One," Theobald said.

Rifle shots erupted above her—at least half a dozen—in rapid succession from the roof, followed immediately by a barrage of gunfire from the parking lot as the Taliban returned fire.

Then, without warning, the entire universe exploded into noise and light and screams—only some of which were hers.

CHAPTER 32

Heavy machine-gun fire exploded windows as a maelstrom of bullets shredded the opposite wall and punched holes in the ceiling. Glass, fabric, and chunks of plaster turned the air into a kaleidoscope of swirling debris and flying destruction. Whitney made herself small on the floor—curled up like a kindergartner hiding under a desk—and prayed for it to be over.

The analytical part of her mind recognized that the barrage was coming from the large machine gun in the bed of the pickup truck—the "technical," the guys had called it. That same part of her brain understood that if the gunner was aiming at their hotel room window, then it was impossible for her to be hit by a bullet because the upward angle was so steep; all the rounds flew into the ceiling. To hit her, he'd have to fire through the wall of the hotel room below them. It was just rudimentary geometry. Thankfully, her left brain reminded her, the Taliban probably did not spend much time studying geometry. But the rest of her brain didn't care.

She was terrified.

Her stomach heaved, but she managed to turn her head to avoid spattering Yi, vomiting on the carpet against the back wall.

Yi rubbed her back. "We got this, Whitney," she said.

She wiped her mouth, then took two long breaths to calm herself—what she had started thinking of as "Chunk breaths"—and then repositioned behind the dresser they had shoved against the wall beside the open door. She sighted over the dresser and down the long hall over her rifle. The floating green dot of her IR target designator bounced up and down, compliments of her shaking arms, and no matter how hard she tried she couldn't still it.

"They'll move cautiously in the first wave," Theobald called over his shoulder. He'd still not fired through the window—not wanting to give away their position, she assumed. "They won't know how many we are or which rooms we occupy. The technical strafed the entire third floor across this side of the building. They know we're on the third floor, but that's it. They'll have to be methodical."

"Who else do we have on this floor?" she asked, not wanting to shoot a friendly by accident.

"Brusk," a familiar voice said on the line. "I'm in a room halfway down the hall, so don't shoot me in the back. Hold fire until they've spotted you or I've fired first, okay?"

"Okay," she said, her voice a shuddering breath.

Her hands were sweaty on the Sig Sauer Rattler's grips, and she let go with one hand and wiped it on her pant leg. She reminded herself that tons of the DIA guys were former operators—some even SEALs, probably, or maybe Green Berets. These guys might not be quite as combat ready or experienced as Chunk and the rest of Gold Squadron, but she was in good hands.

Just like in Benghazi. That didn't work out so well, did it?

Another long breath.

Just when she'd managed to get her heart rate down from out of control to racing, a phone rang and she nearly pissed her pants.

"Yes?" Theobald said softly, taking the call. "Okay, thanks, Mamarad. Now just stay out of their way and hide, okay? You've done all you can."

She looked over at him, eyebrows up.

"Bad guys heading up the west stairwell now. Get ready," he said.

"We're keeping their heads down from up here," a voice said. Stan, she decided. A loud pop followed a heartbeat later—punctuation to his report—the sound of his sniper rifle, she assumed. "Two has the rear element to the south pulled back to the buildings on either side, so the south approach is somewhat clear. If the cavalry is stealthy, they'll be clear coming up the center from the south."

"Eagle, Jackal—we copy your last. We're out of the vehicle and infilling on foot. Five mikes to Home Plate. Get ready to move."

"Call when you're set, Jackal," Theobald said, and he was now standing behind Whitney, leaning against the inside wall by the door, sighting over top of her and aiming down the hall. "We're gonna be engaged any minute."

"Copy," Chunk's voice said. "Hang tough, Home Plate. We're almost there."

She heard the hushed voices in the hall before she saw the approaching fighters. Rough voices and shuffling feet were barely audible over the bass drum pounding in her ears.

And then she could see them . . .

Weathered terrifying-looking men. They were even more frightening in night vision—like aliens or zombies, something inhuman. They were not the color photos from briefings of beaten, angry men they'd captured or killed. Not defeated men in a cell in Guantanamo. These men moved down the hall like coiled springs—full of energy and confidence, straining to see in the dark. The one to the left, the younger one, she thought, was grinning under his thick beard. They had AK-47s and bandolier-style magazine carriers filled with ammo over their shoulders. They wore the round brimless hats of the Pashtun.

"Two just passed me," came Brusk's whisper in her ear.

She wondered why he hadn't shot them. Maybe there were more behind them?

The older one on the right, with gray in his beard and worn, leathery skin, held up a hand. She scanned him. He was wearing filthy sandals. She looked at the other one's feet for some reason—high-top tennis shoes underneath what Riker would call a "man dress." The older one pointed at their open door and growled something in a harsh whisper.

The young shooter raised his rifle.

How the hell could he see anything at all in the pitch black? Did a lifetime navigating the dark mountains of the Hindu Kush train his eyes? Perhaps he could see just slight variations of light and dark, and that was all he needed. Her gaze met his stare, and he seemed to be looking straight into the barrels of her night-vision goggles. His wide-open eyes bore into hers.

The assaulter crept forward, aiming at her over his rifle.

He can't see me, or he would have fired, she told herself.

She took in a long breath to a count of four, held it, and let it slowly out.

He couldn't hear her breathing, right? Not from that far away, and surely not over the gunfire outside.

Her heart rate slowed.

Her mind shifted randomly and abruptly to thoughts of home.

She pictured her college roommate, for some damn reason,

the one who'd gone to law school and laughed when Whitney confessed she was considering going to work for the CIA. She thought of her old boss, Reed Lewis, her friends at NCTC, and having drinks in the bars in Georgetown.

The Taliban fighters advanced relentlessly, leaning forward and straining to see in the dark.

She knew she shouldn't, but she closed her eyes and breathed another long, slow breath. She imagined Chunk leaning over her shoulder, coaching her how to shoot like a SEAL. Centered as best she could, she opened her eyes and tried to place the dancing green dot on the center of the fighter's chest . . . she tightened her grip on her rifle and put tension on the trigger with her shaking index finger.

I won't be taken. Not here. Not like this.

She squeezed.

A blinding flash whitewashed her night vision, and the rifle kicked painfully into her shoulder because she'd let the pressure drift. When her goggles refreshed, the older shooter stumbled backward, but she realized immediately she had missed him, and he was reacting to the flash of her rifle. He quickly recovered and surged forward, his rifle going up and spitting white light at her. She blew out another shaking breath and squeezed again, pressing her shoulder into the buttstock. This time her bullet found a target—not in the center of his chest where she had been aiming, but just above his knee, which he grabbed as he pitched forward. Before she could bring herself to shoot again, there was a crack from above—Theobald, standing over her—and the man's head coughed up a cloud of gray and black, and he crumpled onto the floor.

The younger fighter, covered in blood spatter, screamed something.

She wanted to take a moment and assess what it felt like to have helped kill someone. But she couldn't, because the young terrorist was screaming and firing his weapon at her, the bright white muzzle flashes washing out her NVGs. She didn't know what the bullets were hitting, but they didn't seem to be hitting her. She put the green dot on the head of the boy, who was now pedaling backward while he fired wildly, spraying the walls and doors of the hallway. But before she could pull the trigger, Theobald fired again. The bullet tore off the left side of the terrorist's forehead, and he collapsed.

Without warning, the hotel room exploded with light and glass and screams from Yi.

"The technical has us," Theobald shouted. "They saw the muzzle flashes," he added and dove beside her, just as gunfire erupted anew from down the hall, putting them in a multilevel crossfire. Whitney pulled her head down behind the furniture, her brain screaming that that was stupid, because 7.62 rounds would go right through the dresser made of particleboard like a hot knife through butter, but she cowered anyway, driven by reflex. The hotel room windows were completely blown out now, but plaster and paint continued to rain down on her as the deadly machine gun three stories below searched for the proper angle to hit them.

"Jackal is two mikes out," came Chunk's voice in her ear. "Hang in there."

"Home Plate is pinned down," Theobald shouted from beside her and, a split second later, echoed in her earpiece.

"This is Eagle One—second wave heading in, boss. Get off the third floor now if you can."

She fired again at the same moment that Theobald discharged two bursts. The insurgent dropped his rifle and fell to his knees clutching his neck, eyes wide in terror.

"We're moving out in thirty seconds, one way or the other. Plan is to exfil down the stairs on the east side, though the service area, and out the back. Eagle Two should move now. Eagle One lay down heavy fire. When we hit the exit door, fire grenades, then rope down to join us."

"Home Plate, Eagle Two—I'm gonna hold cover on the roof and rope down with One. We need two pairs of eyes up here until the last second."

The DIA operative's voice sounded so calm, like he was talking about who should stop for beer on the way to the cookout. How did one become such a man?

A double click from Theobald acknowledged the rooftop plan.

Another fighter moved in from behind the man she'd just shot—or maybe missed—and this killer fired over his fallen body. The round whistled past her left ear.

"Home Plate, Jackal—call your movement. We'll hit the Tali shooters at the south corner and cover your exit. On your mark, bro."

A fresh barrage from the technical outside made Whitney cringe.

She fired her rifle down the hall at a shifting shadow, but it didn't matter.

They were coming for her, and nobody was getting out of here alive.

CHAPTER 33

Chunk moved swiftly, leaning forward on his rifle in a combat crouch, his boots silent as he quickstepped across the short wet grass in the vacant lot beside the hotel. Behind him, his teammates were in tight formation, staying in the shadows at the edge of the open field, scanning their sectors for threats. He resisted the urge to look right, where he had total confidence that Spence was advancing his three-man fire team on a divergent line. Instead of hitting the Taliban head-on from the front of the hotel, they'd looped around the back of the property and split into two elements to attack in a pincer movement from the east and west. By approaching from the rear, they'd also avoided the DShK heavy machine gun, which would have to reposition to engage them.

Fifty yards away Saw was getting into position as

overwatch—set for head tapping anyone who tried to flank them or pursue during exfil.

Hang in there, guys. We're on our way . . .

He came to the end of the open field and took position at the corner of a low cement wall that wrapped the perimeter of the hotel property. Opposite the wall, a paved lane looped around the back. He raised a closed fist and scanned the emergency door where Home Plate would exit. The distance between the door and the wall he estimated at fifteen to twenty yards—an uncomfortable gap to have to cross when bullets were flying. Someone had cracked the door open, and he saw no movement through the gap and no shadows disrupting the sliver of light from inside. He shifted his scan to the west corner of the hotel, where an old beat-up black sedan was parked at an angle, blocking access to the street behind the hotel. In doing so, the Taliban had inadvertently provided them cover and slowed their own ability to pursue with the technical.

Nice.

He positioned his green targeting dot—invisible to every terrorist not equipped with night-vision goggles—on the chest of a fighter posted at the rear fender of the car. The terrorist's complete attention was on the action in the front parking lot, where Chunk could hear the DShK strafing the hotel.

"Jackal, Home Plate—we need to go now. You ready?"

He took a slow breath and let the green dot resettle on the torso of the bearded fighter. As soon as he dropped this guy, Taliban would come swarming around the corner. He was just about to check on Spence when the report came.

"Two is set," Spence said in his ear, on time and on target.

"Jackal is set," he said, squeezing the trigger. "Go now!"

CHAPTER 34

EAGLE'S NEST

RELAX HILTON PALACE HOTEL ROOFTOP

MINGORA, PAKISTAN

Andy Burrows hadn't thought about his girls all day—not since his daily video chat, timed so that he could read a story and tell his two-year-old daughter goodnight before bed—but he found his wife and little girl creeping into his thoughts now.

"Reloading!"

He popped up and poured fire from his rifle onto the parking lot of the hotel, as his teammate, Stan, dropped low to swap magazines. It felt like he was firing into a concert light show. More muzzle flashes lit up the night from below than stars shone down from above. He shifted along the three-foot ledge at the edge of the roof, while chunks of cement and stucco began to tear away as the Taliban fighters dialed in on him.

Stan popped up a few yards away, rejoining the fight and drawing fire away from him.

"How many grenades you got left?" Andy hollered, tapping the deep pouch on the left side of his vest.

"I got two," Stan yelled.

Stanley McDonough had been "Mac" in the teams but just "Stan" since he'd transitioned to DIA. They'd been in the same platoon for eight of Andy's twelve years as a SEAL, and for a short time Stan had been his Senior Chief at Team Seven. It was Stan who'd given Andy the nickname "Stalker," and Stan who'd stepped up to be best man in Andy's wedding when his brother got deployed early. He'd been the first friend to visit when little Katie came home from the hospital after being born almost two months early. And he'd gotten Andy the job providing tactical security for the DIA team in Mingora when the teaching job didn't work out and his wife needed to be home with their preemie daughter.

A blessing and a curse.

Julie had cried and held him tight when he told her of the plan to keep money flowing until something else shook loose.

"Make that one, bro," Stan called, dropping down behind the ledge as a grenade detonated in the parking lot. Squatting low, Stan crabbed toward him as chunks of building rained down. "Toss one of yours and we'll keep two for the big bang to cover us when we exfil. 'Kay?"

Andy nodded, forcing his mind back to the job and away from Julie and his precious little Katie—his girls. If he wanted to make it home to them, he'd need to get his Team-guy edge back, like right now.

He scurried left, then popped up, grenade in his left hand and firing his rifle with his right. He tossed the grenade in a wide arc, just as a searing pain ripped through his hip and flank. He fired another three-round burst and dropped behind the ledge.

"Ow, shit, I'm hit!" he hollered to Stan.

"Jackal, Home Plate—we need to go now. You ready?" he heard Theobald say on the comms channel.

"Jackal is set . . . Go now!"

Stan knelt beside him, his face just inches away now.

"They're exfilling," Andy said.

"I know. Where're you hit?"

Andy slipped his hand inside the waistband of his cargo pants, just over his left hip. His fingers brought an electric pain, and he felt hot blood. His left foot went tingly. "It's nothing," he said. "I'm good, man. We gotta go. On my last look, I saw them setting up a fucking mortar. Right beside the truck with the technical."

After the last horrific strafe, he and Stan had managed to keep the heavy machine gun mostly silent, capping the gunner, then taking turns popping the melons of the fighters who tried to take over the job.

"All right, give me your grenade. We're going to reposition to the back of the roof and cover the exfil."

He wanted to protest, tell Stan they needed to keep the bulk of the force pinned down longer to give the inside team more time, but he knew Stan was right. With the gunshot wound to his hip, he would be too slow to hold the north, then sprint to the rope, and exfil by himself. He handed his grenade to Stan and pressed up to his feet. Pain shot through his hip and down his leg as he half jogged, half hobbled, in a low crouch across the roof. He stumbled just as he arrived where Stan already had a rope set, coiled neatly behind the rear ledge, but caught himself before tumbling over the edge. He took an awkward right knee and pushed his jacked-up left leg out to the side, like a kickstand.

He peered over the roof through his gun sight, scanning the side of the building and the little access road that looped around from front to back. He spied four Taliban dug in behind an old black car—engaging the Tier One rescue party who'd snuck behind the building.

Damn it.

"Ten seconds, Jackal," came Theobald's panting voice. "Eagle, get ready to cover us, then slide."

Andy put a green dot on the back of the head of a Tali asshole crouching at the front fender of the sedan. Ignoring the pain and the light-headedness now creeping over him, he focused, correcting the green dot off the man's ear and back into the center of the skull. Behind him, loud, sustained gunfire echoed as Stan strafed the parking lot in preparation to toss his grenades.

Any second . . . boom, boom.

He squeezed his trigger, and the man's head spit a gray puff out the back, and the shooter collapsed. Another terrorist looked toward the roof, and Andy's next round took off the top of that man's head.

"Move now, Home Plate!" he called into his mike.

Before they realize what we're doing.

He sighted a third shooter, who was backpedaling around the black sedan.

Trigger squeeze.

The man fell, dropped his AK-47, and crawled around the corner.

Andy kept his rifle still but glanced right, where he saw movement from the low building across the rear parking lot.

"Jackal, you have movement east," he called.

His voice sounded funny to him—thick and slurred.

"Eagle One is coming to you, Two. Hold until I get there, and I'll cover you on the rope," Stan said, his teammate's words tinny and distant.

Gunfire erupted below, and he heard two explosions farther

away. Directly below him four figures sprinted out of the emergency exit at the back of the hotel. And then on both sides of the open field behind them, Navy SEAL operators materialized as if from thin air, laying down covering fire at the black sedan he had been firing on.

Hooyah, brothers.

Time to go.

Thank God. I'm coming home, girls.

He let go of his rifle and hooked the descender hanging from his harness onto the rope. He checked again and saw the SEAL Team was now guarding Theobald's group who'd just exited the building. Two of the operators had taken knees and were splitting their fire east and west, giving him and Stan the bidirectional cover they needed to rope down.

He stood, his left leg shaking and wet. Below, Theobald was standing in the middle of the cluster, waving him down. He really liked that former Green Beret, though his Navy pride never let him admit it to the DIA man.

"Move now, Eagle," someone barked in his earpiece.

A scream shredded the night as a mortar shell arced skyward.

"Mortar! Get down!" someone yelled. *Stan, yes, it's Stan.*

Andy didn't even try to drop for cover, just turned to watch the rocket screaming toward him. Holding the descender in his left hand, he toppled head first over the ledge, his only possible chance of survival.

And in that moment, he knew he wasn't going to make it home.

He'd known since he'd left three months ago. Maybe that's why he'd written that goodbye letter to little Katie and put it in his footlocker the first week in-country.

A flash of light blinded him, followed by a noise and pressure that burst both of his eardrums. He felt the angry heat of shrapnel from the mortar shell tearing through his body, his arms, his legs, his neck.

He fell and felt the descender bite the rope, slowing him.

And then things got darker and darker, until the ground disappeared completely before he hit.

CHAPTER 35

Chunk watched in horror as the rooftop lit up in orange and red.

Silhouetted in the light of the explosion, a body fell off the ledge.

"Move back! Move back!" he heard someone holler.

He watched the descender bite into the rope, flipping the limp body upright and slowing the man's uncontrolled descent in midair. Theobald turned, the compulsion to go back for his injured DIA teammate obvious, but Chunk stopped him.

"Stay here," he barked. "We'll get him."

Enemy gunfire was picking up, and Edwards was already surging forward, firing to the west where fresh Taliban fighters began to engage them. In less than a minute, the bulk of the enemy force in the front parking lot would swarm around the sides of the building. If the Taliban drove the truck with the technical around, they'd be royally screwed.

"Contact left!"

Spence's call made Chunk turn, but his view was obstructed by the fence line. While Spence and Morales poured fire from the east, he advanced to rescue the fallen DIA man. He took a knee at the corner, sighting around the fence. He counted five Taliban fighters firing from cover behind a black sedan. In seconds, more would be coming from the front.

"Going for our wounded," he called. "Cover the east hotel corner, Three."

"Jackal, Eagle—covering fire, please," came the nearly simultaneous request from the lone friendly on the roof who still needed to rope down. The paradoxical calm of the voice in his headset told him everything he needed to know. The DIA man on the roof was a blooded operator—a SEAL or a Green Beret, in all likelihood.

"Check," came Riker's clipped reply, and gunfire followed.

It was now or never.

Chunk surged forward, sprinting across the gap, and arrived at the motionless body in the dirt at the same time as Edwards, who vectored in from a perpendicular position. In his peripheral vision, Chunk saw a figure sliding swiftly down the rope from above. Fire from Spence and Morales drove the Taliban fighters behind their vehicles.

But that didn't cover them from Chunk's new position . . .

He swiveled and put his green dot on the right temple of a man hunched behind the truck and squeezed. The dead Tali slid down the side of the truck as the men behind him looked around frantically, trying to figure out where the kill shot had come from.

Trip joined the party and, together with Edwards, grabbed the other shoulder of the downed man's kit, and they began dragging the body clear, while Chunk fired and moved, dropping another shithead. The second DIA man from the roof, touched down a heartbeat later and quickly unclipped his descender.

"You intact?" Chunk called, squeezing off a three-round burst that drove several Taliban back around the corner.

"I'm good," the operator called, his own rifle up to help cover their retreat as Edwards and Trip dragged Andy back to the main group.

"Thanks, bro," Theobald said as they fell in.

"Ain't over yet," Chunk said. "Jackal, time to haul ass. Everyone exfil to the van."

Theobald squeezed his shoulder and took a knee beside him, sighting on the front corner of the hotel where undoubtedly the Taliban were regrouping.

"God has the entire lane once you clear the fence," Saw announced in his ear. "Stay on the edges, and I'll cover you all the way to the van."

Chunk double-clicked then looked at Watts. She had taken a knee and was scanning over her rifle back toward the parking lot. Trip and Edwards were already halfway across the field stretching toward the road, south of the hotel.

"Follow Trip and Edwards and cover their six," he told her, squeezing her arm.

She nodded. Her eyes said she had it together, but she was gonna have a lot of shit to unpack when the dust settled. He had never imagined being as impressed with her as he felt in this moment.

"Go now," he said, and she took off with Yi in a sprint.

Chunk cleared the east corner through his sight and saw nothing.

"One, Two—we'll cover, then follow," Spence said from where he was dug in.

"Moving," he said and squeezed Theobald's left shoulder.

A few sporadic pops from Spence acted as a starter pistol, and he and Theobald sprinted—stride for stride—to the east side of the field. They caught up with Watts and Yi, who were trailing Trip and Edwards dragging Andy, the downed DIA operator.

"Two and Six are clear. Crossing to the west side. You got the lane, God."

"Copy," Saw came back.

Chunk glanced over his shoulder as Spence and Morales sprinted to catch up, bringing up the rear. They all cleared the fence and evacuated the field seconds later, leaving the now-pursuing Taliban fighters with nothing but a wide-open, empty green space. He heard the angry shouts from behind him.

"Give us fifteen more seconds before you pull off and join us, God."

Saw answered with a double click, and then Chunk heard the satisfying sound of the suppressed sniper rifle going to work, followed by panicked screams from the field.

They sprinted down the dark street, the DIA man's body now in a four-point carry, Spence and Theobald each holding a leg at the knee and Edwards and Trip at each shoulder. Chunk noted the black, shiny trail of blood that chased behind them on the pavement. Watts jogged beside them, her rifle slung and her hands in the same awkward, half-closed fists as when they'd done the PT run back home.

"God is now Five. I'm off. At the rendezvous in thirty seconds," Saw said in Chunk's ear.

The oversized van waited at idle, slider doors open, and Chunk and Morales took a knee at the front and rear bumpers, scanning every direction for movement as the team piled in, hefting the body behind them. Then Saw appeared in a fast combat jog, coming up the street. Chunk resisted the urge to wave him on.

Pretty sure he knows to get here as fast as he can.

Seconds later the SEAL sniper leaped into the van, then Morales rose, scanned back and forth one more time, and scurried inside.

Chunk followed, and the van pulled away.

The SEALs lined the dark windows on both sides of the van, ready to engage targets. The van, McAllister at the wheel, maneuvered with disciplined slowness through the streets, headed west, back toward where they would cross the Swat River again.

"How's Andy?" McAllister asked from the driver's seat. When no one answered, he called out louder. "Stan . . . Bobby . . . How's Andy?"

"It's bad, bro," Stan said in a tight voice.

"He's dead, Earl," Theobald said gently. "He didn't make it, man."

"Without him, we'd all be dead," Brusk said, his voice cracking.

Chunk became aware of a rhythmic sobbing from Watts, who sat, face in hands, beside Yi toward the rear of the van.

"I'm telling CIA to stand down from moving in, and it sounds like KPP's SCU is pulling onto the scene, which gives even more cover to our exfil," Theobald said. As if to offer a punctuation mark, Chunk heard sudden, intense gunfire in the distance. "I offered CIA to meet up and exfil with us, but they don't believe they're compromised."

"They'll have their own contingency in place," Watts said, shaking her head and gaining control. "Are we gonna be able to get out of here?"

"Calling up the flight guys right now," Theobald said.

"Backup plan is to head west on the N-95 and we'll do a pickup with air from J-bad." Chunk looked over his shoulder. Watts was now five by, because she was up on a knee, her rifle gripped and pointed up, scanning out the windows. "Yi, contact the air out of J-bad and tell them to loiter at the border for now and stand by. No sense in having a border incursion unless we need it."

"On it, boss."

The van turned north, heading up New Road toward the bridge. Chunk tensed. They would cross Fizagat Bypass, only a few hundred yards west of the hotel. There was a chance the Taliban would have the bridge blocked.

But they didn't.

As they crossed, Chunk started to feel like they might actually pull this off.

"The aircrew is in the Beech," Theobald said softly. "I told them not to fire anything up until we arrive. No sense raising an alarm."

"Check," Chunk said. "If there's an issue, they should abandon the plane and clear the airport—I mean, like, any sign of trouble at all. We'll find 'em and pick 'em up."

"Agreed," the DIA man replied. "I'll let them know."

They crossed the bridge at a casual pace—an early morning delivery truck oblivious to what had just gone down a few blocks away, perhaps.

"How's our six?" he asked, and Riker moved to the rear of the van.

"Got nothing," he called. "We're clear for now."

They passed not a single vehicle on the access road as they circled the airfield. The main gate stood open, and they entered without being stopped, the unlit security building apparently unmanned at this hour.

"Never anyone at this gate," McAllister said and drove the van right up to the waiting Beech 1900. "I'd worry more if there was."

Before they'd even gotten Andy out of the van, the Beech's engines began to whine and the propellers started turning. The team loaded quickly and silently—the process of licking their proverbial wounds already underway. Chunk watched it all, standing sentry by the airstair, feeling more than a little numb.

"You coming, boss?" Riker called, his head popping out of the aircraft door.

Chunk nodded and, with a final backward glance at the city lights of Mingora, trudged up the airstair.

PART III

"It's not *what* we do that defines our character, it's how and why we do it."

—LCDR Keith Redman

CHAPTER 36

Whitney clutched the armrests as the twin-engine, nineteen-passenger Beech 1900 flew through a patch of rough air. The flight had been incredibly choppy, which was fitting, she supposed, given everything else that had happened in the past twenty-four hours. She glanced at Chunk, who sat two rows ahead of her, talking in a hushed tone across the aisle with Riker. *Amazing*, she thought, *how completely unfazed by the turbulence they are.* In that moment she couldn't help but wonder what it took to rattle a SEAL. Nothing she'd observed since coming to the Tier One had shaken Chunk's confidence—not the ugly mountaintop mission at the cave, not the al Qadar suicide bomber at the hangar, and not even the surprise Taliban hit at the hotel. One of their own had died, the DIA operative Andy, but even that hadn't broken

Chunk's spirit. The mood of Gold Squadron's first platoon was respectfully subdued during the exfil, but this was no funeral march. She thought that in Chunk's mind, it wasn't even a retreat. To the contrary, this was the team flying home after a hard-fought win on the road.

It didn't feel like a win to her.

She stared out the window, lost in thought for a while, and when she looked up, Chunk was dropping into the seat across the aisle from her. "How you holding up?"

She shrugged.

"You know, Whitney, it's not your fault that Andy died. It could have been any of us. In fact, we're lucky we came out of it with the numbers we did."

"I know, but I still feel responsible," she said. "Is that weird?"

"No. If I had to guess, there's probably a half dozen of us who've been kicking that same thought around in our heads during this flight. Comes with the territory. Just like dying in combat comes with the territory. It's an implied risk we all accepted when we signed on for this rodeo."

She nodded. "I get that, but it doesn't change the conflicted feelings. That's what I'm having trouble reconciling, I guess."

"What conflicted feelings?"

"Well, on the one hand I feel vindicated. That op at the hangar proved my theory. It *was* a drone that attacked our convoy, and they *were* flying it out of Mingora. I was right about the line of sight transmission data, and I was right about the Chinese HJ-10 missiles. And yet, at the same time, if I hadn't encouraged you to act on the NSA SIGINT data, you guys would have been back at the hotel when the Taliban murder squad showed up, in which case we wouldn't have been outnumbered or outgunned, and Andy wouldn't have died."

"You don't know that," he said, shaking his head. "It could

have turned out worse. When we showed up, we were locked and loaded and ready for a fight. But, if we'd come back straight after the hit on the safe house, we might have all been asleep when the Tali showed up."

"Yeah, I guess so," she said, looking down at her lap.

"Nuh-uh. Don't play that game with yourself."

"What game?"

"That alternate-reality crystal ball shit. You'll drive yourself crazy," he said. "I've seen it before, and it ain't pretty. You gotta excise 'what if' from your mental lexicon like it's a malignant tumor, because that's exactly what it is. We make the best decisions we can, with the information we have at our disposal at the time. Period."

She chuckled.

"What's funny?'

"Yi said the exact same thing to me. Must be an NSW thing."

"It's the only way to keep your headspace straight," he said, then narrowed his eyes at her. "But there's something else on your mind. Tell me."

She inhaled deeply through her nose, trying to find the right way to verbalize the ugly reality that her instincts and intellect told her was true. In the end she decided to just spit it out. "I don't think this is over. We still haven't located the drone, and we didn't get Hamza al-Saud."

"It takes time. Commander Day has people looking for the drone, and once we get our photos uploaded into the facial-rec library and get the DNA samples, you'll be able to reconstruct who we bagged," he said.

"Theobald looked at all the pics. None of the dead guys were al-Saud."

"Well, there was that one guy with the ruined face; we still haven't ruled him out."

"I know, but my gut tells me that it's not him."

"There are always question marks after an op, but you need to look on the bright side. We took out their safe house and their command-and-control hangar. Their entire operation in Mingora is blown. On top of that, we got their transmission gear—the laptop, the antenna, the joystick. That was all you, Heels. You *were* right. Your instincts and your analysis were spot on."

"Yes, but what if all we got was what Hamza al-Saud wanted us to get? What if he handed us the proverbial smoking gun—just enough to satisfy our mission criteria and, more importantly, our confirmation bias?"

"Confirmation bias?" he echoed, raising his eyebrows.

"Yes, confirmation bias. It's a powerful logic trap in which each new piece of information we encounter, rather than being evaluated critically, is interpreted entirely through a lens of preconceptions and used to bolster our existing working theory."

"Say what?" he said with a chuckle.

"I'm serious, Chunk. Confirmation bias is something I have to police constantly to do my job as an analyst effectively."

He plunked his elbow down on the armrest and eased his chin into an upturned palm. "All right, I'm all ears."

"We hit his safe house, but al-Saud isn't there. Is that coincidence, or is it because he knew we were coming? We hit his operations center, but al-Saud isn't there and neither is his drone. Coincidence, or because he knew we were coming? Then, Taliban attack us at our hotel—same question yet again. You see where I'm going with this? This is thrust and parry, Chunk. We've been strategizing and operating like we're driving the bus, but that's a dangerous confirmation bias to have, and it's going to get more people killed if we're not careful."

"Okay," Chunk said. "Let's assume for a moment that you're right about all of that—why would al-Saud leave any personnel and equipment behind at all? Why not just ghost the facility completely so that when we show up, we find nothing? Witnesses can be interrogated. Computers can be hacked. He gambled on us taking both off the X and extracting critical information that could undermine his operation and reveal his whereabouts. That's stupid. Look, Whitney, I've spent my entire career chasing down shitheads like this guy. I know terrorists. I know how they think. I know how they react. Most of them are chickenshit hypocrites who use poor brainwashed teenagers to do their dirty work. I know it's tempting to imagine every bin Laden wannabe as the next global terrorist mastermind, but trust me when I tell you that ninety-nine percent of these guys are just angry, deluded sadists, corrupted by power and ideology. Be careful not to put this guy on a pedestal."

"Well, someone makes up that one percent, right?"

Chunk nodded. "That's fair. But our network of intelligence is very mature in this region—more than twenty years old, predating even 9/11. A bin Laden doesn't materialize out of thin air. The one percent you're thinking about are all on *someone's* radar."

Whitney blew air through pursed lips, literally and psychologically deflating. She nodded but refused to concede or walk back her conviction.

"I'm not trying to shut you down here, okay?" he said. "That wasn't my intention. What I'm trying to point out is *your* confirmation bias. You think al-Saud is a terrorist mastermind, so you interpret everything he does through that lens, resulting in your own bias." She raised her eyebrows, and he chuckled. "Yeah, that's right—me read books. Me think big ideas too." Then, holding up his hands as she began to protest, he continued, "The way I see it, on one end of the spectrum there's me, who thinks al-Saud is just another terrorist dirtbag with delusions of grandeur. On the other end is you, who thinks he's the next bin Laden. The truth probably lies somewhere in the middle."

"I couldn't help but overhear your conversation," a voice said behind her headrest. "Mind if I weigh in?"

She rotated in her seat and saw Theobald leaning into the aisle.

"By all means," Chunk said with a nod.

"You said you think the drone is airborne right now," Theobald said, looking at Whitney.

"That's right. I think as soon as we hit the safe house, al-Saud scrambled the drone."

"You think they were using the Mingora runway at night after the airport was closed?"

"Yes," she said.

"Then how are they flying it? Line of sight using another portable transceiver?" Theobald pressed.

"Exactly." She pulled out her tablet computer and navigated to the picture index from the last hit. "These are the images you guys took at the warehouse where you found that control gear. Now if you look, here's the CONEX box with the suicide bomber. But the warehouse is big enough to hold multiple CONEX boxes. In fact, if you look closely, it almost looks like the floor is lighter in a couple of rectangles next to the one Hamza left behind. We know he uses handoffs, and that requires multiple transceivers and multiple pilots."

"But they don't need a CONEX box for that," Chunk said. "They certainly didn't haul a CONEX box into the Hindu Kush when they hit us the first time. All's they need is a laptop, an antenna, a power supply, and peripherals. They can fit all that in a couple backpacks."

"Yes, but you can't fit a dozen HJ-10 AGMs in a backpack. You can't fit spare drone parts and aviation fuel in a backpack," she fired back. "I'm telling you, he took his show on the road. Hamza al-Saud has selected another target, and I'm willing to wager my job that he intends to hit that target before the drone runs out of fuel."

"Have we checked any LOS transmissions in the drone control frequency band?" Chunk asked her.

"Yes, people are working on it," she said.

"I think I'm starting to figure out how your brain works," Chunk replied. "And what did the signal nerds come back with?"

"So far nothing," she said through a sigh. "But I'm still holding out hope. It's much more difficult and time consuming to sift through historical data from multiple sources than to have a dedicated, focused search running in real time."

"Okay, let's presume NSA comes back with no LOS transmissions in the vicinity of the Mingora airport during the time between the safe house hit and the hangar hit. Are you ready to drop it?"

"No," she said.

"That's what I figured," he said with a tired chuckle. "Okay, well, how else could they control the drone?"

"Satellite relay comms is the standard protocol for the Predators," Theobald said.

"Yeah, but I thought we already ruled that out. They might have a drone, but there's no way in hell al Qadar has a satellite, so don't even fucking go there, Miss Confirmation Bias," Chunk said, looking at her.

"Don't worry, I won't," she said, shaking her head.

"Is there any chance they could hack into one of our satellites, or piggyback their signal off a commercial one and control it that way?" Chunk asked.

"I don't know," she said. "That question is outside my area of expertise."

"Understood, but who *can* answer it?"

"We need to talk to a drone guy," Theobald said. "And a

signals guy, and a radar guy, and probably a cyber guy too. More importantly, we need access to folks with the tech and resources to locate, track, and shoot down the drone in real time."

"Where can we do that?" Whitney asked.

"Kandahar," Chunk said. "That's the command and control for all drone sorties in the region, and they have the firepower necessary to finish the job."

"Then we need to go to Kandahar," she said definitively.

"No, uh-uh," Chunk said. "We're regrouping in J-bad. We've got wounds to lick, and if you do find us a target to hit, that's where we want to launch out of. Not Kandahar."

"But I—" she began to protest, before Theobald cut her off.

"I'll take you," the DIA man said. "There's nothing for us in J-bad. Our NOC is blown; we lost Andy. I gotta talk with my Head Shed, but I imagine the plan is to head home and regroup, so going to Kandahar is actually on the way for me. Besides, no offense Whitney, but you showing up there by yourself with your little blue CAC card, harassing everyone with crazy questions, ain't gonna get you far." He turned to look at Chunk. "I'll get her into the OGA compound. I know a bunch of those guys, including a couple of drone pilots. I think we'll get a better response on the spooky side than if we go marching into the Air Force operation center, making wild-ass claims and conjectures."

"You'd do that for me?" Whitney said to Theobald.

"Sure," he said, pinching the skin between his weary eyes. "Because I happen to think you're onto something." She watched the man's eyes tick back toward the rear of the Beech, where the body of his fellow DIA agent lay underneath a camo poncho liner. He closed his eyes, and his jaw tightened. "And anyway, like I said, we need to get Andy home to his girls."

"All right then, it's settled," Chunk said. "When this bird lands, my team will get off, and you guys can head to Kandahar."

"Do we have enough fuel to just drop them and go, or do we need to refuel?"

"We could probably make it, but we need to stop," Theobald said.

Whitney looked at her watch, unable to help herself. The drone was up there—she was sure of it. Every minute could mean the difference.

Theobald saw the look.

"I know we're in a hurry," he said, "but we can't let Andy travel like this. We need to get him properly . . . set up. They have what we need at J-bad. I promise we'll be quick."

She stole a glance at the booted foot sticking out from under the shiny poncho liner. Beside him, Stan sat on the floor against the bulkhead, his face in his hands, openly weeping. She felt her stomach tighten. Maybe if she'd been better on the rifle. Maybe if she'd moved faster, and they'd gotten out of the building quicker . . .

She shoved the thoughts back into the shallow grave in her mind, where she knew they would dig themselves back out in short order, but right now she had no time for this.

"Of course. I'm so sorry, Bobby. So . . . I'm just—sorry. Take your time. I'll wait on the plane. And thank you—both of you," she said, looking between him and Chunk. "For trusting me."

Theobald nodded, stood, and headed to the back of the plane leaving them alone.

Chunk sat with pursed lips, looking at his hands. Finally, he looked up at her. "I don't think we got al-Saud either."

"You really don't?"

"No. My gut tells me he's still in Pakistan."

"Mine too."

Chunk got up from his seat. "I'll tell the guys that when we land they should clean weapons, clean up, and fully reload. If the drone is still up there, and you find that son of a bitch, we need to be ready. I'm gonna move the team to COP Blackfish, east of J-bad and right on the border. It'll cut twenty minutes off the infil back to Pakistan if you find us a package. Plus, there's a whole squad of JSOC army shooters there, and we'll make it a FARP with armed and fueled air from the 160th. We'll use Russian-made Mi-17s the Stalker boys keep handy for this kind of shit, so if we have to go after your boy, we can do it with full-on air, but deniability. You get us a location and a green light, and we'll kill that motherfucker. Okay, kid?"

She smiled and nodded, unsure why her eyes were suddenly rimmed with tears.

Chunk didn't say anything else, just glanced at Andy's body, then back to meet her gaze in solidarity.

CHAPTER 37

KANDAHAR AIRFIELD

AFGHANISTAN

1430 LOCAL TIME

A gust of wind blew dirt in Whitney's face as she crossed the tarmac. She squeezed her eyes shut, but too late. Her left eye stung, and she couldn't open it when she tried to blink.

"Did you get something in your eye?" Theobald asked, stopping a half stride ahead of her.

"Yeah," she said, pulling her top lid over her bottom to try to clear the offending debris.

"There's always shit blowing around out here. Especially on the tarmac. That's why I never go anywhere without shades," he said, tapping his Ray-Bans.

"I lost mine somewhere in J-bad," she said, rubbing her eye with a knuckle.

"You all right?"

"Yeah, I think I got it, but you know how it is—feels like there's something still in there even when you got it out."

"A metaphor for my life," he said with a head shake.

She blinked a few more times, then started walking.

"Hey, Whitney, a word of advice when we go in there," Theobald said, striding next to her. "Try to keep the details of the operation in Mingora to a minimum. The folks we're going to talk to are good people, but these guys love to be in the know. You get what I'm saying?"

"Yeah, I get you," she said, feeling a twinge of irritation at his insinuation that she would leak like a sieve.

"All I'm sayin' is this isn't a swap meet, but they're gonna try to make you feel like it is. Just don't let anybody rope you into an information horse-trading session."

"Sure. Thanks for the heads-up," she said and realized that this was his way of coaching her to avoid a common mistake she might be unaware of.

He nodded, then pointed at the rooftops visible in the gap between two drone hangars. "AFSOC owns those two buildings. Big command center in there. Very busy. Very official."

"Is that where we're going?"

"Nope. We're going to the red-light district," he said with a smug little grin. "OGA has a building in back."

She nodded as she took in the layout. The base was much bigger than she'd imagined, with buildings and hangars everywhere. On their approach in the Beech 1900, she'd made a cursory count of the aircraft on the Kandahar tarmac: one C-17, seven C-130s, two "company" jets, a half dozen A-10s, four F/A-18 Super Hornets, and too many helicopters to count. Theobald, who'd been watching her from his seat, had chimed in that there was even more firepower than meets the eye, because most combat aircraft were stored in ready hangars.

Squinting against the wind and the sun, she followed a half step behind him until they reached a metal building the size of a large construction trailer. Its monochrome desert-tan paint job matched the hangars and most other buildings on base. It looked insignificant from the outside, but if there was one thing she'd learned since joining the Tier One, it was that appearances were usually deceiving.

The entry door was locked, and Theobald used a keycard on a lanyard around his neck to badge in. He held the door for her, like the gentleman that he was, and she stepped inside. She blinked as her eyes adjusted to the modestly lit environment. They had the AC cranking, and the chill embraced her like her handsy uncle and his suffocating hugs at Christmas when she was growing up.

"I heard you were shot and left for dead in Syria a year ago," said a brusque male voice with a down east Maine accent. Whitney turned to see a handsome man, midthirties, with hair the color of burnished copper, emerge from a door to greet them.

A wry smile swept across Theobald's face. "The rumors of my death have been greatly exaggerated . . . It was, as they say, just a flesh wound."

"I heard a building collapsed on you."

Theobald shrugged. "Army strong."

Chuckling, they embraced with synchronized back slaps.

"Whitney, this is Paul Bertrand. He's the tactical operations officer here—responsible for all the mission planning and execution," Theobald said, turning to her. "He might talk like a lobsterman, but don't let that fool you. He's an MIT Sloan Fellow and a helluva covert operator."

"And an International Man of Mystery," Bertrand added, his gaze meeting Whitney's as he extended a hand to her. "One must never forgo honorifics."

"Nice to meet you," she said, shaking his hand, then vacillating on whether to use her real name or NOC, she said, "Whitney Watts—eye candy, reluctant traveler, counterterror analyst."

He laughed at this, then said, "How can OGA Kandahar be of assistance to you today?"

She looked to Theobald, her gaze a question.

"Yeah, go, just lay it all out," he said, but she picked up a subtle undertone in the statement, a reminder of his counsel minutes earlier.

She nodded and walked Bertrand through her theories about Hamza al-Saud's paradigm-shifting drone program and the strike against the convoy. She outlined how she believed al Qadar was controlling the drone and explained her concern that another strike was imminent. She did not, however, share details about the events in Mingora or the Tier One operations that had been conducted recently. Through it all, Bertrand listened without interruption or comment.

When she was finished, he simply nodded and said, "Ayuh."

Whitney waited for him to say something else, but when he didn't she looked at Theobald.

"That's all you got to say? Ayuh?" Theobald said.

"I'm processing," Bertrand said, running his fingers through his red-brown hair, then scratching the back of his scalp. After a moment he said, "You think it's still in the air?"

She nodded.

"Then you should be able to find it with satellite and radar," the OGA man said.

"Yeah, well, we haven't," she said and sighed.

He nodded and looked at Theobald, "Okay, so is that what you're here for? You want me to help you get eyes in the sky to look for this thing?"

"Yeah, that and answer a few technical questions," she said.

"Okay, sure. Do you wanna talk in a conference room, or stand here in our *grand* lobby and chat?" Bertrand said, gesturing to the little foyer between the entrance and a second security door.

"Conference room," Whitney and Theobald said in unison.

"Good call," Bertrand said and badged them through the security door. He led them down a narrow hallway to a small breakout room. "Coffee?" he asked, pausing at the threshold after waving them inside.

"God, yes," Theobald said.

"Whitney?"

"Yes, please."

"Back in a sec," Bertrand said and disappeared.

"How'd I do?" Whitney asked, turning to Theobald.

"Perfect," he said with a nod.

"How do you know Paul?" she asked, tucking her feet under her chair.

"He and I did a joint task force stint a few years back," Theobald said, and with no further elaboration added, "He's sharp as hell."

And that was all they had time for, because Bertrand returned quickly with two cups of black coffee. He handed them over, then dug a wad of powdered creamers, sugar packets, and stir sticks from his pocket and tossed them on the table. Then he flipped a chair around, straddled it, and sat facing Whitney.

"So first off, if this upstart al Qadar asshole is deploying a Pterodactyl using line of sight handoffs and portable transmitters, and you figured it out through SIGINT reconstruct, then you deserve a friggin' medal because that's nuts. Bravo Zulu," Bertrand said, shaking his head in amazement and clapping.

"Thanks, I guess," she said with a little shrug.

"Second, tactically speaking—and I'm talking from al Qadar's point of view now—what a terrible way to have to operate. Talk about Chinese handcuffs. Conducting sorties like that would be a logistical and comms nightmare."

"Yeah, but that's my concern."

Bertrand screwed up his face at her. "What do you mean by that?"

"I mean that if I were in Hamza al-Saud's shoes, I'd be trying to figure out how to get satellite relay control up and running ASAFP. He knows we know he's operating LOS. He knows we're going to be scanning for transmissions in that frequency band in western Pakistan and eastern Afghanistan. He knows that the minute we detect a transmission, we're going to send a Reaper over to check it out. When that happens, it becomes a quail hunt. We just flush and shoot. And the question he'll be asking himself would have to be whether we are going to run out of Reapers with Hellfires before he runs out of drone pilots. I think the answer is obvious."

Bertrand nodded. "Ayuh, that's for sure. The thing is, a terrorist organization like al Qadar will never be able to get satellite relay control because, one, they don't have the money to procure and launch a satellite, and two, no government—no matter how corrupt—is going to give a bunch of terrorists access to one. Not even Pakistan. It's simply a nonstarter."

"Yes, but what about hacking into an existing satellite feed? What if they hacked into a commercial GPS satellite?"

"No, they would need to access a satellite with a Ka-band transceiver," Bertrand said. "You know that hump on the top of the Reaper drone's nose?"

"Yeah."

"That flair in the fairing is to accommodate an upward-looking antenna array for satellite relay in the Ka band. The Pterodactyl has the same array, so they'd need a satellite with the same hardware we use."

"Well, what about hacking into our feed? Could they do that—piggyback their signal inside the transmissions we're streaming already to our drones here in theater?"

"That's a very interesting and terrifying hypothesis you have there, Whitney," Bertrand said, narrowing his eyes at her.

"Is it possible? There are rumors that the IRGC hacked CENTCOM and took control of one of our drones conducting a sortie in Iranian airspace, then crashed it into the desert," she said. "Is that true? Did that really happen?"

Bertrand scratched the side of his neck. "I'm really not supposed to talk about that. It's not my, uh . . . it wasn't my shop."

"So it's true," she said and turned to Theobald. "My God, what if al-Saud's guys figured out how to do the same thing?"

Theobald nodded. "Paul, listen to me. Every hunch she's had has turned out to be prescient. We need to figure out where this drone is and how they're controlling it. And unfortunately, we don't have a lot of time to do it."

"Okay, okay, how much time?" Bertrand asked.

"We believe the drone took off from Mingora sometime between midnight and zero three hundred hours last night. In my mind, one of two scenarios is in play: either they've already landed it somewhere in Pakistan and moved it under cover, or it's airborne en route to hit the next target. Assuming its tank was topped off when it launched—"

"They have maybe twelve hours, give or take, before they run out of fuel," Bertrand said, looking at his watch and finishing the calculus.

"Exactly."

"All right," he said. "Let's head into the Ops Center and talk to some of my guys. We need more brains working this. If my guys are convinced that this is even remotely possible, then I wanna get a pilot's perspective and let you talk to a cyber guy too."

"Thank you, Paul," Whitney said, getting to her feet. "We really appreciate your help."

"Don't thank me yet," he said, rising and moving toward the door. "I have a feeling we're just getting started."

CHAPTER 38

Qasim checked his wristwatch for the tenth time in as many minutes, the behavior more neurosis than anything else. Hamza was pushing the timeline to the limit, and he simply could not stand it any longer. Gripping the armrests of the pilot's chair he blurted, "If we don't fly the drone south in the next fifteen minutes, we are at serious risk of running out of fuel before we reach the target. What are we waiting for?"

It was just the two of them inside the GCU, with Hamza having ordered the small contingent of armed fighters traveling with them to guard the covered garage they were loitering in.

"Timing is important, Qasim," Hamza said, his voice calm and self-assured. "But not only for the reasons you're contemplating. You need to elevate your thinking, consider all possibilities and contingencies. I know the rage you're feeling, but the enemy is smart and more capable than we are. To succeed we must keep them guessing . . . always guessing."

"I understand," Qasim said, but kept his gaze on the monitors in front of him.

Three minutes later Hamza settled into the sensor operator's chair and pulled a burner phone from his pocket and dialed.

"Bring the drone up to cruising altitude and commence the preplanned route south inside Pakistan. Don't forget once you clear the mountains to drop altitude and fly below radar level. Use autopilot as much as possible to minimize your transmissions . . . Yes . . . Have the driver reposition the truck between transmissions while the drone is on autopilot . . . You should go north now, toward Wari . . . Yes, very good . . . May Allah guide and protect you." Hamza ended the call, then removed the battery from the phone. He turned to face Qasim. "There, you can relax now. Rahim has control and is piloting the drone out of the valley."

Qasim nodded. He desperately wanted to connect to the satellite and establish a data link so he could watch the drone transit south as it was piloted by the other crew, who were sitting in an identical GCU strapped to the bed of an identical flatbed truck in Timergara, a hundred kilometers northwest. Qasim wondered if the other crew understood the risk they were taking. Did they know they would be the sacrificial lambs if the Americans figured out al Qadar was now operating the drone over satellite relay? Tracing the transmissions between the GCU and the Pakistani satellite Fun Time had hacked would not be difficult, but only if the Americans first figured out what Hamza had done.

Putting the GCUs on the backs of moving trucks was a stroke of genius. The trucks could drive anywhere in a five-hundred-kilometer radius and the GCUs could maintain the satellite link. They could also instantly hand control back and forth between pilots, further confusing the Americans. Hamza had assured Qasim that a handoff would take place in the final minutes so that he, Qasim, would have the honor of piloting the drone during the attack phase. But Qasim also knew that waiting to shift control until the very last minute virtually guaranteed mission success. If the Americans tracked the signal and orchestrated a strike on the other GCU, it was unlikely they could locate and strike the second GCU in time.

"What now?" Qasim asked, turning to look at the terrorist prince.

"Now, we do the only thing left we can do," Hamza said, unscrewing the cap from a bottle of water and taking a sip. "We wait, and we pray."

CHAPTER 39

OGA DRONE OPERATIONS FACILITY

KANDAHAR AIRFIELD

AFGHANISTAN

Whitney shivered.

The Ops Center might as well have been an ice cave as far as she was concerned.

She'd never been on a submarine, but this is how she imagined the conn would look and feel—with air vents pumping out cold air, technicians sitting at terminals, flat-screen monitors everywhere streaming tactical information in real time, and a big horizontal workstation with maps in the middle of the room. The only thing missing was a periscope and a Navy Commander strutting around with gold dolphins on his chest. She'd been watching the clock hands spin for hours while making little headway finding the drone, but in that time, at least she'd mostly convinced Bertrand that her theory was not only possible but probable.

"Jax," Bertrand said, beckoning a tall and wiry twenty-something who was standing behind a pilot and sensor operator sitting at a drone control station. "This is the guy I wanted you to meet. Jax is the comms supervisor on night shift, but he's responsible for much more than the title implies. Basically, he maintains the security and reliability of all signals traffic this center relies on to execute and support our charter."

"What's up, boss?" Jax said, stepping up. Then, not even attempting stealth, he gave Whitney the face-to-knees survey she'd endured almost daily since hitting puberty.

"Jax, we've got some VIPs visiting from one of our sister outfits, and they have an interesting theory I'd like them to run by you," Bertrand said.

"Cool, whatcha got?" Jax said, automatically looking to Theobald.

"Actually, it's my theory," Whitney said, both hating and commending herself for owning her work.

"Oh, sorry," Jax said, shifting his attention to her.

With a mollified nod, she laid it all out for the new guy. When she finished, he did something she did not expect—he laughed. "What's so funny?" she asked, not even trying to hide her annoyance.

Jax turned to Bertrand. "You see, I'm not the only one."

"I know," Bertrand said, nodding. "Which is why we're having this conversation."

"So you believe me?" Whitney said.

"Of course I believe you," Jax said and shuddered like he'd just caught the heebie-jeebies. "I've been talking about this scenario for months, even before the IRGC drone shit, but did anyone listen? Noooo. But now you're here singing the same tune, and I'm feeling pretty fucking vindicated."

"Jax," Bertrand said, putting a hand on the other man's shoulder. "C'mon, reel it in and focus."

"Yeah, yeah, sorry," Jax said and made a beeline toward the nearest empty terminal.

Bertrand smiled at Whitney and gave her a knowing eye roll before following Jax to the computer terminal.

"So, you said you're convinced this drone hit that convoy up in J-bad?" Jax said, opening an interface Whitney was unfamiliar with.

"That's right."

"What do you think the next target is?"

"I don't know," she said, glancing at Theobald, who was no help. "It could be anything we have in eastern Afghanistan. We don't have any intel on a target. I'm flying by the seat of my pants here."

"All right, all right, that's okay. I mean it sucks, but it's okay," Jax said. A digital map appeared on the screen with slow-moving icons.

"What are you doing, Jax?" Bertrand said.

"Uh, too small. Screw this, I'm throwing it to the plot," Jax said and abruptly shoved back his chair, almost running over Whitney's toes. "C'mon."

They followed him from the terminal to the large workstation in the middle of the Ops Center. Jax shoved a stack of papers and maps out of the way, and Whitney saw now that what she thought was a table was actually a giant Microsoft Surface. The map with icons that had been on the computer terminal now appeared on the digital workstation, expanded over a table-sized area.

"These icons are all the airborne drones and aircraft in eastern Afghanistan at this very moment. They're all squawking unique, encrypted transponder codes, and we just assume they're all ours, because—you know—who the hell else would they belong to, right? Now, the thing is . . ." He mussed up his hair with both hands in a frenetic, almost annoyed manner. "See this drone here?" He slammed his index finger down on a small black triangle with a trailing alphanumeric designator.

"Yes," Whitney said.

"That's an AFSOC drone. I assume it took off from here and it will land here when its patrol is over."

"What do you mean you assume it took off from here?" Theobald asked.

"I mean, simply, that I work inside this black box from dusk until dawn. I didn't go outside and put my eyeballs on this drone as it rolled out of the hanger to confirm that it's an MQ-9, then compare its tail number to today's OPORD. Nor did I call up the AFSOC pilot in Nevada and ask him to verify that Mike-one-seven-two is his bird. You see where I'm going with this?"

Whitney nodded. "Yeah, I think so. We own the airspace, and we're the only ones flying drones in Afghanistan, so of course that drone is one of ours and of course what the computer is showing is accurate."

"Exactly, but if some sneaky bastard had a drone, hacked our system, and started squawking, 'Hey, look at me I'm a friendly,' then it would take an astute and paranoid motherfucker on our side to notice."

"So you're saying it's possible for someone to hack into one of our satellites and not only piggyback a signal in the traffic, but also mimic our protocols and make it appear to be one of ours."

"With computers, anything is possible. Case in point, there was a network breach reported a few days ago at the Diego Garcia RTS. Maybe that was your bad guys."

"What's Diego Garcia RTS?" she asked, but she felt pretty sure she knew the answer.

"It's the Relay Transfer Station for this region," Jax said, confirming her suspicion. "You see, because the earth is round, the control signals for the drones being piloted from Nevada cannot directly reach a satellite in geostationary orbit on the other side of the world. So the signal gets relayed, like a pinball, bouncing off other satellites and Relay Transfer Stations on the ground until it gets where it needs to go."

"If someone hacked RTS Diego Garcia, could they send signals up to one of the satellites we use for drone operations in this theater?"

"Obviously," Jax said, exasperated.

"Okay, then there must be some way to verify these are all our drones," Whitney said.

"There are several," Bertrand replied. "But the method with the highest degree of certainty is to have each drone pilot confirm that they have control of their respective aircraft, while a radar operator verifies. That way we make sure every drone on that screen has an owner."

"How long will that take?" Whitney asked.

"It will take longer to convince my counterparts at the other shops that we need to do this than it will to actually get it done," Bertrand said through a sigh. He pulled out a pocket-sized spiral notebook and began jotting down the alphanumeric identifiers for each of the drones in theater.

"Then we should probably get going," Theobald said.

"All right. I'll take this task while the three of you continue brainstorming other possible exploits," Bertrand said and headed off to make phone calls.

Whitney stared at the display with the slowly moving drone icons and tried to resist rubbing her still-irritated left eye. Then she looked over at the duo seated fifteen feet away, piloting a drone. "Which drone are those guys flying?" she asked.

"This one," Jax said, tapping his index finger on a black triangle, "cruising the Kush."

"What is it, Whitney?" Theobald asked. "I can tell you've got something on your mind."

"I feel like I'm missing something," she said, "but I can't quite put my finger on it."

"Talk through it. I'll see if I can help."

"Okay, clearly that's the ideal way to pilot a drone," she said, pointing at the flight station across the room. "Using a full suite of controls. Now I realize that tactically al Qadar needs to be mobile, but I wonder if we're thinking too small."

"What do you mean?"

"Well, when the guys hit that warehouse they found one laptop and joystick controller, but nothing else. We know al-Saud cleared out before we got there. He had other shipping containers in that warehouse." She turned to Jax. "I thought that the Reaper flight control units were stand-alone things? I didn't realize they were integrated into facilities like this."

"The setup is a little different here because we're not supporting a squadron of drones. On the DoD side of the house, the GCUs are containerized, for lack of a better word. I mean once they drop them in place, they never move them again, but in theory they're mobile."

"What's GCU stand for?" she asked.

"Ground control unit," he answered.

Whitney pulled out her phone and ran an internet search for Wing Loong Pterodactyl GCU, then clicked on the second entry in a list of search results. A web page opened to a Chinese Defense blog showing pictures of a Pterodactyl drone. While most of the pics were of the drone itself, three showed a containerized GCU.

"Those Chinese bastards even copied the Reaper ground station," Jax said, "except I'd say that GCU has an even smaller footprint."

Whitney looked from Jax to Theobald. "What if al Qadar didn't just get their hands on the downed Pterodactyl drone the Pakistani military was testing? What if they got its GCU as well?"

"But they couldn't use it because they hadn't solved the satellite problem yet," Theobald said, finishing her thought.

"Exactly. It's hard to tell the exact dimensions from that picture, but that GCU looks like you could easily load it on the back of a truck," she said.

"Oh, you definitely could," Jax piped up.

She turned to him. "Suppose al Qadar has one of these units hidden somewhere in Pakistan, and it's transmitting . . . Could you find it with SIGINT alone?"

"We know the exact frequency band it transmits in. We know the positions of our satellites and the signal strength they'd need to broadcast at, so yeah, I think so."

"Can you get somebody on that?" she asked.

"I don't have that kind of pull," Jax said with a laugh.

Theobald pulled out a sat phone from a holster on his belt and dialed a number from memory. "Yeah, Matt Chapman, please . . . Matt, hey, it's Bobby Theobald. How are things at the Fort? Good, good . . . yeah, I'm in Kandahar. Yeah, it went bad . . . I'll fill you in some other time, but hey, I got a friend here with the Navy JSOC Tier One element who needs your help. I'm gonna hand her the phone . . . Yeah, thanks, you too."

Whitney took the phone from his outstretched hand. "Hello?"

"Chapman, how can I help you?" said a pleasant voice.

"We need your help to look for a particular signal transmitting inside Pakistan," she said, and as she spoke Jax handed her a sheet of paper with handwritten details about the frequency, modulation, and signal strength of what they were looking for. Without missing a beat, she conveyed the information to Chapman, whom she assumed to be a manager at NSA, though she was learning there were myriad smaller, more secret units with three letter names out there. While she was talking, Jax wrote another note for her.

"What's this?" she asked, pulling the phone away from her mouth.

"The coordinates of the geostationary satellites they could be talking to," he said.

She nodded and passed that information on as well.

"When do you need this?" Chapman asked.

"As soon as possible. This is an imminent threat situation," she said, trying to make her voice as dire as possible.

"Okay. Call you back on this number," Chapman said and the line went dead.

In the interim, Bertrand returned.

"I got good news and bad news," he said. "Which do you want first?"

"The good news," Whitney said at the same time as Theobald said the opposite.

Bertrand looked back and forth between them. "Age before beauty, or youth before wisdom? You guys call it."

"Good news," Theobald said with a wink.

"The good news is that every aircraft on that plot is confirmed to be one of ours. A control verification maneuver was conducted by each pilot and confirmed by our radar operator."

"That is good news," Theobald said. "What's the bad news?"

"We're still not any closer to finding Whitney's rogue drone."

The group nodded and shared a round-robin, what-the-hell-do-we-do-now moment.

Whitney was just about to suggest they brainstorm next steps, when Theobald's sat phone vibrated in her hand. "Hello?"

"Miss Watts?"

She did not remember giving Chapman her name. "Yes?"

"I have something for you. We have a signal that started transmitting twenty minutes ago," he said. "You ready for the coordinates?"

"Yes," she said and repeated them aloud for Jax, who was standing by at the table display to enter them.

"That puts it in Timergara . . . only twenty miles from the border," Jax said. "Shit."

"Is it transmitting now?" Whitney asked into the phone.

"Yes," came the reply. "But there's something else. Those GEOSAT positions you gave me, those are our assets. This transmitter is definitely not talking to any of our assets."

"Are you sure?" she asked.

"Yes," he said with an oh-silly-mortal chuckle. "I'm sure."

"What asset do you think it's talking to?"

"Best guess—PakSat-1R."

Her stomach dropped on hearing this. "Is that a Pakistani military satellite?"

"Officially no; in reality, yes. Islamabad claims it's a SUPARCO owned and operated data satellite, but we know better."

"Can you shut it down?" she said, locking eyes with Theobald.

"Are you talking about the transmission source or the GEOSAT?" Chapman asked.

"Both, either, I don't care," she snapped. "It's urgent."

"The transmitter, no, unless it's online, which I seriously doubt. PakSat-1R, maybe, but that would take POTUS-level authorization," he said.

"Shit, okay, I'll call you back," she said and ended the call. Then she dialed Chunk's number from memory. As it rang, she began to pace. He finally picked up on the seventh friggin' ring.

"Lieutenant Commander Redman," he said, his voice uncharacteristically serious.

"Chunk, it's Whitney," she said, her gaze shifting to the newly added bright red dot on the map. "We found them . . . and this time, we *really* found them."

CHAPTER 40

LEAD 160TH SOAR RUSSIAN MI-17 HELICOPTER

DESIGNATED STALKER ONE

UNNAMED VALLEY OF THE HINDU KUSH

PAKISTAN

2015 LOCAL TIME

Eyes closed, Chunk ran his hand over his gear almost unconsciously, knowing any discrepancy would beg his attention, his fingertips driven by the memory of hundreds of previous missions. It was the quiet time now—a couple minutes after the "five mikes" call from the pilot. He finished the ritual of touching his weapons of war, then opened his eyes and flipped his NVGs into place. The green-gray world that flickered to life was intimately familiar and comforting.

Riker, designated as rope master, was sitting in the front port corner. His booted foot was propped up on the large green bag beside him, his body motionless except for the slow, rhythmic rise and fall of his shoulders. Behind him, his chin almost on Riker's shoulder, was Saw, gloved hand up and ready to be first to slide down the thick rope and into the fight. His head was bowed, his left hand wrapped around the silver cross he wore on a thick chain around his neck. Chunk watched as his friend pressed the cross to his lips, then dropped it back inside his shirt. Trip waited beside the sniper, rocking back and forth to the heavy metal music streaming from his iPod Shuffle, which he'd had one of the tech guys hardwire into his Peltors so that any radio call muted it instantly. The young SEAL tapped a gloved hand on his thigh to the music. *His own prayer ritual of sorts*, Chunk guessed.

He looked at his watch, then over at Spence, who was sitting on a canvas bench at the aft end of the cabin. Spence nodded and gave him a "hang loose" surfer wave.

Chunk glanced at his watch again and keyed his mike.

"Mother, Jackal—two mikes from Mako."

He couldn't help but chuckle. Riker had insisted that the checkpoints for this op be sharks. He loved that asshole more than he could say.

"Jackal, check. Signal is still transmitting. Stationary at same pos in the truck lot south of Wari. Our drone pass still shows three semitrucks and one oversized king-cab pickup in the lot. No other movement or thermals. Center truck has three thermals in the rear and two in the cab—all the others have single thermals. Pickup has three thermals. No potential QRF detected outside of Wari itself or Timergara farther south." Yi's voice was all business as she coordinated from the TOC in J-bad.

"Check. Thanks, Mother."

"Happy hunting, Jackal," said the unmistakable baritone of Captain Bowman—a little nod to let them know he was watching.

Chunk was pretty sure Watts and Theobald were looped in from the OGA compound at Kandahar, but they'd been radio silent since the initial comms check.

He glanced out the side of the helo and fixed his gaze on the center truck—the target. But they couldn't just pop up and hose it down. If they were wrong about this and they killed innocents, it would be international-incident-level shit, especially after their last unsanctioned operation in Pakistan. Flying in a Russian helicopter would only give them so much plausible deniability.

Unless they killed *everyone*. And that wasn't who they were.

Though the option occurred to you, didn't it?

He switched his radio to vox.

"Stalker, Jackal—target is the center truck. Pop up from the rear and put fifties through the engine block, then hover dead center, and we'll fast rope on either side."

"Copy. One mike," the pilot announced, and the doors slid backward on rails inside the fuselage, revealing an opening much smaller than what they were accustomed to in a Blackhawk. The night air whipped inside the cabin, tinged with the smell of kerosene.

Saw and Morales would hit the ground first and move to either side of the target truck's cab, while the rest of the SEALs headed to the rear. Stalker would hang in a static hover with the starboard side fifty, ready to hose down anything else from the truck and the port side focused on anything approaching from the road.

Between them, they had trained and executed a mission set like this a hundred times.

Chunk felt the helicopter drop almost to the ground, then watched the cloud of dust kick up in billowing, curling waves as the pilot pulled up, the g-force making him heavy on his seat. He held his NVGs in position, clutching his helmet, as the pilot kicked the right rudder and spun the helicopter hard clockwise. There was a loud burp and flash of light as the starboard-side .50-caliber machine gun tore the truck's engine compartment to trash in a half a second. The pilot kicked the nose forward again and slipped the bird backward, just as Riker and Edwards kicked their heavy bags of rope out the doors. Saw and Morales gripped their respective ropes, locked feet on, and stepped out to begin their slide. Spence and Trip were on the ropes before the first two heads slipped from view, and Chunk moved forward and gripped the rope just as Edwards took the same position across from him.

He slid fast and felt the friction build to scorching levels under the double gloves and in the arch of his top foot, as it always did. As he neared the ground, he watched Saw and Morales moving forward on the cab. Chunk landed in a crouch, pulled his rifle up, and immediately moved to the rear of the truck, shadowing Trip. Then, he felt the double tap of Riker's hand on his shoulder and heard the soft belch of suppressed 5.56 gunfire behind him, as his two teammates engaged a threat from the cab—a confirmation in his mind that they had the right truck. He heard the thump of the heavy ropes hitting the ground behind him as Stalker released them, pulled up, and moved off to his left.

He tapped Trip's shoulder, then followed him around the rear of the truck with the CONEX box strapped to the bed. Trip and Spence moved in on the double doors of the modified shipping container, while he and Edwards stepped three paces back and offset by forty-five degrees. Riker positioned himself dead center between them and a few feet behind, crouched over his rifle, the muscles in his heavily tattooed forearms bands of tension.

Four rifles targeted the container's double access doors while Trip pressed a charge into the center seam.

Chunk held his green dot on the door, projecting in his mind where that would place his round once the doors were open.

"Preserve the tech but don't get blown up," he said, reminding his guys to kill anyone who might be wearing a vest.

Riker was the only one who answered, having just played this very game less than twelve hours ago. "Riiiight."

Trip and Spence pulled back to the corners and averted their eyes.

Chunk closed his eyes just as the *whump* shook the truck and smoke filled his nostrils. When he opened them, Spence and Trip were pulling the CONEX doors open.

They surged forward, Chunk narrowing their wedge-shaped formation. Riker fired twice from his left, and a fighter fell forward out of the container, a puff of dust rising around him as he belly flopped beside Chunk's boot.

Two left.

A figure moved in a crouch from deep within the container, and he fired twice. The shadow dropped.

"Jackal, the pickup truck is coming around now."

"Stalker has him."

A burst of .50 caliber exploded from the hovering helicopter and a tongue of fire licked out of the sky in his peripheral vision. A fireball belched skyward as the incendiary rounds ignited the fuel in the pickup, and what was left of it evaporated with the fighters inside.

Trip crouched by the rear door of the flatbed, right behind Spence. Small arms fire lit up the smoky interior of the CONEX box, and both SEALs returned fire.

"All tangos are down, but pull back. The container could be booby trapped like the last one," Spence called, and he and Trip jumped off the flatbed, putting distance between themselves and the CONEX box.

"Two tangos down in the cab," Saw said. "No vests or explosives up here."

"One of the other trucks in the lot just started its engine and is heading for the exit."

"Stop him?" the Stalker pilot asked.

Chunk considered. Most likely just some poor dude in the wrong place at the wrong time.

"Let him go, Stalker. Mother, track that truck for us. Five and Six, secure the other truck while we sweep here."

It took only minutes to confirm the CONEX was not rigged to explode. While the rest of the team held security, Chunk and Spence pulled hard drives and photographed everything inside. The cargo box looked more like a Tactical Operations Center than the slapped-together flight controls they'd found in Mingora. It looked almost identical to, though somewhat smaller than, the drone flight control center he had seen once in Kandahar.

"Mother, Jackal—Jackal is Bull Shark and secure," Chunk reported.

"Roger, Jackal," Watts came back. "What did you find?"

"The CONEX on the flatbed appears to have drone controls inside, but not like the one in Mingora. This is super sophisticated shit we have here. Sending you video now," Chunk said using his tablet to stream live imagery inside the container to her via satellite. "This is what you had us hunting for, right?"

"That looks like it," Watts said in his ear. "Photograph everything and pull whatever hardware you can."

"But quickly, Jackal One," Yi chimed in. "We're seeing truck movement in Timergara headed your way. Looks like Pakistani National Police. You need to be out of there in less than three mikes."

Chunk grimaced as he pulled hard drives and computer components from the two workstations, while Spence collected mobile phones from the dead, photographed faces, and scanned fingerprints.

"Trip, get in here and rig this thing to blow up. We need to destroy everything we leave behind."

"You got it boss," the SEAL replied.

"Stalker, Jackal One—low hover for pickup in ninety seconds."

"Roger, Jackal," the helo pilot came back.

As Trip rigged the charges, Chunk took one last look around the ingenious mobile drone control center camouflaged as a shipping container and shook his head.

What the hell will these assholes come up with next?

CHAPTER 41

Qasim sat, quite literally, on the edge of his seat, using his legs to stabilize himself as the truck swayed and bounced. He'd taken control of the drone only moments ago and was still getting the feel back. The Americans were engaging the other GCU at this very moment, which probably meant his own time on earth was coming to an end soon.

Snapshot images of the people he'd lost flashed across his mind's eye. His father, Eshan, Saida . . . It was only right that Allah allow him to be the one who pulled the trigger and avenge the deaths of those he loved. Rage flared in his chest, and it took a long, slow breath to steady his hand on the joystick.

An unexpected jolt slammed his ribs against the right armrest of the pilot's chair. He winced, releasing the control stick, as he was jostled violently back the other way.

"What the hell is the driver doing?" he demanded, quickly retaking control of the drone and stabilizing the altitude. "The drone is at five hundred feet. We're lucky I didn't crash it."

Teeth gritted, Hamza radioed the driver in the cab. "What is going on?"

"Bad road, heavy traffic," the driver replied.

"We need to move!"

"I know, I know, I'm trying."

"Try harder," Hamza said and clipped the radio to the breast pocket of his shirt. To Qasim he said, "Turn the drone now."

"But it hasn't reached the waypoint."

"I know, just do it. Vector toward Kandahar, maximum speed with terrain-following altitude control to avoid radar detection," Hamza ordered, gripping the armrests of his chair.

Qasim nodded and did as ordered, turning the drone west and engaging the autopilot. In the corner of his eye, he saw Hamza skillfully working the controls on a navigation screen.

"Two hundred and thirty-four kilometers to the Kandahar Air Base," Hamza murmured. "Speed over ground is two hundred and seventy-nine kilometers, which puts us on target in . . . fifty minutes. Forty-eight minutes to the earliest opportunity to fire the missiles. Damn it, that's too long." He turned to Qasim. "Are you still transmitting?"

"I'm not issuing flight commands, but the data link is active."

"While the drone is on autopilot, is the information flow only one way? Is the data streaming from the drone to the satellite to the GCU only, and if so, could the Americans track us?"

Qasim rubbed his chin. "The truth is I don't know. I imagine that ninety-nine point nine percent of the data flow is unidirectional, but I can't say for certain. There are probably intermittent handshakes between the GCU and the satellite to maintain connectivity."

"How do you not know these things?" Hamza snapped. "You're the system expert."

"This drone was designed and programmed by the Chinese, not me. If you were to print the operating system, you would have tens of thousands of pages of code. I told you from the beginning, even with Fun Time's help, it was going to be impossible for me to understand everything they did," Qasim fired back.

"Sever the link," Hamza said, the veins standing up on his neck.

"You think the Americans are coming for us?"

"Of course they're bloody coming for us! Our only chance is to reposition so that forty-five minutes from now when they show up here, we're somewhere else, but that plan won't work if they're tracking our signal, and if our bloody fucking driver doesn't get the truck moving. The road will get better when we pick up the N-80 west. There will be plenty of trucks to get lost in then, but we have to get out of this traffic jam first."

Anxiety washed over Qasim. He'd never seen Hamza rattled like this. He reached for the console, then hesitated. "You understand that if I do this, there is a small but distinct possibility we might not be able to reestablish the data link with the satellite or the satellite with the drone? Networks—especially satellite networks—can be finicky. The signal is good here, but if we move fifty or eighty kilometers, it could be poor. All I'm saying is that there's no guarantee when I try to log back in and reestablish our connection with the drone that I will be able to do so in the window of time necessary."

"There are no guarantees in life, Qasim," Hamza said, reclaiming his composure. "Risk-reward calculus is the only thing that matters. Do it."

Qasim nodded and severed their connection to the satellite. Then, as if the universe acknowledged and approved of Hamza's decision, the truck lurched forward, and they were moving again. He set a countdown timer on his watch for twenty-five minutes. As they rumbled along, his mind conjured imagery of an American Apache helicopter materializing over the horizon and launching a Hellfire missile at the GCU—a missile they'd never see coming from inside this windowless box. What would it feel like to be blown to pieces and incinerated? That was what these missiles did to the human body, after all. He's seen it first-hand . . . watched his sister and his father ripped apart and burned to ash.

I don't want to die that way.

"Put it out of your head," Hamza said, as if reading his thoughts.

"What are you talking about?"

"I know what you're thinking, and you need to put it out of your head. We're not going to die today. There's much work still to be done, and I have plans for you, Qasim."

"What kind of plans?" he heard himself ask, feeling almost separated from his body.

"Big plans," was all the terrorist replied, before keying the radio clipped to his chest to call the driver. "What is the situation now?"

"The road is improving, and we are moving more quickly now," came the driver's reply. "Don't worry, I know what to look for. If I see a roadblock, a tail, or anything I don't like, I'll radio you. This is a mountain road for now, and we will be hard to spot. Once we get close to Kohat we can lose ourselves in the traffic."

Hamza turned and gave him a tight smile.

"You see? It is as I have said. Allah is with us, and we will succeed. It is not His will that you die here today, my brother."

Time passed, and with each minute the road became smoother. Soon, Qasim released his death grip on the control desk and even slipped farther into his chair.

He nodded at Hamza, who smiled again, then turned to the two armed fighters who were sitting on the floor at the far end of the GCU. "Are you wearing your body armor?"

Both men nodded, the one on the right tapping the center of his chest with a closed fist.

"If an American SEAL team tries to breach this container, they will probably breach through that door behind you, so I would not sit there," Hamza said. "I want a two-meter setback with your back to me and your rifles trained on that door."

The two shooters acknowledged the order and moved to defensive positions. A bead of cold sweat ran down Qasim's side as his nerves began to get the better of him. He checked the timer on his watch. *Nineteen minutes.* Time was passing at a crawl now, and he cursed not having a window to look out. It was terrible, riding around in this box without being able to see.

He looked at the two fighters, kneeling with their rifles pointed at the doors. There was no chance that these men, no matter how committed, would stop a team of American Navy SEALs.

Again, Hamza appeared to read his mind.

"Don't worry, I have several surprises in store for the Americans, should they come for us, Qasim," the man said in English, grinning. "There is more firepower between us and the Americans than these two brave men."

Qasim nodded.

Pull yourself together, he told himself.

He checked his watch.

Eighteen minutes.

He closed his eyes and said a prayer. When he finished, he checked his watch.

Sixteen minutes.

"Power on the laptop and sync it with the GCU," Hamza said. "But do not reestablish the satellite data link."

Qasim nodded and grabbed the laptop with the cellular modem from the floor. He opened the screen and powered it on. Once the boot sequence was complete, he opened a screen-mirroring application and connected to the GCU via cellular network. The laptop screen flickered once, followed by the GCU flight monitor interface, and then they were synchronized.

"Laptop synchronized with the ground control unit," he said, looking at the simplified digital control panel on the laptop screen that mirrored the physical GCU interface. This little miracle was their final contingency plan should they be forced to abandon the GCU in the next ten minutes. As long as both the GCU and laptop had a cellular signal, and the GCU was connected to the satellite, he would be able to relay basic flight commands from the laptop to the drone, even if they were separated from the truck.

"Very well," Hamza said. "Reestablish satellite link between the GCU and the drone."

Qasim nodded. This was the moment of truth . . . if he could not reconnect with the satellite, the mission failed. Cold sweat pouring from his armpits, he logged in and started the initialization process.

"Is it working?" Hamza pressed.

"I think so," Qasim said, staring at a stalled progress bar on the screen. Ten uncomfortable seconds passed.

"It's not working. Try again," Hamza snapped.

"Hold on . . . give it a moment, or we've wasted this time."

"I said start over," Hamza barked, just as the pop-up disappeared and the connection was made.

"Data link established," Qasim said, exhaling with relief.

"Good job," Hamza said and gave his shoulder a squeeze. "Now test the laptop. Send a relay command to the drone."

After a quick validation maneuver with the pilot's stick, he took control of the drone via the laptop, changing altitude smoothly with a press of the up and down arrows on the keyboard.

"It's working."

"Excellent," Hamza said and murmured a quick prayer, while Qasim confirmed that both of the drone's air-to-ground missiles were armed and ready to be launched. More than enough firepower to kill the Americans at the base they'd built only hours from his ancestral home. And if the Chinese missiles failed to do the job, he would fly the drone itself right down their throats.

Either way, in less than fifteen minutes, vengeance will be mine . . .

CHAPTER 42

Whitney had finally relaxed and was going to ask Bertrand about sleeping accommodations on base for the night, when Jax sent her blood pressure skyrocketing.

"Hey, everybody, I think we got a problem," he said from where he sat at a terminal, a headset on one ear so he could hear the room.

"What's going on?" she asked.

The OGA drone wizard looked up from his computer. "The signal's back."

"What do you mean the signal's back? My guys just blew the GCU to kingdom come and killed the pilot team."

"Yeah, well, hooyah and all that Navy SEAL bullshit, but the signal is back. It moved, but it's the exact same signature, and it's bouncing off the exact same PakSat-1R, so . . . yeah, it's back. Transmitting from . . ." Jax tapped his computer keyboard like he was a court stenographer. "A hundred and twenty miles south of the truck your supermen just hit."

"In Mardan?" Theobald said, taking a seat beside Jax, who was pulling up a satellite map.

"No, south of Mardan. Right here . . ." He tapped a winding road just north of where it intersected highway N-80, twenty-five miles southeast of Peshawar. "Oh and giddyup, yo, check this out—the signal is moving."

"Moving?" Whitney said, feeling the blood drain from her face.

"Yep."

She yanked the headset off Jax's head, taking a pinch of his curly hair with it.

"Hey . . . Ouch! I mean, just help your fucking self to my stuff."

"Get me back on frequency with the strike team," she said, ignoring him.

Theobald was already leaning over Jax and opening the encrypted comms program.

"Damn it, this is exactly what I was afraid of. It's like a fucking shell game. They have multiple transmitters, and they're moving the command and control around like a hot potato," she said, talking a mile a minute. "They must have handed off while Chunk was hitting the first transmitter. That means the drone is still airborne and en route to a target right now. We need to retask Jackal, but we really, really need to find that fucking drone before a whole lot of innocent people die."

Jax nodded and headed to the oversized workstation. "I'm on it," he said.

"You're patched through," Theobald said, his voice tense.

"Jackal One, Jackal One, this is . . . um . . . Heels," she said, unsure what call sign to use. "Repeat, this is Heels."

"Hey, Heels," Chunk said, amusement in his voice. "Go for Jackal."

"Jackal, you're not going to believe this, but they've passed control of the drone to another GCU. We have a new target package near Nowshera. Urgent you strike now. Hurry."

"Mother is live," came Yi's voice immediately. "Jackal, I show you just four mikes from Dogfish," she said, using the call sign for the border waypoint they were about to cross, the Durand Line between Pakistan and Afghanistan.

"Yeah, well, we're changing heading and going back for more, Mother."

"Understood," Yi said. "Charlie Oscar authorizes retasking."

"Coordinates sent directly to Stalker," Theobald said from his computer.

"Coordinates received," Chunk said. "Estimate target in twelve mikes. Designating it Great White."

Watts let out a long shaky sigh. This job was going to take years off her life. She rubbed the knot tattoo on her wrist and closed her eyes.

"Oh God, I know where the drone is headed," Jax announced. "I know what the target is."

"What?" she asked, looking at him, but the expression on his face answered the question.

"Us," he said, his voice cracking. "This compound."

Theobald looked from Jax to her. She nodded her concurrence, and he pulled out his sat phone and dialed from memory. She felt time slow, like in a bad dream, and for a moment she wondered if it *all* was just one long nightmare—the new job at the Tier One, the hotel attack in Mingora, the Pterodactyl drone cruising toward her with missiles at the ready. Could somebody just pinch her already so she could wake up at her desk in McLean, Virginia and go back to her old safe life as a CIA staff analyst working at NCTC?

Theobald pulled the headset from her head and spoke into the mike.

"Mother, you have the hit. Home Plate is off air temporarily," he said, using their call sign from the prior op. "Good luck and happy hunting."

"Copy, Home Plate," Yi came back.

He looked at her. "I'm calling the watch officer."

She felt a surge of adrenaline, then anger.

It is not going down like this. I'm not gonna unravel this whole puzzle knot just to have it end like this.

"Sir, I have an immediate, credible airborne threat to the base," Theobald said sharply into his phone. "This is Robert Theobald, a Task Force guy, and we need you to scramble a fighter to intercept a hostile drone immediately . . . Yes, sir, I said a drone . . . Sir, I know, and I just simply don't have time to convince you. This base is going to be under attack in minutes, and we need a fighter up . . . Additional confirmation? Seriously?" He looked at Watts and shoved the phone into her hand. "Tell him."

"Sir, this is Whitney Watts. I'm the N2 for the JSOC Navy Tier One, and the unit is engaged in a counterterror operation in Pakistan as we speak. You can vet me through the JSOC commander, but by the time you do, we may all be dead. We have identified a hostile drone inbound from Pakistan. We're sending the track details to you via intranet on the high side right now . . ." She snapped her fingers at Jax, who nodded and began to tap on his keyboard.

"Tell him to ready any antiair defensive countermeasures," Theobald told her. "It'll be in firing range in under two minutes."

She relayed his instructions, finished the call, and looked back and forth between Theobald and Jax. "I'm not sure if he believes me."

"I don't think he has much of a choice," Jax said, typing furiously at his terminal. "Because I just sent an alert to every damn terminal on this base."

CHAPTER 43

MOBILE GCU

HIGHWAY N-80

FIVE MILES EAST OF KOHAT, PAKISTAN

2130 LOCAL TIME

Qasim could not help but grin as he held the joystick gently, with three fingers and his thumb. He made subtle corrections as the ground streaked by on-screen, streaming to him in real time from the high-def camera in the nose of the Pterodactyl. The weapons data at the bottom of screen was green, indicating both missiles were armed and ready to fire once the targeting data was in.

"Final targeting data loaded," Hamza said from the sensor operator's chair, and a flashing red circle appeared on Qasim's screen to the left of the projected track of the drone.

Qasim applied gentle left pressure on the stick and watched as the red circle slowly moved right in the display, until it was just above the green crosshair circle. Next, he leveled the wings and looked at the range to target.

"In sixty seconds I can execute the pop-up maneuver and deliver the missiles."

"Excellent," Hamza said, the satisfaction in his voice matching Qasim's elation.

Three kilometers.

Two.

One.

He pulled the stick back and watched as the night sky filled the screen, and the red flashing circle dropped to the bottom of the screen, still directly below his track indicator. He watched the altimeter scroll up on the right side as the airspeed to the left of the display fell away. At ten thousand feet, he pushed the stick forward, crossing the horizon, the lights of the city of Kandahar in the distance. The red circle moved up slowly from the bottom of the screen until it overlapped the green crosshair circle again, stopped flashing, and became brighter. A warble announced missile lock on the target Hamza had designated—the American drone compound on the southeast side of the runway at Kandahar Airfield.

Qasim took a deep breath.

He thanked Allah for the honor of meting out his vengeance on Americans and squeezed the trigger.

White light filled the screen, and he watched the first missile scream off into the distance.

He counted to fifteen very slowly, then selected the second missile. Immediately the red circle flashed once, then locked and became solid, and the high-pitched warble confirmed target acquisition.

He squeezed the trigger again.

Hamza rose from his seat and kissed Qasim's right cheek. "It is done, brother."

"Almost," Qasim whispered and pressed forward on the

joystick, lowering the nose and dropping his altitude quickly. He stabilized at five hundred feet.

"What are you doing?" Hamza asked curiously.

"Crashing the drone into the airbase. There is no recovering it now . . . I intend to kill as many of them as I can."

"Lock it in with the autopilot, Qasim."

"No. If the American SEALs come for us, I want them to see my hands at the controls. They will know who killed their brothers at Kandahar." He felt tears—of joy and pain, of rage and satisfaction—streaming down his face.

Hamza whispered in his ear. "That is not your fate, brother. Allah has other plans for us. This attack was only the beginning."

Qasim looked up at him. Now, he felt only love and brotherhood for the man he had days ago feared and maybe even despised.

"Is that true?"

"Yes, brother. Do as I say. Lock in the autopilot." Hamza said, then radioed the truck driver and instructed the convoy to slow. "Our work is done here. We're separating from the convoy."

"And if the Americans come anyway?"

"Then I have one final surprise for them . . ."

CHAPTER 44

OGA DRONE OPERATIONS FACILITY

KANDAHAR AIRFIELD

AFGHANISTAN

Whitney tried to swallow the lump in her throat, but it stubbornly wouldn't go down. Sirens wailed outside as Kandahar Airfield woke up. For the first time in its history, the joint base was under aerial attack.

"Two minutes until the hostile drone can fire missiles," Jax said, pacing around the surface display like an agitated tiger. Everything had been handed off to the base air wing and security teams now.

They were helpless.

Jax's announcement unleashed a burning in the pit of her stomach. It was like being told you had cancer—only it was a cancer that would kill you in two minutes instead of months or years.

"It's locked on us," he announced.

"You don't know that, Jax," Bertrand said, arms crossed over his chest. He sounded calm—almost soothing.

"Yes, I do. What the fuck else would they target?" Jax's voice was tight and rising. "They didn't fly the damn thing all the way down from the Hindu Kush to hit a civilian hangar. They're targeting the drone operation. They're gonna fire their missiles at us—at this building—because, you know, we're the great Satan, and no one is more satanic than the C-I-fucking-A!"

Whitney stared at him, his hysterics having a paradoxically calming effect on her. Strange, in the span of sixty seconds she'd cycled through the gamut of emotions—terror, then anger, then despondent depression, and now peaceful resignation. Perhaps she had, in her last minutes, discovered the secret to living in Chunk's world. Perhaps in those moments—when life and death boiled down to only action or reaction, when planning and strategy and intellect were impotent—humans were hardwired to slip into a Zen-like state. From an evolutionary perspective it would—

"The C-RAM will engage if they fire missiles," Theobald said, interrupting her thoughts and looking at her with a tight smile.

"What's that?" she asked, her voice far away and somehow not hers.

"It stands for Counter Rocket, Artillery, and Mortar," Jax said, almost absently, then started barfing out facts for her. "It's really called the LPWS, but that's harder to say. It's the Land-based Phalanx Weapon System—like the Navy CIWS." He pronounced the last acronym *sea whiz*.

"It fires twenty-millimeter incendiary rounds at a rate of three thousand a minute, forming a cloud of bullets the inbound ordnance has to fly through. It'll stop the missile," Theobald insisted.

"It'll have to stop two missiles," Jax said. "The drone is an

MQ-9 clone. It'll have two missiles onboard." He rose suddenly, knocking over his chair. "Fuck this. I'm going outside. Anyone else going outside?"

"Aren't we safer in here?" Watts asked and looked at Theobald.

Jax laughed hysterically, already trotting for the door. "No way. This is ground zero. I'm outta here. You guys do what you want."

"Should we stop him? Or is he right?"

"He'll come back," Bertrand said, his Maine accent thicker than usual.

She glared at Theobald, demanding an answer to the real question.

"If the missile hits this building, then Jax is right," Theobald said. "We're goners. But the C-RAM will stop the missiles. And we're much safer in here from any shrapnel that makes it through, and way, way safer if the missile hits another structure nearby."

Bertrand slipped into Jax's seat and watched the track of the drone. "Less than a minute till they'll be in range."

"You want me to go get him, Paul?" Theobald said.

"Either he comes to his senses or not. There's no persuading him when he's like this."

"I'm gonna try." Theobald jogged off after Jax, perhaps just needing a task—any task—instead of watching the second hand sweep around the clock.

Whitney stood motionless, watching Bertrand in his seat, eyes glued to the monitor. She felt something grab at her pant leg and looked down to find it was her own hand, shaking badly and clutching at the cargo pocket of her tactical pants.

Me, tactical? What a joke. Who the hell do I think I am?

She stared at her shaking hand, intrigued because she felt preternaturally calm, but her hand just kept shaking and grabbing at the flap of her pocket like it had a mind of its own.

"Missile away," Bertrand said calmly. He looked up at her and smiled that same calm smile these guys all seemed to use. "Thirty seconds . . ."

She nodded and looked up at the clock, where the second hand was sweeping past the nine. When it reached the three . . . *boom*.

The door burst open, and Theobald came running back in.

She raised her eyebrows again—apparently, her new form of communication.

Theobald shook his head. "He said he wanted to see it coming."

She nodded and returned her gaze to the clock.

The second hand was sweeping past the eleven. How was it moving so slowly? She couldn't tear her eyes away. It swept across the twelve . . .

"Second missile in the air," Bertrand said.

The clock's red hand swept past the one . . . then the two . . .

Something roared outside, like an electronic version of a chain saw tearing through wood. It lasted two seconds, there was a pause, then it happened again.

"That's the Phalanx," Theobald said.

The second hand crossed the three.

"Take cover," he shouted and grabbed her wrist and pulled her down with him, pushing her under the table, just as the entire building shook, and a sound like metal wrenches dropping on the roof filled her ears.

"Shrapnel," Theobald hollered over the din. "From the missile. The C-RAM must have got it!"

The lights flickered but stayed on.

A dinner plate-sized hunk of metal tore through the table and embedded itself in the floor, not two feet from her. She scanned the floor and saw a half dozen smaller holes spread out away from her, little tendrils of smoke rising above them.

"Stay where you are," Bertrand said. She looked past Theobald and saw the CIA man huddled under the workstation he'd been seated at. Blood trickled down his temple from a wound somewhere above his hairline. "Second missile in a few seconds."

She heard the burst of the chain saws again—the Phalanx shooting at the second missile.

Then she heard a maniacal laugh of satisfaction and realized it was her. She looked at Theobald, whose eyes were closed. She tried to say something, but her mouth was so dry that her tongue stuck to the roof.

A second or two passed, and she tensed in anticipation for the incoming shrapnel.

Luck, or fate, or whatever, held them now.

But the shrapnel didn't come.

Instead the entire world shook, and she heard—then felt—the massive explosion.

They were plunged into darkness.

She heard what sounded like wrenches being slung against the side of the building.

"Holy shit," she said through a breath.

"The second missile got through," Theobald said, both horror and relief in his voice. "I think the building next door took a direct hit."

She didn't answer. What was there to say?

He found her hand with his and gave her a squeeze. She squeezed back. They waited in pitch-black silence for what felt like forever before Bertrand called out.

"You guys okay?"

"Yeah," Theobald said. "You?"

"Smashed my head on the desk, but I can't blame that on the missile."

"We need to get outside and help," Theobald said. "There's gonna be a shitload of casualties."

"And we need to find Jax," Whitney said, her statement more a question.

"Yeah," Theobald said without conviction.

A mobile phone rang.

"That's mine. Hold up a minute, guys," Bertrand said. "Bertrand—yes, sir, at least here at the Task Force compound, but we're headed out now . . . Oh, shit . . . No, sir, but we'd like to help out with. . ." His voice trailed off.

A third explosion rumbled outside, only this time farther away.

"What was that?" she said, grabbing Theobald's arm.

"Oh, thank God, I'll let my people know . . . Yes, sir. I wish I could say you're welcome, but it was a Navy JSOC analyst who figured it out . . . Understood . . . We're headed out to do our own BDA right now, sir, but you can get me on this phone at any time . . . Thank you, you too, sir." Bertrand ended the call, and she felt herself relax. "That explosion was one of our F/A-18s destroying the drone. Nothing else incoming on radar. Base is on lockdown. Initial reporting is that the AFSOC compound was hit by the second missile. Damage control and emergency medical are mobilizing . . ."

"Let's see what we can do to help," Theobald said.

"What about my guys?" Whitney asked.

"No power right now, so unless you can call them on the phone, we'd best just wish them Godspeed and pitch in outside."

She pictured Chunk's response if she made a blind call to his sat phone in the middle of his op. *Not an option* . . .

"Okay," she said. "Let's go."

With Yi in his ear, Chunk would hit the target and bring everyone home safe.

Because that's what Chunk and his boys did.

Better than anyone.

CHAPTER 45

"Mother, this is Jackal," Chunk said into his mike. He hated the tension in his voice because it was unfamiliar. But so was being blind and deaf. "You got anything yet from Home Plate?"

"Negative, Jackal," came Yi's calm but equally tense reply. "Negative comms with Home Plate."

In the pause Chunk thought about what the subtext in Yi's reply could mean.

"Talk to me, Mother," he demanded.

Silence hung on the line for a moment.

"Jackal, the al Qadar drone just executed a strike on Kandahar," Bowman said, making one of his infrequent appearances on the radio. "Two missiles were launched. All comms are down. We don't know anything more than that."

Shit, we were too late.

"Check," he said, trying to sound professional. "Let me know when you talk to her."

"I will," Yi came back. "What else do you need?"

"We need you to deconflict the target for us. There are multiple trucks on the N-80, and we're less than five mikes from last pos of the target."

"Working on it, Jackal. I'll have an answer in one mike."

Chunk looked up to see six pairs of NVGs staring at him like alien invaders, with six pairs of concerned eyes lit in dull green behind them. They'd heard.

Message received.

We're no longer stopping the attack—we're exacting revenge and killing these assholes so they can never do this again.

Chunk let out a slow raspy breath and, unable to think of anything either inspiring or witty to say, turned and looked out the dirty oval window of the Russian Mi-17 special operations helicopter. He knew what he needed to do and that meant pushing Watts's image out of his head to focus on the mission.

"Jackal, Mother," Yi said. "We have your target. I'm sending imagery to Stalker now, but be advised. Based on spacing, we believe the target is traveling in a convoy. Expect resistance. We will light the primary with laser from our drone overhead . . ."

"Our drone's still on station?" he asked, his voice now full of hope. If Kandahar's OGA drone operation was still functioning, that must mean Watts was okay, right?

"Control shifted to AFSOC in Colorado, operating on a two-second delay," Yi said, reading his mind and stealing his hope. Then she was back to business. "The primary target is similar to the last—an eighteen-wheeler with two containers strapped to the bed. Not sure what the lead container is, but it has one thermal inside. Three thermals in the cab, the driver and two passengers, and four thermals in the rear CONEX, two in apparent defensive positions in the midsection and two seated forward in the box—presumably, the drone pilot and his RSO. We have a pickup truck fifty yards in tow with three thermals and a tarp-covered cargo area suggesting a technical in the bed. Convoy is moving forty-five miles an hour."

"Jackal—check."

Chunk's mind was racing. The drone attack was apparently already over, so no matter what happened here, they weren't preventing shit. Which meant the objective for the operation had just changed dramatically, from nuking the GCU from the air to taking crows and collecting intel. They needed *living* bodies who could be questioned, something he and his team had failed to deliver thus far. He needed to do it this time for Whitney. Only then could they find Hamza al-Saud and cut the head off this snake before al Qadar regrouped and tried this again somewhere else.

"Jackal, three mikes to target. What's your play, bro?"

"Give me a second," Chunk said to the pilot, his temples throbbing.

He clicked on his NVGs and scanned the faces of Gold Squadron, the best warriors he'd ever served with, and the plan coalesced in his mind.

"Here's the play," he said. "Stalker, you swing wide and come up behind them from the east. We ain't stealth in this flying tub, so that'll give us the best chance at surprise. First order of business is to take out the tail pickup with the technical. We hit it first with the fifty. Then you reposition, and we put more rounds into the engine block of the target truck. Gunner, you can take out the driver and riders in the cab, but do not hose down the CONEX boxes. That second container has our HVTs; we want to take them alive. We've got no ropes since we dropped them on the last hit, so you're gonna have to hover once the target is stopped. Thoughts?"

"Roger on your plan, Jackal," the pilot replied. "Can hit the pickup, stop the truck, and kill the bad guys in the cab. Drop you when it's bricked. Show starts in three mikes."

"Roger, Stalker," he said, then briefed his guys about how to assault the GCU while minimizing the risk of getting blown up.

"Jackal, Stalker—one mike and I can engage the security truck."

Riker and Spence pulled back the old-style doors of the Russian medium-lift helo. The two helo gunners greeted them with nods, gripping the handles of their respective .50-caliber machine guns.

"What am I missing?" Chunk asked as everyone moved to positions on either side of the open doors.

"What about the CONEX in front of the GCU?" Spence asked. "One thermal inside, what the hell's going on in there?"

"Gotta be where the boss is hiding?" Saw said. "Saying prayers on his rug or meditating or some shit."

"That, or some poor sonuvabitch they kidnapped. Let's try not to strafe that container if we can help it. I really want Hamza al-Saud alive, and if it's a captive, we want to rescue them intact," Chunk said.

Everyone nodded.

"Jackal, we can hit that pickup anytime. They don't seem to know we're here yet."

Spence nodded. Saw kissed his cross. Riker gave Chunk a grin and a thumbs-up.

"Hit it, Stalker," Chunk said and tightened his grip on his rifle.

The helo dipped slightly, and Chunk leaned into the night wind, affording him a perfect view of the pickup truck tailing the target semi. He watched as the pilot fired a rocket from the portside weapon's pylon. It stretched out from them on a long red-and-orange tail.

The entire cab of the pickup truck disintegrated in a fireball, and the rear half—with a huge DShK machine gun now visible as the tarp blew from the bed—veered off the road in a cloud of sparks, crashing into the ditch and ejecting a man who had apparently been hidden beneath the tarp. The helo yawed in midair, and the starboard-side gunner gave a short burp of his .50-caliber machine gun, destroying the DShK and cutting the enemy gunner in half.

The pilot dipped the nose and accelerated toward the back of the target semitruck, and Chunk went heavy as the helo ascended sharply. Seconds later his stomach fluttered, and he became weight-less for a moment as they reached apogee and transitioned to a hover. The pilot kicked the tail left, opening a nice firing lane on the cab and engine compartment now one hundred feet below them.

Chunk whipped his left hand across his gear a final time, just as the gunner let loose a long burst, and a tongue of red tracers tore across the hood of the truck.

Sometimes a plan comes together.

He gripped his rifle just as Riker hollered, "What the fuck is that?"

Chunk leaned out the door and saw a panel suddenly fly off the top of the lead CONEX box. In horror he watched the twin barrels of a dual KPV machine gun rise out of the opening, the barrels angling toward their helicopter as they rose.

"Break right," the copilot screamed, but it was too late.

Twin streams of 14.5-mm rounds shot toward them, miss-ing the cockpit as the aircraft jinked right, but ripping across the main rotor mount.

Something exploded, and they were falling.

Chunk hit the ceiling with his helmeted head, then crashed painfully back to the deck as the pilot executed a modified auto-rotation maneuver to slow the descent. The ground rushed up outside his window, but the world was spinning in a blur.

For a moment, his mind flashed back to Iraq, when he was spiraling to earth in another helicopter, only two years earlier.

Same damn Russian piece-of-shit helicopter as the last time.

"Mother, Mother—Stalker One is hit," he called, somehow managing to key his mike "We're going down. Send Stalker Two—"

And then they hit.

Hard.

CHAPTER 46

Whitney had seen unspeakable carnage in her life, but this was different.

The difference was the smell—sulfur and kerosene mixed with burning plastic and a coppery stench. Across the ramp the AFSOC drone hangar burned fiercely, flames spiraling upward with twisting tendrils of black smoke. Then she caught a whiff of something else, an odor that reminded her of a cookout, of a burger on the grill . . .

She gagged at the epiphany.

A ruined body to her left caught in her peripheral vision, and she turned toward it.

"Is that?"

"Keep moving," Theobald said, grabbing her by the upper arm and hurrying away from the horror.

That was . . . that was Jax.

She vomited bile in her mouth, but somehow managed to swallow it. Blue lights streaked toward them across the runway as a massive emergency response mobilized. Her head cleared as they reached a patch of fresh air, and she patted the pockets of her cargo pants, suddenly in a panic.

"Wait," she said. "I lost my sat phone. I have to check on Chunk—on Jackal . . ."

She began to turn back toward the OGA drone ops building, and Theobald grabbed her sleeve.

"Hold on—use mine."

She punched in the number from memory. There was a single ring, then:

"Go for Mother."

"Mother . . . it's me. It's Watts," she said, her voice catching in her throat. "SITREP on Jackal, please."

"Whitney? Oh, thank God . . ." Yi took a long breath that was loud on the phone. "Jackal is . . . on target." There was something unspoken in Yi's message—something a part of Whitney's brain told her that she needed to tease out, but she just couldn't.

"What's your status?" a gruff baritone voice interjected. *Captain Bowman*, she realized.

"I'm . . . I'm . . ."

What the hell is my status?

"I'm intact," she finally managed. "The base was hit. Heavy casualties. We . . . we weren't able to stop it, sir."

"Understood," he came back. "From what I understand it could have been much worse."

"We're going to try and help here however we can," she said, gazing at the last of the burning fires. "Loop me in when Jackal is clear, please."

"Wilco, Home Plate. Mother out," Yi said, answering for Bowman. The line went dead.

Theobald's eyes bored into her as she turned to face him.

"Well?"

"They're hitting the target now," she said, her voice quivering with raw emotion.

Theobald nodded, but he looked concerned.

"Don't worry," Whitney said, aware her voice was now quivering with rage. "Chunk will get the bastards who did this, and when he does, this will all finally be over."

CHAPTER 47

Chunk blinked twice.

Which meant he wasn't dead.

Yet . . .

His eyes weren't closed, but he couldn't see. He reached his left hand up and pulled his NVGs back into place, and the world rematerialized in bright gray-green monochrome. He was lying on his right side on the floor of the helo. No, not the floor—the starboard cabin wall. He rolled onto his belly, felt his weapon beneath him, and pushed himself up onto hands and knees, the maneuver causing his right shoulder to flare with pain.

"Jackal, call out," he said, the effort bringing a coughing fit and tearing pain in his right chest, confirming he had multiple broken ribs. He dragged his left hand across his body, searching for other pain and wetness. "One," he said, starting the roll call.

"Two," Spence called, a grimace of pain in his voice. "I'm in the fight."

"Three is five by," Riker called, strong and clear.

Of course you are . . .

"Four. Hit my fucking head and bleeding."

"Five . . . in the fight, but I think my leg is broken, bro. Down by the ankle." Saw's voice was not that of a man with a bad fracture, but he was a SEAL after all.

"Six is intact," Morales called, and Chunk saw him moving forward to the cockpit. "Checking the pilots."

"Nine has busted ribs, but I'm in the fight," Edwards called from the back.

"Six, check on Stalker and report. Everyone else, exfil the bird and set up security ASAFP."

The port door above him looked up at the night sky, and he didn't figure he could get the aft ramp open easily, so Chunk stepped on the side rail of the starboard bench seat. With a grunt of pain, he hauled himself up by the webbing and seatbelts on the port side. His shoulder burned like it was on fire as he pulled himself through the doorway and onto the top of the wrecked, smoldering helicopter.

The Army door gunner looked up at him, stretched prone on the side of the bird, scanning through his gunsight at the truck that sat sideways on the highway, smoke pouring out of the engine compartment.

"No movement," the Special Operations soldier whispered. "The gunner on that heavy machine gun must have been killed by our fire. We shot at about the same moment, so I must have gotten him."

"You good?" Chunk asked, his head swimmy for a moment.

"I'm good," the gunner said. "How the hell is that possible?"

"A great friggin' pilot and a lot of luck," Chunk said.

"One, Six," Morales called. "I got one angel—the starboard gunner—and one urgent surgical CASEVAC in the pilot. He's awake but unstable, lots of fractures, and I think he's bleeding in his belly. Copilot is banged up but intact. Team's coming up."

Saw popped his head through the gap first, crawled past him, and immediately set up on his sniper rifle. His left boot was turned at an unlikely angle, and he winced as he set the foot down. Spence and Edwards crawled up through the door and immediately slid off the edge and dropped down onto the ground, spreading out in either direction and scanning over rifles for threats. Riker followed a moment later, sprawling beside him, then Trip peeked his head up. Chunk saw blood running down the bridge of the SEAL's nose.

"Mother, Jackal One . . ."

"Mother—lost you a moment. SITREP? Are you Great White?" Yi came back.

"Negative, Mother. Stalker One is down. Repeat—Stalker One is down. One urgent surgical CASEVAC and one KIA. We need Stalker Two immediately. We are moving on the objective."

"Roger." Her voice said she was desperate for more information, but her professionalism won out. "Comms with Home Plate. Strike confirmed. Heavy casualties, but Home Plate is intact. Repeat, Home Plate is intact."

Chunk let out a long exhale. *Thank God, Watts survived.*

"Jackal, Stalker Two—we're inbound. ETA is twelve mikes," the pilot of their standby helo announced.

"Jackal," he said in acknowledgment.

Trip was beside him now. "Let's kill these fuckers, boss."

He nodded at the younger SEAL and squeezed his arm.

"Six—stay with the urgent surgical. Five—hold here as over-watch for security. Four, Two, Three, and Nine are on me."

He slid painfully down the belly of the wrecked helicopter, moved left, and took a knee. In seconds his teammates fell in and he was surging forward as the lead of an arrowhead formation—Trip and Edwards flanking him close and Riker and Spence fanning out a few paces behind.

"Talk to me, Mother," Chunk said into the mike as he swiveled left and right, clearing the center lane.

"Four live thermals in the GCU container. Three in the cab are cooling and motionless, and one thermal appears KIA on the pavement beside the truck," Yi reported.

"That's the heavy gunner," Saw said in his ear. "Got him on my scope. He's dead as shit."

"Two and Nine, clear the cab, then join us at the rear. Four tangos inside, and we absolutely must take someone back alive," Chunk said.

Their wedge-shaped element split, with Spence and Trip peeling off toward the cab of the truck.

"Movement in the back, Jackal," came Yi's calm voice. She was in the zone now, and Chunk was glad they had her. "A door on the side of the GCU just opened, and you have two tangos ready to surge."

Chunk took a knee, the once-hot pain in his chest and shoulder now just background noise. He brought his laser targeting dot up just as two figures charged out of the GCU. They wore military kits with plate carriers over their long shirts, heads wrapped in shemaghs that left only their eyes exposed. The left one slipped off the side of the flatbed and dropped into a crouch. He opened fire at the same time Chunk put a round through his forehead. Beside him, Riker's rifle burped in time with his own, his bullet striking mere inches below Chunk's.

"Mine," Riker said, as the fighter pitched forward into the dirt.

The other shooter, who wore a bulkier vest, drew his arm back—apparently ready to throw a grenade—when Saw's sniper rifle barked from behind them, and the man pitched backward onto the ground. The grenade landed beside him. The explosion was mostly dirt and noise, but the grenade ignited the man's suicide vest, and he was consumed in a fireball.

"Two squirters out the door, heading south," Yi announced.

"Me, Two, and Three," Chunk barked and began sprinting after them with Spence and Riker.

His ribs screamed at him as he ran. He rounded the corner at the rear of the truck, cleared left and right, then circled wide.

"They're heading south across the field, toward the tree line," Yi said. "They're keeping the truck between them and Five."

Smart. They know we have a sniper.

He saw them now, running full speed without looking back, arms pumping and apparently unarmed. He saw movement to his right, and Riker was closing the gap. One of the fleeing fighters whirled, stopped, and threw his arms up in surrender. Chunk took a knee, his momentum sliding him across the rocky ground painfully as he aimed. Not taking any chances, he put a bullet in the man's right thigh. The terrorist dropped to the ground instantly, clutching his leg.

"Tango two appears unarmed," Riker called.

"Then take him alive," Chunk said.

Spence angled wide, leaned into his rifle, and fired. The 5.56 round tore through the running man's ass, and he fell to the ground.

Riker pulled up at a safe distance, and he and Spence covered both wounded terrorists in case either was ready to martyr himself for Allah. But neither asshole did. Jihadi leadership was consistent on this point, always leaving the blowing-themselves-up part to the kids. His chest throbbing, Chunk moved in slowly, his green dot floating on the closer man's forehead.

"Lift your shirt," he growled, first in English, then in Arabic. The man did so, very slowly and carefully, exposing his bare abdomen and chest and rolling side to side to show he had no explosives strapped to his body. "You speak English?" Chunk barked, but the man didn't answer, only glared at him, his eyes venom and his face rage.

"Checking the other guy," Spence called, and in Chunk's peripheral vision he saw a similar scene playing out. "He's clean too."

Riker moved in and put his booted foot on the first man's left forearm, and Chunk now did the same on the man's right.

"Yes," the man said finally answering as he leaned his head back to rest on the ground. "I speak English. My name is Hamza al-Saud, leader of al Qadar, and I demand you turn me over to the Pakistani authorities. I have nothing to say to Americans operating illegally in this country."

Riker chuckled, took a knee, and frisked the terrorist's sides, groin, and legs. "Oh, don't worry. I'm sure you'll think of something to say in the dark hole you're headed for," the Senior Chief said. He pulled flex cuffs from his kit. "Everyone talks."

"There is nothing else you Americans can take from me," the man said, his dark eyes burning through the barrels of Chunk's NVGs. "I will say nothing because you have nothing with which to compel me. I will wait and watch until Allah's final judgment wipes you from the face of the earth."

Riker pulled the man into a seated position, his hands behind his back in the flex cuffs.

"You do that, bro," Riker said, stepping back now and holding his weapon trained on the man's chest. "A week from now I'll be drinking a beer, grilling burgers, and having sex on the beach, and I won't even remember I ever fucking met you."

Chunk smiled. *Man, I love this guy.*

"Two, how you doing?" he called to Spence.

"My guy is clean and cuffed," Spence replied. "Won't give me his name, but I think he speaks English."

"All right," Chunk said. "Get him up. We're leaving."

"Truck's clear, boss. We got tons of shit, including hard drives, a laptop, and two cell phones," Trip reported from back at the tractor-trailer.

"Check. Stalker, SITREP?"

"Stalker Two is three mikes out," the helo pilot called in.

"Roger, Stalker Two. Set down beside Stalker One. We have nine to exfil, two crows, and one KIA. We blow the downed helo, and we're out of here in five mikes."

"Copy all, let's get you home."

Chunk shifted his gaze to Hamza al-Saud who was lying at his feet.

"Looks like your terrorist days are over, motherfucker," he said and pulled a can of Kodiak from his pocket. Packing the tobacco with rhythmic snaps of his wrist, he regarded the man wholly responsible for this nightmare that would forever be his first Tier One operation. "Oh, and in case you were wondering, we shot down your drone."

Holding his rifle in a combat carry, he turned and started the short trek back to the crash site. Despite the throbbing pain in his chest, he walked tall and with swagger, refusing to give even the slightest consolation prize to the terrorist mastermind whose dark, haunted eyes he could feel burning a hole in his back.

CHAPTER 48

"We did it, brother," Hamza said with a broad smile from the driver's seat of the nondescript getaway sedan they'd used to flee minutes before the American Special Operations helicopter hit the convoy. "Allah is smiling down on us tonight."

Qasim nodded and watched the lights of Peshawar zip by outside his window.

He wasn't disappointed to be alive, but neither was he elated.

Apathetic, he supposed.

He felt Hamza squeeze his right shoulder. "Are you okay, Qasim?"

"Yes," was all he could muster.

"Good," Hamza said, as if the matter were settled once and for all. "Because you have a wedding to get ready for. I don't know about you, but I, for one, am looking forward to returning to London."

"London?" Qasim gasped. "Impossible. My life in London ended the day I walked through that hangar door."

"Now you're just being melodramatic," Hamza said with a laugh. His good-natured chiding reminded Qasim of Eshan—speaking with the comfortable intimacy of a lifelong friend rather than a terrorist who, only an hour ago, had directed the first air strike against the United States since 9/11.

The very thing that drove America into Afghanistan in the first place.

"I'm not being melodramatic," Qasim said, his mind spiraling down an abyss of worry. "The British and the Americans share intelligence, and the Americans photographed me and Eshan at the border. They know we were together. It is only a matter of time before they come for me."

"If you recall from the video, Eshan's death was a messy one. I do not think what was left of his face was enough to satisfy facial recognition parameters . . ."

This comment hit Qasim like a gut punch as the macabre video clip of Eshan taking a round to the face at point-blank range played in his mind.

"So put these thoughts out of your mind," Hamza continued. "Think about your future. Think about your new life. Diba, your lovely bride, and her parents and sister are already in Kabul, waiting to meet you at the airport. Their tickets to London have been paid in full."

"What? How is this possible?"

"What did you think Eshan was doing while you were configuring the drone? He was working the entire time: securing travel visas for Diba's family, making reservations at a mosque in London for your wedding, preparing the wedding announcement, checking and replying to your emails, updating your Facebook page with pictures from your time in Afghanistan, and creating a virtual fairy tale for anyone who might be interested in knowing what you did while you were on holiday." Hamza smiled. "It is our gift to you, for everything you did for us."

Qasim looked at the terrorist prince, speechless.

"What is that look? Did you think all of this was just to have you pilot the drone one time, then go into hiding in the slums of Pakistan? Did you think I would send you home to the Hindu Kush, to join the ignorant Taliban fighters in some cave? Don't be ridiculous, Qasim. This was always the plan. Eshan wanted to bring you into our family and help you have a family of your own. It has always been about family. Nothing else matters. Your life is finally just beginning."

Despite not wanting them to, Hamza's words moved Qasim. He felt warmth inside. Was this what hope felt like? It had been so long, he had forgotten.

"So you want me to continue working at British Aero?" he asked tentatively.

"Of course. Take some time, settle back into your job, and be the best damn engineer that you can. Try to get promoted. In the meantime, get married and make love to your wife and have a son. Enjoy life. When I have all the chess pieces in place for the next operation, I will contact you . . . but not as Hamza al-Saud. As of this moment, I am Asadi Bijan."

"I don't understand?"

"Hamza al-Saud was captured by the Americans. He will be taken to a black site and interrogated, broken, and possibly disposed of."

"I don't understand," Qasim repeated, screwing up his face.

"One of our brothers martyred himself today, taking my place—my identity. He has made the ultimate sacrifice for Allah. It is a living martyrdom, but martyrdom in the truest sense."

"Your bodyguard?" Qasim asked, remembering how the man shadowed Hamza virtually everywhere and climbed into the GCU when they were escaping.

"Yes," Hamza said. "Razaq asked for this privilege. He has been protecting me and training for this for two years."

"He looks nothing like you!"

"Similar enough. I have kept a very low profile. Besides, he is a good actor. Conviction is the ultimate mask."

"But how do you know they did not shoot him? They killed everyone on every raid."

"There was a motion-activated camera inside the GCU. They took him."

Qasim looked into Hamza's eyes—eyes of a man he'd once feared, then admired, and now held in reverence. How was such an intellect possible? How could a mind be so strategic, so deliberate, so prescient? It explained how someone so young could have risen so fast. Hamza al-Saud was the Steve Jobs of their jihad. Brilliant, driven, groundbreaking . . .

"I see I've left you speechless," Hamza said with a laugh. "What is my name?"

"Umm . . ." Qasim hesitated, not wanting to fail this test. He had heard the name but not committed it to memory. "Uh . . . Bijan," he said finally. "Asad Bijan."

"Asadi Bijan," Hamza corrected and parked along the curb at the airport. "Time to go, Qasim. See that man standing by the pillar? His name is Jani. He has your tickets, passport, and all the paperwork for your trip home. Good luck."

Qasim opened the passenger door. "What happens next?" he asked, unable to stop himself from asking the question he already knew the answer to.

Hamza smiled, his dark eyes full of purpose. "Next . . . the real work begins."

CHAPTER 49

Chunk looked aft, toward the back of the C-17 cargo plane where First Platoon from Gold Squadron in the Navy's newly reconstituted Tier One SEAL Team had set up a campsite on the raised ramp of the workhorse transport jet. He looked at his banged-up crew, shook his head, and smiled. They should probably be stopping at the military hospital in Landstuhl, Germany, but telling bullheaded frogmen anything of the sort was like telling a cat to breathe underwater. Saw's leg had been placed in a cast by the JSOC medical unit after a painful closed reduction. A follow-up with orthopedics would be required once they were home, but a full recovery was all but guaranteed. Trip had had his head sewn up, and everyone else had checked out okay except the pilot, who'd had emergency surgery in J-bad and was probably already in the ICU at Landstuhl.

As for Chunk, his ribs were taped—broken in three places—and he would need rehab for his shoulder. Riker, as usual, had walked away with hardly a scratch. Only Edwards was a concern, with his own set of broken ribs, but also a pulmonary contusion. The surgeon had explained that it was really just a bruise of the lung, but unlike a soft-tissue or skin bruise, this could have devastating complications. The SEAL also had a small amount of fluid in his pleural cavity—what the surgeon called a hemothorax. In the end, the lead surgeon from the JSOC had cleared Edwards to fly back with his team while grumbling something about "fucking SEALs." Chunk would insist that the Edwards be admitted at Portsmouth Naval Hospital in Virginia before the last leg of the trip to Tampa. For now, he watched the frogman tip back a longneck Budweiser and say something that made the entire team laugh, then grimace and grab his chest as he laughed, himself.

Seeing Chunk looking on, Riker tipped his beer in his direction and smiled. Chunk gave his friend a two-finger salute off the brim of his ball cap. Then he grabbed a beer from the cooler and walked over to where Saw lay in a hammock, a ball cap over his eyes.

"Sleeping, bro?"

"Not anymore," Saw grumbled and pushed his hat up with a thumb. He scratched his thick beard and yawned.

Chunk took a seat.

"Whaddya think, Senior Chief?" he said, kicking up his feet. "You make the right call?"

"Which one?" Saw asked, intrigued.

Chunk laughed and took a pull of his beer. "Coming over to the Tier One? You were kicking around retirement when we got tapped to screen. Don't tell me you weren't planning on dropping your package after our last deployment."

Saw laughed and kicked a flip-flop-covered foot over the cast on his other leg. "Dude, what we did in the last week was more than we accomplished in the whole last deployment with Four," the sniper said. "I miss my wife and kids like crazy, but this—what we did here—is why I became a SEAL to begin with. We saved an assload of lives and made the world a better place. That's my calling, Chunk. I think this is what God created me for—stopping these evil assholes and helping people that can't help themselves. Ellie has my six, as long as what I do matters."

Chunk nodded and smiled, not sure what else to say.

"All in, bro," Saw added, definitively answering the question, then pulled his hat back down over his eyes.

Enough said.

Chunk thought of walking to the back and hanging with the team, but maybe those days were gone. He was the Skipper of Gold now, right? He'd always loved that the Teams were a place where you were judged by your operator skills more than rank, but still. Would his guys decompress better if he hung back?

"Can I talk to you?" a female voice said behind him. He turned to Watts, who saved him from having to make a decision.

"Yeah, sure," he said.

She turned and headed toward a handful of airline-style seats, anchored forward of the nylon benches that filled the mid portion of the cargo plane. She slid into one of the chairs, pulled her legs up under her, and dropped her hands in her lap.

"What's up?" he said, taking the seat beside her. "You look like you just lost your puppy, while the rest of us are celebrating our first big win as the new Tier One." When she nodded but didn't look up, he added, "You did an incredible job—you know that, right?"

"It's weird," she said, looking at the cluster of SEALs drinking beer at the other end of the cargo bay. "One minute you guys are grab-assing and joking with each other like a high school football team, and the next you're doing things—I'll just say it, *impossible* things—with purpose and precision, the likes of which I've never seen before. To step into the line of fire, without fear of death and consequence, over and over again . . . I just . . ." He watched as she traced her fingers across the knot tattoo on her wrist. Chunk let her have the moment and waited for her to organize her thoughts. She looked up again. "I'm not sure I belong here, Chunk. I'm just an analyst. I don't think I was made for this type of work."

He took a long breath, knowing how he responded mattered.

"I know that the pace and intensity of what we do is overwhelming, but you are a vital part of this team. The door-kicking, bad-guy-shooting component is only half of this equation. It took your brain to identify the drone threat, then untie the knot. It took your conviction to drive the mission forward. If you hadn't taken the initiative to study the convoy aftermath and come up with a theory about what really happened, we'd still be in Tampa with Bravo Platoon doing workup exercises."

She shook her head and looked up. "Nine men and one woman died in Kandahar. Three dozen were wounded."

"And if you hadn't unraveled al Qadar's plot, that number would have been hundreds, maybe thousands."

He sighed and leaned back in his seat, felt the dull ache from his jacked-up shoulder and the fading burn from the gunshot graze in his upper arm. Shit, what else could he say? Working in this environment *was* insane. And she'd been thrown in the deep end of the pool. She looked at him, and he tried to see something other than the shock of her last few days. And he thought he did—maybe he'd told her what she needed to hear.

"Look, the world we work in is a shitburger," he said, making her laugh. "Oh, you like that one?"

"Yeah, that's fire," she said, shaking her head.

He wasn't really sure what "that's fire" meant, but he went on, "Look, what I mean is, if this world is not for you, then I can get you back to your old job with a phone call, and it won't hurt your career, I promise."

"I don't care about that—" she began, but he held his hand up and continued.

"I know you don't. I've seen how you work. But here's the question I have for you." He leaned an elbow on the armrest they shared. "Do you know of another job—including your old job in McLean—where your drone-strike theory could have been chased up an operational chain, generated tasking for a direct-action unit with the capability to stop the threat, and implemented in time before the next attack? I'm not dissing the IC here, not at all, but the bureaucracy of the system would have prevented a direct-action tasking like ours from happening in time to save Kandahar. Do you agree?"

"Yeah," she said, nodding. "And I can't think of another command where I would have been given so much leeway."

He rubbed his beard, not sure how to say it but charging forward anyway. "Look, I let you down, Heels . . ." She smiled at the nickname—*a good sign.* "I didn't adequately prepare you for what you would face in the field, and that goes double for this operation. Tier One SEALs have a term for ops in places like the one we just pulled out of. Maybe you've heard it—the suck."

"Oh, yeah. I've heard it, all right."

"Well, I threw you into the deep end of the suck without teaching you how to swim first. That was my bad, and I won't make that mistake again. If you want to stay with us, we'd be honored to have you. I can't promise the next op will be any less dangerous, but what I can promise is that when we work together, we accomplish serious good for mankind. And I will personally make sure you're ready before you go downrange next time."

She sighed and opened her mouth to answer, but he cut her off again.

"Nope . . . I'll tell you the same thing I would tell any SEAL in my command. Don't make a decision this important on the fly, and sure as hell not in the waning fog of combat operations. Take a few days. Think about it, then let's talk again when we're back home, okay?" He rose and smiled down at her. "We *can* still do our job without you, Heels, but I'm not bullshitting when I say it would be a helluva lot harder."

"Thank you," she said, flashing him a genuine smile.

A strong hand squeezed his shoulder from behind in just the wrong place, making him wince.

"What're we talking about?" Theobald asked, stepping up beside Chunk, oblivious to the stinger he'd just inflicted. "Oh, and thanks for the ride home, by the way."

"Least we could do, bro," Chunk said. "We were just talking careers."

"Oh, jeez—let me chime in, then. Run, Watts! Run far away as fast as you can!" the DIA man said, then let out a chuckle. He edged past Chunk and dropped into the seat beside Watts. "I'll take the career counseling from here," he said with a grin, crossed his legs, and looked at Watts. "Let me tell you my personal experience with these SEALs. About a year and a half ago I was in Syria, just minding my own business, running a nice established NOC, when I get a call from this dude named Smith asking me for a favor. Yeah, really, Smith. Next thing I know, this SEAL character shows up. Over the next twenty-four hours, the dude talks me into assaulting a terrorist compound. Just the two of us, I might add. I get shot, blown up, and a house collapsed on top of me, while he rides off into the sunset chasing down a gang of kidnapping terrorists single-handed. Meanwhile, I lose my NOC, spend three weeks in ICU, and don't even get a box of chocolates. I'm telling you, if you meet a SEAL named John Dempsey, run away and never look back."

Chunk barked a laugh. "You know Dempsey? Oh, shit, let me tell you. I got roped into an op with that guy in Iraq once, and he gets me blown up *and* crashed in a Russian helicopter. Same piece-of-shit bird I crashed in yesterday, come to think of it. But that's not even the craziest shit—if I could only tell you about the last op . . ."

"It seems to me, Lieutenant Commander Redman, that your crew and Dempsey's crew have a lot in common. You're both bad news. Case in point, you and this skinny young girl show up, destroy my new NOC, get our hotel ambushed, then fly me to Kandahar just in time to be on the receiving end of the first UCAV attack on an American military installation." Theobald looked over at Watts, who was smiling now, enjoying the banter. "Maybe it's not a Dempsey thing—maybe it's a SEAL thing."

They all laughed at this, including Watts, and the look in her eyes told Chunk she was already in a better place.

"Excuse us, Chunk," Theobald said, shooing him away with a wave of his hand. "I'll take it from here and give her the *real* inside scoop."

Chunk shrugged, wincing in pain because he'd forgotten about his shoulder, and headed toward the back of the C-17 to finally join his men. As he left, he heard Theobald begin his counseling session. "You see, Watts, the thing you have to remember about SEALs is . . ."

Thank you, Bobby Theobald . . . I owe you one, brother.

CHAPTER 50

The air in the mosque smelled depleted . . . if there was such a thing.

It was as if the stale exhalations of hundreds of men still lingered from the last prayer service, and the air had not yet been renewed. Qasim pushed the thought from his mind and adjusted his necktie. He'd chosen to wear a bespoke three-piece suit for the ceremony, adopting the official uniform of the enemy on this most momentous of days. He'd wanted it to be a private affair and to issue no invitations for the ceremony, but Hamza had been clear. It was absolutely essential for their mission that Qasim completely reintegrate into his old life in London and return to work at British Aero. Of course, Hamza had no way to know that Qasim had never had a *real* life in London. His coworkers were courteous, but they were not friends, because none of them had ever known him, not really. Regardless, the man who'd returned from Pakistan was nothing like the man who'd left on that well-earned and long-overdue holiday all those weeks ago.

New Qasim was confident.

New Qasim had charisma.

New Qasim embraced the Western life.

"It is for Allah that we must live this lie. It is not an apostate life when lived in service of the Quran, brother," Hamza had said. "What we do, we do for Allah, but also for Eshan, for it is only by his sacrifice and foresight that we are alive today."

Oh, Eshan . . .

It was Eshan's absence today, of all days, that brought him the most pain.

He scanned the faces of the assembled, nearly two dozen coworkers from British Aero, more than half of them with guests. And then there was Diba's family—all of whom he vaguely remembered from his childhood, but none of whom he knew well. Would it upset them to know that their attendance meant little more to him than that of his coworkers? The only guests in attendance today that mattered to him were ghosts: his father, his sister, and Eshan.

He felt their presence, cold and pitiable.

And finally there was Hamza—radiant and regal as a prince—whose attendance had taken him by surprise. Qasim had almost slipped and called him Hamza twice, catching himself both times without anyone the wiser. Hamza al-Saud was in American custody, probably being interrogated to death in some dark hole. Asadi Bijan was in London now. It was the perfect name: Asadi, meaning "strong as a lion," and Bijana, "lonely place." An apt metaphor, as if chosen by Allah himself.

Standing across from Qasim, Diba looked positively radiant.

This was the wedding she had dreamed of since she was a child, he knew. Perhaps, at one time, this was the wedding he had dreamed of too. He could no longer remember. It was certainly not the wedding he deserved.

Not anymore.

The imam smiled at them. After all, weddings were supposed to be joyous occasions, but Qasim was having none of it. His heart was a star imploded—a black hole after a supernova, voraciously consuming all light, warmth, and joy in the universe. When the time came to speak his vows, he felt an upwelling of emotion, but instead of love for the woman across from him, he was boiling with hatred for the Americans who'd robbed him of everything that was good and happy and true in his life. And so it was for this reason that the vows he spoke fulfilled a dual purpose—committing him in body to Diba and in spirit to Allah's army.

He was a terrorist now . . .

No, not a terrorist—that was *their* label for him, he reminded himself.

He was a trusted leader.

An enlightened warrior.

A shadow soldier.

The once and future prince of House al-Saud, the visionary leader of al Qadar, had promoted Qasim after the events in Mingora. He had also given him a precious gift, which had arrived via courier at Qasim's flat in London the afternoon of his return. The package had contained an antique Saudi Arabian dagger with a mother-of-pearl handle gilded in eighteen-karat gold. The curved blade was nine inches long and forged from Damascus steel. It was the most beautiful thing Qasim ever seen. He caressed it every night, running the pad of his index finger over its cold, smooth, polished surface. The undulating ripples in the gunmetal-gray steel had a hypnotic effect on him, like watching swirling eddies in a stream.

The imam said Qasim's name, snapping him out of his fugue. At the imam's prompting to seal their vows with an embrace, Qasim leaned in and kissed his bride, but when he pulled away, he saw that her eyes were rimmed with tears, which made him angry.

None of this was his fault.

This had been done to him.

She looked at him strangely. He forced a smile onto his face. "I love you, Diba," he whispered, reading his lines in a play.

Her smile broadened, and she kissed him again.

Everything that happened after that was a blur—the reception, the dancing, the thank-yous and goodbyes. Back at his flat, in the new queen-size bed he had purchased for them, he consummated the marriage quickly and robotically. And when he was finished, only then did he feel compassion and empathy for his new bride.

"I'm sorry, Diba," he whispered to her back. "I know I am not behaving as you imagined. It's not fair, I know . . . I am not the man you thought I was."

She said nothing, just sniffled and covered her nakedness with the bedsheet.

"I will find a way to make it up to you," he said. "I promise."

"Can I talk to you, or will you hit me?" she said, her voice small but steadfast.

He was taken aback by the comment. He had never struck a woman in his life. *Where was this coming from?*

"Of course you can talk to me. You can say anything." He gently coaxed her to roll over and look at him. "I would never strike you."

"What we did today was not a wedding. It was procedure," she said. "The stage was set, the players in place. Everyone was there—my heart was there—everyone was there but you." Voice cracking, she added, "And it broke my heart."

"I know."

"Then why did you do it? Why did you punish me like that?"

"You misunderstand. It was not a punishment. It is not that my heart does not belong to you, my love. It does—I am your husband now and forever. I retreated out of necessity. I refuse to give the Americans the opportunity to do to you what they did to my father, my sister, and my best friend. What I do now, I do to protect you. To protect us—*all* of us."

She closed her eyes, and a little laugh escaped her lips.

A flash of anger stirred in his chest, but he swallowed it down. "What is funny about that?"

"Fate has a cruel sense of humor, it seems," she said, opening her eyes, her voice suddenly weary.

"What is that supposed to mean?"

"I have loved you from afar for as long as I can remember. I was drawn to you because I thought you were not like the other men, always chest-pounding, settling their disagreements with their fists and their guns. In you, I saw a compassionate and wounded soul. A man with inner courage and conviction. A man not afraid to turn the other cheek. A gentle man. A studious man. I told my father this. I told him my greatest fear was being married into the Taliban. My greatest nightmare was to be a terrorist's wife."

"I am not a terrorist," he said, trying very, very hard to keep his voice measured and calm.

"We are married now, Qasim. Please don't lie to me," she said.

"I'm not lying."

"You think of me as the shy girl who stands at the wall and watches everyone. That is true, I am shy, but it does not mean I am stupid. I may not be educated and worldly like you, but I could have been, had my circumstances been different. I knew what Eshan was doing. I also knew that he was using me as a pawn to manipulate you. That he was trying to recruit you . . ."

A pit formed in Qasim's stomach as it hit home that Diba understood everything. "Then why did you agree to marry me?"

"Because I did not, in a million years, think that he would succeed," she said, the dam finally breaking as she began to sob. "I guess I am a stupid girl after all."

He didn't touch her for a moment, just watched her chest heave as she cried in front of him. Eventually, pity got the best of him, and he pulled her in for a hug. She did not resist his embrace, but she did not reciprocate either, her body wooden against his.

"Can you get out, Qasim?" she asked, her breath hot on his chest. "Tell them you've changed your mind and you want to live a simple life."

"I don't know," he said.

"You don't know if you can, or you don't know if you want to?"

"Both," he said, finally being honest with her.

She nodded, then after a long silence asked him, "Will you try, for me . . . please?"

He let out a long exhale. "Okay," he said, caressing her hair and wondering if he was lying to her and to himself. "I will try, Diba . . . for you."

EPILOGUE

"What the hell is this place?" Whitney said, putting her hands on her hips and squinting as she took a measure of her surroundings.

Chunk grunted a laugh as he set the two heavy Pelican cases on the wooden firing stand. She hadn't offered to help carry them, because, well, so many reasons.

"This is the range where they do initial quals for junior airmen on the base," he said, snapping the gun cases open, "and the best place for other units just looking to put some lead on paper."

She looked around the heavily scarred and weathered outdoor range, a facility she imagined would be put to shame by any of the civilian shooting clubs in the Carrollwood suburbs north of the base. Plywood dividers separated the simple wooden shooting stations, with dirt lanes leading to target stands at seventy-five yards. Unmowed grass grew between them, probably tall enough to reach her knees. A hill behind the target stands served as a berm to absorb rounds that found—or didn't find—their mark. Behind the berm, unoccupied marshland stretched for hundreds of yards, a secondary backstop for any bullets that sailed high.

She brushed a sweep of bangs out of her eyes and folded her arms across her chest. She was wearing a short-sleeved T-shirt today, which exposed several of her more intricate tattoo jobs, but did nothing for her waifish physique. She'd never cared about her "task-chair fitness level" before this assignment, but upon seeing Chunk's gorilla arms rippling in the afternoon sun, she suddenly felt self-conscious. No, not self-conscious . . . inadequate?

Not inadequate . . . something else.

"But shouldn't I be practicing in the kill house? I need to learn how to shoot and move—isn't that's what you said? We have to train like we fight—that I need muscle memory. Remember?"

"I did. You're right," he said and pulled a short-barreled Rattler from the case. He set it down on the wooden stand and placed a magazine beside it. Then he walked the lane, carrying two targets—simple circular things that flashed neon when hit with a bullet—while talking to her over his shoulder. "But I made a mistake. In the Teams, when we first start weapons training, we break the weapons down and put them together again, over and over. Then we fire rounds, three at a time, at a simple target, dropping the magazines and reloading, over and over." He secured the targets on the target posts at the end of the two center lanes. "The point is there is *lots* of muscle memory we need to train into you before you're ready for the kill house," he said, walking back. "We need to make the weapon into an extension of you. Then the shoot-and-move component will be easier. Better to think of muscle memory in terms of layers. Weapon familiarity and handling first, aiming second, shoot and move last. Make sense?"

She nodded. It made perfect sense.

She picked up the assault rifle, feeling both apprehensive and determined. This was the first time she'd touched a weapon since that night in the hotel. He watched her check the chamber clear by pulling the charging handle back a few inches. Next, she looked at the spine of the magazine, counting her rounds. Satisfied, she snapped the magazine into the receiver, tapping it twice, just like he'd shown her. She checked the safety, then chambered a round with the charging handle, checked the safety again, and set the weapon—barrel pointing downrange—on the table.

She cocked an eyebrow at him.

"Good," he said.

She nodded, but her gaze fell to her feet and the dirty Oakley boots she'd worn every day since they'd returned from Pakistan . . . she wasn't sure why.

"Did Theobald tell you I shot a man?"

Chunk took a deep breath, like he'd been waiting for this. "Yes," he said.

"Did he also tell you I missed?"

"He said you hit the guy in the leg."

"Like I said, I missed."

"A hit is not a miss."

"Oh, don't patronize me. If Theobald hadn't been there to back me up, I'd be dead." She lifted her head and let her mind's eye take her to the hotel hallway in Mingora. The image was so real that she could almost smell the sweat of the approaching terrorists and felt her pulse quicken. She squeezed her eyes shut ,and the image evaporated—for now. She looked over at Chunk, who was watching her without staring. "I'm glad I didn't kill that man, but I'm also glad that Theobald did. Is that crazy? It sounds like a contradiction. It's the strangest damn thing, Chunk. I tried to kill the other one, the younger fighter, but I couldn't. Or didn't. I'm not sure which. But I'm glad he's dead too."

He didn't say anything, seemingly content to let her talk through her first combat experience uninterrupted.

"I was so scared," she said and felt her eyes rim with tears. "I was certain I was going to die."

No, you're not doing this in front of him, Whit, she silently chastised herself, shifting a quarter turn so he was in her peripheral vision now.

"And I didn't want to die . . . but I didn't want anyone else to die either. I didn't want to kill those men who were trying to kill me, but I wanted them dead . . ." She shook her head, frustrated that she couldn't properly articulate what she was feeling.

He touched her arm, and she turned to look at him, eyes wet but unashamed.

"People who like killing have no business here," he said. "Contrary to what you might think, we work hard—very hard— to weed out those who like killing. Because we are not in the *killing* business. We are in the *intervention* business."

"Are those your words," she said, "or someone else's?"

"You know I ain't smart enough to come up with something like that all on my lonesome," he said, cranking his Texas twang up to eleven and flashing her a self-deprecating grin. "Nah, it was something Captain Bowman told me, that Kelso Jarvis once told him. He said that every Tier One mission is a preemptive strike. We kill so that innocents can live. We conduct violence on a small scale to prevent violence on a mass scale. We fight battles to avoid fighting wars. It's violence, for certain, but it's a violence of action."

"Sounds very Machiavellian. The ends justify the means and all that."

He thought for a moment, then said, "Yeah, well, I guess I'm a pragmatist, not a philosopher. In my humble opinion, it's not *what* we do that defines our character, it's *how* and *why* we do it. Show me a pacifist who defeated a terrorist and saved lives, then we can debate methods and means."

"I'm not trying to pick a fight," she said, meeting his gaze. "I'm just trying to figure out where I stand on killing. In that hallway I was conflicted, and it almost cost me my life. Right here, right now, I'm still conflicted. A man named Andy, who I never even knew, died on that roof in Mingora. Jax died in the drone strike on Kandahar, and so did others. Do you think—"

"No," he said, immediately cutting her off.

She gritted her teeth and pushed. "But if I had put the pieces together sooner. If I had anticipated the enemy's next move before . . ."

"Don't do it, Whitney. Remember, those questions go nowhere," he said, then under his breath, "nowhere good." He looked away, contemplating his own demons, she surmised. After a long pause, he fixed his eyes on her. "You're smart. And bold. And not afraid to give your best self and risk being wrong. We had setbacks, and you didn't quit. Without you, there wouldn't have been a mission in the first place, and a lot more innocent people would have died."

"But I didn't stop it. A missile got through."

"One missile, yes, but the other missile was destroyed and so was the drone before it crashed into the barracks, or the chow hall, or a C-17 loaded with soldiers. If not for you, the Phalanx might never have been activated. If not for you, an F-18 would not have been scrambled. We could have lost hundreds—even thousands—had the attack on Kandahar been executed as planned. You did good, Whitney. We're damn lucky to have you."

"Do you really mean that?" she said.

"Hell yes, I do. And I'm going to make damn sure that next time, you're ready. Out here," he said, gently squeezing her biceps, "up here," he added, tapping her forehead, "and in here," he concluded, pointing to her heart.

She looked at him—really looked at him—and in that moment she thought maybe she saw the real Lieutenant Commander Keith Redman for the first time. He had peeled back the layers, both hers and his, to give her the counsel she needed. He was not a mindless killing machine. He was not a cowboy with a machine gun. He was a leader, by example. A motivator, by force of will. A teacher. A brother.

A hero . . .

He was a Tier One Navy SEAL.

Chunk picked up his unloaded rifle and checked that the chamber was clear. "First lesson. For now, don't worry about aiming." He sighted on the target in a combat stance. "Just concentrate on trying to not move the weapon when you squeeze the trigger."

He squeezed the trigger three times in rapid succession.

Click, click, click.

"See how my trigger pulls did not impact the attitude of the weapon?"

"Show off," she grumbled and lifted her Rattler off the table stand.

She aimed down range, adjusting her stance and noting the feel of the weapon against her shoulder and cheek. She squeezed the trigger three times, concentrating on not moving the weapon as she did, and three rounds barked out. She watched three neon flashes appear on the target—wide apart and almost random, but all of them on the paper.

That was something, she supposed as she set the smoking rifle back on the stand.

"You'll get there," he said with a laugh. "I have no doubt about that."

An awkward pause hung between them, until she said, "Thanks, Chunk."

"For what?" he said, fishing a tin of wintergreen snuff from his pocket.

"For today," she said, giving him her best bro nod, "and everything else."

"You're welcome."

"Oh, and also for not calling me Heels."

Chunk laughed, "Today only." Then he gestured at her rifle. "Go again."

ACKNOWLEDGMENTS

We would like to thank far more people than space allows, but in particular, we wish to thank our families for their endless support of our work. Without them and their love and encouragement, none of these books could happen. We love you.

Thank you to our phenomenal agent, Gina Panettieri of Talcott Notch, who continues, day after day and month after month, to deliver more opportunities to share our work with the world.

Thank you to our new team at Blackstone for proving to be among the very best in the business, taking our story and turning it into a novel.

A special thank-you to you, our loyal readers, for following us on yet another adventure and for encouraging us to find a way to bring Chunk and his team to the front and center of their own series. Hope we did it justice for you.

And thanks to our many of brothers, and some new friends, from the Special Operations community for your support, advice, and encouragement. While our work is fiction, we strive—always—to bring to our characters a realism that honors the work you still do and the sacrifices you and your families make. Thank you . . . You know who you are.

GLOSSARY

AQ Al-Qaeda

BDU Battle Dress Uniform

BUD/S Basic Underwater Demolition / SEAL training

CASEVAC Casualty Evacuation

CIA Central Intelligence Agency

CO Commanding Officer

CONUS Continental United States

CSO Chief Staff Officer

DNI Director of National Intelligence

DoD Department of Defense

Eighteen Delta Special Operations Medic

EOD Explosive Ordnance Disposal

Exfil Exfiltration

FARP Forward Area Refueling Point; a forward staging area

FOB Forward Operating Base

GSW Gunshot wound

HALO High Altitude, Low Opening

HUMINT Human Intelligence

HVT High-Value Target

IC Intelligence Community

Infil Infiltration

IR Infrared

ISAF International Security Assistance Force in Afghanistan

ISR Intelligence, Surveillance, and Reconnaissance

JO Junior Officer

JSOC Joint Special Operations Command

JSOTF Joint Special Operations Task Force

KIA Killed In Action

LZ Landing Zone

MARSOC Marine Corps Special Operations Command

MEDEVAC Medical Evacuation

NCTC National Counterterrorism Center

NOC Nonofficial Cover

NSA National Security Agency

NSW Naval Special Warfare

NVGs Night-Vision Goggles

ODNI Office of the Director of National Intelligence

OGA Other Government Agency; frequently refers to CIA or other clandestine organizations

OIC Officer in Charge

ONI Office of Naval Intelligence

OPSEC Operational Security

PJ Parajumpers; pararescuemen of the Air Force Special Operations Command

QRF Quick Reaction Force

RPG Rocket-Propelled Grenade

RTS Relay Tracking Station

SAPI Small Arms Protective Insert

SAS Special Air Service; British Special Operations Forces equivalent to Green Berets

SCIF Sensitive Compartmented Information Facility

SDV SEAL Delivery Vehicle

SEAL Sea, Air, and Land teams; Naval Special Warfare

SecDef Secretary of Defense

SF Special Forces; refers specifically to the Army Special Operations Green Berets

SIGINT Signals Intelligence

SITREP Situation Report

SOAR Special Operations Aviation Regiment

SOCOM Special Operations Command

SOF Special Operations Forces

SOPMOD Special Operations Modification

SQT SEAL Qualification Training

SWCC Special Warfare Combatant-craft Crewman; boat teams supporting SEAL operations

TAD Temporary Additional Duty

TS/SCI Top Secret / Sensitive Compartmented Information; the highest level security clearance

TOC Tactical Operations Center

UCAV Unmanned Combat Aerial Vehicle

UAV Unmanned Aerial Vehicle

USN United States Navy